THE
PROPHET
OF
COBB
HOLLOW

MINGO KANE

SUA SPONTÉ #9

Mingo Kane

The Prophet of Cobb Hollow by Mingo Kane

Copyright © 2016 Mingo Kane

Cover and interior design by Jacqueline Cook

ISBN: 978-1-61179-367-3 (Paperback)
ISBN: 978-1-61179-368-0 (e-book)

10 9 8 7 6 5 4 3 2 1

BISAC Subject Headings:
FIC000000 FICTION / General
FIC002000 FICTION / Action & Adventure
FIC014000 FICTION / Historical

Address all correspondence to:
Fireship Press, LLC
P.O. Box 68412
Tucson, AZ 85737
fireshipinfo@gmail.com

Or visit our website at:
www.fireshippress.com

SUA
SPONTE

For my family and the
Happy Travelers...it is what it is.

To: 1st SGT. John Tompkins.

" May WE forever share in
the solemn understanding,
that once upon a time,
long ago & far away,
WE walked beside, And
in the shadow of men
far greater than ourselves."

WE shall remain, faithfully

The talons of Freedom

Martin Fields

B1/75

Acknowledgements

I'd like to thank Fireship Press: Mary Lou, Jacquie and Margi for their faith, patience and diligence.

I'd also like to extend my appreciation to Dr. John O'Brien for his undying support over the years.

My deepest gratitude to Karyn, this novel would not have been possible without her enduring loyalty, confidence, and encouragement.

Lastly, to the military men and women who protect this Great Nation...*Sua Sponte*.

THE
PROPHET
OF
COBB
HOLLOW

MINGO KANE

FIRESHIP
PRESS

1

San Francisco, 1975

I waited in the hospital cafeteria among the doctors and staff as they chatted over their morning coffee, health care's opportunists fashionably dressed in plain white compassion. This was how life ended for the terminally ill, no code blue or crash-cart revival. No second chance for the miracle of recovery, just the smell of disinfectant blooming from sterile rooms followed by the finality of a sad and eternal silence. I let the depressing chemistry of their antiseptic world fade and poured over my notes on the man I was writing about, a lost legend of American mythology.

Reuben Shadrack Judah was born in 1837 and died on his birthday in 1955 at the age of 118. Raised by a Cherokee shaman, he eventually married Jessamine Spitler and had three children. His wife and daughter were killed during The Civil War while Reuben was serving as a Confederate spy for John Mosby and his band of Rangers. Knowledge of the revenge Reuben wagered on the men who killed his family was sketchy, but what transpired during that time helped create a legend. At one time he owned close to 35,000 acres and was considered the richest man on the East Coast. He became Teddy Roosevelt's closest friend and was the first man selected for Roosevelt's Rough Riders during The Spanish-American War. He

1

had traveled off and on with Wild Bill Hickok, was inducted into Harvard's secret Porcellian Club, and was reputed to have killed close to three hundred men. For every man Reuben killed, the legend said he heated a gold cross and burnt a scar into his flesh as a means of self-redemption. Reuben later served in World War One with New York's Lost Battalion and was awarded The Medal of Honor. Several years later he was incarcerated and placed in one of California's State Mental Institutions and supposedly died penniless.

A practiced voice announced over the intercom that patient visiting hours were open. I rechecked my notes a final time and went to room 313A to see Reuben's personal male attendant. He was the last man alive who knew the truth about Reuben Shadrack Judah, *The Prophet of Cobb Hollow*. Paul Tandy looked up at me when I walked into the room and blinked his deadpan eyes. The frailness of his thin and wasted body was outlined beneath the sterile hospital sheets, and tubes ran in a series of disturbing tentacles from his emasculated arms to a host of beeping monitors. He punched the button on his morphine drip like a trained and starving parasite.

"Please forgive me should I begin to wander; opiates do have such disorienting effects," he apologized with a tight smile, already riding the narcotic buzz ever closer to that absolute infinity he fought against.

"Understandable," I answered.

A nurse in white scrubs came in and checked the monitors and IV drip. Death's white-clad helpers, debt collectors until all accounts are paid in full. The dying man watched the woman go about her clipboard duties and waited until she left the room before he continued.

"Tumor," he said, tapping his freshly shorn skull.

"Excuse me?"

"I had a malignant brain tumor removed but the cells had already spread throughout my body," he explained and closed his eyes. "Cancer is such a lonely death."

"I'm truly sorry, Mr. Tandy." He waved off the apology.

"Let's not talk about that horrid disease. Let's talk about The

Prophet. Reuben Judah said someone would come, wanting to know about him and his life." He paused and shifted in his bed. "I think that is partly why Reuben asked to be cremated when he passed."

"So a curious novelist like me wouldn't seek out his grave?"

The frail man gave a feeble laugh and shook his head no. "Actually, I only found out about the request for cremation after I read his final will. Reuben wrote that he might as well fan the fires now rather than face the Hell of his eternity later."

"Reuben sounds like he was a hard man," I said and smiled down at him.

He looked towards the window and nodded slightly. "In some ways he was, and yet Reuben had an odd compassion about him that drew you in."

"Such as?" I asked.

"Even way back then, everyone suspected what I was."

"That you're a homosexual?" I cut in.

A sheepish smile slipped across his face. "How did you know?"

"I did some research before I contacted you. I knew that while Reuben Judah was at the sanitarium, he would only allow you to care for him towards the end of his life, and only you knew he was living under the false name, Luther Eli Cobb."

"Considering what I am...I suppose that delicious sliver of information strikes you as odd?"

"I'll admit that knowing what little I know about The Prophet of Cobb Hollow, it does pose some unanswered questions. Is this the hospital where Mr. Judah stayed?" I asked, changing the subject.

"Oh, my, no. This facility is a private hospice that caters to the wealthy upper crust of our shrinking society. Reuben was confined to a state facility where I was employed, a truly dreadful place. But since Reuben had no known relatives and was living under the assumed name of Luther Eli Cobb, he was placed there as an inmate of the state until his death."

I looked around the room where framed art work adorned the papered walls, lacquered floors were spotless, and the staff was neatly dressed and courteous—a final passing of the empty karma cup where the patients have nothing left to ante up, fares and tares when facing the sterility of death's cold grip.

"How could someone afford a place like this?" I asked, looking down at him. He held my gaze then relaxed and closed his eyes.

"Please tell me you're not being bashful. You're a novelist doing research for a book, so spit it out and ask. How can someone like me be here instead of a community hospital?" He let a thin slice of his tongue slide across those pale and waxen lips, almost as if he were tasting, or perhaps testing the answer he was about to give. "Shall we say that here in San Francisco I made certain lifelong friends with connections both political and otherwise. In my younger days, I catered to powerful men who had secret desires in their guarded lives. Therefore I was taken care of for my innate ability to keep quiet their petty indiscretions."

"I see," I replied and smiled in spite of myself. I liked this fragile man; his demeanor was polite, and it had me thinking that maybe this was why Reuben Judah trusted Paul Tandy. Mr. Tandy had come from a time when one had to keep secrets if they were to survive in a masculine world that frowned upon the dissimilar.

"You know we haven't been properly introduced," he said, holding out a feminine hand. I took the offered hand and we shook. The bones beneath his porcelain skin felt like those of a fragile child.

I made the introduction. "I'm Martin Carlson. We spoke on the phone earlier this week."

"Martin is a name Reuben admired greatly. Of course, you already know I'm Paul Tandy."

"I'm curious, why did Mr. Judah like that particular name?"

"The name Martin is derived from Mars." I looked down at him lost in the translation. "Mars was the Roman God of War," he explained.

"Mr. Tandy, weren't you ever the least bit frightened of Reuben Judah?"

"Why heavens, no. Mr. Judah treated me kindly when the rest of the world sought to do otherwise. As I said earlier, he had an odd compassion about him very few ever saw. In some ways I loved him

4

like a father, queer as that may sound," he explained.

"So tell me, Mr. Tandy. What did you find so compassionate about, Reuben Judah?"

"Compassion it was, but before I regale you with my explanation would you be so kind as to provide me with a sip of water? Morphine is such a wonderful drug but it leaves me terribly parched." I took the container and held it to his pallid lips and watched as he took a shallow sip through the straw.

"Do you want another drink, Mr. Tandy?"

"No, and please call me Paul. I feel we're almost friends now that we have made the proper introductions."

"Okay, you were telling me about Reuben's generous side."

Paul smiled at my choice of words. "I am not sure generous is the word I would use, but perhaps it does apply in a strange way. It was 1940 when I was first employed at the state mental asylum and found myself caring for Reuben and a few other veterans suffering from post-war shell shock. I was warned about him of course; he had already made quite the impression by that time. He was a condemned prisoner in that institution, an inmate for life… incarcerated for strangling a man to death with his bare hands."

"You mean outright murder?" I asked.

"Not exactly. Apparently a gentleman by the name of Rudolf Hauer tried to rob Reuben and our dear Mr. Judah took exception to that indecent foray. During his preliminary court proceeding, the appointed district attorney made the argument that Reuben had acted with excessive and undue force, and therefore the state sought a second-degree murder conviction. Of course, this was before the court system had pat-down searches, and I believe it was the local papers that wrote—at some point, Mr. Luther Eli Cobb sprayed the court and district attorney with gasoline, and then struck a match to both."

"Was the attorney killed?"

"No, but his legs were burned to a point that he was confined to a wheelchair. It took six months to repair the court room, and by that time Reuben was declared legally insane and therefore committed."

"And that's your idea of compassion, Paul?"

"No, that is how Reuben came to be at the asylum, his compassion is what he did for me. A deed begat of trust, and in return he earned my confidence. Quid pro quo, Martin." Paul closed his eyes briefly and then reopened them and asked for another sip of water.

"If you don't feel up to this I can return tomorrow when you have had more time to rest," I said as he drank.

He shook his head and then swallowed before he spoke. "I'm afraid the morphine has begun to sink the fangs of lethargy into my failing revival of thoughts."

"Reuben did something for you and in turn you did something for him," I said, trying to get him back on topic.

"Oh, yes, I was at that dreadful asylum less than a week when an inmate by the name of David Allen Macy attacked me. Mr. Macy was a convicted molester and a very nasty man. Of course the brutish lout tried to rape me but several orderlies were able to pull him off before that unpleasant incident occurred. Mr. Reuben had a great distaste for this oafish beast and that night the gruesome pedophile apparently hung himself with a belt. The odd thing was, Mr. Macy did so from his door knob and he was found in the sitting position on the floor with no pressure on his crushed neck from the noose. No one either cared or investigated the matter, and the suicide was quickly put to rest, and the body donated to a local college as medical fodder for dissection."

"I'm lost, Paul. How did this suicide bond you and Reuben Judah?"

"It was Reuben's belt that Mr. Macy had supposedly used to hang himself. Of course I knew Mr. Judah had done the murder himself and only doctored the scene to make it appear as a suicide."

"You saw him kill Mr. Macy?"

Paul Tandy shook his head. "No, actually I did not witness the crime."

"Then how can you be sure, Paul?"

"I let Reuben use my Zippo lighter as he explained how he used his bare hands to crush the throat of Mr. Macy. I watched as he heated a gold cross he wore around his neck and then used the hot crucifix to burn a scar across the back of his hand. I kept quiet about what Mr. Reuben had confessed to me, and a friendship was born of that bloody trust." Paul Tandy looked up to where I stood over him, our eyes met, and he held my curious gaze. "You do know about the cross he wore and those ghastly scars I presume?"

"I heard rumors about those crucifix scars burnt into his skin from a very distant relative, but I couldn't confirm that aspect of the legend."

"The scars were no legend I can assure you, Martin. In accordance with his final will only I was permitted to wash and prepare Reuben's body for cremation."

I was curious about the morbid practice. "Did you count the number of scars Reuben had burnt into his skin, Paul?"

"It never occurred for me to try, dear fellow."

"Why?"

"Those hideous burn marks covered every inch of his body with the exception of his palms, face, and the soles of his feet. The scars were actually quite small; the crucifix had a smaller raised cross of thin wire in the middle and he only heated that section. The fresh scars looked like the feet of shore birds, and the older scars were burnt in so many overlapping layers they had outstretched spines like sea urchins. Those hideous burns gave his skin a scaly look that almost shimmered and reflected light when the sun caught Reuben at the right angle. The deepest scar Reuben had was on his chest, just below the nipples."

"Just the one?"

Paul continued explaining. "Yes, the deep scar on his chest was for his wife and daughter. Mr. Reuben said it was his way of remembering them. I remember how he would tap his chest whenever he spoke their names. It was so odd to watch at times, almost as if he suffered each time his finger touched their personal scar." Paul Tandy had now pulled me into a story I was eager to know and he could sense that excitement in me. "Be careful what you seek, Martin. Greed is such a hard emotion to wield, and it will ultimately possess what you are if you cannot control its pull," he cautioned.

I placed my hand on his shoulder and gave it a squeeze. "I'll be careful, Paul."

"We all start out as cautious creatures by nature, dear fellow. I told Reuben the same thing when he warned me about allowing greed to guide my heart. Reuben knew what I wanted most of all and he dangled that prize before me like bait. Of course, I took everything The Prophet had to offer, and because of that—I was trapped by the secret jewels of my own desires. Mr. Reuben captured me like he captured everyone. He offered us the opportunity to taste our greed." Paul Tandy closed his eyes and exhaled his next statement like a whisper no one should hear. "In the end...I did him."

"Did what to him?"

"I killed Reuben Shadrack Judah, also known as inmate Luther Eli Cobb...upon his request, of course."

"Mr. Tandy, if you are telling me you murdered..." I started to protest when he cut me off with another wave of his slender hand.

"It was Reuben's request, my dear fellow. I think he would have lived forever had he not gotten sick. Pneumonia, you see. He caught it in that damp and dreadful place and was drowning in his own fluids. Mr. Reuben did not want to die like that. Hard men live and die such hard lives."

"How did you...?" I started to ask, when Paul waved me off again.

"Reuben planned the whole event out. He put his private affairs in order, his will and any loose ends that may have needed taken care of before he summoned me. It was October 31, 1955, his birthday. Just before I started my normal midnight duties, I slipped into room 13A where I administered to the inmate known as Luther Eli Cobb a lethal dose of morphine. I stayed with him beyond the end of my shift and cleaned his body before I escorted it to the crematorium.

"The final remains of Reuben Shadrack Judah, his military medals and all personal effects, other than the manuscript he wrote covering his life, were incinerated on November 1, 1955. I remember it was a crisp fall day, cloud-free with a bright and heatless sun, a cool breeze coming off the ocean moving inland. In accordance with his will, I took the remains of Mr. Reuben to the high mountains along the Pacific coast and let the Santa Ana winds carry his ashes eastward to his home. I was only twenty-eight back then," Paul said and closed his eyes, "I was so young and I never knew how many hard miles I had yet to face."

"Did Reuben say anything, any last words?" I asked, urging his drugged mind back onto the subject.

Paul Tandy opened his eyes and tried to smile, his waxen lips stretched tight like waxed paper. "Odd that you mention it; he did ask for a few minutes before I injected the drug. Reuben closed his eyes and told me to do what I had to do once he nodded his head. He never once opened his eyes, and then Reuben did something I had never seen him do. He smiled and said five final words before he nodded his head. I administered the drug and Reuben kept that smile on his face until he stopped breathing."

"What were Reuben's final words?"

"He whispered: '*I am because we are.*' I do not know where Mr. Reuben was when his eyes were closed and he spoke those words, but it was one of the few times I ever saw him honestly smile. I hope he is now in some faraway place where that smile first developed."

"Reuben Judah is the one who paid for your care in this facility, isn't he?" I asked.

Paul Tandy stared up at me, eyes suddenly sharp and guarded. "Like I said, Martin. I made powerful friends and I took care of them."

"Are you sure what you have told me is the absolute truth, Paul?"

"Every word dear fellow, every word," he answered and took a raspy breath. "I am so dreadfully tired, so tired of the pain and procedures…so tired of it all."

"I'll come back tomorrow and we can finish up, Paul. I think you need to rest and if my questions have upset you in any way, please forgive me," I apologized. He dismissed the apology with a toss of his hand.

"You haven't asked me about Reuben's manuscript." Paul Tandy's eyes were closed again, but a tight smile teased the corners of his mouth.

"We can talk about the manuscript Reuben Judah wrote about his life tomorrow, after you've rested," I replied, but he knew I was lying. I was hooked with the story, and I desperately wanted that book. It was the only reason I was here. "Tomorrow, Reuben's book will be waiting on my bedside table for you, dear fellow," he said in a groggy voice.

"Okay, Paul." I wrote the phone number of my hotel room down and turned to leave when his small voice stopped me.

"Before I forget, this may as well go with the book." Paul Tandy opened his gown and removed a thick chain from around his wasted neck. He held out the necklace and let it slide like a forbidden serpent into my hand, metal still warm from his pale and gothic flesh.

I couldn't leave without asking. "Paul, everything you told me about Reuben Judah's death went against your Hippocratic oath. Why'd you do it?"

"You ask me why I did it…I did it because I loved him. It was the only way to give him peace and the only way to free him from himself. Life can hold such pain for some. Rueben deserved better."

I walked into the hallway looking at Reuben Judah's chain with the dark and blackened cross. I rubbed the metal with my thumb and the years of soot disappeared, leaving a thin stain on my finger like a burnt and holy avatar. Bright yellow wire gleamed beneath the blackened crust and I realized that the crucifix and chain were solid gold.

2

I was in my hotel room standing at the window, looking out over the bay, watching the sun resurrect itself from the awakening horizon and thinking about Paul Tandy, when the phone rang.

"Hello?"

"Is this Martin Carlson?" a sterile voice inquired.

"Speaking, may I ask who is calling?"

"This is the Meadowland Hospice Facility and I am sorry to inform you that Mr. Tandy has passed during the night. I know you are not a relative but a box of personal items was left on his table with your name and this phone number written on it. It will be made available for your procurement at the front reception desk."

I felt only the vain sympathy of knowing that Paul Tandy's suffering had finally ended. "Thank you for calling, I'll be there shortly."

"You're welcome, and I am sorry for your loss."

I caught a cab and made the trip to the Meadowland facility and back to my hotel in less than thirty minutes, curbing my curiosity and waiting until I was alone in my room before I opened the box Paul Tandy had left. The book was carefully wrapped in a large rack of brown butcher's paper and was the approximate size of a family bible. Inside, another smaller box was covered in decorative paper with an envelope attached to the outside. I opened the parcel and read the attached letter:

> *My Dear Martin,*
>
> *It is with great regret that I must put my last words to prose as I fear the pulling tides of death now guide me to fabled shores elsewhere. Please care for Mr. Reuben's manuscript as I admired and loved the man greatly. Take caution with what you may discover, for I fear Mr. Reuben's words are far more reaching than his deeds themselves. Sometimes lives are sacrificed so fortunes can be made, but from within the discovery of our mortality...we all die broken and alone.*
>
> *I would like you to accept the other enclosed item as a gift from myself and Mr. Reuben. Forgive my deceit, but as I told you...I have my own connections and I knew more about you than you could have possibly known about me. I believe this particular brand of scotch is among the rarest, and one that you have coveted fiercely. Please enjoy and I bid you a safe and prosperous journey on life's troubled waters, my friend. Remember dear fellow, never let greed guide the soul...or your fate shall become an inescapable reality.*
>
> *I am because we are,*
> *Paul Tandy*

I opened the slender box and pulled out a bottle of Royal Brackla single malt scotch, aged for sixty years. That alone made this bottle one of the rarest vintages of scotch on earth. It was Paul Tandy's final jest, to prove that he had the secret friends he seemed so proud of. I peeled back the sterile wrapping that covered the manuscript, then I poured three fingers of vintage scotch into a tumbler. I opened Reuben Judah's book to the first page that held the last words written by his hand, and then toasted Paul Tandy and the secret discretions he had taken to his grave.

Last Will and Testament of Luther Eli Cobb

It is the final oddity of my life and the unknown gambles I have wagered that I now find myself writing the end of my story. I have come to understand that a man is born but his reputation is earned, that it matures through the years as the inescapable chains which bind him to the acoustic shadow of his past deeds. It is the beguiled character of such validity that will live long after the feebleness of his life and the bread of his table has subsided.

Whether or not I am perceived as a just man I cannot say; no person can control the course or opinions of others. What human truths should be whispered of me shall fade beyond that veracity to leave but a scar of half-legends in the wake of my death. Whether I am right or wrong, believed or not, and beyond that of my scarred flesh I leave only my words and the cross I have borne as both blessing and curse. Only my male attendant, Paul Arthur Tandy, shall be permitted to attend my body, I shall be cleaned a final time and then face the flames of cremation.

I have come to accept my choice to fan the fires now, rather than face the Hell of my eternity later. Know that my ashes are to be spread upon the Santa Ana winds so they may be carried eastward to my home, on those reeking winds of faded wars I will live forever. My ashes will infect the blood of this reawakening land and infuse the bones of all things whether hallowed or hated. Beware to those who would seek to gain fame or profit from the burden of

*my tale, I am as I am. My revenge will become what
you fear most. These are my final words as they are
so written by my hand.*

*My name is Reuben Shadrack Judah, I am also
known as Luther Eli Cobb.*

I am—The Prophet of Cobb Hollow.
October 31, 1955

3

California State Mental Institution
San Francisco
Alpha Block, Ward Thirteen
Monastery of Mad Monks

Reuben Shadrack Judah
January 2, 1940

The emptiness of my prison-barred window has become an unforgivable nuisance to me. It is nothing more than an isolated and unchanging link to the outside world I am forbidden to touch. Many times I've caught myself listening to the network of screams echoing against these walls of steel. I feel the cold vibrations of decay while those in anguish are lost to hard eyes that forgot how to feel. The people in this place have closed off their minds to the resonance of normalcy. They have forgotten how to laugh and they bear the lash marks of mental and physical injustice like medals of valor. Their scarred backs endure beatings from the guardsmen until their subconscious uncoils its mental restraints, just so to bleed and bruise themselves free again.

But in this place so dark that the demons themselves share no heavenly access—there is an unspoken connection in the chambers of their free-thinking minds. That if it were not for the nightmare of the procedure, they would conquer this realm and make real the possibility of wicked things. So let the light dawn on another torturous continuum while I sit here before my window, alone and unkempt. It is the same each night when nothing stirs in my small world except the voices of insanity, speaking in poetic whispers like sad little pigeons. My personal male attendant is new and he watches me with curiosity. Interesting young man, this Paul Tandy. He will not survive in this revolting place without my help. I have already saved him once and made things right on his behalf. Mr. Macy, the molester—I should have met that gruesome bastard twenty years ago.

Paul Tandy saw me sitting alone, mustered up the courage, then walked over to where I sat looking out the window. "You're not sleepy, Mr. Cobb?" he asked, taking a seat in the chair beside me.

"I am quite alert."

"I wanted you to know that what you did for me will not be forgotten. Mr. Macy would have probably raped or killed me," Paul said in a low voice.

"Mr. Macy's days of causing pain to the innocent are over."

Paul smiled. "Indeed they are, Mr. Cobb."

"I would appreciate it if you would address me as Reuben," I said.

He looked confused. "I'm not sure I understand?"

"My given name is Reuben Shadrack Judah. It's been years since I've answered to that name," I explained and added for my personal insurance: "Of course, this information remains between us and goes no further."

"Of course, Mr. Judah." Paul leaned in close to me and whispered, "And don't worry, if there's one thing I've learned about this place, it's how to keep a secret."

"Paul, do you know how old I am?"

"No…actually I do not," he stammered.

"I am 103 years old, and the long life I've lived has become a nuisance."

"Nuisance? No indeed, look at all the wonderful things you must have experienced, Mr. Judah."

"Wonderful no longer exists in my world, and who will know of me and my life when I am gone?" I asked in return.

Paul tried a polite counter. "But you're in your golden years, Mr. Judah,"

"The only thing golden about these years is the color of my piss."

Paul smiled and softened his tone. "I already owe you a personal debt so I'd love to hear more about you. Where were you born?"

"I was born in Augusta County, Virginia, in the year 1837."

Paul looked at me in disbelief. "So you were alive before the Civil War when slavery still existed?" he asked.

"I was and I can still remember the scenes of those days with vivid perfection. The first time I saw slaves was the day of my accident."

"Accident?"

"I was kicked in the head by a mule. That crazy bastard damn near killed me, but I survived. It was after I healed that my memory became perfect and these eyes of mine changed color," I said tapping my cheekbone.

Paul was drawn into the story with his sleepy expression and hypnotic stare. "When was this?" he asked, stifling a yawn.

"Do you really want to hear my story?" Paul Tandy nodded a little too eagerly. He was hooked. "Are you sure?" I enticed.

"Absolutely, Mr. Judah," said Paul smiling. "We're alone and it's not like you and I have anyplace to be."

"Then listen to my voice, let me take you back to where it all began. Take the long cool drink from the well of my memories."

The Day
Augusta County, Virginia
October 31, 1850

The first time I saw slaves was on the day of my thirteenth birth year, 1850. My father and I were on our way home with a half-broke mule, a callous animal whose soul seemed darker than the man who had sold him to us. We walked the empty roads under a blue sky and cooling weather, small clapboard shacks dotted the landscape of harvested fields where the slaves were kept in bonded confinement.

I would sometimes catch a flicker of movement from the doorjambs, and within those thorny creases of darkness is where the children of servitude clutched the shadows which claimed them. Their walnut hide stretched taut across their overworked bones of dissension like doll skin, avatars with white eyes blinking in and out of the gloom, dark-skinned sprites with polished teeth like ivory wind chimes set against some pale and moonless night.

We walked with the mule in tow down a dirt road that split the aboriginal workers in their respective fields of labor. Those black voices would call out to one side of the road and the workers on the far side would answer back in a united voice of hardship amid the clinking of hoes upon their seasonal ground.

It was the harmonized singing coming from those fields of sadness that truly captured their shared religion of pain, the way their voices called out a story of despair from one field to be answered back with a tale of deprivation from the other. Some conjoined moment of combined inspiration to take their illiterate minds off the sad cadence of their day. But it was more than a song to these abused and shackled people, it was the soul of a dark and forgotten continent that spoke with dignity and pride through their tribal ancestors. It was that affection which would one day infuse the hearts of men and then change the course of a nation. I looked down at my work-stained hands as black as the slaves I passed, and knew that today—slavery existed and no opinion had changed in this deep and gothic south.

The final memory of that day was the mule being hitched to our barn stall when I walked around the blind side of the napping animal. The sudden movement of my shadow startled the mule and it kicked straight back, both hooves catching me in the head.

Instead of an instant death there began the slightest quickening of time somewhere deep within me. An abnormal reawakening, a religious laying of healing hands to keep me alive while the dark agents of fate pulled me between the conflicting lines of life.

The doctor was summoned but the old sawbones told my father there was nothing to be done, to let the course of life work the magic of recovery, but I would need to stay asleep or I would die. My father was an overly devout man of the cloth, and his Appalachian parishioners were not in favor of the Indians. But my father broke down and allowed the Cherokee to administer any natural remedy that might save my life. How quickly God is forgotten and all taboo alternatives to death become validated in those cruel dark hours.

In the days that followed I remained unconscious and became a solitary mental molecule within the fabric of creation, a prevalence of voided animation, a quanta phasing in and out like a supernova offering life to a new world while giving death to mankind's earliest system of reason. I broke free of the nothingness and became a divine specter rising upon the glassy planes of an unknown era, to a permeable time before all religions. I was moving unhindered through trees as big as long-extinct dinosaurs, above mountains that arose like unnamed icons and across grassy plains where cold glacial streams flowed untainted as blue as opals. I was the Pan God living in an elemental place where wind and rocks and water still ruled unquestioned, a time of inflection when the first man and woman lived upon the land like biblical prophets.

I was a free spirit between two wolves, one white and the other black as midnight. The wolves spoke and I answered.

"Your heart is your first teacher. Tell us why you are here, tell us what you desire," the wolves asked.

"Am I dead?"

"All who have died are equal. Life is our gift to give and yours to live. You are not dead, so ask from the heart and we will answer from the heart."

"If I am not dead then what is my life?" I asked them.

"What is your life? It is like the flash of fireflies in the night, a soft brilliance winking in and out. It is your icy breath in the wintertime and the shadow that follows you across the grassy plains of your youth and loses itself in the unspoiled sunset of age. Your life is what

19

you give our world, not what you receive. "

The image and voices began to blur as I felt the hands of life pulling me back, purging my existence from the pulse of this world—and in an instant of bright awakening—I was washed away from them like an unspeakable sin.

I opened my eyes and stared into the leathered face of an old, Cherokee man. "I saw two wolves," I said.

"The motivation of your heart lies within those twin wolves," the old man answered.

"Where is my father?"

"He will be gone for several months preaching in the white man's churches. I will take you home to our people."

I was groggy and confused. "Our people?"

"You have much to learn," he said, picking me up in his arms.

He was the man who would become my adopted father. His name was Three Crows, and I cannot tell the story of my life, without in part...telling his.

4

Fatherless
1852

It took three months for the swelling in my mule-stomped head to subside, but in the two years that followed my recovery, an unexplained transformation occurred. The rest of my body had grown abnormally large and unhindered; at fifteen I was already a head taller than grown men twice my age and thirty pounds heavier. The doctor thought my rapid height and muscular development was due to the initial head trauma I had suffered from the mule kick, which somehow influenced a small gland inside my brain. The doctor was partially right. But no one could explain why my eyes had changed color, or why my memory had become flawless. I was a malformed and odd-eyed variant, brown eye on the right side while the left eye had changed to the oddest shade of blue.

But—with divine change there is a divine penalty. The people in the town of Waynesboro, including my father, could not accept or understand my abnormality. I was the hidden albino living in the black world of normalcy, standing out like an untraceable shadow against a pure white canvas. I was shunned by a strict culture that saw me as nothing more than an introverted and malignant giant.

All conversation in our house became nonexistent and the only physical interaction between my father and me was his daily list of chores, which I was handed before he left—and the nightly whippings when he returned home because I did not meet the guidelines of his stern expectations. Two years of neglect and physical abuse creates a callous on the heart that never completely softens.

"What did I do wrong?" I finally asked one night. It was after a particularly brutal whipping for a minor transgression of some unspoken faith. That night, Father had used a leather strop. The beating finally stopped when his arms had grown too weary to swing the instrument of his anger.

"Look at what those red savages did to you," he answered in a voice reserved for his sermon. "You're nothing more than a monster with the mind of an imp," Father said, hanging the strop on a wooden peg.

"Savages and imps?" I pointed to his leather strop. "Tell me, Father…in this house, who is the savage and who is the imp? I am no different than you or the people who attend your church."

Father clenched his jaw and grabbed my shirt by the collar, trying to pull me closer. I did not budge. His hands were small and soft. Weak. His hands were made for turning the pages of his Bible, or beating an obedient child. I was a head taller and heavily muscled from the demands of his daily labor. My hands were square and blunt, made for holding a shovel or breaking the bones of abusers.

"Those red niggers are heathens, no better than the dirt they sleep on. That's why they have to scratch out a living in those mountains, because no decent Christian in Waynesboro would ever allow them into our community," said Father as his puritan anger began to control the tempo of thoughts. "I have talked with the church elders and we have decided the Indians have no place in our society, or anyplace else for that matter," he said.

"They saved my life and tried to save Mother's. They came to help when you, God, and your church had all but turned their back on us…or have you forgotten that?" I replied.

My father went to grab his strop, but instead, he turned and backhanded me across the face. My head never moved. I did not blink. He began quoting obscure scripture in a blind frenzy, spittle flying from his mouth like flakes of tarnished snow. And then my father did something odd, even for him. He mentioned my mother's death for the first time.

Father wiped his fleck-covered mouth with the back of his shaky hand. "You are a lover of those Godless heathens, just like your mother was. She let those red savages bewitch and seduce her when she was in the pains of your childbirth. God's punishment on her was swift and just, and yours will be no different."

I could see it then, written in his eyes. I was cast out of his shadow and he had now become wed to the true matrimony of his motivations. My father had always blamed me and the Cherokee for my mother's death. I would forever bear the responsibility for the life she surrendered when I took that first breath. As long as I remained in his house, I would endure the wrongful beatings of his guilt and wear his shame—it was *that* intolerance which I could not abide. I turned and walked through the door and stood on the porch when my father spoke to me for the last time.

"Go ahead and leave, go tonight and you'll become the Godless bastard you are. Run away, Reuben. Run away and live a life of poverty with your heathen saviors. I will never utter your name from this day forward and you will die forgotten." The silence that followed was molten. I sucked in the hard air and waited. I wanted my father to ask me back into the house. Instead, my father walked to where I stood on the porch and slammed the door. "You are an abomination," he yelled. Those were the last words I heard from my father.

I never wanted to leave that cool October night. It was forced upon me. Bigotry is a mighty tool which the just wield unjustly. Like a dark coat with the harsh pockets of disparity, I would learn to wear the prejudice well. How deep those pockets were. I was never the son my father wanted so I became what he made me—a byproduct of abuse and rejection. It was like stitching together a puzzle with thread, sewing the pieces of your life together one stitch at a time. But, so frail was my thread and so dull was the prick of my needle. Everything I'd sewn together began to unravel until I was stripped naked. To my father I would forever be the homeless hobo martyr—the mendicant beggar who was banished to rule a stained and tarnished world.

So many years have passed and the indelible purity of my truth has faded with them. My father was the most devout man I have ever known, and I was summarily raised in the shadow of his likeness, but in his eyes I failed to hear that final calling of Godly servitude.

The only relative of my father's family I knew was his grandfather, Keller Judah. He was a Spanish pirate who fought in The French and Indian War. I have never mentioned my father's name, and though I will never know—I will always wonder where I was when my father died.

5

The Cobb Hollow Divide
Three Crows
October, 1855

The Cobb Hollow Divide was named after a legendary madman who was lost in those mountains in 1780. Silas Cobb took shelter in a cave during a snowstorm when he lost his bearings while hunting. After building a fire, the legend said that upon the illuminated walls were pictures and runes written by a lost and ancient race, but it was deeper inside the rocky hole where Silas Cobb found the gold. Rich yellow veins as thick as tree branches. The fire he started began to melt the snow around the small opening, loosening the rocks above causing a great landslide—trapping him inside his personal treasure tomb for thirteen days. He survived by eating bats, bugs, and roasting the laces of his moccasins. When he finally dug his way out, Silas Cobb staggered back to town half-starved and mad telling the quaint population about his wondrous find, but nobody ever found that fabled hole of worldly riches. Silas Cobb finally went insane in those mountains, searching day and night for that lost cavern full of gold. He disappeared one winter's eve and was never heard from again. To this day the lonesome beauty of those ridges and plateaus is known as the *Cobb Hollow Divide*.

* * *

The night my father abandoned me, I made the mountainous trek to Three Crows' cabin by daybreak and found him rocking in a chair on his porch. He only nodded a greeting as if I were expected. "I have nowhere else to go," I told him.

The old Cherokee lit his pipe then pushed the door open from where he sat. "Then you are home," he said.

The next day was a typical mid-October morning, cool and fresh and a time when the painted leaves of fall had begun to register its unspoiled grandeur upon the mountain's gentle curves. It was the month when the Cherokee celebrated their New Moon Ceremony. Since autumn was the season when Cherokee legends say the world was created, it represented the New Year celebration and began a rebirth of life. There would be a communal feast, dancing, and a purification ceremony that involved immersing oneself seven times in the cold mountain stream, called "going to water." For me, the purification would include predictions of my future and I would be given a Cherokee name. Three Crows would conduct the baptism, but an old Cherokee woman would do the prediction. I was baptized by Three Crows that evening and then sent naked towards the high mountain peaks for my telling.

"How will I find the old woman?" I asked Three Crows.

"Look for her fire," he said.

The Cherokee people called her The Dove and even Three Crows paid reverence to the blind woman. She took my hands as we sat ringed around her fire pit, those milky eyes like cold white stones from a lifeless hearth. She opened my hands and placed crystals of clear quartz in my palms. The old woman closed my hands and brought them to her temples…

"You still fight what is unknown to you. You must find a balance in this life," she said.

"Balance for what?"

"I see what I see, and I see a long hardship," she said and clenched her eyes in tight concentration.

"My life is already one of hardship," I replied.

The old woman kept her eyes closed and spat to her left. "Hardship comes in many forms, and the long life that awaits you is one of death if you continue to struggle against your anger. If you fight the living world you will be lost to us forever, and your days will have hate as a guide and regret as your shadow. And like me, you will outlive all that loves you and you will one day bury all those who ever knew the man you could have been. Choose wisely which desire you surrender to; if you feed your heart with hate you will walk a path with no end."

I could see that honest poverty was the old woman's custodian in a world where it was both her salvation and her curse. The Dove was an outdated obstacle to the industrial society that had forgotten her and the sacred domain she once ruled. She was a remnant, a timeless dreamer who now had deprivation as her savior. She thought and then smiled before she blinked open those chalky eyes.

"On this day I give you a Cherokee name, a name that will represent your inner struggle. The answer is behind your miss-matched eyes. It is behind those eyes that a war is being waged. From this day and for all time you will be known as *Nahi Kaga Di'lsti Uwasa*. You are, *he who fights himself*," she translated.

"Why this name?" I asked.

The Dove tapped her chest. "Go and ask Three Crows about the two wolves," she answered, rising to her feet, and then she looked down to where I sat. "You will one day become the mountain that life will break itself upon. But remember, some will always die so others may live. This life is about learning to let go, even when you hurt the most you must learn to love the hardest. That will be your hidden balance, if you can find it." She stood and walked from the fire into the darkness of her blind world. Her last words trailed from the edge of that eternal night...

"I am because we are."

After that night, I began to notice the first of many changes in Three Crows. He seemed lost in his own brand of thoughts, almost withdrawn. It was during the early spring when the Cherokee on the Cobb Hollow Divide were busy gathering and packing goods to sell at our upcoming Lily of the Valley festival. But Three Crows still seemed to occupy himself with some unspoken agenda. The old man finally came to me with his usual intelligent focus and self-conscious awareness. As if he alone knew the secret of some indefinite event.

"Pack enough provisions for a week," Three Crows told me.

"Where are we going?"

"To a special place so we might talk of things past and those that are yet to be." I had come to expect these cryptic answers; all Cherokee were like that.

We left the following morning and I followed Three Crows deep into the mountains where the steep slopes gave way to deep gorges, where large rocks sat wind ravaged and scarred like some horrible plague had sought them out. We ceased to talk and let the beauty of those distant wilds speak of its immaculate conception, where the hidden histories of the mountains and those unsung ballads of mankind were forever woven upon their seasonal winds.

The quiet ridges above seemed to welcome us as if we had reawakened something primitive in their ancient and silent voices, perhaps a similar tale forever inscribed of the short and violent lives of men and their wild ways. We were here among them, their stony days a passing of seasons beyond all counting, where only the native breeze bespoke of them in a diatribe none could know—silent narrators each in this static testimony of change.

We made camp in a place unknown to me, and the old man and I built a fire as the night dropped its blanket upon our dim and clock-less world. I watched Three Crows from across the blaze as he held his palms upward and then gestured towards his chest, as if he were pulling some unknown thing to him.

"Go ahead and ask," said Three Crows.

"How did you know I wanted to ask you something?"

"My hearing is fading but I am not as blind as The Dove," said the old man with a smile. "So let us talk and your heart will find peace."

"The Dove told me to ask you about the two wolves."

The old man nodded his understanding and explained. "Before

28

man there was nothing, it was in the beginning of time when the earth was all water. There was no land and all the animals lived up in the sky on the clouds. They were waiting for the land to dry but it would not dry. They would send down one animal at a time but it would never come back. Finally, they sent down the water beetle. The water beetle dove into the water, grabbed a handful of mud at the bottom and brought it up then placed it on top of the water. It was then the mud started to dry and land was born. The animals decided to send the buzzard down to the earth, and as the buzzard flew close to the land he would flap his mighty wings and formed our mountains and valleys. All the animals came down and settled on the earth. And the Great Spirit placed among them one man and one woman."

"Where do the two wolves fit into this story?" I asked.

"Inside our hearts there is a conflict between the black wolf and the white wolf. The black wolf is thought to be evil—he is anger, envy, greed, arrogance, self-pity, and ego. The white wolf is thought to be good—he is peace, love, hope, truth, compassion, and faith. The fight between the two wolves is going on inside you, and their appetites are ravenous…so they must be fed."

I was confused. "How do I decide which wolf to feed?"

The old Cherokee simply replied, "That is the conflict which forces you to choose. But if you learn to feed them right, they both will be content. You see, if you only choose to feed the white wolf, the black one will always be angry and always fighting the white wolf. He is hungry. But if you acknowledge the black wolf and feed him, he is happy and the white wolf is happy. The black wolf has many qualities the Cherokee admire: tenacity, courage, fearlessness, and planning when it comes to war. You will sometimes have need of these qualities which the white wolf does not have. But the white wolf has compassion, caring, strength, and the ability to recognize what is in the best interest of all."

Three Crows pointed to his chest and continued. "To feed and care for both means they will serve you well and do nothing that is not a part of something greater, something good, and something you will use to build a better way of life. Feed them both and there will be no more internal struggle for your attention. And when there is no battle inside your heart, you can listen to the voices of a deeper understanding that will guide you in every circumstance. Peace, my son, is the Cherokee mission in life. A man or a woman who has peace inside their heart has everything. A man or a woman who is pulled apart by the wolves inside him or her has nothing," he said, then looked skyward before adding a final thought. "The Cherokee have always said a special prayer to calm the two wolves when they fight."

"What is it?" I asked.

"*I am because we are*," he replied.

I changed the subject. "Why did The Dove name you Three Crows?"

"She foretold my future and said that I would walk three dark paths, as black as a murder of crows. Three paths, three crows."

"Have you walked them?" I asked.

"I have walked two and I am walking the third and final path now."

"What were the first two paths you followed?"

"The first path was when my family died. They went to the lowlands in the valley to live among the white settlers. They were welcomed and adopted the white way of life, but all things change. As more settlers moved into the valley they were cast out and made to leave."

"Where did they go?" I asked.

"The white people wanted more than we had to give. They took our children and cut their hair, put them in the white schools, and changed their names. Our children went to their churches and began to worship their God, but even that was not enough for them. They stripped our Cherokee identity and then we became the invisible people with no heritage. It was then the white people realized they did not need us anymore and their government sent the Cherokee away. My family died on the Trail of Tears near Oklahoma, and their death is what began my second path."

"What did you do?" Three Crows looked at me, his face darker.

"I left these mountains and became a hater and hunter of men. I fed only the black wolf and my days were filled with hate. For many years I wandered the land until my heart was so black that I only knew hatred as my compass. I finally came back to my cabin and learned to feed the white wolf again."

"And you are walking your third path now?" I asked. He nodded and poked the fire with a stick, sending red motes skyward like hellish sprites.

"Yes, my third path would come to me in the shape of a lost boy child. This boy would become our people's salvation…but he would also bring death upon me." I looked at him as he took a deep breath, and then he exhaled the finality of his remaining path with a curt smile. "My third path is you."

I shook my head in objection. "If I am to bring you death then I will leave the Cherokee tonight," I said.

"You came to me as my son, seeking knowledge so you could walk the good path. And who now is your father if it is not me? I am the river of life from which you flow. When I am gone, you and our people will live. What would your world be without me and our people? I do not fear death, Reuben. I await its cold touch so I may see those I have always loved. Life will always be harder than death," said the old man.

"I can change my path so we both might live. The Dove is wrong," I argued.

Three Crows only smiled and shook his head in silent objection before he answered. "How can you change what is already foretold?" he asked and swept his hand across the ground. "How can you change your shadow that is cast by the sun? You will soon hold the light of our lives, Reuben. To the Cherokee people, our honor, courage, and virtue mean everything to us. It is our way of life. We do not covet power or gold, these things mean nothing to us—and they mean everything to the white man. They will kill for both and justify their actions through God. But, I want you to remember this for all times. That love…true love never dies. Your flame of life will one day burn away the darkness and ignite a path to greatness. There will come a time when the stars shall cease to sparkle and all gold will lose its luster, a time when the government will become a prison to the people. Then and only then, all that will matter is what we have tonight."

"What's that?" I asked.

"All we have tonight is a father's love for his son," he said. Three Crows then did something that I will never forget. He laughed. It was different, not genuine. Like a man facing the hangman and a laugh is his final jest.

6

The next morning Three Crows and I left the camp and hiked deeper into the nameless scale of our surroundings. The old man's route led us through endless tangles of briars and mountain laurel, thick as despair, down and across rock ledges that made it seem as if we walked upon the very brim of this world. Three Crows only stopped once. It was when he caught a small butterfly and I watched as he observed the insect intently while the creature crawled across his hand, and even this minute piece of perfection was not lost to the old man. We moved until the sun's arc had lengthened and we found ourselves upon a great ridge of boulders. A sacred place where it seemed the rocks themselves were stoic sentries in this true order of creation. Beneath our feet stones fell from the roof of some unknown grotto and dropped silent and long into the deepest bowels of a dark and terminal world. Three Crows took a knee and pointed to where a bald and limbless tree stood out upon the ridge like a crucifix.

"Watch until the sun hits its peak and then we will dig at the tip of that tree's shadow," he explained.

I walked to the spot and waited as the shadow moved across the ground like ink. "Here?" I asked pointing. The old man nodded and I began to move the stones until a roughly fashioned trapdoor was uncovered.

"Let me help you open it," said Three Crows. We pulled the wooden door until a rush of fetid air escaped, what lay beyond was dark and humid and smelled like the lair of a predator. "Inside to the left is a torch," he said.

I found the torch and struck steel to flint until the pitch ignited and handed it to the old man. "What now?" I asked.

"Follow me," said Three Crows as he disappeared into the darkness. "Watch your step," he said over his shoulder. I stepped down onto the soft floor as the old man dropped his torch into an ancient fire pit.

The seasoned wood sparked to life and upon the lit walls were pictographs of ships with enormous heads carved in the shape of mythical beasts, and on the ground laid thirteen skulls bleached white as marble. Across the cave's floor were large battle axes and pikes and breastplates with helmets made from the horns of some unknown animal.

"Vikings?" I asked.

"Our ancestors called them, the 'the bearded ones.' And when they found this cave they decided to make war upon the Cherokee, but in that time our people were as many as the stars and the bearded ones were killed and placed here," explained Three Crows. "Look deeper," he said pointing beyond the fire pit.

I looked past the old man and down a dim corridor to where something sparkled, like...Gold. The walls held veins of the yellow metal as thick as tree trunks, and littered about the ground were nuggets the size of a quail's egg. I glanced at the old man with wide eyes and he only smiled in return. "Then the story of Silas Cobb is true?" I asked. He nodded mutely.

"Yes, but the truth died here and it is buried with him," said the old man.

"If anyone else should find this cave the government would take every acre. And you know this, don't you?" I said to him.

"Yes, and this is why only you and I will ever know of it."

"Then why did you show it to me?" I asked.

"Like The Dove foretold, you will be the savior of our people.

34

That is why I brought you to this place...I am selling you our land and all of this goes with it," he explained, sweeping his hand about the room.

"But...but, how can I afford?"

Three Crows cut me off before I could finish. "Afford? But you have not asked the price," he said and stepped closer to me.

"What could I possibly have that could buy 30,000 acres...and, all of this?"

The old man looked at me and then at my feet. "Take a handful of dirt and pour it into my hands," he instructed cupping his hands together. I did as I was told and Three Crows rubbed the sifted soil between his hands, and it fell away like a blessing. "Sold," he said.

"A handful of dirt?"

Three Crows smiled. "Dirt is worth more than gold if the right man or government wants it bad enough. Gold does not float on air, it's in the soil and rocks. If you own the soil and rocks, you own the gold."

"But why?" I asked, confused.

"The days of the Cherokee are almost gone forever. You are Cherokee, but you can also walk freely in the white world. If you own this land they cannot take it from us and we can live here in peace until our time is done." I shook my head to object, but the old man waved me off and continued, "Know that I love you as much as my own sons, perhaps more. But I also know in my heart, The Dove spoke the truth...you will save our people, Reuben."

"But I will also bring you death."

"Perhaps, but I will not die today," Three Crows said and grinned. "Do you know the lawyer who owns the bank in the town of Waynesboro, a man named Stoddard Quillen?" he asked.

"I know the man. My father used him all the time. Father didn't like him or his brash attitude, but he always said Stoddard Quillen was as honest as the day is long."

"Good, because he has drawn up the legal documents to make this land yours."

"But what about the gold?"

The old man only laughed and explained. "I do not think Stoddard Quillen will work for free. So we better take some of this back with us. We have an appointment with him at his bank tomorrow morning before our Lily of the Valley Festival starts."

7

Present

"You never saw your real father again, did you?" Paul Tandy asked, wiping away his tears.

"No."

Paul nodded his understanding and sighed. "It was much the same with my father once he found out about me."

"That you are a lover of men?"

Paul Tandy looked at me with weepy eyes and shook his head in silent confirmation. "I guess this means you disapprove of me and my lifestyle too?"

"Love knows not the gender, only that it is," I replied.

"Thank you for understanding," he said and shifted in his chair beside me. "Like you, I was asked to leave his house and never return," Paul said and sniffed before changing the subject. "So the gold is still there?"

I shook my head, no. "I rode through my land for the last time some thirty-odd years ago. The land is now a dedicated wilderness area owned by the federal government, The George Washington National Forest. It's as untouched as when I owned it. Teddy Roosevelt made sure my land would be preserved through federal law. I served with Roosevelt. Teddy was a great friend and a great man."

"Then what happened to the cave and the gold?" Paul asked.

"When Franklin D. Roosevelt became President he established the Civilian Conservation Corps. A dam was built to hold back the spring snow runoff, and the Cobb Hollow Reservoir was created. When the Cobb Hollow Divide was flooded, part of the mountain collapsed and everything in the cave was buried forever. The gold and all that I ever loved are now under more than eight hundred feet of water and rocks."

"You knew Teddy Roosevelt?" Paul asked wide-eyed.

"Knew Teddy well. I served under him during the Spanish American War."

"What was Roosevelt like?"

"We have years to go before we get to Roosevelt. I haven't spoken of Jessamine, and how we met."

"Jessamine? You've never mentioned her," said Paul rubbing his thin face.

"She was my wife."

"I didn't know you were married. I always thought you were…" He paused and searched for the word.

"Unmarried?" I cut in. Paul nodded. "No. I was married and raised a family once upon a time."

"Then I want to know about Jessamine." said Paul.

"Then come and see me when your ears are thirsty, and I will tell you how we met."

* * *

I sit and watch the neon sign across the street winking in and out. I hear the static buzz of electrical current igniting the gas into an orgy of pink pulsating light. It is the same, night after long night. When the other inmates have gone to sleep to find that secret place where their dreams are cruel and free. I sit here and replay my life. Good or bad, I ponder the anti-blessings of my own design. It's hard to know what is true and righteous in this world. Hard to know if the full moon glowing and grinning like some ancient hieroglyphic rune is nothing more than a gateway to an alien world I have yet to explore.

There is an elderly couple shuffling along under the lamplight. The woman is crippled and frail, the man's arm is around her shoulder for support as if they were both tarnished refugees. There is music playing, somewhere far down the street…faint as a wish, but just loud enough. The man and woman stop and begin to move in a lonely sidewalk dance comprised of unsure steps. The old woman's leg and arm are misshapen and useless from some unknown affliction—but still they dance. They dance to remember what was, and they dance to forget that the old man has become the crutch in her life.

Through my window there is a slim cataract of life that slowly winds down this dim tabernacle of time. I have no recourse but to ask, "Do I measure my remaining time in days or in these tragic scenes from my window?" These old eyes beg to see and relive a single moment of shy perfection, something so precious to me. My first dance with Jessamine…

"Good evening," said Paul sitting down.

"Why pink?" I asked.

"Pink?" Paul looked around. I pointed towards the neon sign across the street. "Oh, it's some kind of a gentleman's club," he explained.

"You mean it's a brothel."

"A brothel to the poor, a gentleman's club to the wealthy," Paul clarified with a smile.

"It's all the same, rich or poor," I said.

"What's all the same, Reuben?"

"The price you pay."

"You were going to tell me how you met your wife, Jessamine," said Paul, changing the subject.

"We met just before I was coaxed into a fight."

"What was the fight about?" he asked.

"The fight was more of a contest the mountain people called 'King of the Pit.' Just relax and feel my energy. Let my voice carry you away, stay with me…I am close."

Mingo Kane

40

8

Lily of the Valley
Sunday
May 13, 1855

I stood above the Bee Rocks waiting for Three Crows as a rack of clouds rolled across the valley like a great white misfortune. The cold stone of the Bee Rock jutted from the landscape as if the spine of the world itself arose from the fallow soil, quiet and cold as hate itself. The silent sentinel, unvoiced in its stony existence while forever tasked with surveying the ever-changing landscape below.

The Bee Rock was first used by the Cherokee as a lookout vantage point. A midsummer feast would be held and the children would douse the honey bees with corn flour as they flew by. From the high rock, lookouts would call down through the valley and give directions so that walkers could follow the ghostly homeward flight of the bees. Once the hive was located and night fell, the bees would be smoked out and the wildflower-scented honey harvested.

It was the day of our Lily of the Valley festival and it would be the day that would set the mechanics of my life into perpetual motion. Three Crows stopped beside me and caught his breath before speaking.

"I think it's best if we slip into Waynesboro from the far end of town," he said.

"I reckon that means you don't want anyone seeing us," I noted aloud.

"It makes my heart glad to see that all these years of creating a smarter Cherokee is paying off," the old man replied.

* * *

"Your father won't be at the festival?" asked Stoddard Quillen. He was much as I remembered him, robust and barrel-chested with a face that seemed perpetually red, as if he was always angered.

"No, he'll never have anything to do with me or the Cherokee," I answered.

"Are you going to compete in our best man of the valley contest? Lord knows you have the size and muscles to win it," said Stoddard sizing me up.

"I honestly haven't given it much thought."

"He should compete," said Three Crows looking at me. "All men need to establish the pecking order among their peers."

"Guess that means I'll likely enter," I replied with a shrug.

"Good, damn good to hear," said Stoddard. "That bastard Günter Kruger will be there and I'd like to see someone finally put him on his arrogant ass."

"Why?" I asked. Stoddard looked at Three Crows for direction.

"Tell him," said the old man.

"Günter Kruger is the son of Hermann Kruger, German immigrants who amassed some wealth through their South River China Clay Company…but they're cruel sonofabitches. And that includes the whole lot—men, women, and children," Stoddard explained. "They wanted the Cherokee's land bad, and they'll voice their opposition when they find out who owns it now."

"What good would mountain land do for them?" I asked.

"Trade route," answered Stoddard. "The Krugers would cut three weeks' worth of travel off their route to Atlanta where they do business with the Spitler family. Gunter has taken a shine to the oldest Spitler girl, Jessamine."

"But Three Crows and I would give them full access to any route they want."

Stoddard shook his head in objection. "You don't understand this kind of people, Reuben. All the Kruger family cares about is what they want and who they gotta' run roughshod over to get it. The women are equally cruel bitches, always pushing their way around town and running the good womenfolk off. So do me a favor, if you get the chance."

"What's that?" I asked.

"Knock Gunter Kruger on his German ass. I'll have good money wagered on you."

"What kind of event is this?" I asked. Three Crows cut in before Stoddard could explain.

"I'll tell you about it later," he said patting my shoulder. Something told me I was not going to like this contest, but I kept my concern private. "How about the other agreement we spoke of?" Three Crows asked Stoddard.

"Oh, yes, Matthew is set up in my private study, let's finish our business with him and we'll head over to the festival."

"What kind of agreement?" I asked.

Stoddard explained over his shoulder as we walked. "My bank loaned Matthew Brady the money to open a new photography business a few years ago. Matthew came here to take a portrait of me and my family, so I asked him to do me a small favor…which he agreed to." I could tell by Stoddard's tone he had planned this land venture out, far in advance. And it made me wonder how long Stoddard and Three Crows had plotted this secret acquisition.

We entered the study where Stoddard Quillen, Three Crows, and I were placed against metal poles to keep us unmoving and rigid while Matthew Brady took the picture. In our hands, we each held a copy of the deed and bill of sale. Once the daguerreotype was taken, we smeared ink on each of our right thumbs and that fingerprint went in the upper corner of each copy. I would retain a copy, one was entered into the courts through Stoddard's law office, and the final copy was locked in Mr. Quillen's private safe. Once we completed the transaction, I had become the richest and largest land owner in the state of Virginia.

* * *

I watched the Cherokee labor as both organizers and hosts for our Lily of the Valley Festival, their muscled and red-boned arms sweating with their work. They strived in vain hope to better form a pure and mythical world in this, their unblessed land. The Cherokee are the survivors of the inhospitable—they are the artists, lovers, and dreamers hidden among the ruthless white masters who control their lives with a flip of the unearned coin.

The Cherokee worked all year gathering berries that eventually became colorful jars of jams and jellies. They dried wild apples to sell for baking pies and cakes, old women made moccasins from their supple brain-tanned leather, and even the children dried assortments of medicinal plants or made flower arrangements to sale or trade.

But the prizes among the townspeople were the Cherokee's smoked hams and the heavy slabs of cured bacon. The Cherokee's hogs were raised by hand and allowed to freely graze in the mountains where they grew fat on wild chestnuts and acorns. Once the swine were decently slaughtered, the thick white fat was rendered down for cooking lard or used to make cakes of lye-scented soap—all of which the Cherokee made with great care, and every item was sold to only the earliest of buyers. But the hams and bacon gave the Cherokee a devoted and almost fanatical following. Both were spiced and salted heavily before they were wrapped in layers of cheesecloth saturated with dark molasses and brown sugar—all of this was done before the meat was properly hung, and then smoked slow and low over seasoned hickory all winter long. There were no other hams or bacon like them anywhere, and every pork product was already sold by the time Three Crows and I arrived.

There were small platforms set up where local musicians played, and the while the men sipped homemade bust-head whiskey, the women gathered in a collection of braying gossips to barter their own brand of wares.

The majority of patrons awaited the festival's climax, a brutal contest of strength to decide the best man in the valley. A large corral of logs was built in the festival's center point, and only two men would face each other in this pit when the competition began. After that, it was all grit and no quit until one man was either knocked unconscious, or he submitted. The locals called it, *King of the Pit*. In the evening there would be a community feast, then torches would be lit, and the entire festival would culminate with a dance that night.

I stood beside Three Crows and Stoddard Quillen who were engaged in their own variety of tittle-tattle while I watched the charade of juvenile passion unfold in its finery.

The young males were gathered in their own adolescent tribe as the girls walked by with their coy appetites for flirtation. Some of the boys flushed like mercury rising with their circus smiles running wild. Others were aloof or indifferent, tall and gangly and so close to becoming men. There was an untainted confidence in some of the brassy young men, and others were so bashful they never cracked a smile. To them, the girls were the exotic dreams of their suppressed fantasies, dressed in their colorful pastels with fine hair that curled to the shoulders. Some of the girls were delicate or statuesque, others tiny as dolls. And when male and female eyes met—thoughts collided together and made an amazing sound like lovers blowing a backhand kiss. They each savored a kind of wonderment they had never known, as if they were lifting their voices together in a united prayer.

But my sound was in my head and my audience was loneliness, and then Jessamine Spitler walked into view. Stoddard Quillen elbowed me in the ribs when she stopped before me and made an introduction.

"I believe you're Reuben Judah," she said, extending her hand.

She was slight of build and, while the other women wore the wide hoop skirts of the day, she wore a slim summer dress which outlined her sleek figure. "I am, and you are?" I replied shaking her delicate hand.

"Jessamine Spitler. My father's business sold your family the material for your church."

"It was my father's church, not mine."

"I see," she said and pointed towards the circle of logs. "Are you entered in the contest?"

"Hell, yes," Stoddard cut in with a slur. Jessamine looked at the red-faced attorney and nodded politely.

"Nice to see you again, Mr. Quillen," she said and curtsied to the inebriated man. Jessamine turned back to me and started to speak when a heavy voice from the crowd cut in.

"Head back to your mud hut! No decent woman is interested in a shit-smelling, half-breed hog farmer." If Jessamine Spitler heard the insult she did not acknowledge it. She simply turned and walked back into the crowd without a word.

Stoddard Quillen leaned over and whispered in my ear. "Get ready to meet Gunter Kruger."

I said nothing and watched as the German loudmouth pushed his way through the crowd. He was big, and he wore his Germanic heritage in both size and weight. A head taller than me and twenty pounds the greater, he was thickly made with a foul temper to guide his bulk and little in the way of brains to regulate any moral direction. Gunter Kruger stopped in front of me and rubbed his wide chin, then spoke over his shoulder to the gathering crowd.

"What's the matter with him? Can't he talk?" Gunter said with a laugh, and all those of ill-manners laughed with him. Three Crows made a hooking motion with his index finger across his nose. It meant disgust. A sign among the Cherokee people signifying someone immoral and deceitful. But even this obscene gesture was lost on the crude monster now facing me.

Gunter and men like him were used to muscling their way through life—it is the way of bullies the world over—to be seen and feared because of bold threats or mere physical presence. Gunter Kruger leaned towards the man on his left and spoke loudly enough for everyone to hear. "I wonder if the hog farmer has tapped Jessamine Spitler's cherry."

"The truest juice comes from the first squeeze of the berry," another man added.

"Well...have you sampled her juice yet, injun' lover? Or maybe you're gonna' let that cherry rot on the vine?" Gunter asked me. He grinned like a villain and crossed his arms as if my answer was required.

I felt the flush of rage stripe my face and took a step towards Gunter Kruger when Three Crows touched my arm and spoke soft in his native tongue. "If you lose your temper you forfeit reason and all of your mistakes will be manufactured by anger. Wait until the pit."

"You have a little competition this year, Gunter. Reuben's name was the first one I put on the ledger for our best man in the valley," Stoddard Quillen said loud enough for the crowd to hear. The big German smiled and stepped close to me with his unearned swagger.

"Good," said Gunter sizing me up. He then turned and elbowed his way through the crowd as if he were parting some obstacle.

I looked towards a gloating Stoddard Quillen. "How many people are entered in this contest?" I asked. He grinned and took a long drink of whiskey, then burped his answer.

"It's just you and that other arrogant sonofabitch because no one else in their right mind would think of fighting Gunter."

"Why?" I asked.

"That cruel bastard broke a couple jaws a few years back when he won our best man in the valley, and no one has challenged him since." I looked at Stoddard and then Three Crows, both were smiling. "Relax, you're a strong healthy lad, you can take him," said Stoddard, patting my shoulder.

Mingo Kane

9

I was looking over the caged circle, trying to find knots or burrs in the rough-cut logs to avoid if my back was pressed against them when I faced Gunter. "I wanted to wish you good luck earlier," a voice said. I turned and Jessamine Spitler was behind me. "But I decided to wait for a proper time," she explained and leaned against the ring.

"Thank you," I replied and looked at her closely for the first time. Her face was smooth with delicate elfin structures, nose soft and turned slightly upward as if she snubbed the world with an odd and magnetic vanity.

"Is that a thank-you for wishing you luck, or a thank-you for waiting?" Jessamine asked. I liked her sharp attitude immediately. I smiled at Jessamine Spitler in spite of the circumstances.

"Thank you for the wish of luck," I said and motioned with my chin to where Gunter stood watching us. "From the looks of his size I may need more than good luck. A stout club would help me even things up."

"You'd ruin a good club on Gunter's thick head," she said and laughed as Three Crows walked over.

"We need to talk before the fight begins," he said and looked at Jessamine apologizing. "I beg your pardon for the intrusion."

"I thought this was supposed to be a wrestling match," I noted aloud.

Jessamine and Three Crows both shook their heads no and answered in unison. "Not when you're in the pit with, Gunter."

"It was nice talking with you, Reuben," Jessamine said and started to walk away when she stopped and turned around. "Before I forget, Gunter is left-handed and he never uses his right, watch out for his head butts if you work in close…he's mean-tempered, just so you know," she said and walked back towards the raucous horde of revelers.

"Good woman, that one," said Three Crows watching her until she disappeared in the crowd. Gunter Kruger stood off to the side and watched the entire scene between us unfold then followed Jessamine into the mob with an odd expression.

"This isn't going to be easy, is it?" I asked to avoid the subject of Jessamine.

Three Crows tapped his head as if the secret to winning was lodged there. "All you need is the advantage of knowing his weaknesses, and then you have to do what no other man has done."

"What's that?" I asked.

"Beat him," he said. As if his explanation was a well-known fact.

Three Crows led me back to the Cherokee camp where I removed my shirt and was smeared from head to waist with pork grease. "Once you're in the pit, take off your shirt and this grease will stop him from grabbing you," said Three Crows. The old man then rubbed my elbows and forearms with fine sand.

"What's this for?"

"Heads are hard so save your hands, just hook his left arm and pin it against your waist. You got to keep him close and use your forearm or elbow to hit him with glancing blows. If you catch him right, the grains of sand will cut him. If there is blood in his eyes he will have to blink more often," the old man explained, and pointed at my feet. "Keep your moccasins on to protect your toes, and tie the legs of your trousers tight around the ankles so nothing loose can be used as leverage if he grabs it." A dinner bell began to ring and

Three Crows grinned, "I think that is for you."

We walked over and stood across the pit from Gunter as Stoddard Quillen began to introduce the fighters. The old man continued with his advice. "He will try to hurt you from the start and not be shy about the manner he will use," said Three Crows.

"I don't plan on being none too shy about this fight my damn self," I answered. The old man smiled and leaned in close.

"Let him think you are scared, avoid his punches and wrestle with him instead."

"Why?" I asked swinging my arms, getting them ready.

"You have to let his confidence weaken him first."

I started bouncing on my toes. "How do you figure?"

"Gunter's size is a gift from his ancestors."

"Still makes him big," I replied.

"True, but Gunter didn't earn it. All his life others did the work for him. He's weak in the middle and has no wind. Don't let him hit you, but stay in close. Grapple with him. Gunter won't be able to grab you because of the grease, and he'll use all his wind trying to get an advantage. Grab his trousers and lean on him with all your body weight, hold him in tight then pin his arms to the side to make him use his legs for leverage and support. All it will take is three minutes and after that, he'll be spent. When Gunter starts talking to you or the crowd, he's trying to bide his time to get his wind back… that's when you do it."

"Do what?" I asked.

"Let loose the black wolf," Three Crows instructed.

"Sounds good to me; is there anything else?"

Three Crows leaned over and started massaging my shoulders. "Don't lose. I wagered the last of my personal hams on you."

"I reckon we both might starve," I said stepping across the logs and removing my shirt. A low whistle swept through the crowd. Bets were being made, odds were given. I was an underdog to the heavily favored German jaw-breaker. I was going to change that. The bout would begin when the bell rang once and end when one man went down, or conceded. I watched Gunter flex his arms and shadow box like a trained pugilist. I turned to the old man as the crowd began to cheer in anticipation.

"He's a might bit taller than I thought he was," I said.

Three Crows grinned at me just before the bell rang and the fight began. "Remember, the tallest blade of grass is the first to be cut."

The crowd went silent as we faced each other, the local bully against a godless mongrel. The blue hills arose undisturbed behind us like a grand arena, ever stoic in this ageless showdown of philandering repetition. Locusts chirped in the pending twilight, their song as ancient as the Bible, and in this moment it was as it had always been—just another day in the eye-blink of all creation. The battle for king of the pit had begun.

Gunter shook out his arms and stared at me with fanatical eyes, like he was a part of some strange initiation in the brutal light of this day. "Time to lose a few teeth, hog farmer," he said and spat to his left.

"Well, come ahead and take them, you big ugly sonofabitch. I'm not going anywhere," I answered back.

We met in the center and Gunter was quick to throw a series of stiff jabs. I ducked under each punch and stepped back keeping my distance. "You gonna' fight or run?" he laughed, and the crowd laughed with him.

Gunter came at me again and we clashed together in a rush of gristle and bone. I did as Three Crows instructed and pinned the German's left arm to my side and made him work for his advantage. His right hand slid across my greasy back as he fought for a hold. He gave me a vicious head butt cutting my eye just above the brow. Blood ran in dark steams down the side of my jaw. I answered his head butt with a savage punch to the ribs and Gunter backed off.

"Didn't think it was going to be like this, did you?" I asked, and this time, Gunter said nothing in return.

We stood there facing each other like abused and drunken revelers. Gunter made no move nor sound, like some reckoning or truce had been silently made between us, and the knowledge of this truth had escaped me.

"Stay on him," Three Crows yelled above the crowd. And we clashed again in our pit of future sorrows.

I held tight against Gunter and took three more head butts as my price, but he was panting under the weight of my body. I brought my forearm against the side of his head and I felt the full weight of him dissolve as his knees buckled. The big German was hurting and tried to break free, but I kept him tight and close. He dropped his hands and I caught him with a right cross to his cheek, knocking him backwards into the logs. This time it was Gunter's turn to bleed.

There is no mistaking the thrill of driving a bare fist into the human body out of savage anger. It takes the desire to win out of your opponent, weakens him, creates doubt in his ability, and devours his confidence when first blood is drawn. Gunter looked at me with uncertainty in his eyes. Being hurt was foreign to him. My pain was earned, and at that moment, the tide of the crowd began to turn in my favor.

This time he came towards me on cautious feet, slow and unsure. There was an unspoken malevolence to Gunter's eyes and in that instant—I knew that Gunter had broken with reality and become the most dangerous of all men. A man beyond desperation and without conscience, a man who no longer carried any link to the reality that might otherwise temper desperate actions. Gunter Kruger was afraid of losing this fight and the unearned ego he thought to gain.

We stared at each other as creatures reborn from some dark past that had only begun walking upright, an ageless and primordial competition between alpha males—driven not by survival, but by sheer bloodlust to become the dominant of the species. I knew the big German was close to going down. Gunter's arms were heavy and hung low beside his waist. His punches were slow and empty as a birthday wish. He had neither the direction nor defense against Three Crow's strategy.

I heard the old Cherokee yell from the side. "Let loose the black," he said. I looked at Gunter, his ribs working in and out like the broken bellows of a forge.

"Do you concede?" I asked, and received a grimace from the

German.

"Go to hell, hog farmer," he said and spat out a clot of blood.

We closed the distance a final time and circled each other. I could see my reflection in his cool blue eyes, the smell of stale sweat and sour beer mixed with the mud and sawdust of the pit. The crowd was yelling in the background like feasting wolves wanting blood for their primal payment. Gunter reached out his arms as if to connect and grapple, I stepped in close and gave him a sharp uppercut instead. His head snapped back and I saw the ground seem to roll under his feet as he staggered back. I stayed on him, the sound of meaty fists crashing into the flesh of men.

Gunter hooked my neck and tried to butt me but I ducked under his arm and sent a crashing right hand to his jaw. The big German went to his knees and tried to stand on wobbly legs, looking about with glazed eyes. I grabbed a handful of hair and threw a series of forearm strikes to the side of his unprotected head. Each time my elbow crashed into the German's head he sank towards the ground a little more, as if I were driving a human nail into the earth itself. Gunter went limp and his arms relaxed, I hit him flush behind the ear with a hard right hand and I was ready to hit him again when a deep guttural voice spoke from the side.

"Let him up...he concedes." I looked at the man who spoke and knew it was the father, Hermann Kruger.

I was covered in blood, drenched in sweat, and wearing a coating of grime. I stood over the broken and defeated Gunter Kruger in savage triumph as Three Crows entered the pit and held my hand aloft in victory.

"Reuben Judah, best man in the valley," Stoddard Quillen yelled, and the crowd erupted.

Three Crows checked my bloody head and pinched the cut flaps of skin together. "Never be ashamed of this scar, it is a symbol that you were the better man on this day," he said.

The truest light of your ambition provides an honest balance until that which you wanted most becomes the residue which binds you to your achievement. The day was mine and the victory I won set all things into motion…and it was the mechanics of this contest, which began to turn the wheels of revenge against me. The pride of men is hidden behind stubbornness and stays cloaked within the shadow of arrogance.

Jessamine Spitler leaned against the log barricade with her hands clasped as if she were in prayer. She waved me over. "I told you Gunter liked to butt heads and you still took three before you caught on," she said, and smiled.

I spat a clot of mud from my mouth and eyed her. "It's not like I wanted them."

"That was something to see. Folks will be telling the story of this fight to their grandchildren," she said.

"Telling them what?"

"They'll tell them how you wore Gunter down and peeled his face like a peach," Jessamine explained making a noise like a low whistle.

Before I realized it, the words came out. "I would like to call on you," I offered.

"I would like that," she replied.

* * *

Gunter Kruger and his family left before the evening banquet began, leaving Jessamine and me free to survey the sights and sounds of the event. Most of the festival goers were dressed informally, while the Cherokee danced about in the decorations of their forebears. The Native women wore colored sashes tied about their waists while men were adorned in simple buckskin breeches and moccasins; it seemed as if time had turned back and a lost culture of aborigines were now reborn in living indigenous flesh.

Rows of cook shacks let loose the aroma of food that was either roasting or broiling, and people walked about holding tin plates loaded with meat ranging from venison or pork, to a diverse assortment of wild fowl.

I found an empty table next to a long rectangular fire pit made from stacking flat river rocks together. A rack of old wire was woven and stretched lengthwise across the stones for a cooking surface and next to the crude structure sat an elder black man basting a variety of foodstuffs. He seemed to work the homemade grill with some handed-down Negro philosophy as he watched the assorted victuals sizzling to the heated embers below.

The old Negro looked at me with sad and abused eyes as he basted the charred skin of his fare. "Mistah' Judah, that sho' was some fight, I swear afore God and three 'sponsible witnesses, I ain't never seen the like of it."

"Thank you," I replied and looked about. Everyone had their respective places to dine, but no one was sitting here. I said to Jessamine, "I don't know about you but I'm starved. If this spot suits you, it's fine by me."

"Works for me, I'm hungry too," she answered.

The old black man shook his head in objection. "White folk don't take their dinner with the cook niggers, Mistah' Judah."

"These two white folks eat where they please," Jessamine answered sharply.

"I sho' don't wanna' cause you two young'uns nary a bit of trouble," he said, ladling two plates full of cooked meat. "I's just cook'n up a lil sump'in in case some black folks happen by."

"I think the best man in the valley has earned the right to pick where he eats," said Jessamine.

The old man seemed to relax. "I reckon you right missy, Mistah Judah sho' 'nuff did…that Gunter Kruger is an ornery feller. Never thought I'd see the day when he got bested in a fight. He whupped me near to death with a tobacco cane once."

"Why'd he whip you?" I asked.

"'Cause I said morn'n to him and his kin when their buggy passed me by. I was just walking along when they happened by and never meant no disrespect to Gunter or his folks, but he beat me anyhow…and but good. Had me some horrible whupping scars on my back that didn't heal for a month or more. Yup, he's a mean'un."

Jessamine handed me a plate full of food then gave the black man a smile. "This time it's Gunter who's healing from a whipping,"

56

she said. The man smiled back and nodded his gray speckled head in agreement.

"And I'd say he be eating soft food till that jaw of his'n heals," added the old Negro.

We sat across from each other and ate as the black man sang an old hymn while tending his fodder. "Do you feel sorry for them?" Jessamine asked looking towards the elder black gent. She split a chunk of meat with her hands and handed a piece to me. "Try this," she said, putting the other slice in her mouth. "I've never had anything so good."

I took the meat and held it between my fingers, thinking about my reply. "I don't think any man should own another. If a man is willing to work for you, he deserves a decent enough wage to provide for his family."

"Exactly," Jessamine agreed and looked the scene over before posing another question. "Did your family ever own slaves?"

"No, my father considered slavery an abomination."

"Your father didn't come to the festival, did he?" she asked. I shook my head and finished chewing before answering.

"No, he never cared for the Cherokee...or me for that matter," I said, hoping she would change the subject.

"Your father doesn't agree with slavery on one hand, but he can't tolerate the Cherokee on the other. I find that odd," she said and paused. "I don't mean to pry, but why doesn't he care for you or the Cherokee?"

"I think he blamed both of us for my mother dying when she gave birth to me. How about your family?" I asked as the evening torches were being lit.

"My mother and father are still overcome with shock because they had a pre-arranged marriage between me and Gunter Kruger, as if I had no say in the matter. Of course I let them know I would refuse the Kruger's offer before one was made."

"Why?" I asked.

"It's not about love to any of them," she answered with a hard edge.

"Then what's it about?"

"Business," she said, and then added with a harsher tone. "To Gunter and my father it would be a business proposition. My father and his brothers are heist merchants with warehouses in South Carolina, Virginia and Atlanta. Hermann Kruger needs his goods transported to my family's warehouses for distribution. If we marry, my father would get the Kruger's business and my mother would gain more status in her community of gossiping hens. Everyone would win, except me," she explained.

"I've not heard kind words about the Kruger family," I said finishing the last of my meat.

Jessamine stacked our plates together, split a slab of cornbread, and handed me a thick chunk before answering. "Yeah, the Kruger family tends to get what they want, no matter what it is or who it's from. And Gunter Kruger doesn't like being second best at anything," said Jessamine.

I was about to reply when the music started and the final assembly of festive hopefuls began dividing up into a collection of singles. The young females stood to the side in one faction while the adolescent males convened in a congregation of their own across from them, each side awaiting a gesture of courage from the first male brave enough to seek out a dance partner. Stoddard Quillen used his fingers and whistled, then waved his arm in my direction as if he needed my assistance.

Jessamine looked at me and said, "I think Mr. Quillen wants you to lead the first dance." She wiped her hands on a cloth napkin. I felt my body become rigid. I found myself groping for words, but I could find none. "What's the matter?" she asked with her coy eyes alight and defiant. "Don't tell me you've never danced before."

I struggled to say something, anything in my defense, "Well..." I managed to stutter, but no other words followed.

Jessamine's hand stretched out towards mine. I resisted the sudden instinct to recoil. She closed her hand around mine. "Come on," she whispered in confidence. "I'll show you. All you have to do is ask."

"Ask what?" I responded.

"Ask me to dance," Jessamine said in a mischievous tone.

I cleared my throat. "Jessamine Spitler…may I have this dance?"

She smiled and replied with something akin to triumph in her tone, "Mr. Judah, it would be my pleasure."

I realized my hand was still in hers as we walked towards the circle of fresh cut grass that had been prepared by the slaves a day prior. The smell of greens and wood smoke still lingered in the air. The sound of music gained clarity and volume as we approached the band. I felt Jessamine's hand pull mine gently, causing me to turn my body towards hers until we faced each other.

"Now," she said with a gentle authority. "Place your right hand on my left shoulder and take my other hand and hold it with yours."

I stretched my right hand out. Almost like I was reaching for a hot stove. My hand found Jessamine's shoulder and moved around to the gentle sway of her back. My other had held hers and we were closer than I thought possible, I could feel the outline of her breasts brush against my chest. "Like this?" I asked. She gave me a curt nod and took a step towards me.

"Now just move with me," Jessamine said with confidence.

My body was at her command. She coaxed me backwards, and then we drifted to the right. I felt her pull me forward. And then we flowed left and then back again. It was a box-like pattern that our feet drew into the fresh grass. She moved with grace. But also with a refined and deliberate ease. We were in perfect harmony with each other amid the music's tempo, our fingers intertwined in a union without vows, sharing a trust born of mutual hardship in this apostate land. Other couples began to dance and we were crowded and pressed more closely together; her body had a rich firmness and her hair was scented with the spring air and sunshine, fresh and earthy, as if she were born of these worldly elements. The torches wrapped around us as the new moon clenched the night sky…and we danced. It was mystical and magical—star-crossed lovers so passionately unhinged. Beneath the gilded Heavens and those yet to come, under the watchful eyes of God and those deities like him now nameless and forgotten. We danced for ourselves as we created a new cadence to this hard cruel world. We danced until Jessamine looked up at me.

"Maybe it's time for a break," she said. I thought I did something wrong.

"Why?"

"The band quit playing a while ago, Reuben," Jessamine said and smiled up at me.

It seemed as if we had only touched hands and whether it was four songs or twenty, it mattered not. We danced unaware. I don't know why I said it, but before we parted I looked down at her, her face serene and smiling up at me. I will never forget that look, that moment so flawless in time, the brevity of perfection.

"*I am because we are*," I said. Jessamine smiled and put her head on my chest. And for the first time in my life I felt complete, and I smiled back…

10

Hermann Kruger started passing a petition around town insisting that all land owned by the Cherokee was to be sold at a public auction. Stoddard Quillen produced the legally signed documentation of my sole ownership along with a stern warning to the Kruger patriarch. Should he contest the legality of my land rights, Stoddard would use any means necessary to absolve the unjust claim at the full expense of Hermann Kruger's assets. The elder Kruger conceded with a warning of his own—"Today is yours, Quillen, enjoy it while it lasts. Tomorrow will be mine." And therein the seeds of greed were planted, and I would one day harvest the bitter fruit of that transaction.

I was now a man of considerable means, and began clearing a piece of rich bottomland for my house. Jessamine came daily to help with plans and kept the books so that all who labored for me would be paid. The house would sit against the mountains below the Cobb Hollow Divide with the Bee Rocks directly overhead. Across the front would be green pasture to the South River, and beyond that, fenced corrals for horses and other livestock.

The months Jess and I spent working side-by-side together to complete my house mortared our relationship. Jess had a fierce independence when women were expected to be anything but. She bypassed the meat and went straight for the gristle. Jess didn't mind getting her hands dirty building something and it wasn't long before we began calling it *our* house—making plans for a library full of books on geography, history, and other areas of learned interest. Jess designed a barn to keep horses of solid stock she would personally select, and I mapped out a penned area beyond a grove of wild chestnut trees for the Cherokee's hogs. We decided the remaining fields would be cleared for planting and harvesting a wide assortment of seasonal crops.

Fall was fast approaching and we were less than a month away from completion. Jess and I were working side by side, chinking the stone foundation of the horse barn she alone had designed. "Do you want to take a break?" I asked her. Jess had been unusually quiet all day.

Jess sat down in the sawdust and crossed her legs. "Doesn't it bother you?" she asked.

"Does what bother me?"

"That I've taken over all of this, the layout of the house, the barn…everything. And what bothers me is you've never said no to anything I've suggested, or even questioned the reason why I wanted it that way," she explained. Jess stood up and wiped her hands across her dress front then planted them on her hips. "Well?" she said.

I stood there and shrugged off her demand for an answer out of playful spite. "Well, what, Jess?"

"Well, it just seems to me that you're counting the chicks before your clutch is hatched," she said. I gave her a look of mock confusion.

"Jess, we haven't talked about buying chickens or even building a hen house."

At my reply Jess kicked a rock with her foot then crossed her arms. "You know damned good and well I'm not talking about buying chickens. I think you've become a bit high-handed and presumptuous, Mr. Judah." I started to tell her I was joking when she cut me off with a wave of her hand and continued. "It seems nowadays you've become somewhat cocky and overconfident by allowing me to plan all of this. Maybe it's because you're counting on me being here without my say so in the matter," she said and then pointed her finger at me. "I think that maybe you're taking for granted a little something you haven't even asked me for."

"Jess, I couldn't have done any of this without you, keeping the books and paying the carpenters, placing an order with the sawmill for lumber and fencing material. I wouldn't be anywhere close to finishing this project without you and your help. I always sorta' figured it was ours because we did it together."

"And that's it?" she said rather harshly. Jess threw her hands up in exasperation and walked in a tight circle. She stopped and put a hand on her hip and cocked a leg. "I'm just an unpaid worker to you? Why don't we build an extra stall in this barn and you can pen me up here. Keep me locked away and pull me out from time to time when you need something else planned or built." Jessamine was full blown mad, looking me straight in the face, holding my stare as if the staggered space between us demanded my reprisal.

"Jessamine Spitler, would you do me the great honor of becoming my wife?" I asked. The abruptness of my proposal caught her off guard.

"You've got to do better than that," she replied with a softer edge.

I stepped behind the barn stall and retrieved an object I'd been working on for the past few weeks. It was wrapped in a rack of brown oilcloth and tied shut with twine. I untied the knot and pulled a large walnut plaque free of its wrappings. It was hand sanded and stained with acorn hulls by the Cherokee women. It wasn't much, but the words engraved across the surface were done by my hand alone—*I am because we are.*

I handed the finished mantle piece to Jess and told her I planned to hang it above our stone fireplace. Jessamine smiled and walked over to me, looking up to where I stood over her. She shoved me back against the barn stall with her hand and stuck her finger in my face.

"It sure as Hell took you long enough," she chastised. I pulled Jess close to me and kissed her.

"It's hard for me, Jess. You come from a good family and could've had any man in the valley."

Jess looked up at me and wrinkled her brow. "My family is not so great, Reuben. We have more skeletons in our closet then there are bones in a graveyard." I laughed and pulled her tighter then kissed her again.

We parted and looked at each other. "I forgot to tell you we need to pack a picnic lunch and hike up to the Bee Rocks tomorrow," I said.

"Why?" she asked.

"We're meeting Three Crows so I can ask him to perform a Cherokee marriage ceremony for us…after we're properly married in a civilized church to appease your family. And I was kinda' hoping that maybe you could talk some sense into Three Crows about moving down here with us. I thought he could live in that guest house we built."

"So you had this whole thing planned all along. And here I was, worried to death day and night that Gunter Kruger would have to ride up and sweep me off my feet before you'd ask," she said, shaking her head. Jess gave me a playful shove and said she would have the old Cherokee in our guesthouse before the first frost.

I thought about what she said before I replied. "I honestly never had a plan, Jess. I just needed to find the right words and the right time to ask you proper."

"You did just fine. And what you inscribed on this plaque is impeccable, Mr. Reuben Judah," Jess replied and gave me another kiss. "This barn should be finished by week's end. And after that, we have furniture to order," she said and then thought for a second before adding. "I was thinking that maybe we can order something else, something special I have always wanted."

"What's that, Jess?"

Jessamine looked down and answered as if she were embarrassed to ask. "I'd like to have a piano and a violin."

"Well, now, it seems to me you did a little planning of your own, Miss Jessamine Spitler." Jess brought a hand up to cover her grin. "Do you play?" I asked.

"I have never touched a musical instrument in my life. But I want our children to be educated and musically inclined," she explained. It was my turn to be caught off-guard. I hadn't planned that far ahead or given any thought about us having children.

"Children…I would like that, Jess."

* * *

We made it to the Bee Rocks just as the sun crossed the peak of the mountains and ate a lunch of bread, cheese, and thick slabs of Cherokee ham.

"When will Three Crows be here?" Jess asked after we'd finished eating.

"I'm not sure. He said that it would be after he was finished digging ginseng and sassafras roots. It's hard to get a straight answer out of that old man." Jess nodded and leaned close against me.

"Promise me that you will always be honest," she whispered in my ear then kissed my cheek. I put my arm around her and pulled her close.

"I promise," I answered and kissed her back, our two hearts separate but as one in the descending light of our new world.

"Can we just sit here together until the sun sets, Reuben?"

"Yes, ma'am." She nodded and wiped her eyes, the acorns in the trees clinking like a soft choir. "I love you," I whispered and kissed her again.

"I know, Reuben. I love you too," she answered, taking my hand and putting it to her face. Our fingers were intertwined in a union without vows, sharing a trust and caring born of hardship in a visceral land which we so wanted to change. Jess stood up and pulled me to my feet.

"Feel my heart," she said. Jess took my hand and placed it inside the opening in her bodice. I felt the consistency of her soft skin as I let my fingertips trace the dips and curves of her neck, along the outline of her clavicle, and down to the space between her breasts. As I moved closer to her, I could smell the scent that was uniquely Jessamine Spitler, my future wife– if I were to lose my sight I would forever know her by that fragrance.

"Maybe we should wait until we're properly…" I started to say when she put a finger to my lips.

"Don't say anything, Reuben," she whispered. It was as if she held within her, all the knowledge of those maternal ancestors dating back to the time of Eve. Jess slowly began to undress, her eyes never leaving mine. Knowing her natural beauty was her greatest power, she shared this awareness with me. My eyes were following her every move, my ears listening to the soft scrapes and rustlings as her clothes slid down the perfection of her body. Jagged shards of sunlight created mysterious shadows around Jess like a halo. I watched and memorized every look, every gesture, and every unnamed emotion to sustain me for the unknown times ahead. My heart pounded faster, and my mouth dried as she reached up and placed her hand on my cheek. Jess seemed to reach into me with her essence, and then she slowly began to undress me. Every hardship I knew was erased. There was no memory in my past, as if it were suddenly wiped clean by this single moment in time. All that mattered was what we were creating together…right here, right now.

I ceased thinking at that moment and gave myself to Jess. I felt the need to feel her body, to make it a perfect fit within mine. The tree branches seemed to create a symphony of privacy and fellowship, as if they alone bore witness to our lovemaking. And I wanted this one thin cataract of time to last forever. So distinct it was. Flawless and unspoiled, this perfect reflective point that would live within me—forever.

We were dressed and lay woven together on the warm autumn leaves, talking of things yet to come as lovers do when their future is vast and buoyant before them. Jess and I put away the ruins of our past and began building our own library of memories. The house we had built, a library soon to be full of books, a nursery, and the livestock that would eventually grace our land. I pulled her against me, the smell of our lovemaking and promise on her hair—crushing her to my chest, inhaling the foundation of what she meant to me. I looked at Jess long and hard. My curious stare made her uncomfortable.

"What is it?" Jess asked self-consciously.

"Do you think you are beautiful?" I asked.

"What?" she laughed.

"I watch you and the way you not only see the beauty in your life, but somehow you are able to feel it. I have always thought you have to feel beautiful to truly understand its worth."

"And you do not?"

"I am a man," I replied.

"And men are so different from women, Reuben."

"Maybe not all men…but I am."

Jess cupped my face in her hands. "I see and feel beautiful because you see that trait within me. I know you are beautiful because I can see that rarity in you as well, Reuben. And that is all you need to know," she said and looked into my eyes. "Your different colored eyes become darker when you are excited."

"Three Crows says it is because of the fight going on inside me," I explained, letting my index finger trace her fine lips. As if upon them was the blind and unspoken language of a lover's Braille.

"And your eyes changed colors because of your accident?"

"Yes."

"I hope Three Crows decides to move in with us. I'd like to get to know him better," she said, changing the subject.

"We'll find out soon enough."

"When?"

"Right now, he's standing behind the trunk of that hickory tree," I answered as the old man stepped out and came forward. "Your feet are quiet but you reek of ginseng," I told him. The old man smiled and sat down between us.

"Reuben and I would be honored if you would conduct our marriage ceremony," Jess said to the old man.

Three Crows looked at her and shook his head in mock disgust. "I once told a man that you were a smart woman, but it seems I was mistaken," he said.

"Why?" asked Jess.

Three Crows smiled and tilted his head in my direction. "No decent woman with a lick of sense would want to be partnered with such an ugly man."

My mouth dropped open at the brash insult—and for a moment, Jessamine sat stunned. Three Crows slapped his knee and guffawed and then Jess laughed with him at my expense. From that moment until the day he died, Jess was the old man's favorite. The old Cherokee accepted her offer without question when she asked him to move into our guest house. There were only a handful of families left on the Cobb Hollow Divide, and each household was making plans to move to the lowlands before winter. Under Jess's direction, each Cherokee family was transplanted and given paid employment on our farm.

Jessamine Spitler was the only person to have ever loved me for who I was to her, the only one who showed me what true beauty meant. We were to be married a month later, and though Wilbur Spitler was not overly pleased with the prospect of her marriage to me, he was not necessarily opposed to it. To have his daughter marry outside their strict Irish clan, and to a man with strong ties among the mountain Indians was unheard of. The Spitler family came from a long line of wealthy heist merchants, and the inner core of their Catholic family was cemented in material wealth.

But, to have his daughter betrothed to the man who not only owned the entire Shenandoah Valley, but a man of serious means who could guarantee safe passage across the Cherokee lands made all pledges of love possible. Wilbur Spitler was a vain man and that conflict was his balance. It was like an internal gyroscope that forced him to choose. God is all but unknown when fortunes are to be made and that fact did not go unnoticed by me.

We were wed late October under a red and clipped harvest moon, brought together like the cold water of an emotional glacier. Three Crows spoke the old words of our people then we joined our hands and became one soul.

11

Present

"I'll never have the memories of sharing something so intoxicating as your first dance," Paul Tandy said.

"Sometimes, I think back and remember so little of my time with Jessamine, as if someone took the stones from her grave. And yet, to this day, my ancient blood still whispers her name. Jess gave me life, a reason to be more of a man."

"I don't think I'll ever understand the beauty of a love like that," said Paul.

"Nobody can truly love their lover unless they love you back. It's the only way."

Paul nodded his agreement and smiled. "Another year soon comes to an end. Do you make any New Year's resolutions, Reuben?"

"The end of another year means nothing to me. Long ago, after Jess was gone, I resolved not to make any more resolutions."

"You said you had children. How many?"

"Three total, almost nine months to the day we were wed, a set of twin boys was born. Luther and Eli. A year later we had a girl that Jessamine named Molly."

"So that's where you got your name, Luther Eli Cobb...from your son's first names and Cobb Hollow." I nodded in agreement as Paul closed his eyes as if he were dreaming. "I can almost see everything you've described," he said.

"It was the greatest time of my life, but all things change. As happy as we were, war was just beyond the horizon with its false pretense of peace. The Country was changing its views and the general population was under the grand illusion that the coming war would be a nice and tidy affair. It wasn't and my life would change forever because of it."

Paul checked his watch and stretched his bony arms. "Mr. Reuben, I have to get back to my rounds, but tomorrow I'd like to hear more about your children and the Civil War."

"And so it goes," I replied and watched him go.

* * *

We got a new admission yesterday, an old Negro man who looks to be in his eighties. He watches this place with rheumy codger eyes as if the finality of his jaded life is but a nightmare. He is frail and weak and no fight for life remains within his abandoned soul. I look at his hands, the skin like brown seaweed draped over the brittle limbs of an abused puppet. Paul Tandy said he was a shipyard worker until he caught some disease from the insulation. A *three-weeker* is what the staff calls them, such a cruel medicinal metaphor— therapeutic validation for another clock-less life winding down to the last three weeks of certain uncertainty.

The female nurse that attends the black man is a new arrival to this wonderful tabernacle of insanity. Her starched white uniform is without the stains of her under-appreciated trade. Blood, fecal brown marks, and those yellow patches of urine that never fade are absent from her attire. Those stains will become her battle scars, contaminates that will symbolize her initiation into deviance and dementia. She stands off from the wheelchair bound black man as if he might be contagious. Little miss sunshine the white-clad savior. She comes fresh from some paper doll factory in the perfect city, with the perfect family, and the perfect high school attendance. Daddy's little princess still feels the electric air of her new profession but cannot fathom the possibility of incurable.

Stay here in this place, my precious. Stay with these passionate fanatics and they will take that dream from you. Stay here and earn the hard edge of your life after seeing the darkest fetishes and desires of the insane come alive. Stay here long enough and you will begin to taste this place and its bitter palate of mental deceit. Spit it out and runaway while you can, or the flavor of dementia will linger forever.

The lunatics call her kind of a *three-weeker* as well. Three weeks to decide if she will endure or succumb to the evil she never knew existed. Little miss sunshine steps away to clean a fresh puddle of vomit, the old black man watches her go about the nastiness of her chore. I notice the old Negro has hearing aids in both ears.

"Do they help?" I asked him.

"Come again?" he says, cupping his ear.

"The hearing aids, do they help?"

"They work for about a week," he answered and gave me his best codger smile.

"The batteries only last for a week?" I ask.

He shook his head no. "Not what I meant at all. When you first get these hearing devices you begin to hear everything, all the sounds you had forgotten or paid no mind to. It's all in your mind, you see. Your mind tells you what to hear and what is important, so after a week the worst silence in the world begins to happen. You realize the only sounds you really need to hear are the voices that made your life livable. But when you grow old and all the people you loved are finally gone, any sound after that doesn't really matter," he said with a feeble laugh, and then went silent.

An old man's laugh is a wonder to hear, but it is a dishonest sound. Old men never laugh with the honesty of a child. I have to agree with the old Negro man. The only sounds you need to hear in life are the voices of your loved ones. Once those voices are silent, we are all deaf to a certain degree.

Little miss sunshine grabs the wheelchair handles with her dainty hands. "Time for bed, Mr. Jenkins."

The old black man turns to me as he is wheeled away. "I might as well turn these things off forever," he says tapping his ear. "Like I said, there's nothing important to hear anymore. All I ever hear in this wretched place is when it's time to eat, time to wash, and when it's time for bed. The only thing I haven't heard them say is when it's time for me to die."

I watch the old black fellow as he is wheeled down the hall past Paul Tandy. "Good evening, Reuben," said Paul, walking over and sitting down in a vacant chair beside me.

"How long does he have?" I ask.

"Who?"

"The old black man."

"Mr. Jenkins?" I nod. "Perhaps a week, two at best," Paul said.

"Two weeks is a lifetime, I once saw 5,000 men die in one day."

"The Civil War?" asked Paul.

I nodded and closed my eyes. "It was at Gettysburg."

"I'd love to hear how it all started. It's rare to have first-hand history recited by a man who lived through it."

"Then walk with me into the shadows of my yesterday listen to my words and you will see a truth that is all but forgotten…"

12

War
1861

On a mid-April morning in 1861, Stoddard Quillen paid me an unexpected visit before he boarded a train to Richmond for a meeting with Virginia's Secession Committee. The pause in his itinerary came with an unwelcome benediction. Fort Sumter had just surrendered to the newly formed Confederate States of America. Stoddard never got out of his buggy, just a brief stop and a cautious word of advice before catching the train. "Best be making plans in case the railroad shuts down if this war gains momentum," was all he said.

I was faced with few options and made the hard choice to divide my family for their security should I be called to enlist. Luther and Eli left that afternoon on a train bound for Atlanta where they would live with Jessamine's father. Wilbur Spitler had already made the move to Atlanta for the very same reasons we were sending Luther and Eli—for safety should a full-scale war break out.

Stoddard returned five days later with the hard news that Virginia had seceded from the Union, with one exception. Fifty western counties would split from Virginia and remain loyal to the United States.

"You best be watching Hermann Kruger," said Stoddard as we finished dinner.

"The reason being?" I answered as Jess cleared the table.

"I'll leave you two to discuss business," Jess interrupted with her arms full.

"Thank you again for dinner, Jess. I don't get fed quite so well at home these days," Stoddard replied and then looked back to me as Jess left the room. His face had a thin smile. "To answer your question…Hermann Kruger's South River Clay Company is a slave-operated company and falls across the divided lines into what will soon become the anti-slavery State of West Virginia. Hermann owns less than a hundred acres of land here in Virginia. So think on this—that small section of land he owns borders your property on three sides and Hermann has no legal way to cross back and forth between the two States. Hermann is trapped. In other words he has to choose which side he's on, and Hermann knows full well…this is the one time he can't play for both teams. It seems that arrogant bastard is on the fence and either choice he makes will cost his uppity ass a fair price."

"What do you think he'll do?" I asked as Stoddard stood and stretched then started for the door. He thought as he walked and put his hat on before answering.

Stoddard cocked his head and winked at me. "Let's just wait and see what happens. Let Hermann play his hand first," he answered before leaving.

We found out in less than a month which hand would be played. A small parcel of Hermann Kruger's land may have bordered mine here in Virginia, but his slave-driven South River Clay Company fell beyond the segregated state lines of conflict. The entire Kruger family changed their view on the legality of slavery and sided with the newly formed West Virginia. Virginia had become a Border State and close to 10,000 acres of my land helped create two new counties in West Virginia. Every acre I owned beyond those revamped state lines was quickly confiscated by West Virginia's temporary government in Wheeling. And before I could contest the forfeit, 2,000 acres of my land was resurveyed and legally deeded to Hermann Kruger.

Hermann now had the option of staying on the middle ground and playing both sides. He could keep his retail office in Virginia and run his business in West Virginia. Hermann Kruger could now sell his goods to both sides of this conflict, and he had just acquired all the available lands routes between the two.

I was caught up in that instability of turbulence and left without a surrogate option—and though we were both aggressive in our opposition to the legality of slavery—Jess and I were left with no sensible alternative. We would side with Virginia and remain loyal to our home.

I held firm to my conviction that no man should be shackled to another. Black skin or white, we were all barefoot servants to the same masters and we each swore an oath of servitude under the pretense of revolution. The North only provided the rope—it would take both sides to tie the knot that would unite them to war.

I enlisted as a private in the first Virginia Calvary under William "Grumble" Jones, July of 1861. Ten days later I would be in Prince William County where The First Battle of Manassas would hold center stage, and once the smoke cleared, the temple of freedom would come crashing down upon the heads of a blind and bitter Nation.

Though our boys were Jessamine's greatest joy, it was our daughter Molly who truly captured the attention; at four, a constant and consistent commotion of curiosity drove her young mind. She was driven by an endless and perpetual hunger to explore the miracle of life, and though the world would sometimes slow for her—Molly did not slow down for anything or anyone, except for Three Crows.

The old man would take whatever creature her prying hands may have found and tell her the Cherokee story of its creation, how that particular being came to be, and what purpose that creature had in this world. To Three Crows, Molly was his devotion, a student of life with the same miss-matched eyes of her father.

That last morning before I left, Jess and I hiked up to the Bee

Rocks at daybreak and we sat overlooking our homestead and the broad expanse beyond. By the summer of 1861 our farm had doubled in size and now swept into the brilliance of our Shenandoah Valley. The ground fog hung low over the scene as if the defeated land slept beneath a seamless and unavoidable plague. We sat and watched the bright and golden sun arise like the angry eye of God.

"Can we just sit here until night," Jess asked leaning against me.

"We can sit here as long as you like, Jess."

"We can stay until dark, you're leaving for Northern Virginia tomorrow," she said. I nodded and pulled her close.

"The Federal troops are gathering near Manassas, nothing more. We'll march our army there and exchange insults and come home royal drunk and weary of menfolk altogether," I replied, trying to lighten the mood.

"I hope so, but promise me you'll be careful," Jess said and gave me a kiss. We had both worn britches and work shirts that day. Jess pulled a necklace from her breast pocket and put it around my neck. It was a double cross, a thick beamed crucifix with a smaller cross of wire layered on top. Both the chain and crucifix were solid gold.

"Where did you...?" I started to ask when Jess put a finger to my lips.

"I found some nuggets in your chest of drawers and had Stoddard Quillen melt them down so I could have this cross made for you. Bricks and mortar, do you remember?" Jess asked.

I held the cross in my hand and nodded my head. "I would never forget that, Jess. It was the day we were building the foundation to our barn. It was the day I asked you to marry me."

"Yes, you supplied the bricks and I supplied the mortar. We built it together, that's why the big cross symbolizes the brick and the smaller cross made of wire represents the mortar."

"Thank you, Jessamine Judah," I said and gave her a kiss. She stepped back and grinned, odd glint in her eyes.

"Did you find Silas Cobb's cave of gold?" she asked. I shrugged my shoulders. Jess gave me a shove. "You're not going to tell me, are you?"

The Prophet of Cobb Hollow

"You'll have to ask Silas Cobb that question and find out for yourself," I chided back.

"You're not getting off that easy, Reuben Shadrack Judah. And besides, I didn't pack a few extra blankets in your knapsack for nothing, so get a fire going. It's too cold this high up to be naked, even under blankets," she said and winked.

"I 'spect we're gonna' make enough heat to keep us both warm," I answered back with a wink of my own. Jess laughed and pulled me down beside her.

"Just be careful, Reuben. Don't worry about me and Molly. Just promise *me* you'll be careful," she said.

I left that morning on a dark bay stud Jessamine had picked from her personal stock. Jess had a subtle way about her when she worked with horse flesh. She broke her horses the same way she broke me and the rest of her fishbowl world; Jess wore you down with kind hands and patience. She named him, "Sampa." It was the closest word in the Cherokee language for, The Prophet.

"I call him Prophet because he's just like you," Jess told me.

I swung my leg over the saddle and brought Prophet around to face her. "How so?" I asked.

Jess walked over and hugged my leg. "He's quick to start and can run as fast as any, but he's got a slow sure gait that will wear down even the best."

I leaned down and gave her a kiss with my cross dangling in the static air between us. Jess closed her eyes and touched the double crucifix to her forehead, and then gave it a kiss before tucking it back into my shirt. "I want you to promise that you'll always come back and take care of me," Jess said and gave me a final kiss.

"I promise."

"You best keep your promises, Mr. Judah."

Jess smacked Prophet on the rump as Molly stepped outside to watch me go. She wrapped her arms around Jess's leg with her wet hair in a tangle of leftover dreams. The bay lurched up the mountain path toward the Bee Rocks. I looked back at Jess and watched as she put her feet together with Molly's and they held their arms out

77

to make an overlapping human cross.

"*I am because we are,*" Jessamine yelled. They were both like a house with a thousand tiny rooms. And each door was opened one room at a time to reveal another hidden beauty. How many doors did I leave unopened that final day?

13

I sat on the Bee Rocks waiting to say goodbye to Three Crows before I dropped off the other side to my assembly point. I was examining the cross Jess had given me. It was large as a silver dollar with a thin wire mounted on top of the main crucifix, two crosses forever touching each other—Bricks and Mortar—two hearts intertwined in a union beyond mortality, a symbol of faith and the firm belief that even once…just once, the odd-eyed man could feel the true honesty of love.

"I am getting too old to walk these trails. I remember when I could run top to bottom without stopping," Three Crows said coming up from the path. He bent hands to knees and caught his breath, then sat down on a log. He rubbed his face and looked up at me sitting on Prophet with my arms crossed over the pommel.

I looked down at him and said, "You picked the spot, old man." Three Crows grinned then waved me off my horse to come and sit with him. I dismounted and straddled the log beside him. The old Cherokee closed his eyes and wove his hands over the valley as if he were casting a spell.

"I remember days like this when my father took me to the forest and we ate wild blackberries. More than ninety years ago. I was just a boy of four or five. The leaves of those blackberry bushes were so dark and green, briars thick as needles. The grass always smelled sweet with the seasonal wind those long years ago. There were buffalo here back then, and we would have a great hunt and we would kill only one for a feast," he said and opened his eyes, they were wet. "And now, the buffalo are gone. And the blackberries are not as sweet and the wind smells like the stagnant air before a storm. All of this will be gone soon enough, and I am truly glad my eyes will not live to see it."

Three Crows thought for a moment and then held out his hand to me. "Come and hug an old man before you leave," he said, wiping his eyes on the back of his hand.

I gave the old Cherokee his hug and mounted Prophet then swung around to say goodbye…Three Crows was gone. It was the last time I would ever see the old man. By day's end everything would change, and my life would soon become a series of unmarked tarot cards blowing in the wind, unread and meaningless—the hanged man or the broken King without a Queen. A beautiful muse of failings without penitence, solace, or solitude. Whether right or wrong, I would soon have war as my ultimate guide.

I was met at the assembly area by "Grumble" Jones himself, who took one look at Prophet and reassigned me to the Washington Mounted Rifles. His moniker was justly earned—"Grumble" Jones had the personality of a fencepost and the humor of a mute ghost. We were herded, man and beast, on a train already loaded with General Joe Johnston's men and set forth towards Manassas Junction. I squatted beneath Prophet in the cramped boxcar and took a seat next to another private. The men on top of our rail car began to holler out obscure comments like we were set forth upon a scavenger hunt: "Gonna' get me a Yankee jacket," someone would yell and another would holler back, "I'll be sure and plug a few holes in it so Billy Yank won't object to you taking it."

We sat back against the wall and the nameless private said to me, "I'll tell you one thing…if you wanna' hear the honest truth of it."

"What's that?" I asked.

"Those loudmouths up top," he answered, pointing towards the ceiling. "They're nothing more than dumbass farm boys with cow shit in their ears. They're of a mind we're riding off to a choir recital. Well, this sure as shit ain't gonna' be no church social," he said and kicked a pile of fresh horse dung. "No, sir, not by a damn sight. Men are gonna' die on this day, and they're gonna' die on both sides."

"I surely hope not," I said, taking my hat off and wiping the sweat away before replacing it. "I don't think either side is ready for a fight."

He laughed and shook his head in objection. "Oh, there's gonna' be a fight. Ole Joe Johnston is here to throw his hat in the ring, but he's just as content as we are to solve this without firing a shot. We'll be with J.E.B. Stuart and no finer man will you find in the saddle. But the one to watch is the new General we got fresh from VMI, Thomas Jackson. We belong to Stuart and Stuart belongs to Jackson, and make no mistake about it…Jackson is here to fight and he aims to have it his way."

I stuck out my hand and we shook. "I'm Reuben Judah."

"John Mosby, pleasure given these circumstances," he said and stretched his arms. "Now here is what I propose to you, Mr. Reuben Judah."

"I'm listening."

"I say to you that a lot of men are going to die this day. So let us stay close together and watch each other's backs. Fair enough?" he asked, this time extending his hand. We shook again and our handshake forged a bond.

"I reckon you're right…fair enough, John Mosby."

14

Bull Run
Manassas, Virginia
July 21, 1861

We off-loaded near the farm of Wilmer McLean and gathered in the front yard of his Yorkshire Plantation. The Confederate Generals looked like glass figurines in their grey uniforms and bright red sashes—an arrangement in their finery of war. I was beside Mosby as J.E.B. Stuart rode the lines repeating orders. Drums and bugles sounded and across Bull Run Creek, in a long green meadow…the Federals began to line up. Mosby and I watched the sheer numbers and I heard John say to no one in particular, "Dear Lord, I reckon we're gonna' either shit or get off the pot this time around."

"I sure as hell hope we're not going to charge them across this field. We'll get cut down before we make the creek," I said aloud.

Mosby pointed toward a group of blue-clad riders, one hundred strong breaking for the wood line. "Nope, there's our quarry," he said.

Stuart pulled up, his horse sliding to a stop on its haunches and then it stood prancing about. "Let's run'm down before they breach our left flank," cried Stuart. We were off across the field as firing commenced and men begun shouting and dying in the heatless afternoon.

Mosby was right about Stuart's horsemanship. I watched as Stuart took the reins in his teeth and read his map at full gallop, then folded the map neatly and tucked it away in his breast pocket as if it were nothing of consequence. Men were firing blindly and breaking ranks as we rode through their confusion, other men just quit fighting altogether and ran away from the engagement once the first blood was spilled upon the dry summer grass. We charged down and away from a small bluff where General Thomas Jackson sat on his horse overlooking the scene, sucking a lemon with his hand raised to the sky above as if he alone were divinely touched.

General Barnard Bee rode up to Jackson in a panic. "The enemy is driving us," Bee shouted over the gunfire as we slowed our approach.

"Then, Sir, we will give them the bayonet," said Jackson, unsmiling.

Bee wheeled about and rode off shouting to his men. "There is Jackson standing like a stone wall. Let us determine to die here, and we will conquer!"

These were his last words. Mosby came beside me and we bore off to our left as Bee went down with a musket ball to his chest. And those final words of his—whether spoken out of contempt or admiration gave Jackson his epithet, Stonewall.

We paralleled the creek bottom and galloped into a patch of scrub woods and met the Federal Cavalry as they tried to cross at Blackburn's Ford. Stuart drew his pistols and shouted, "Let's be quick about our business!" And then he fired into the group and I was initiated into the cavernous arms of war.

I was better equipped than most and pulled one of my twin Navy Colts and fired into the melee, both man and beast came crashing down the far bank and into the water, and all scenes of this violent transaction were lost to the gun smoke, splashing, and chaos of the moment. The Federals lost a dozen men in the exchange and they spun their mounts around then raced back down the creek with us on the opposite side, matching them stride for stride like a disconnected shadow…and all the while firing back and forth at each other from horseback in a beautiful catastrophe of killing. Off in the distant, artillery whistled down a deadly tune as barrage after barrage exploded like the thunderous clap of God's own hands. The Federal mounts finally broke away and went back up and over a hill as we came through the woods within view of the main battlefield.

Hundreds of men lay dead and dying on the long green slope before us, others hobbled around or sat bleeding. The Federals had retreated and now the Rebels came out on the battlefield and the real killing began as they went man to man and stuck each through the breast with their bayonets. They talked and joked among themselves as they went about this ghastly chore as if they were killing bugs in a garden plot. I looked to my left to where a man was sitting down holding his battered shoe aloft with the amputated foot still inside it. The old fellow looked at his bloody stump and kept screaming over and over, "You sumbitch!" as if he were mad at the severed appendage itself rather than damning the vile war, which now claimed it. How odd and morbid those grizzly sights were. And only then did I pause to catch my breath and decipher these atrocious scenes as they unfolded before me.

It felt as if the power of battle had exhausted me and I was temporarily spent. But then I felt its slow magic of revival, as if God himself was massaging my neck, whispering to me as if I were nothing more than a tool in this grand enterprise of war.

The day was closing and the shade of night fell dark and lonely upon our encampment. Torches and oil lamps were lit to guide the wagons loaded with corpses to their final destination. Tarps were pulled over cut pine boughs and formed row upon row of covered domiciles, places of respite where saints and sinners could escape the never-ending misery and despair. Some sat by oil lamps with their gear scattered out before them like tokens, as if they alone could puzzle together these sacraments of war. Others were either cleaning, honing, or repacking for what would become a nightly repetition to match their daily tedium of killing. On a distant ridgeline a bonfire was lit where broken men could gather like ancient pagans participating in a ritual, their shadows as warring leeches from a nightly dream they seemed to conjure. To the side a host of old Negro slave women stirring their blackened kettles over a fire, cleansing the blood from used bandages amid the clink of crude metal tools scratching out a shallow grave for yet another nameless occupant… and all the while came those horrid screams from the wounded being treated by the unsure hands of weary and unapologetic doctors. And still those old Negro crones sang their gospel and stirred their black and bloody kettles in the sepia tinted lamplight like a covenant of witches. Their freedom was mixed in the blood they stirred and this fact was not lost to them as they applied their awful trade. These were the scenes I would see nightly—once the killing was done.

Present

"It sounds so utterly dreadful, but you have the most poetic way of relating your story," said Paul. He looked at me and shook his head in wonderment. "It must have been horrible at Manassas. Was that your only battle or did you fight in more than just one?"

"I was in all the major battles, including Gettysburg, by accident. I was reassigned to a special Ranger unit John Mosby put together in January, 1863."

"Were you ever wounded?"

I shook my head, no. "Never a scratch."

"Amazing," said Paul, and he thought for a moment. "Which battle was the worst?"

"As bad as Antietam was, I'd put Gettysburg above it for the sheer stupidity and brutality. I was only there to deliver information to Lee and watched the battle from his viewpoint."

"You actually talked to Robert E. Lee?" asked Paul.

"I sat beside him through the first day of fighting and never fired a shot," I replied.

"I'd like to hear that story," said Paul. He leaned over and whispered, "I was hoping to ask you a personal question, not meaning to change the subject."

"What is it?"

"Did you hear about Mr. Trusloe?" asked Paul.

86

"Who?"

"Mr. Trusloe, the new inmate on this ward who raped close to a dozen women in San Francisco. The smarmy little man who is always bragging about the women he's been with. His father is a newspaper magnate and his mother's family has deep pockets as well. Very deep pockets."

"Not deep enough to save the monster they raised," I replied with a slight grin.

"No, they weren't that deep. Then you do know that inmate Simon Trusloe is dead." I shrugged my indifference. Paul only smiled and went further with his explanation. "It seems Mr. Trusloe's family hired enough lawyers to get him a sentence of three years with our institution, instead of a life sentence in a state prison. From the first day he was admitted here, Simon Trusloe was very adamant that soon as he got out he'd go back to raping women. It's not like any of the staff much cared for the lout. But it was so odd how he did it."

"Did what?" I asked.

"Committed suicide, it seems Mr. Trusloe locked himself in one of the lavatory stalls and slit his own throat. Our investigation thought it strange that he locked the stall from the outside."

"Maybe he wanted to do the job right so he locked the door and crawled under?" I offered.

Paul smiled and shook his head in confirmation. "We thought the same thing and put that in our report. But, I noticed something different that no one else saw. Of course, I kept the observation to myself," Paul explained. He was baiting me, getting smarter. Paul Tandy was learning.

"What did you discover?" I asked.

"Mr. Trusloe slit his throat with a razor-blade. We found the blade in his bloody right hand, and the odd thing is…I knew for a fact the Simon Trusloe was left-handed."

I turned in my chair and looked at Paul. He held my gaze and I offered him my own bait. "Ambidextrous are the hands of retribution," I replied.

Paul dropped his head with a thin smile. "Reuben, can I ask you something? If you promise you won't get upset?"

"Ask," I told him. Paul took a deep breath then looked out to where the night was now darker than his thoughts.

"Does it bother you at all?" he asked.

"Does what bother me?"

"The killing, all of it. In your past, yesterday, today, or tomorrow. Does the violence ever bother you at all?"

"No…not one damn bit," I said.

"How can that be?" asked Paul.

"Answer me this," I said and looked at him. "Have you given any thought to your personal rapist, your Mr. Macy?"

Paul wore an odd expression, like he was caught in a personal lie. "No…not once since he was found dead," he answered in a quiet tone.

"You are safe because there are certain men willing to do acts of horrible violence on your behalf, so you won't have to. The women your Simon Trusloe raped, do you think they will feel safer, maybe sleep better at night knowing their private boogeyman is dead?"

"Yes," said Paul softly, "I'd say they will feel much as I do."

"And what *do* you feel, Paul Tandy? What secrets do you share with those women Simon Trusloe violated? Do you still hide from the world when you are alone? What feelings do all of you share knowing your personal demon is gone," I asked him.

Paul looked down at his feet and sighed. "A sense of relief; in an odd way it's almost like you found a part of yourself you thought was lost forever. You feel the strength of life because the nightmare is over and you don't fear the dark anymore."

"Tonight all of you will sleep safely without ever having to raise your hand in violence. Tonight I'll sleep better because I did. That is my balance."

"I can find no fault in your logic, Mr. Reuben," said Paul, rising and stretching his bony arms. "I'm off for the next three days, but when I come back I want to hear more about John Mosby and Gettysburg."

"Fair enough," I answered and watched him go back to the uncertain drudgery of his wafer thin life.

* * *

They brought horses into the courtyard today. I overheard the orderlies talking about how the animals will soothe the savage beast within the patients. They are ancient steeds, holdovers from a forgotten war once proclaimed, "The War to End All Wars." The dishonesty of that proclamation does not escape me. War was here before all creation, and war shall remain ever present until mankind calls forth the force of its conflict from the shadows of peace. I sit at my window, watch the swayback mounts graze in the pallid moonlight, and I remember when animals like these charged across the field at Gettysburg. Eyes of both horse and rider wide and scared, nostrils flared as the tarnished blades of the cavalrymen were pointed toward the front of their pulsating heads like great iron spikes. The rumble of their uniform hooves pounded the ground as the animals broke through the smoke- and doom-like caricatures from some apocalyptic novel. How truly magnificent they were.

The volley of continuous fire and the plumes of that cruel gun-smoke as the mounts were cut down with their cargo of mute flesh like an obscene rodeo of chaos. Struck down as if they were a part of some beautiful prayer. The rip of bayonets being pulled free of scabbards and the cries of those final oaths of love to a now sonless mother, lost in the air to the maternal ghost amid the curses now frozen on the dead lips of those who claimed them.

It has been near a century and I can still hear the sounds, feel the shudder of the beaten ground, and I still curse the heat of battle in my veins. My greatest fear is that my eternity will be to revise and relive those days.

Paul Tandy came over and sat back in his chair defeated. "I've given a lot of thought about what you told me a few days ago. I've thought about what you are doing in this horrible place, maybe you're doing it to make their lives safer. But I'm curious and I have to ask...Why do you bother? Why do you even care at all, Reuben?"

"Because I can, and why would I not? What else do I have to favor in this retched life? It is my amusement."

Paul looked at me with unsure eyes, wanting to push the issue further. His expression softened and then he changed the subject with a reminder. "You said before my three-day shift break that you'd tell me about John Mosby and the Battle of Gettysburg."

I turned and looked at him then brought my fingers to his eyes and touched his brow. Paul shivered at my cold touch and I spoke softly. "Wipe your mind free of thoughts and listen to this tale, feel the breath of war and taste the fragrance of my life. This story is the beginning of the end…"

15

Richmond Virginia
October, 1862

In the fall of 1862, true to his promise of Confederate reorganization following the heartbreak at Antietam—Jefferson Davis and Robert E. Lee set the pendulum of my life into motion. By General Lee's directive, John Mosby and I were hand-selected by J.E.B. Stuart and given a new set of orders. Our instructions were to disengage from our current unit, wear civilian attire while moving with caution and discretion across Union lines as a two-man team. We were to separate and use any means necessary while scouting and observing Union supply routes, encampments, and then report back our gathered intelligence.

It was during those harsh months of overland travel when John and I began to notice a subtle change in both the Union, and the Confederate soldiers. We would often pass the troops of both sides as they marched away from one conflict and walk foot weary into another. What the men carried varied out of necessity, but every man shared a certain communion in this unruly tabernacle of combatants—no matter which side the soldiers were on—they each held, within themselves, the innate ability to kill.

Spotsylvania County, Virginia
May 2, 1863

I crossed the Rapidan River as sunlight filtered through the forest where tree limbs laid their shadows upon the rippling water like hands clasped in a prayer. Wild cherry blossoms littered the glassy surface and were swept downstream until they gathered in a swirling chaos of soft pink petals. I made the far shore at a shallow point and the commotion of horse hooves sent trout darting upstream in dark flickers. Prophet scrabbled through the wet shale and up the bank as a young Confederate sentry stepped out from behind a hickory.

"Mister, unless you wanna' be sport'n a musket ball in your head, I s'pect you best stop right there," he said bringing his long rifle to bear. He was barefoot and dirty, sunken eyes and a wolfish smile that was best served to shy maidens at a dancehall.

"Easy, friend," I said, bringing my hands up slowly. "I'm a known man to General Jackson and only here to give him my scouting report."

"You some kinda' spy?" he asked in a snotty tone.

"I personally think that's a somewhat aggressive and distasteful question. So instead of this idle chitchat, why don't you just have your runner inform the General that Reuben Judah is here. And a piece of advice," I said before he could protest. The boy looked up at me and waited. "Don't let the clothes fool you, son. Whether I'm in or out of uniform, I'm still a soldier. So the next time you address me it will be out of respect, or I will step down off my horse and knock you on your prissy little ass."

"Kinda' bossy, ain't ya, feller?" he said as he lowered his musket. The boy put two fingers to his tongue and gave off a short whistle. Another boy not much older trotted over from the far woodline and then left at a run with his instructions. "We'll just sit and wait till I hear back. So you just get real comfortable and keep your hands away from those Navy Colts," said the boy with an easier tone.

I smiled and relaxed back into my saddle. "I'm only here to deliver a message and receive a new set of instructions," I said politely. The runner appeared from the edge of a long green pasture

The Prophet of Cobb Hollow

and waved his arm.

"You just ride on ahead and he'll take you to that crazy, lemon suckin' sonofabitch directly," the sentry said, plugging his jaw with a wad of tobacco. He started walking back to his post when I stopped him with a question.

"I take it our good General's temperament hasn't changed since I last rode with him?" I asked.

The boy paused and turned around then spat a brown stream. "Naw, Jackson's still crazy as a shit house rat. Nothing ever changes in this damn war. It's the same ole horseshit, our blood and guts get spilled following his orders while he grabs all the glory," said the boy as if this were a well-known fact. He mopped his brow and spat again, then looked skyward at the sun. "You best be get'n along, Ole Lemonhead Jackson don't like to be kept waiting," he said, walking back to his post.

I tipped my hat and kicked Prophet into a gallop across the field and looked towards a hillside where the runner was pointing. The General and his staff were on their horses looking over the Confederate positions, Jackson with a map in one hand and a slice of lemon in the other. I rode up and saluted Jackson.

"Good morning," I said, dropping my hand. Jackson didn't budge in his saddle or bother to look up and acknowledge the gesture.

"The fighting has already started. Why weren't you here earlier?" Jackson finally said with his head down.

"For that very reason, General. I was on the other side of the river in Union territory when the fighting broke out," I explained.

"Well, whatever information you may have had is rather useless since I have already seized the initiative and struck the first blow." Jackson finally looked up and took a bite of his lemon then made a face as if he might be distasteful with my presence. "You ride for Stuart, do you not?" he asked.

"Yes, sir, John Mosby and I were the first two men selected for his new Ranger unit."

"I know John Mosby on a personal basis so you must be the other one," said Jackson.

"Reuben Shadrack Judah. I rode with you at First Manassas."

Jackson looked at me and winked at his entourage of young staff officers. "General Lee and I want to lure the Yanks further into Virginia near Chancellorsville so we can divide our forces and take care of them on our own soil," explained Jackson. "What do you think of that, Reuben Judah? Let's see if your military expertise qualifies for the honor of my consideration," said Jackson, removing his hat in a flourish.

"Well, sir, no man should invite the enemy to shit in his own backyard," I said.

Jackson replaced his hat and looked at me as if I had just showed him my bare ass. He dropped his head and chuckled sarcastically then rode off. One of his young aides yelled after him, "What now, General?"

Jackson pulled up and looked at me over his shoulder then answered the man. "We're going to scout the Union positions until nightfall. Tomorrow, I'll offer them a shady spot under the trees in our backyard so I can personally wipe every one of their asses after they've taken a shit."

Less than an hour later Jackson was shot while returning from his scouting mission, shot by a man in the 18th North Carolina Infantry, mistaken for Union cavalry. I was perched by an open window on the Fairfield plantation when I heard the last words Jackson would ever speak.

"Let us cross over the river, and rest under the shade of the trees," he whispered and died. I was standing with Mosby when they loaded Jackson's body for transport back to Richmond where he would lay in state. Jackson got off easy. While he was being praised by the public masses as a dead hero, John and I were given a new set of orders.

We were to ride further across Union lines into Pennsylvania and scout for Lee's advancement into the heart of Northern territory. Two months later, Mosby and I would be in Gettysburg where the war would get bloodier...

The Prophet of Cobb Hollow

Gettysburg, Pennsylvania
July, 1863

John Mosby and I met with General Lee and his entire staff well before daylight on the morning of July 1. And based on the intelligence we had gathered, the Union forces were set up in a fishhook defensive position around Gettysburg—which Lee took into calm consideration—and then decided to divide his forces yet again. John Mosby and I thought the plan would result in heavy Confederate losses, but we kept our concerns mute once Lee overruled our advice and gave out his directives to senior officers.

At daybreak, I was on Prophet while Lee and his staff were looking down to where the Union camp sent bacon-scented cook-smoke through the sleepy town of Gettysburg. In the pre-dawn gloom, those plumes of smoke made it seem as if God himself had chosen this point in time to pen his new commandments for those about to be ruined and forgotten.

I broke away from Lee and his ill-fated counsel and rode over to where a Baptist preacher was giving his pre-battle sermon. He was dressed in all black, a saintly man peddling his version of salvation like a black clad gargoyle. It was the same religious pre-battle fodder I've heard before, and I wasn't so sure either side was doing the work of God. The old pulpit puppet was ranting about righting the wrongs of injustice in the name of our blessed Father.

"Injustice indeed…preach away old fellow," I said riding up. The preacher stopped mid-sentence and looked up at me.

"Do you have something against the word of God?" he asked.

"I can assure you I have nothing against God or his words. I'm just not real fond of those who falsely worship him, present company included. It seems to me that mankind has some ulterior motive when he begins to preach about doing God's will." I swept my hand in an arc over the rolling hills of Gettysburg. "Would you say this pending act of war is God's will, or is today's grand show of fighting injustice nothing more than unharnessed aggression brought forth by the motivation of men?"

"If it were not for the suppression of our state rights we would not be here upon this field of imminent death," the preacher replied in his best sermon voice.

"State rights have nothing to do with this, and you know it."

"May I have your name?" the preacher asked, noting my civilian attire.

"Reuben Shadrack Judah, I work for Marse Robert."

He looked me over and then asked with a slippery smile, "Then you tell me, Reuben. Why are we here?" The small gathering of men inched closer to hear the conversation.

"We are here for peace," I replied.

"I do not believe that," said the preacher smiling. I smiled back and set the hook.

"We're gathered here to prove peace was drawn from the blueprints of war. Tell me I am wrong, preacher man. Show me the error of my ways and I will surely pronounce you a savior to these men and proclaim your words as gospel to the masses that gather before us." I stopped and smiled down at the Godly servant then waved a cautionary finger at him. "But be forewarned my good preacher, the last savior to speak of God's will some 1,800 years ago left his perch vacant. Are you ready to fill his worn sandals? The cross is bare and it hungers for another savior to take his place. Are you sure you're ready to bear the burden of that deliverance?"

The preacher pointed his knurly finger at me. "The Almighty knows what is in your heart from the day you are conceived, Mr. Judah."

"Then we are doomed when we draw that first breath," I replied.

"You don't think the Almighty will deliver us to victory?" asked the preacher.

I grinned at the man and said, "I think God will be nothing more than a spectator watching his grandest sport, war and killing." I looked at him and the crowd of faces around us. Waiting for another rebuttal but received none. "I have a question for you, preacher man."

"What is it?" he asked as the men formed a semi-circle around us.

"If God created all men equal, wouldn't a black man share in this Biblical version of equality?"

There was a quiet murmur through the gathered mass. "They're not equal," a voice said and then another chimed in. "They're dumber than a box of hammers and nowhere near as smart as white men."

"Not as smart," I laughed. "They're smart enough to plant cotton, smart enough to pick cotton…but not smart enough to count the profits. Is that what you mean by a black man not being as smart as the white man?" The crowd went silent and I surveyed the curious faces looking at me. "Besides that, all men are half black, no matter what color they are on the outside," I said to them.

"Says who?" a voice from the crowd asked.

"Step out into the sunlight where I can see who I'm talking to," I answered.

A Georgia farm boy with a powder burn like a birthmark on his right cheek stepped out and removed his stained bucket hat. "I'm white as they come with nary an ounce of nigger blood in my veins," he said thumping his chest. The men around us laughed. I waited until the commotion died down.

"White as they come," I smiled and shook my head in objection then pointed to a bare patch of grass behind him. "I want you to wave your right hand and watch the ground at your feet."

"I'll give you a good piece of advice, Mr. Fancy Mouth…it's best if you don't make a mock of me," said the boy bristling.

"I can assure you I am completely earnest in my request, now do what I said. Look down at the ground and wave your arm," I replied. The farm boy did as I instructed and those gathered around watched as his shadow mimicked his every move. "What color is your shadow?" I asked.

"Blacker than the ace of spades," an old codger yelled. The group and the boy with the powder burn erupted into laughter until I raised my hand and quieted them.

"Bah, you're a madman," the rebel preacher cut in before I could speak. He waved me and his broken congregation off as if we were both a nuisance, then pushed his way through the crowd as the men laughed and smacked him on the back good naturedly.

"If we are to fight and die on this day, let it not be about the color of our skin. Goddammit, let us fight for each other," I said as the bugle blew for them to assemble their battle lines.

I looked out over the field where the men were lining up like infantile sheep being led to slaughter by a deceitful shepherd. Down the long ranks the men readied themselves, adjusting their gear and fixing bayonets. As the command to march was given, destiny on that day would soon become a flagrant desecration to all humanity. Through the cheerless gloom they went as if they were about to face down some incurable curse, and the heat of the day mixed with the sordid tempo of pre-battle did not touch them as they went unnoticed into this odd climate of war. In the midst of surviving the pending harshness of this day, these soldiers would forever remember an unpaid debt to those men who would not survive upon these sacred fields of aggression. I thought to myself, battle will always arrive on the air of a single whispered word, and then it will end no less as quiet.

When the solitary word *fire* was whispered, the first twenty minutes of Gettysburg became a blur of smoke mixed with the charge of white-eyed madmen. And in those precious moments the very air itself held a soiled and polluted odor, a violent vacuum surrounding the stagnant vapor of men dying.

Hour by hour another thousand men down and the beaten ground around them—a formless waste of life as if this battle alone was to be the last conflict on earth, and it too would one day be lost to the ages and ashes of its ruin. The soldiers on both sides came and they fell like doomed lemmings, dropping to the troubled waters as if to pacify some misguided prophecy. Gettysburg would rage like a timeless clock without hands for three days. Lee would gamble on all three days and thrice be denied...and I would bear witness to it all.

By the fourth day Lee was retreating while Mosby and I stood in the rain overlooking the quiet battlefield where the bodies lay undisturbed in the very spot they had fallen. We watched in silence as two buzzards circled in slow greedy arcs, floating on the humid updrafts while waiting for their turn at the leftover scraps. Through the ruined streets of Gettysburg church bells rang their dull sad song, as another local lad was being carried to his place of rest. We watched in silence and I noted that the funerals for those lost to the grip of battle were always a measured procession of mourners, sad songs and slow walking. The old women, cowled beneath their bonnets like disciples of some vague religion, sitting graveside in silence with wooden and calloused hands, clasped in their apron laps as if they held some unknown divinity there. Their shadowed faces beneath their bonnets were etched with the lines of age like tree bark—and each ceremony thereafter would become just another poignant stone placed on the sad path of my life.

"Look at those damn buzzards. I truly do hate those wretched birds," Mosby finally said after the last icy ring of the funeral bells.

"I admire them for their impartiality," I replied.

"Admire what?"

"The buzzards," I said.

"You admire buzzards? What in the Hell does that mean?"

"They eat the dead on both sides. And if times are hard, buzzards will eat their own," I explained.

"You truly are a scary sonofabitch sometimes. Do you know that?" said Mosby.

"It is what it is, John."

"Well, I hope after this war is over every one of those damned birds starve," growled Mosby in disgust.

We sat and watched as a wagon creaked by with its cargo of bloody Confederates piled high as if this were some contest to harvest the dead. On the top, looking back at me with cold unblinking eyes lay the Georgia farm boy with the powder burn. At that moment, I bore witness that his blood was just as red as the blackest of men.

"Reuben, I want you to stay near Gettysburg for a day or two then head south towards Winchester," said Mosby. I shook off the sight of the dead farm boy and shrugged my shoulders in confusion.

"And do what?" I asked.

"Watch out for General Sheridan and report all of his movements."

"Why would Sheridan be as far south as the Shenandoah Valley?" I asked. John shifted in his saddle and looked at me.

"He's looking for me and any man who rides with me," said John as if it were nothing worth noting.

"If he's looking for you in the valley then where are you going to be?" I asked.

"I'll stay further north and work my way back and forth into Washington. When we need to meet, we'll use the town of Culpepper and stay at the Buckhorn Inn the first week of each month and decide what to do next."

"Okay, what time?"

"I'll let you know. Reuben," he said and paused. "There's one more thing." It was the way Mosby said my name. I looked at him with tight eyes. "I want you to stay away from your farm," he said.

"Why? I've not been home for two years. I'd only be a day's ride from Jess and Molly."

"That's not the only reason Sheridan is in the valley, Reuben." I waited for him to explain. John took a deep breath and exhaled as if the words were formed on that exchange of air. "Phillip Sheridan's latest directive from Ulysses Grant is to not only hunt down and find the men who ride with me. He is to further seek out the families of these men and take those family members—neither harmed nor molested—and to use them as hostages. I'm doing this for you, putting you as close to home as I can while being certain you and your family are safe. Just stay away from your farm, Reuben." John waited for my reply. I looked past Mosby towards the mountains and thought of Jess and Molly. I thought about my boys in Atlanta and Three Crows. "Okay?" John asked again, waiting for my answer.

"I'm getting tired of this war, John."

Mosby nodded and took a deep breath. "Everyone is, Reuben. The sun doesn't shine up the same dog's ass twice. Gettysburg broke the Confederates, Lee is done," said Mosby exhaling and relaxing. He had my answer without me saying it. Mosby knew I would follow his order and stay away from my home until he said otherwise.

"How much longer do we have before it's over?" I asked.

Mosby shrugged.

"A year maybe, not much more than that. Jefferson Davis has already tried to get Lee to disband into small guerilla units and continue fighting along the mountains. But ole Bobby Lee ain't having none of that chickenshit."

"Why not?"

"Honor," said Mosby tugging his reins.

"What are you going to do after this is all over?" I asked Mosby, changing the subject.

Mosby spun his horse around until he was facing me, and he thought for a second before answering. "I'm not too damn sure, but I do know one goddamn thing."

"What's that, John?"

"I'm sure as hell done with being a soldier," grinned Mosby.

"Yup, I reckon we've both had our fill," I agreed. Mosby started his horse across the wet and bloody field then pulled up and twisted around in his saddle.

"Be careful in the valley and watch the skyline, Reuben. Grant would like nothing better than to see either one of us shot or hanged," he said. I nodded and let Prophet take me a little deeper into the nameless and savage landscape this war had created.

Two weeks later, I would be disguised as a Union officer and sit across from Ulysses Grant at a dinner he was hosting for his junior officers. I rather liked the man. While the young officers clamored about the process and the profound strategy of war, Grant only listened. And then he said something over dessert that I would never forget.

"The stratagems of war are best served as fodder for conversation over smooth Kentucky bourbon and a fine cigar," said Grant exhaling a plume of smoke.

The table toasted his words and I raised my glass with them. No truer words were ever spoken, but war will always be served with the whisper of blood.

One year later, Grant would accept Bobby Lee's surrender at Appomattox and put an end to this awful war. The surrender was signed in Wilmer McLean's parlor, and the irony of that particular deed will never escape me. By the time Lee had signed his name in forfeit, Jessamine and Molly would be gone and I would be in the smoldering ruins of Atlanta—searching for my sons.

16

Present

"I wonder what would have happened to our country if the South had won?" asked Paul.

"It wouldn't have mattered. The end result would have been the same, but with less bloodshed," I replied.

"You said Jessamine and Molly were gone. Where'd they go?" asked Paul. And his question, though I was ready for it...hurt.

I touched the deep scar on my chest and replied, "They were killed just before Christmas in 1864."

"Mr. Reuben, I am so sorry. I never meant to bring up something so horrible," apologized Paul. He covered his mouth with a hand and spoke through his fingers. "Reuben," he started to say in a soft voice. But I cut him off before his lip-quivering questions continued.

"It was deemed an accident," I said tartly.

"An accident?"

"There were ulterior motives. Lives were sacrificed so fortunes could be made and everyone involved paid a fair price, but I paid the greatest price of all."

"If you care to talk about," Paul started to say.

"Not tonight, maybe tomorrow," I said quickly. Paul was hurt by my sudden rejection. I could see the pain of my abrupt refusal in his eyes.

"Tomorrow I'm taking a personal day off. But I'll be back the day after and I'd really like to hear the rest of your story. But only if you feel like telling it, Mr. Reuben, I don't want to upset you or cause any pain," said Paul softly.

"Today after tomorrow it is."

Paul stood and put his hand on my shoulder, gave it a squeeze and then walked back into his unguarded fishbowl world.

* * *

Know this—to see death is to know that throughout the history of human conflict, after the dead are buried it, is the living that shall bear those silent scars. I remember one summer day as I picked my way through Orange County, Virginia after the Wilderness Battle. I came unexpectedly upon a silent meadow of death and what an appalling spectacle it was. In the cover of red clover laid the unburied remains of soldiers—skeletons side by side almost touching each other like the joined cheeks of long dead lovers. Confederate and Union skulls met skulls, bleached white with those grim and deadly faces still stitched to the very expression of their macabre destruction. Now and then, all war veterans will relive their battles and the brave days of nameless men. They shall recall with great solidarity those ghostly brothers who lay beneath cold stones. Old warriors take new courage from those shrines of great sorrow. Those who are untested in the ways of war venture into these fields of the stony dead and see only the monuments, but the men who fought on that hallowed ground still see with great clarity where bones of the dead once littered the scorched earth.

I was on my way back from Atlanta at the war's end when I traveled through a sleepy no-name town. I remember how the stars along the dark mountain ridgelines were as crisp as silver apples dangling from the night sky, passionate buttons of the blind and muted Gods. I walked Prophet down the deserted street where unfilled coffins were ready-made and stacked along a store front. The pine wood fresh-cut and the citrus smell still evident in the stale night air. But it was the windows in the small shanty town that defined the times. Each window was lighted by a solitary candle to mark the loss of a soldier, like gold stars each wink of flame became a flickering symbol of the heartache that stained the very cusp of this sleeping community.

One house near the end of town had four candles burning, and the significance of that mother's sacrifice did not go unnoticed. The Queen of Angels must have surely wept because the depth of that burning sorrow had no known length to those candlewicks of grief, no toll for a parent's absolute resolution to such a sudden and excessive forfeit.

If there is a God in some aft and gilded Heaven, I would like to face him. I would like to have him come down from his thorny throne and answer my simple question. Why war? Why put the curse of destruction within the very marrow of man? I would be ever curious as to the answer.

I watched Paul Tandy punch the time clock early and walk to where I was sitting. "I forgot to tell you the other night, I'm working a double today," he explained sitting down beside me. "It's the monthly visitation for the non-violent patients on our ward."

"The once a month time when family members feel the need to visit those who are forgotten," I said, noting the strangers in clothing other than patient-issued gowns.

Paul nodded and said, "I see it all the time, it truly is sad for so many who have no one."

An elder female patient passed us by talking in the gibberish of the insane. "I had such a grand time with little Ellie today," she said to the well-dressed woman beside her.

"Momma, Ellie's been dead for years," the fashionable woman answered.

"When did she die?" asked the old woman.

"Died when Teddy Roosevelt was President. Let's get you back to your room so I can leave. I've got a lot of errands to run, but I'll be back next month." The dressy woman held up a popsicle and used it to bait the old woman into another windowless room with the same view of dead imagination.

"Using a popsicle to bribe her. It truly is a shame," Paul said watching the scene unfold.

"To the insane those popsicles are gold," I answered back. Paul shuddered.

"Her entire world has come down to nothing more than a popsicle," he said.

"Perhaps, but that popsicle gives her life an advantage."

"How so?" asked Paul watching the well-dressed woman leave.

"The dressy woman can either feed the beast or fight the beast."

"Very true," said Paul. His voice got nasal when he got excited. "They say those with dementia revert back to their childhood as the disease progresses," Paul explained to me.

"Would God have it any other way?" I asked.

Paul looked at me, odd expression on his face. "I cannot say you are wrong, it's just a hard way of looking at the final days of her life. She lives in a world that she cannot touch and watches helplessly as the real world passes her by."

"Like I said, would God have it any other way?"

Paul shook his head and changed the subject. "I was hoping you would tell me about your time with Teddy Roosevelt."

"We'll get to Teddy in good time, but we have a few years to go until we get to the Rough Rider's grand day in Cuba."

"I'm working a double and have nothing but time. So lead me on and make it a good one," said Paul sinking down into his chair.

"Then open your heart and free your mind. Let go of your thoughts and listen to my words. Feel the sway and the verve of emotions and let your imagination guide you back to when the darkness of my life began. Breathe deep the gathering air of my memories and pluck the petals of my life from their stem. Walk with me and see the magic of western expansion and relive this unwritten history as it unfolds."

The Darkness
1864

While traveling the Confederate States I had no cause for

personal alarm and went by my given name. To those I conducted business with I was Reuben S. Judah, direct wholesale supplier for the Confederate Army. I had with me all the necessary credentials which I obtained through John Mosby and his growing network of bipartisan contacts.

When I traveled in the North I was known as Luther Eli Cobb, a fully authorized procurer of supplies for the Federal quartermaster. I was given credited paperwork allowing me free travel which was personally signed by the Union Quartermaster General, Montgomery Meigs. I carried with me a Union lieutenant's uniform and would sometimes dress the part to obtain any vital information I deemed pertinent. It was easy to pass myself off in their encampments as a newly commissioned Union officer. Walk around with a confused and befuddled look on my face, act important, and remember return salutes from time to time as a way of showing my unearned superiority.

By the time December arrived in 1864, the war was hopelessly lost for the Confederates. Lee was hemmed in; Grant and Sherman had cut off any chance for reinforcements. While Atlanta was burning under Sherman's scorched earth policy, Sheridan was carving his own path of destruction through the Shenandoah Valley.

Culpepper, Virginia
December 19, 1864

I skirted the cold Rappahannock River for two days until I crossed over at dusk and rode frozen and saddle-weary into the town of Culpepper, Virginia. I kept Prophet clear of the cobbled road and went straightaway to the far end of town where the Buckhorn Inn sat nestled against a bend along the slow churning river. I was a regular monthly guest at the Buckhorn and swung by their livery to feed and rub down Prophet before I checked in. I was formally acquainted with the owners and always left them generous tips so no one at their establishment or in the town of Culpepper questioned my profession. Once per month I was here to deliver my financial statements to General Meigs and to meet with Mosby. Simple logistics. I stole from Meigs and funded Mosby's operations with the garnished supplies and acquired information.

Room thirteen was already reserved and paid for by one of Mosby's men. It was John's way of telling me the first day of the week and the third spot of four designated locations we had already agreed upon. I'd meet John tomorrow night at the cemetery, two days early. This was odd…even for John Mosby.

I had a quiet dinner with the Buckhorn's owners, complete with idle chit-chat on the subject of our nation's war and what hardships might come afterwards. "The uncertainties of both have given me a slight case of heartburn. I feel certain a cool walk in the winter air may help aid in the digestion," I politely explained to them and excused myself. I'd rather spend my time with Prophet, rubbing him down and thinking of Jess and Molly. Other than our letters and a rare telegraph when the lines were up long enough to send one— Prophet was the only link that kept me connected to my family since the war began.

The following day I walked into town as the mid-morning sun sent arteries of cold mellow light through the streets and alleyways. I stopped outside the Culpepper General Store where a girl sat in a wagon seat stroking the head of a mongrel pup.

"Your dog?" I asked scratching the pup's ears. She shook her head no with childlike defiance. "Then whose dog is it?"

The girl shrugged indifferently. "Danged if I know, we found him outside of town and he just kinda' followed us. I wanna' keep him but my pa said no."

"Why'd he say no?"

"Pa said since ma died, feeding two mouths is hard enough."

"Why would you even want that ole dog?" I asked.

"It's just me and my pa; it'd be nice to have a friend," she explained, giving the pup a pinch of her biscuit. I looked around and found a used gunny sack in the grain bin. I took the burlap sack and shook the stray oats out before handing it to her. "Whatcha' want me to do with this ole poke?" she asked, scratching her nose. The pup whined and licked her hand for biscuit crumbs.

"Wrap your dog up in that sack and hold him close to you. That way he'll get used to your smell. Let him sleep at the foot of your bed on that ole tote sack and take him outside every time he wakes up. Be sure and tell him to do his business, and make sure he does before you take him back inside."

"I told ya,' my pa already said no. Told me I could hold him until he paid for our goods but he'd rock the dog if he tried to follow us home," she replied with a tart shrug of her shoulders. I liked her straightforward attitude and thought of my daughter. I made myself a promise to buy Molly a dog of her own once I got home.

"I'll talk to your pa," I told her. She looked skeptical but nodded and stroked the pup's head as I walked inside the store. There was only one other customer, a man wearing hardscrabble overalls talking with the shop-keep about seed prices. "Is that your daughter out there in the wagon?" I asked him. The farmer turned and looked me over but didn't answer. "The one with the stray pup," I added. The man seemed to slump at my question.

"Yes, sir, if that's your dog I'll take him from Libby directly and get him back to you. She's only holding him because he followed us."

"Not my dog at all, matter of fact I'd like her to have him. Every girl needs a friend," I said and he started to object until I held my hand up. "Your daughter told me that you said feeding a dog cost money and I agree with you completely." I looked at the shop-keep and asked. "How much would a hundred pounds of dry rations for that pup run me?" He looked at me over his spectacles while doing the numbers in his bald head.

"Three cents a pound, but I'll do two cents a pound if you buy in bulk," said the shop-keep.

I laid twenty dollars on the counter. "This will cover food for the dog. Let this man take what he needs today and subtract it from the balance each time thereafter until the twenty is spent," I told him. The shop-keep gave me a confused look then shook his bald and knobby head.

"If you say so, but twenty dollars would last five dogs three lifetimes," said the shop-keep.

109

Mingo Kane

"Yeah well, I happen to know that all dogs like table scraps a little more than dry food. And the twenty is exactly for what I said it was for...to buy food. I'll leave the buying part up to the new owners, as long as both are fed."

"Mister, you're gonna' make Libby a happy young'un and I sure do thank you. It's been hard on us since her ma died, but seems a mite bit harder for her," the farmer explained.

"Every puppy, at least once in its life, deserves to be loved by a little girl," I said and walked back out to the wagon.

"What'd my pa say?"

"The dog is yours."

She squinted at me. "You're funning me, ain't you?"

"Nope, I made a deal with your pa. The dog is yours." Instead of jumping up and down like most young girls, Libby reacted the same way my Molly would have. She cocked her eyes and gave me a cynical look.

"Mister, just what kinda' deal did ya' make with my pa?" she asked.

"In a week or so I'll be coming back through Culpepper. So the deal is, you owe me one plate of fresh biscuits," I said spitting into my palm then sticking out my hand. Libby thought for a second.

"Pa says my biscuits are almost as good as ma's," she said, looking at my hand before spitting in hers and shaking. "Mister, I reckon we got a deal."

"I reckon we do," I said tipping my hat.

When night fell, I checked on Prophet and left him with an extra ration of oats before walking to the cemetery, always careful to check my back trail for anything that appeared out of place. John was waiting at the far end of the graveyard with his body wedged between a tree and the retaining wall, breaking up his outline and presenting a small target. If confronted he could vault the wall and escape, or use the tree for cover and fight. I stopped beside an unmarked plot and waited for John's prepared greeting. I didn't need the code, I knew John Mosby by his stance. He always stood with an air of swagger that was unknown to him.

110

I took another cautious step forward. "Are you a friend of Jesus?" asked Mosby. I stopped and answered him from the shadows to complete our code.

"I am a Brother," I replied. It was Mosby's way of being certain our meeting was known but to us. If I had answered with anything else, John would know I was compromised and leave.

Mosby spoke in a low tone so the sound of his voice wouldn't carry much more than a few feet. "I wasn't sure you'd be in town this early so I took a chance and reserved you a room for three days. I hope you don't mind."

"Not at all, John. Why, is something wrong?" I asked. Mosby put a finger to his lips as if he were a salesman selling me a secret.

"I am in room twelve, right next to you. Meet me there in one hour and cough at the door instead of knocking," he said and vaulted the wall.

I watched as Mosby melted back into the shadows and disappeared across the cobbled street with my mind racing towards some sensible conclusion, perhaps the war had ended or maybe we were being disbanded and sent home. I had no way of knowing that within the next hour I would break free of my exiled obscurity and begin to hand-forge a lifetime of personal wars.

Mingo Kane

112

17

I sat in Mosby's candlelit room while he poured us two glasses of sipping whiskey. "I shared a glass of good Kentucky bourbon with Grant himself less than two weeks ago," I said as John poured.

Mosby grinned and handed me a glass then tipped his in a quiet toast. "You shoulda' shot the bastard in the face. I've heard more than once that Grant has a fondness for his drink."

I took a sip of my whiskey and waited until the burning sensation in my gut subsided. "I don't know about that, but I rather liked the man. Not what I'd call a typical officer."

"How so?" asked Mosby.

"He listened more than he talked."

Mosby chuckled then set his glass down on the small table between us and rubbed his face as if to free it from weariness. "I hope you feel the same way about Grant after I'm done talking," said Mosby. I could tell by the tone of his voice he had labored long on the unspoken subject between us. I could see he was still struggling with the right choice of words.

"Then spit it out, John. What is it?"

"Reuben, we're like brothers so I'll not barter words with you. I'll tell you everything I know up to this point, and then I'll help you in any way possible. I owe you that."

"John, what is it?" I asked again. But I knew. I could tell from Mosby's tense posture that what he was about to tell me was hurting him.

"Reuben, two nights ago there was an attack," Mosby started.

"I've been tied up in Fredericksburg but I haven't heard anything through our network about an attack."

Mosby shook his head and held up a hand for me to let him finish. "It wasn't near Fredericksburg. Reuben, I'm sorry…the raid happened at your farm." I sank down in my chair.

"Jess and Molly?" I asked and Mosby dropped his head. The room grew dark and the world seemed to shrink within itself. Mosby sighed and spoke the words in a whisper and they swallowed me up.

"They were killed immediately in their sleep, Reuben. I don't know any other way to soften this blow, and I know there are no words I possess to help ease the burden of grief you must surely feel. But know this…I am here for you. I am here to help you do what is needed to make things right."

I would not break down nor would I cry in front of John Mosby. I knew he would expect that much of me. "There was an old Cherokee man there, my adopted father. His name was Three Crows." Before I could finish I knew the answer by the way Mosby's posture remained unchanged.

"He was bayoneted; as far as anyone was concerned, he was just a filthy old Indian that didn't matter to a living soul."

"He mattered to me, John." I clinched my eyes shut and swallowed back the grief as best I could. "Why?" I asked. My voice thin as homespun thread.

"I met with Phil Sheridan under a flag of truce to find out the answers. It was an accident by his account, a misfired flare that exploded inside your house and caught fire. I have our Rangers dressed as civilians scouring the Union camps looking for any additional information. But what I do have is the straight gospel from an attorney named Stoddard Quillen, a business associate of yours if I am correct." I nodded my head in recognition and John continued. "Under Grant's orders, the families of those who ride with me were to be captured and used as hostages. It was Sheridan's job to carry out these orders and he passed the buck down to his junior officers. Sheridan made camp just outside of Waynesboro, Virginia and began to burn crops, bridges, and barns until one man came forward and offered Sheridan information about you if he would spare his business." Mosby stopped and waited for me to grasp what he had said.

"I don't know a soul who would've turned me in," I said in a shaky voice.

Mosby looked at his notes. "Let's take it slow and get it right before we act, Reuben. It is my understanding that you are somewhat familiar with a man named Herman Kruger?"

"Kruger snatched a few thousand acres of my land just before the war broke out. After this is over I aim to get every inch of my property back."

"Well, you might have to get it all back as it stands right now. Hermann Kruger is the one who turned you in to Sheridan. And because your land is now vacant and unattended, you have thirty days to rebuild or sell. If you don't, then Kruger will likely get it all," said Mosby.

"John…" I started to say when Mosby waved his hand and cut me off.

"Listen to me first, Reuben. Kruger isn't even sure if you're alive but there's no doubt he's waiting for you, and if you do show up at his place you'll be cut down on sight, or hung for some trumped-up charge. Do as I say and we'll get you through this," explained John.

"We'll?"

"We're brothers. If those bastards hurt one of my men they best kill every damn one of us," said Mosby, draining his glass.

I stopped by the livery and had the stable boy saddle Prophet while I went back to my room to pack my possessions. I'd give some excuse about urgent business and promise the owners a quick and safe return when I checked out. In my room, tucked into the hidden compartment of my personal travel case, was a quick letter from Mosby.

Reuben,

My thoughts go with you, but take heed that nothing good is ever done in haste. Plan your operation three times and execute it but once. In seven days we shall meet in the same room at the same time. I am already working on the additional information we'll need.

Always remember what I said:
'Brothers'
It is what it is...and so it goes...
JM

I burnt the letter and left with all I owned, and that thought suddenly struck me. I had nothing and nowhere to live. I had no one to share it with. I was alone. These thoughts stayed with me as Prophet and I traveled the bleak countryside toward the burnt husk of my life. The horse somehow seemed to know, perhaps the odd mood or sullen vibe I was giving him as we rode in silence. Maybe it was the sound of me choking back the sobs but Prophet rode the whole way both roguish and hard, and we were bone weary of travel and each other's company altogether when we made the Quillen residence just before daybreak.

I knocked and Edith Quillen lit a lamp then met me at the door. She was slight of build and bent from years of raising a family of three boys while helping her husband succeed. "Reuben, thank the Lord, you're alive," she said giving me a hug then breaking down and sobbing. Stoddard came up behind us and put his hand on her shoulder.

"Mother, he's had a hard ride; let me talk with the lad in private while you make us some strong coffee," he said guiding her towards the kitchen. Stoddard nodded his head for me to meet him at the door to his study.

Mrs. Quillen gave me a kiss on the cheek and a final hug. "I'll have the coffee ready directly so get comfortable and rest. I'll bring it in to you with sugar and a spot of fresh cream," she said, leaving.

"Thank you, Mother," said Stoddard, opening the door to his private room. It was the same decor I remembered from the day Three Crows and I signed the deed to my land. The bookshelves with hardbacks on the topic of law, a musty odor of tobacco and leather mixed with the rich memories of old men playing poker. Stoddard closed the varnished door and wiped his eyes, then spread his arms. "Come here and give me a hug before you sit down."

I gave him a hug and I could feel the weariness of my loss in his embrace. "What happened?" I asked as we broke apart. Stoddard walked over and dropped down into his high-backed chair.

"It's the damndest thing, Reuben. Here in this part of the valley we never once saw a soldier from either side or heard a shot fired in anger. I guess we got used to feeling sheltered. So when Sheridan got here, people panicked."

"I don't need the long history, Stoddard. Just tell me what happened," I said in a darker tone than I intended. But Stoddard could be long-winded and I wasn't ready to hear the small details just so he could hear himself talk.

Stoddard rubbed his eyes and sighed. "Alright, son. I always knew the truth about you, but everyone else only suspected it."

"Suspected what?" I asked.

"Everyone suspected you rode with Mosby, but even before that—it was talked about around town that you," Stoddard paused and searched for the right words before he continued.

"That I what?"

"That you found Silas Cobb's cave of gold." I started to protest but Stoddard cut me off. "Don't try and bullshit me, son. You came out of the mountains with nothing but the land the Cherokee gave you. You built a grand house, barns and fences, bought prized horseflesh, and had solid livestock filling your pastures. In our small town people began to ask questions about where all the money came from but nobody knew for sure. You up and married the prettiest girl in the valley, right under the nose of the family that hated you for it. And you've got to admit, Reuben. You've been pretty quiet about all of it."

I felt my temper rise above the anguish. "My house and family is gone because I built a life with my own two hands. My wife and daughter were killed because Jess had an eye for quality horseflesh. Three Crows is dead because the Cherokee brought their livestock to my pasture, which was rightfully their land to begin with. The life I knew is burnt to nothing because of some legend about a cave of gold?"

"I know you're smarter than that, son. That's just an excuse for what happened and you know it. Hermann Kruger has wanted your land since the day he came here. And Sheridan made it clear that his intentions were to, first and foremost, scorch everything in sight. Kruger used you to spare his house and business with information. Hermann struck a deal because he thought you were already dead and anything else that came after his bargain with Sheridan was another bonus for him."

"Well, the whole Kruger family is gonna' find out that I am very much alive."

Stoddard softened his tone. "Reuben, I'm truly sorry. Sorry as I can be about this. I loved Jess and Molly like they were my own. Three Crows was as good a man as I have ever known and we were friends for many years. But they're gone, son. They're gone and there's nothing you or I can do that will bring them back. If you go off hot-headed and hunting revenge, then you're doing exactly what Kruger wants you to do. You've got to be smarter than that," said Stoddard, using his hands to emphasize his words.

"What am I supposed to do, Stoddard? Stand by and watch everything I have ever loved become lost and forgotten? Or maybe you think I should run away and hide? The war came to me first; I never sought it out," I snapped.

"Alright, just calm down and tell me what do you want to do? Because I want to fight them legally, in court. But if you're opposed to that, then I am all ears," Stoddard explained. I handed him my leather travel purse. He opened the flap and thumbed through the papers. "What's this for?"

"Inside are all my written instructions and I want you to follow them to the letter. After I'm done with the Kruger family, you and I will meet in your office two days from now…four hours before sunrise. No matter what you see or what you hear, you be at your office without fail. I'll give you enough money to cover the inconvenience, and there will be enough funds left over to last your family two lifetimes," I said and stood to leave. Stoddard Quillen was honest but if his integrity could be bought, he would be there.

Stoddard got up and put his hand on my shoulder then gave it a squeeze. "I'll do as you ask but I want you to think about this before you act."

"I have it planned out, Stoddard." I opened his front door and stepped out onto the porch as Prophet started prancing by the hitch-rail. Stoddard's voice stopped me at the steps.

"Reuben, I hope you're not talking about the outright killing of Hermann Kruger. I know you've seen the devil's own day, but forget what this war and riding with Mosby has taught you. These days we're living in a border state and what happened to your farm was considered an act of war by the Union investigation…it's over, son."

I shook my head in anger and fought back the tears. "If Hermann Kruger can bring his personal war to my doorstep, there's nothing wrong with me bringing my war to his."

"Forget this nonsense, Reuben."

"How can I forget, Stoddard? The only choice I have right now is to remember my family, or forget them. How can I rebuild a life with nothing, tell me that. How can I learn to forgive and love again? Can you teach me how to absolve my past and move on, to understand the perfect weight of redemption while forgetting the memories of my mind? Can you show me how to cry away the pain, softly at first, and then in bitter rivulets like cold rain down a foggy window. Can you or the court make everything right when it's all been taken away?"

"No, I reckon not." Stoddard dropped his head and seemed lost in thought before he continued. "Reuben, before you go there's one more thing. I didn't want to tell you because it's mostly hearsay, but I'll not lie nor keep it a secret. Gunter Kruger enlisted in the Union as a lieutenant and his father pulled some strings to get him reassigned to Sheridan, and because they both knew where you lived—it's rumored that Gunter gave the order to open fire on your house. After your farm was in flames Gunter's younger brother killed Three Crows. I overheard some of the Union soldiers talking about it outside the bank. The Yanks said the old Indian kept saying a Cherokee chant over and over before he was bayoneted by Wilhelm Kruger." Stoddard tried to repeat the native words as best he could. I knew the phrase Three Crows had spoken just before he died. I stood there letting the story Stoddard had just told me sink in as Prophet shook his head and snorted, as if he understood that we were now in this personal war together.

I stepped off the porch and swung into the saddle. "The black wolf hungers," I said looking towards the mountains. Even in the crisp winter air, I could feel the slow burn of rage building inside, giving me an odd sense of warmth.

"What's that you said?" asked Stoddard.

"The words Three Crows spoke before he died. That's what they meant, the black wolf hungers."

"No wolves around here," said Stoddard watching me adjust my stirrups before gathering the reins.

"Three Crows wasn't talking about a real black wolf. The old man was talking about me," I said and looked down at him from my horse. "You just remember what I said, two days time at your office. And don't be late, Stoddard. There are lives and fortunes at stake."

I made it to my farm as the sun crested the ridgeline and sent rays of tawny light over the burnt landscape like some malfeasance from a soiled brush. A thin veil of smoke hovered over the trampled ground where clusters of warped tin lay draped like a blanket overtop the charred timbers. It seemed as if some great beast had suddenly crushed the memory of my life from existence. No buildings were left standing nor did one fencepost remain upright. Everything was leveled by man and fire alike. All that I had ever owned was dead, burnt, or stolen.

I climbed down off Prophet and stood in the archway of my ruined home. How badly I wanted to walk through that burnt door into another time. I wanted to stand before the gilded throne of God and spit in his hard ugly eyes. I wanted to cry at his feet, beg his forgiveness, and ask him why?

But nothing stirred except the dead ashes blowing across the scorched ground as if some horrible stain was sent forth to torment me. I took the rope from my saddle and looped it around a wedge of charred tin and used Prophet to pull it free. I had my Navy Colts with me and I wanted someone, anyone to come and protest my actions. But none came and I alone would have to endure this grievous task.

I walked to the back corner of my burnt house where our bedroom would have been and yoked the timbers free. I found the seared and blackened remains of Three Crows first. The soldiers had thrown his body on the fire as if it were nothing more than trash to them. I took his bones and placed them on the ground and then went back to continue my search through the rubble.

I found Jess and Molly together, side-by-side as if they had slept through that ghastly night in a cocoon of innocence. How hard it was to look at them, to touch what was left of their cold lives. I cradled their bones, hugging them to my chest, and I let them alter my heart. My wife and daughter lay with the old man and I placed their remains in a crude box I fashioned with leftover wood. There was no time for a proper funeral and I was without surrogate options. I made the decision that my family deserved to be buried together in the cave, and once I finished I would seal that vile hole, forever. I strapped the homemade ossuary holding my family's bones to Prophet's saddle and walked beside him into the mountains, and it was at this moment when the sudden weight of my loss became so overpowering that I broke down and wept. In my life, I would shed tears of sorrow for another human being twice. This was the first.

On that long walk, my time seemed to recalibrate itself until I realized that in the midst of my life, I was faced with my inability to forget—and that until the day I died there would be these special moments, memories that are relived like they just happened. That is the curse of my perfect memory—to forever remember that final day when Jess and Molly's faces came before me as I left. I remember the exact camber of their stance as they stood mother and child, hip to hip, and made a human cross of remembrance for me. The smell of their wet and stormy hair that morning still overpowers my nostrils. Sometimes, in the dark days ahead of me—in the awful glare of future battlefields so far away—I would awake cold and hungry, eyes red-rimmed and raw from nightmares. And all of the light in these gloomy days ahead would become a funnel of darkness trapped inside head. I would grit my teeth and fight nameless men I would never know and still the exact timber of Jessamine's voice would haunt me beyond this harsh prism of time. Jess spoke five final words that were to become my motivation:

"I am because we are."

On that walk to and from the cave I became a man with nothing to live for and nothing to lose. I let myself go and gave in to the rage of my inner black wolf. I would sacrifice the remaining beauty of my life by denying it existed, and I would imprison myself behind a gold cross and the bloody crusade that came with it. At this crossroad, I was without a sensible conscience to act as my moral compass, so I surrendered to hate and let that emotion replace the pain of my love.

I had removed enough gold from the cave to ensure that I and my sons would be secure for the rest of our lives before I placed that final stone over the entrance. Half of the gold would be buried under Three Crows cabin, and the other half I would give to Stoddard Quillen for future expenses. When I walked into Three Crow's cabin that final day, on the mantle were three black feathers from a crow sitting beside the old man's medicine pouch. It was his way of telling me that he knew the words that were foretold to him those long years ago had come true. I alone was responsible for his death. But somehow the old man knew more. Somehow, Three Crows knew I would follow his path and become a hunter of men, and as I rode off that mountain with the black feathers in my hair and his medicine pouch around my neck—I also knew for certain the old Cherokee woman would be right about me as well. Once I took the dark path of revenge, there was no going back. I would, as she foretold:

"Become the mountain that life would break itself upon."

18

Birth of a Legend
December 24, 1864

When I left the old man's cabin that final day I carried two hundred pounds of gold to give Stoddard as an initial deposit, and buried twice that amount under the cabin's foundation. I allowed myself enough time to bury several smaller caches scattered throughout the mountains for future emergencies, should they arise.

I rode to a remote rail station near the budding town of Staunton, Virginia and made a reservation to leave the following morning just after daybreak. No matter what happened tonight, by tomorrow morning the telegraph wires would be cut and I would be headed back towards Culpepper to meet with John Mosby.

I had no doubt that Stoddard had scrutinized my paperwork and questioned the very legitimacy of what I wanted him to do. Stoddard would receive my land for exactly what I paid for it, with the clause that I could purchase it back from him, or his heirs, for the exact same price—a single handful of dirt.

I rode into my personal history that night with nothing more than two gallons of lamp oil I took from Three Crow's cabin, a handful of torches, and enough ammunition to fight half of Hell if need be. I rode Prophet to where Hermann Kruger's house and his South River

Clay Company sat near the border of my land, and waited. I watched as one by one the candles and lamps inside his house smoked out like dying stars, and I waited another full two hours before I moved closer. I listened for another hour before I tied Prophet to a fence rail and removed the lamp oil and torches. I took the oil and soaked the porch of the Kruger business and residence before I went inside their house through an unlatched window. I wore my moccasins and had stripped to the waist with war paint crisscrossing my torso and face, around my neck hung Three Crow's medicine pouch and the cross Jess had given me.

I went upstairs, being careful to step with light pressure on the wooden boards, testing their soundness to see if they would creak or pop. All of the upstairs doors were ajar to allow the heat from downstairs to move up and keep the second story warm. I went by the first two doors where the daughters were sleeping and stopped at the third door where Hermann Kruger and his wife slept. I stepped beside the old woman and put one of my Navy Colts to her temple then took my other pistol and rapped Hermann Kruger on the head with the barrel. He sputtered awake and wanted to protest until my voice stopped him.

"Who in the hell?" he started to ask gruffly. I nodded towards the pistol barrel resting against his sleeping wife's head.

"Go ahead and talk a little louder, if you do and this snoring bitch wakes up. Then I can promise you that the last words your wife will ever hear are going to be blown out the back of her goddamn head," I whispered, cocking the weapon.

"If you're gonna' rob us, do so and be damned in the process. Just don't hurt the women," said Kruger in a harsh whisper. I put a finger to my lips for him to be quiet and grinned at the man in the small light of the room. With my war paint on and standing amid the dim shadows, I realized Hermann Kruger did not recognize me.

"I'm not here to rob anyone, Kruger. I'm here for you," I said.

"Me?"

"We have a little unfinished business," I said stepping to his side of the bed. "Now get up and put your hands behind your back."

He did as he was told and once I had his hands tied I pointed the pistol barrel towards the door. "Let's go, we're going outside," I whispered in his ear. He started to move but my hand held him back. I leaned in close and spoke clearly so he would fully understand my intentions. "And if you make any sound whatsoever I'll kill you where you stand."

Hermann Kruger nodded his understanding and walked both quiet of foot and mute of mouth until we were outside and I had him securely tied to the hitch rail. "What now?" he asked me as I started back towards his house.

"We need a few witnesses to make our transaction legal," I answered over my shoulder.

I went back to the master bedroom and awoke Mrs. Kruger and informed her that if she and her daughters wished to live another night, they would remove themselves from the house and walk in front of me until we were outside. The Kruger women were like the men, hateful and tight-lipped in their paltry gaze towards me and my native associations.

"I hope you catch a death of a cold," mumbled the eldest Kruger daughter, noting the war paint and my bare chest.

"Don't worry, I'm getting ready to warm your night up to a grand scale," I said as we walked through their front door and outside into their yard. They saw Hermann tied to the hitch rail and each one of the women cried out and ran towards the patriarch as if they were interrupting a sacrifice. I walked over to where they were trying to chew through the leather straps binding his wrists and leveled my twin pistols at the women. "Let's go, over here by the fence."

The women stopped and turned and then each one glared at me before they hobbled on bare feet and stood side by side against the fence. I walked over to them and had each of the women sit down and tied them to their own personal post. "You're him, ain't you? You're the injun' lover that rode with Mosby," said old lady Kruger before I tied the gag around her mouth.

"I've been called many things, but I'll never apologize for anyone or anything I have ever loved. Now," I said cinching down her gag until she retched. "Let's get this deal started so we can build a fire…it's getting chilly."

I walked back over to Hermann Kruger who stared up at me. "I wasn't sure, but it's you," he said in a sour tone.

"Glad you remembered me, so now that we're all reacquainted, let's get started and finish our business. I'm afraid I plan on being a rather busy man after tonight. A lot of travel plans need to be made," I said.

Hermann Kruger shook his head and screamed up at me. "What business do we have? You're a madman. You have nothing I want and I have nothing I'd be willing to sell someone…someone, with your absolute insanity!"

"Your little agreement with Gunter and Sheridan cost my family their lives." I held up a bucketful of dirt for him to see. "You wanted what I owned, so here it is. I hope you still have the appetite for it."

"No one was supposed to be hurt, Gunter was told to fire a warning shot only…what happened was an accident," Kruger tried to bargain. His wife chewed through her gag and yelled over to her husband.

"Hermann, don't you dare grovel before this heathen lover. If you're gonna' die then be a man to the end and damn that murderous bastard to Hell," she said. Her words seemed to revitalize Hermann Kruger and give the condemned man a brief moment of resolve. But when he looked up at me, I saw it in his eyes. Hermann Kruger knew he was about to die.

"Go ahead, get on with it, nigger lover. You are the devil himself, Reuben Judah."

"I don't know about being the devil, but tonight I'm using your property to burn a hole in the door to his domain," I said, striking a match and dropping it to the oil-soaked ground. I lit the torches and tossed them through windows and to the rooftops. Hermann Kruger watched in silence as the flames came to life and licked the ground at his feet then slithered like a fiery serpent towards his house. The women began squirming and screaming through their gags like a horde of bleating goats.

The Prophet of Cobb Hollow

I watched the fire grow and mopped the false sweat from my brow as Hermann Kruger shivered and said nothing in his defense. "Are you cold Hermann? Not getting warm enough for you yet?" I asked. Herman titled his head back and watched mutely as the flames burnt through the roof of his house and business. Through the crackle and spit, the women's lamentations could be heard over the splitting and crashing of wood work. "Watch the flames and get used to seeing them, you sonofabitch." Kruger said nothing in return and his false arrogance forced me to break with reality when I realized, he truly did not care what had happened to my wife and daughter.

I rammed my knee to Hermann Kruger's groin and when he arched back against his bindings to scream—I shoved a handful of dirt into his mouth and began to repack the muddy hole each time he tried to spit it out. The women were screaming in horror and Prophet began rearing as the flames licked the night air and lit up those mountains for miles around. I stopped and watched as Herman Kruger suffocated on the dirt of my land and choked to death because of his greed.

I walked over to the fire and placed my coffee pot on a block of embers and sat down watching Hermann Kruger die while his women cried. When I leaned over the fire to pour myself a cup, my necklace dangled over the coals until the cross itself was cherry red. As I sat back, the molten crucifix fell against my chest and the sound and smell of my own skin sizzling and popping made the Kruger women scream that much harder. I cannot explain what a violent release the burning sensation had on me. Like a wrist cutter freeing her inner demons with blood, or perhaps a suicide jumper kissing the silent air as he fell. I had become a mortal Phoenix shedding one fiery skin to reemerge and live violently in another.

I can close my eyes and still feel the pain of that first scar to this day. The cross itself was actually quite small and the scars themselves, smaller still. Like raven feet making their path in the snowy flesh of their meal, or perhaps the obscene freckles of a mad man hiding behind the insanity of his art. I learned that night to burn away the guilt and use my pain as a form of self-redemption. It would become a lifelong habit to add an odd and immoral balance to my newfound cruelty.

I took the still molten cross and burnt another scar above the first for the old man and then walked towards him. Herman Kruger's body slumped over and his head hung limp as blood dropped from his nose to the rocks below. The stains upon those ghostly stones were like poisonous flowers from a fairy world, and those blood blossoms would now and forever—mark the course of my life. The Kruger women were wailing as I stood and pulled the imbedded cross from my scalded chest before mounting Prophet. I rode over to where they were tied to their posts squirming like salted leeches in the sun. I sat on Prophet watching as their entire world seemed to burn before their eyes, and I was about to offer the women some rare form of condolences, not that it would have mattered to them. At that moment, it might have mattered to me and tipped the scales to nullify my hatred. I was willing to stop the killing and let it be, I had seen enough bloodshed in the war to last me a thousand lifetimes… but the eldest Kruger daughter looked up at me and glared her hatred like a curse.

"There's more of us than there are of you. My brothers will hunt you down and see you and yours dead," she said. The women took turns spitting on the ground where Prophet and I stood.

Looking into their vulgar eyes, I realized the cross would never again symbolize me and Jess. What our union in life had meant. It would now represent her and Molly. The cross would be my personal reminder that they would not be forgotten. And should I be the only one to remember them, then so be it.

I looked down at those mean-eyed crones and met their gazes one by one. I wanted to make sure that they understood I would match their hatred of me ounce per ounce.

"I hope every last one of you bitches suffers," I said leaving them tied to their misery and rode off.

I stopped just outside of Waynesboro and threw a rope over the telegraph wires so I could pull them down for cutting, and took the extra time to wash myself clean of war paint and grit in the

South River before changing into my travel clothes. Once I finished my transaction with Stoddard there would be a final meeting with Mosby. After that, I was on loan from life…

Stoddard Quillen was sitting at his desk looking out the dark office window when I rode up and stopped Prophet beside his ornate buggy rail. He yanked the door open and motioned me inside with a flurry of his hand. "Quick! Get off your horse and get your ass in here before someone sees you. You've busted the hornet's nest wide open with what you did."

I stayed seated in my saddle. "Did you take care of everything, Stoddard?"

"Yes, everything…as per the instructions in those papers you gave me. Now get inside."

"And you know what to tell the people when I leave here this day?" I asked.

Stoddard shook his head empathetically. "Yes…yes, now inside quick or they'll hang the both of us."

"Last chance, you're absolutely sure everything is complete and you know what to say when questioned?" I asked a final time.

"Yes, damn you." Stoddard was losing his patience. "And if it makes you feel any better, you're right about all of this."

"Right about what?"

"What you did to the Kruger's. You did what any man would have wanted to do under similar circumstances, but that's what separates you from other men. You crossed the line and did what the rest of us wouldn't have had the guts to do. And not that I condone it, mind you. But God forgive me…I sure as hell envy you for doing it."

"Good of you to admit that," I said, drawing my Navy Colt and shooting him where he stood.

Stoddard Quillen grabbed his wounded ear, a chunk of flesh gone as blood ran down his neck to the pressed collar. "Have you completely lost your goddamn mind?" screamed Stoddard, gingerly touching the gap in his ear.

"Quiet man, I mean you no harm. We need the townspeople as

witnesses and there's compensation if you'll hear me out," I said quickly as lights were being lit in windows.

"Couldn't you have told me or written it down without shooting my ear off? My goddamn new hat is gonna' ride crooked on my head thanks to you," growled Stoddard.

"I've not much time so listen carefully. You wait a few months until my business from last night dies down. Make an excuse sometime in early spring and leave town for the day to do a little fishing. I want you to go alone and make sure no one follows you."

"Go fishing where?" asked Stoddard, looking around as more lights flickered to life.

"To Three Crow's cabin, dig under the rear foundation stone and finish what I wanted done with the extra gold you find buried there," I said spinning Prophet around to leave. Every window in town was suddenly aglow and the townspeople sat watching us through their curtains. "Raise your hands and lay down," I said quickly to Stoddard. I watched as he dropped to the open doorway before I fired three shots through the wooden frame left of his head.

I rode out into the street and addressed the entire town. "I'll kill any man, woman, or child that comes hunting me in those mountains. They're mine," I yelled. Heads disappeared from windows as the townspeople ducked from view. I fired a parting shot into the floorboards, inches from Stoddard's brow, and pointed my pistol at his prone body. "And I aim to kill every sonofabitch who had a hand in stealing my land or killing my family," I shouted, and then I spurred Prophet through the center of town.

Stoddard would later give a statement to Union authorities that I had come to his business seeking revenge. That he had barely escaped with his life by playing dead when my first shot went wide and clipped his ear. The story Stoddard gave was…

I must have gone insane over the death of my family and losing my land to him at such a cheap (undisclosed) price. That my religious upbringing caused me to see my sudden forfeit as God's retribution because of what I had done while riding as a spy for John Mosby. Stoddard added a few extras about me having a necklace of human teeth, holding a Bible and quoting scripture with burn marks covering my grimy body. None of which were remotely plausible at the time he gave his statement. The version about those teeth being gold came long after his original lie. Stoddard finished his statement by telling the law and Union officials that I had proclaimed myself: *"The Prophet of Cobb Hollow."*

From that day forward, any person who was lost near Cobb Hollow and never heard from again was blamed on *The Prophet.* Lovers who eloped, unsolved wayward robberies, random murders, and missing livestock were all levied upon *The Prophet.* Two young children told the townspeople a tale that I had bewitched them by playing a satanic flute made from a human leg bone, music so pleasing to the ear that they were hypnotized by the demonic melody. In their version, I'd become the Appalachian pied-piper, a stealer of children and souls. I was the boogeyman every parent threatened their children with as a way of making them behave in church. My legend grew until I became the hidden monster that made boys and girls mind their manners, and wash behind their ears. I was the cave-dwelling mad man and the evil chore-master. You did what you were told or The Prophet of Cobb Hollow would steal you away in the night.

I will forever wonder how many dreams my legend may have corrupted because of Stoddard Quillen's backwoods propaganda.

Mingo Kane

19

Culpepper, Virginia
December 27, 1864

I was in Culpepper a full day before my meeting with Mosby and found the Buckhorn's owners pleasant as ever, inquiring about my personal well-being while grubbing for any news about the horrible Confederate raid near Waynesboro. "Nothing of note has graced my ears," I told them, signing their ledger. I took Prophet to their livery and left him saddled, then went back to my room to pen a quick letter to Wilbur Spitler with the news of Jess and Molly, and for him to expect my visit in the very near future. There wasn't any reason to mention Three Crows in my correspondence; Wilber Spitler wouldn't have cared. I walked back to the livery and rode Prophet into town to finish my deal for the pup. A plate of homemade biscuits was getting harder and harder to come by these days.

The shop-keep was behind his counter reading a periodical when I walked in.

"Something I can do for you?" he asked as he looked up and creased the corner to mark his place. I handed him my list and he went to work filling it while talking over his shoulder. "Did you hear about the house fire and murderous raid near Waynesboro?"

"Nope."

"Heard tell a feller went crazy because of the war and killed another man while his family was tied to a fence and forced to watch."

"What happened to the crazy man?" I asked. The shop-keep turned around with an excited look. I realized too late that I'd just found the town gossip; I could tell by the shrill change in the tenor of his voice.

"Folks down in those parts said the crazy man rode with John Mosby, learned his war craft and brutality from the Grey Ghost himself. I heard tell that he up and killed a man over a land dispute, and then burnt his place to the ground while his wife and daughters watched at gun-point. Last anyone heard, he walked naked into the mountains with his musket and a Bible, nothing else. Those hill people are a strange bunch indeed. Already talk of the search being called off because no one wants to die trying to find him in those spooky hollows. I guess they figure if he's naked in those old mountains nature will surely do the work for them. Makes you wonder what it would take to set a man off on a murderous path like that."

"Did you happen to catch the crazy man's name?" I asked.

"Reuben Shadrack Judah, and they're starting to call him, the 'Prophet of Cobb Hollow,' " said the shop-keep with a smug grin. "They've even made up a song about him, goes something like,

> 'He owns the night and he rules the day,
> His skin is cold to the touch.
> He has no blood in earthly veins,
> But blood is what he wants.
> Scalps of hair and a harvest of teeth,
> Jewelry of the mad.
> Reuben Judah craves them both,
> And your soul is what he will have.' "

"Sounds like a mighty mean man," I replied as he started bagging up my goods.

"You just never know about folks these days. It'll be three dollars and a half," he said, hitting the register keys. I paid my bill and the shop-keep kept eyeing me. "Not meaning to pry or offend, but can I ask you a question? Why'd you do it, why did you buy food for that ole mongrel dog the other day?" I thought about my answer for a second.

"Personal reasons," I said and changed the subject. "I'd like to check up on that pup; do you happen to know where those folks live by chance?"

"Yessir. Follow the road out of town until you come to a small wagon road on your right. Take that and follow it to the end and you'll find their house smack dab against the mountains. If you wanna' go check up and see if he spent the money you gave him, I'll save you the trouble. Jim Carver and Libby might not have much, but they're both honest."

"I don't much care about the money, shop-keep. I had a deal for a plate of homemade biscuits and I mean to keep it. I won't be back until tomorrow morning so keep my goods behind your counter until I fetch'm."

"That'd be fine, didn't mean to offend you with my question about the dog," said the shop-keep.

"None taken."

I followed the shop-keep's directions and rode up the rutted trail until I came to a small field. The farmer was loading his winter crop of turnips and cabbages into a wooden barrow. "Howdy again," he said as I rode up.

"Howdy back," I replied, swinging down off Prophet.

"Your horse can graze right there if you've a mind to let him." The farmer wiped his dirty hands on his pants then stuck out his hand. We shook and his hand was hard and dry, cracked from the weather and harsh work of his trade. "Come on up to the house and set a spell. I'll unload these ole turnips and such later on."

"I've been in a saddle off and on for near four years. Push that old barrow up to your root cellar and I'll help you get'm in and dusted with lime."

"Well, I'm obliged to you once again," he said, pushing the wheelbarrow to the cellar door. "Libby is gonna' be sorry she missed you."

"When will she be back?"

"Sometime after dark. I sent her up on the hill to run the milk cow back down here to the barn." We got to the cellar and I threw the door open and began unloading turnips and cabbages and putting lime on each row.

"Did the dog go with her?" I asked. The farmer stopped as if the question offended him. He went back to work at a slower pace, contemplating his answer.

"The dog's gone."

"Run off?" I asked.

The farmer unloaded the last turnip and closed the trap door. "No sir, the little feller is dead. Killed by a mean sonofabitch for no reason other than he was barking at him when he walked by the other evening. Little Libby threw rocks at the bastard but he beat the dog to death with his hands." I stared at the farmer and he shook his head in disgust. "I'll tell you one thing, and I've given it a lot of thought…it takes a cruel sonofabitch to kill a pup in front of a child."

"Who is this man and where might I find him?" I asked.

The farmer looked left and spat in objection. "Mister, I rightly thank you for what you've done for us, but let this'un go. The man's name is Joe McGee. He works as a loader down at the freight yard when he decides to show up. He's mean enough sober but he's meaner when he's drunk, which is most of the time."

"I have his name, now where can I find him besides the freight yard?" With a train to catch, I didn't want to bring any undue attention to myself near the rail station.

"Takes his breakfast every morning at the store around eight."

"Thank you," I said and started walking off the hill towards Prophet.

The farmer fell in beside me. "Libby is sure gonna' be wound up 'cause she missed you. She had some choice words she wanted to share with you about what happened to her pup." I flipped the man a ten dollar gold piece. "What's this for?" he asked.

"Buy her another dog," I said, swinging into the saddle. I gathered my reins and looked down. "Did she give the pup a name?"

The farmer looked up at me with his sad overworked eyes. "Yessir, on the way home and I asked her why she wanted to keep that little rascal. Libby said that was the perfect name for him... Rascal."

"I reckon so. You best remind Libby she still owes me a plate of biscuits." I spun Prophet around and started to leave.

"I never got your name," he said.

I started Prophet off the hill. "My name doesn't matter, but you can tell Libby I'll be seeing that cruel sonofabitch about her dog," I told him over my shoulder.

I got back to my room and napped on the bed until the sound of footsteps and a man's cough came from outside my door. It was Mosby's secret way of letting me know he had arrived. Later, in his room over a bottle of brandy, we talked about my past few days. I told him what had happened to Jess and Molly, and what I had done afterwards. John never said a word, only nodded his approval until I finished talking.

"Well, I hope you brought your pretty blue Union uniform," said Mosby.

"Why?"

John smiled at me and tipped his glass. "Wilhelm Kruger has deserted and headed west by last accounts, but I have firsthand knowledge that Gunter Kruger is staying at the Peterson House in downtown Washington. Believe it or not, that was his punishment for burning everything you owned—house arrest for one month. And the odd thing is, Gunter's room was paid for in advance. A full three days before he lit the fuse and destroyed your farm. It seems the Kruger clan had this whole thing planned out from the start. The best part, ol' Gunter is completely unaware of what you've done to his family."

"His brother Wilhelm can wait for now, but how do we handle

Gunter without getting our asses shot off?" I asked.

"One of my men has a contact just outside of Washington who will help us get into the Peterson House."

"A contact?" I asked.

John wrinkled his nose in distaste. "Yup, a smarmy little turd named Booth. I recall his birth name as being John Wilkes…anyway, he's the type that's too chicken shit to actually fight so he fancies himself as a dashing Confederate spy."

"Is he any good?"

"Hell, no, but he does know exactly which room Gunter and another high-ranking Union officer are in. My man in Washington has done some background work and verified Booth as being a second-rate actor and self-proclaimed southern sympathizer. Booth is staying at the same boarding house awaiting auditions for a new play, 'Our American Cousin.' I'm told the play is actually quite entertaining. It's supposed to start at The Ford Theater sometime around mid-April. Ole honest Abe is supposed to be there himself; maybe we can catch the opening night together," John said with a wink.

"Maybe, now what do you have in mind?" I asked, getting him back on the subject.

Mosby laid out his plan and I found myself standing at a crossroad again, and once more I would let retaliation decide the course of my actions. I could have walked away, but I didn't. Gunter Kruger had given the command to fire, and his brother Wilhelm had killed Three Crows. I thought hard about my choice before I agreed to Mosby's harsh plan of action.

"When do we leave?" I asked. John laughed and slapped me on the back, then refilled our glasses.

"I've already made our travel arrangements for tonight, it'll be grand," said John draining his glass.

We arrived on the outskirts of Washington two hours before Mosby's plan went into operation and moved towards a large blaze along the Potomac River. "What's going on up ahead?" I asked.

John answered without stopping. "It's a tent city for refugees called, 'Shanty Town.' "

"Shanty Town?"

"It's nothing more than a shithole where lives and trade goods are for sale. Just remember to be careful and stay close; should a man wanna' disappear or buy anything from women to information, Shanty Town is the place to be. Once I see the signal I'm looking for, we'll cross over the river into the city, so be ready to move," John warned.

"What happens once we've finished our business at the boarding house?"

Mosby stopped and patted my shoulder. "We come back here. Shanty Town will be our central rally point if we're compromised or separated. Like I said, Reuben. Whether it's a hideout or protection, if you have the money it can be bought in Shanty Town. Hell, even the Union officers walk lightly in or around that putrid shithole."

We moved towards the growing inferno with the stealth born of our newfound action, as guerilla warfighters. Those revelers who were around the bonfire were now asleep in their own waste and vomit with a whiskey stench on their foul-snoring breath. They were mothers none and landless all, beneath the fading harlequin of stars with the gray light of day forever dawning on grayer faces. Mosby skirted the fire and slipped between rows of tents then down a black mud alley where fecal holes and the ammonia stench of urine soaked the air. Some of the denizens sat by small fires with pots boiling the coming day's rations, cornbread with watery beans—a vagrant's feast in the dead king's land.

We came to a multi-colored tent used as a brothel by a host of drunken women. Mosby and I stopped and looked toward their coy smiles with their tasteless offer of disease-flavored flesh. One of the women showed me a saggy teat, her nipple like a burgundy sand dollar wilted in the baking sun. The women drank from a clay jug and passed around the sloshing concoction, giggling. They gave passersby deceitful smiles and ribald remarks, all of which were designed to entice a man with the false promise of pleasure—an ageless recreation offered at the expense of these desperate women and their sad misfortune of employment.

A heavy-set woman with rolls of pasty fat cleaving from her shirt saw us standing there and waved us closer. "Hey, sugar, you wanna' drink?" she cooed.

"I'd rather swallow a mouthful of horse piss," said John. The offhand comment seemed to have no effect on her.

"How about you, a little sip?" she asked me.

"No, thank you, Ma'am."

"Ma'am?" The prostitute laughed.

"I'm looking for a small, well-dressed man with a thin mustache that probably walked by here a few moments ago," Mosby said to her.

The fat woman flashed her wet green teeth at her friends. "What's it worth to you?" Mosby gave the woman a hard look.

"You have no idea what the hell I'm even talking about," said Mosby.

The fat woman smiled and took a sip before answering. "If you're gonna' be that way about it, then find'm yourself. Window shopping might be free, but everything else has a price."

"If you know where he is I'll pay," I said to her. A husky female voice came from inside the tent and answered me before the drunken woman could respond.

"It's not that, sweetie. We just don't care. Now, if you have the money and want some action then come inside and enjoy everything we have to offer. But if you're going to stand around and ask questions about your boyfriend all night, run along home," the voice advised.

"The hell with these mule-faced hags...let's go, I'll find him," said Mosby.

We turned back the way we came and ducked through a side alley where two men were fighting over some misunderstanding. They rolled in the polluted filth underfoot, cussing and scratching while a small crowd cheered them on. Mosby spotted Booth across the muddy road standing near a shabby tent, touching his nose and tugging at his ear each time a Union officer walked by. He was wearing a tailored suit with a flamboyant red-lined cape tied around his thin neck. We watched as Booth walked in a small circle spinning his elaborate walking cane, as if he wanted to be seen by everyone who passed him by.

"Look at that dumb bastard," Mosby said.

"Kinda' flashy for a spy," I noted aloud.

Mosby rolled his eyes. "And that's his problem. Booth stands out and he talks too damn much."

"Why in the hell is he going through the trouble of giving the signal to every damn officer that walks by?" I asked. Mosby chuckled.

"Those were his instructions. Booth doesn't know either of us or what we look like, and I mean to keep it that way. His acting career is going downhill and he's in this game for money and fame, nothing else. The ignorant bastard has no honor, absolutely none. Matter of fact, once this night is over with I might just pay someone in this hellhole to slit the bastard's throat for the general principal."

We both watched as Booth went through his ear and nose routine each time a blue uniform walked by. "So that means Gunter is there?" I asked.

"Yup, touch the nose and Gunter is in his room. Touch the nose and tug the ear, both of the men we're looking for are there. It looks like we have all our eggs in a basket, so let's go crack a few and make us an omelet."

We went through Shanty Town and crossed the Potomac and came out on a cobbled street where a carriage sat waiting like a funeral hearse. "I've had enough of this walking shit," said Mosby opening the door and climbing in. "Get in and we'll ride the rest of the way."

"How far do we have to go," I asked.

Mosby's contact answered from the driver's seat. "Two blocks, once you two are out I'll circle around and wait on a side street until I see your signal," the man replied. Mosby pulled out a flask and took a small pull then offered it to me. I declined as the buggy came to a stop in front of a large brick building.

"Here we are; good luck," said the driver. Mosby looked over at me and grinned before we got out.

"Time to earn your money," he said.

We walked straight into the Peterson House as if we owned it, and that night—we did. "Upstairs, first door on the left is yours. The last door at the end of the hallway is mine. Be quick with your personal business then meet me back here," said Mosby stopping at the staircase.

Up the stairs we went like old chums ascending a watchtower, our boots clopping against the polished boards and us talking in a loud, carousing tone. To anyone in the rooms, we were two young officers returning from a drunken night of merriment. At the top, Mosby stopped and pointed to my door then handed me the key. "How in the hell could you already have the key?" I asked putting it into the lock. Mosby shrugged the question off.

"The key to life is having the key," said John. I unlocked the door and started to slip inside the room when Mosby touched my shoulder and whispered. "Be quick and no gunfire unless all hell breaks loose." I nodded and stepped inside Gunter Kruger's room and closed the door—I wanted this to be a very private affair.

The room smelled of sex and smoke and cheap whiskey; on the table a candle had burnt down to the wick leaving a puddle of wax. I looked at the bed and as my eyes adjusted to the low light, a girl sat up and started to speak. I put a finger to my lips and opened the door for her. She slipped out of bed half-naked and walked out the room then disappeared down the hall as if this were normal in her nightly profession.

I stood over Gunter Kruger and watched the man sleep until I remembered Mosby wanted this to be quick. I whistled and Gunter opened his eyes and asked, "What took you so long getting back from Shanty Town, Booth? Did you bring me another girl? She better move her ass more than the last bitch you brought me. That little whore didn't move an inch until I slapped her around." I could smell the raw booze on his breath.

I pulled my saber free of its sheath and rested the cutting edge on Gunter's exposed stomach. "It's just the two of us, Gunter. Like it was when we fought in the pit." The realization of my statement brought the situation into focus.

Gunter's eyes cleared and he tried to sit up but I pushed him back down flat with the blade. He sputtered and tried to explain, "It wasn't my fault, Reuben."

"Yes, it was, but I wanna' know why?" I pulled my arm back and pressed the tip of my saber into the soft spot between his naked legs.

"It was my father's idea because you embarrassed our family in front of Jessamine and the entire town. He blamed you and that old Cherokee for stealing the land that shoulda' been ours."

"It's funny that you put the burden on poor ol' Hermann. Your father did the opposite and blamed you just before he died," I said and pushed the blade into him.

I put my knee on his chest and covered his head with a pillow to quiet the cries of pain. I pushed the sword harder until the tip of my saber came out just above the breastbone and arced upward in a curvature until it split Gunter Kruger's chin to the bone, wedging his mouth shut. Gunter tried to reach for my arm to stop the blade's progress, but he was groggy from sleep and booze. I pulled the pillow free and his eyes closed slightly as a sticky bubble of blood plopped out of his mouth. I felt him going limp, body relaxing in the final seconds.

I pulled the blade free and wiped it clean on the bedding then placed Three Crow's medicine pouch across his chest. The three black crow feathers would be for his brother, when I found him. I heated the cross by the dim candle flame and burnt another scar beside the first then walked back out into the hallway to wait until John finished his own brand of unsavory business. Like a stone cast into a well where the ripples never find a shore—I had now honed my blade of retribution and became a pauper living on the unearned currency of life.

A voice in the hallway startled me and I drew my Navy Colt, cocking it. The half-naked woman who was in bed with Gunter stood in the doorway of a vacant room. "Is he gone?" she asked with distant eyes.

"Yes."

"Did you kill him?"

"I know how you must feel, how confused you must be," I started. She stepped towards me and asked again.

"Did you kill him?"

"Yes."

"Are you going to kill me too?"

"No." She nodded and went back into the room and closed the door.

Mosby stepped into the hallway and had with him a scantily dressed Union officer. Tears fell from his jolly cheeks as he wept for Mosby's redemption and received none. "Having a bad day?" I asked him as they walked up. The officer looked up at me and ground his teeth without answering.

"Allow me to introduce General Stoughton. It seems this poor fellow must have run out of female entertainment and fell asleep," said Mosby smacking him on the backside with the flat of his saber. The General winced and John laughed. "Let's go, loverboy. I think you'll fetch me a fine price in a prisoner swap with Grant."

"What about me?" I asked Mosby.

"What about you?"

"I'm not sure what comes next, John."

"As far as the Union is concerned, what happened to you was an unfortunate act of war. So, as far as the Confederacy is concerned, what happened to the Kruger's is an unfortunate act of war. There's nothing either side can do about it, and they know it."

"No charges of murder or arson?" I asked.

"No, but that doesn't mean you're gonna' be safe by a damn sight. What you and I have done with this unit has created a lot of enemies, on both sides. But here's what I say to that…the hell with them. We take care of our own, by God." Mosby smiled and handed me a roll of papers.

"What's this for?"

"Your discharge orders," said Mosby. I started to protest but he waved me off with a flourish of his hand. "I'll not hear how your duty comes first and all of that other military bullshit. We started as privates together and we go out as colonels together."

"I never thought about my rank," I admitted.

"Well, you're being honorably discharged as a full colonel," John explained then added with a wink. "But I don't think you'll be drawing any back pay when this is over."

"Wouldn't want none anyway," I replied. Mosby laughed and put his arm around my shoulder.

"Nope, I reckon not. Now let's get pretty boy some place safe so we can enjoy a late farewell dinner together," Mosby said pushing the half-naked general forward with a laugh.

"Farewell dinner?" I asked.

"I know you're worried about your two boys, so I took the liberty of having reservations made for Luther Cobb on the nine am train bound for Atlanta, Georgia, tomorrow morning. That gives us plenty of time tonight so we can celebrate in true Virginia fashion."

"I guess that means mulled wine and roast chicken," I said falling in behind him. It was Mosby's favorite meal. He stopped and looked at me over his shoulder with a shit-eating grin.

"Why Reuben, so good of you to offer...I humbly accept. If there's nothing else I can be of service for, then I think we better move a bit more quickly. The Federals are feeling the strain of my raids these days. Grant has gone so far as to order the planks taken up each night on the bridges leading in and out of Washington." Mosby chuckled at the thought and then pushed the general towards the staircase.

"There is one more thing you could help me with," I said as we walked down the stairs.

"Name it," said John snapping his fingers.

"I could use one of your men to watch my back tomorrow morning before I catch my train."

"Really," said Mosby stepping into the street with his human cargo. "In regards to what might I ask?"

"I need to see a man about a dog and I could use one of your men to keep anyone there from moving until I catch my train." I told

John what had happened as he lit a cigar and took a drag.

"The cruel bastard killed a pup with his bare hands for no good reason. There just ain't no damn call for that." Mosby exhaled and blew across the ember then made a circle in the air with the lit cigar.

"It's my understanding he has breakfast every morning at the store in Culpepper before going to his job at the freight yard," I explained.

"Consider it done," said Mosby as the covered buggy pulled up. The door opened and a large hand snaked out and pulled the general inside. The door closed and John tapped the wheel three times and the buggy with its precious cargo sped off into the night. "Done and done," said Mosby extinguishing his cigar on his boot heel.

Mosby started to cross the street when my voice stopped him. "Thanks for all your help, John. You're about the only friend I have left."

"Damned if we ain't had quite a ride together, Reuben," said Mosby offering his hand.

We shook and I grinned at him. "Damned if we ain't."

"I'll have a man in the store for you, but do me a favor," said Mosby looking at the crisp night sky.

"What's that?"

"Beat that sonofabitch's brains out and then kick him in the bleeding crack where his balls used to be," Mosby answered stepping into the street.

"Back for your goods?" asked the Culpepper shop-keep as I walked in.

"I'll get them directly; right now I'm looking for a man that takes his breakfast here."

"Who might that be? I know most everyone in town."

"A man named Joe McGee. Do you know him?" I asked.

The shop-keep's demeanor changed at the mention of his name. "I know him, can I ask what's it about?"

"None of your damned affair," I said. I didn't like his prying into business that didn't concern him. "Let's just say I need to see

Mr. McGee about a dog." I could see in the shop-keep's eyes that he knew what had happened, and he saw in mine—I knew that he hadn't told me about the dog when I bought my goods the day before. A large surly man walked through the door and flopped down at one of the small tables near the back edge of the store. A gaggle of old men were playing a game of checkers by the pot-belly stove. "Morn'n Joe," they said and went back to their game.

"Tell your ol' lady to get cooking," said the lout to the proprietor.

"Mother, Joe McGee is here waiting for his breakfast," said the shop-keep through the back curtain. "Did that answer your question?" he asked me in a whisper.

"Yup," I said, surveying the interior for one of Mosby's men.

"I don't want any trouble; this store is all I've got," the shop-keep whispered across the counter.

"Then go in the back room and help your wife cook."

"No, sir…this is my store."

"Suit yourself, I'm getting ready to change Mr. McGee's outlook on what it means to be civil, and when I'm done…that ugly bastard is gonna' understand the importance of small animals."

I stepped away from the counter and began browsing through the store, walking the aisles and checking the stocked items. I heard a rich baritone voice with a soft southern drawl speak from the other side of the shelves. "Are you a friend of Jesus?"

"I am a Brother," I replied through the shelves. I moved some canned goods until a hard face with dark brown eyes stared back at me. The man on the other side smiled before he spoke.

"Mosby sends his regards, so get to it and do what you gotta' do. I got your back," the man said.

I walked over to where the dogkiller was sopping up his runny eggs with a biscuit and stood beside him looking down, saying nothing. Joe McGee finished his meal and wiped his dirty hands on his greasy pant legs then looked up at me. "Something I can help you with?"

"As a matter of fact there is. I bought a dog awhile back and paid twenty dollars to a man and his daughter to feed and care for the critter until I got back. I rode in yesterday and what do you think I hear. I'm told a story that my dog was beat to death by a man named Joe McGee."

The fat man leaned back and put his hands behind his head and grinned up at me like a depraved jester. "And that would mean exactly what to me?"

"So that means you owe me exactly twenty dollars and I mean to have it, one way or another." The men playing checkers stopped their game and leaned forward, watching and listening. The shop-keep stayed behind his counter and peered at us sideways over the register. Joe McGee feigned a yawn before he answered me in an off-handed manner.

"Well, my mouthy friend. Here's the way I see it…it's all your fault. You shoulda' told the little bitch who threw rocks at me to keep your damn dog tied up. The little bastard was always running off the hill barking at people and shit," he said and looked over to where the checker men sat as if they were his private audience of approval. "And beside that, I don't owe you a goddamn thing." I didn't wait nor did I want to argue further with the cretin. I had a train to catch. I stepped forward and hit him square in the mouth, sending him ass first through the chair in a shower of splinters and blood. Joe McGee hit the back wall and slid to his side unconscious.

A black cast iron skillet hung on the wall behind the stunned shop-keep's head. "Hand me that skillet," I said to him. The man stood motionless, refusing to move from behind the counter. "Hey shop-keep, if I have to get that skillet myself, then I swear to God, when I'm done using it on this sonofabitch…I'll use it on you."

The men playing checkers started to get out of their chairs when Mosby's man pulled his pistol. "Enjoy the show, gentlemen. But I'd much prefer if you were to stay seated," he said, motioning them back down with his gun barrel.

The shop-keep handed me the skillet and I brought it down on Joe McGee's head, the sound like a dull church bell. I hit the man three more times until his head seemed almost lopsided and full of malleable clay. "Goddamn," said one of the checker players.

"They hellfire," said the other. Mosby's man laughed at these antics and seemed to enjoy the thrashing unfolding before him.

I handed the skillet back to the shop-keep who stood holding it and looking down at the beaten man. I pulled out my travel purse and thumbed through the bills. "How much for the damage to your chair and skillet?" I asked the proprietor.

"The chair is on the house but the skillet's gonna' fetch you a dollar," he answered without looking up. I put the money on his counter and a few extra bills for the added trouble.

"That'll cover the damages and buy them breakfast for interrupting their game," I said pointing to the checker players. I walked over and took my goods from behind the counter and started to leave when the shop-keep asked if I wanted the skillet I just paid for.

"Hang it back where it was and any time someone asks to buy it, you tell them it's not for sale," I told him and left.

Years later, I was on my way to meet with Teddy Roosevelt and join his US Volunteer Calvary unit just before the Spanish-American War broke out. I stayed the night in Culpepper and marveled at the city's progress since the early days of post-Civil War reconstruction. Joe McGee was there, the same as when I left him. Blind in one eye and shuffling along the railroad tracks with a clawed hand whistling for a stray dog that would never return. The dog-killer may very well have been a "cruel sonofabitch" to some, but not to me. Joe McGee got what he deserved and I have no regrets.

Mingo Kane

150

20

Present

"What happened to the Kruger family?" Paul's thin voice asked. "I didn't mean to startle you, but you stopped talking and you've been staring straight ahead for some time now," he apologized.

"The Kruger women were ruined because of what I did. They sold what little they had left and sailed back to Germany. The old woman died on the ship but the daughtcrs made the voyage. All three of those hateful bitches married military men and raised like-minded families of their own. It's so odd how time has its way with you," I answered. Paul gave me a confused look and squinted.

"How do you mean, odd?" he asked.

"I would meet the Kruger's again in France. And once again they would be on one side of a war and I would be on the other."

"What do you mean, in France?"

"World War One...I received an overseas telegram from those Kruger bitches when the United States announced their involvement in the war. I was told by them in no uncertain terms that when the war was over and Germany was victorious, their boys would be coming here for me and my sons. It didn't matter to them who was still living; they were going to erase the Judah name from existence."

"What'd you do?" asked Paul.

"I saved those high-handed whores the trouble and went hunting them on their land instead of them hunting me on mine."

"Speaking of which, what happened to Mosby?" asked Paul. I thought back to my time with John Mosby. I thought about our long friendship and the hard years I'd lived since he'd died.

"John went on to campaign for Grant in Virginia when he ran for President, and the two became rather intimate friends. The South never forgave Grant, and Virginia saw John as a traitor. His boyhood home was burnt to the ground and at least once someone tried to assassinate him."

"But I looked him up in our library. John Singleton Mosby never surrendered."

I shook my head in agreement. "Mosby and those who rode with him didn't surrender nor did we take an oath of allegiance. Most of us just quit fighting and went home."

Paul was curious. "So some of you still believed in the South?"

"Hell, no, we never believed in the South, or gave two shits about the Confederate cause. What would we have gained by either? We fought for our homes and for each other because we believed in both," I explained.

Paul smiled. "Mr. Reuben, would you mind if I ask you a very personal question?"

"Ask."

"Did you ever remarry, and if you didn't, why not?"

"In all of my years I never took to my bed another woman. I had only enough love in my heart for one, and when Jessamine died she took that love with her."

Paul was crying; unashamed, he wiped his eyes. "I can understand that kind of love, I truly can. It's amazing that you've seen so much death and hardship and yet you survived it all."

"Others in my long life sacrificed themselves to the cause of war or the misadventure of blind justice. They were all taken down, the stardom and heroics they so desired was always just out of their reach until each man became a tarnished star falling from the sky. I feel no sense of vindication as one of the handfuls of survivors. I would rather have seen them all succeed, catch the brass ring. Ride the full-time limit and cross the line with a whip cracking overhead. As it turned out, it was I who would outlive them all."

"What happens next, Mr. Reuben?"

"My first concern was for my sons, Luther and Eli. I found them and made sure they would be taken care of. I left the outskirts of Atlanta not long after John Wilkes Booth murdered President Lincoln at The Ford Theater. I will always wonder what might've been if Mosby had made good on his plan to kill Booth."

"I guess our history would have changed forever, Mr. Reuben."

"It doesn't matter now," I said and shrugged. "It is what it is."

"Can we pick your story up tomorrow night? I have to do my security check before shift change." Paul asked, standing and stretching his arms.

"Tomorrow it is," I said.

* * *

There are such wretched creatures in this place, poor souls who are forced to relive the eternity of some life-altering enterprise. They each walked a fine line of conflict in their dismal lives until they lost their balance. Some slight weight shift in the mediocrity of life that tipped the scales to some insane finality—jilted lovers with scarred wrists or those who hid their unchecked and jaded addictions, perhaps some horrible accident thrust them here among the elderly who forever reside within their colliding worlds. Each of them slipped and fell upon the razor's edge, the thread of their obsessive life too fragile and the dynamics of their halved and unbalanced world now altered forever.

I sit here night after night…and I listen to them. I hear the secrets uttered by both men and women, ever remorseful for their exploits of malfeasance which cannot be undone. I see the lowest of life here in this place of forgotten whispers.

I hear the cries of a mother who abused her children, now condemned to die desperate, alone, and unforgiven for the crimes of neglect. Her tears are shed for what she cannot hold. They are meaningless.

I see the abuser of young women and I hear his shifty lies of seduction. I listen to the curse of his jealously for those he can no longer touch or defile. I mark his hard words of deceit and await a time when I will not be bashful. I will right the wrongs of his injustice.

I sit and listen…and I see these things, here in this place.

I see broken men of war who will forever fight the inner workings of their private battles. I hear their screams from the nightmares, and I share with them a mute kinship of understanding. I see them as the pilgrims of pestilence. They are forgiven and shall remain, faithfully—prisoners shackled unto themselves.

At midnight, the guard checks the doors and his keys will jingle like a stick being pulled across the iron rungs of a fence, grinning like terrible teeth as he pushes them into door-locks. Locked or unlocked, time flows through all doors at an equal pace. In my prison the thought of passing seasons no longer exists but I measure them anyway, in moments such as these. When I sit at my window and watch those gleaming keys with untold fascination, looking for an exit from within these inner walls of torture.

Paul mumbled a greeting to the night watchman and walked over to where I sat. "Are you busy with your thoughts, Mr. Reuben?"

"No, just sitting here watching the world go by."

"Everyone went to bed three hours ago. The world is asleep, Reuben."

"The world still moves…even in your sleep," I said.

"Is there anything I can get for you?" asked Paul. I looked up at him and decided to test the water of his conviction.

"As a matter of fact there is. I would like to hold your keys," I said. Paul gave me an odd look.

"My keys?"

"Yes, just for a second. I'll return them." Paul unlatched his keys and handed them to me. I felt the cool metal and let my finger trace the dull peaks of the teeth, wore down from years of abuse. I shook them on the ring just so as to hear their metallic jingle and handed them back to Paul. "That was oddly gratifying for me, thank you," I told him.

"Why the keys?" asked Paul.

"I honestly don't know," I replied as a minimum security inmate stepped into the hall. He drew out his hand and made a gun with his thumb and index finger. His hand recoiled as if he had just shot Paul. The inmate blew across the tip of his barrel finger then holstered his imaginary weapon and disappeared back into the thorny recesses of his room.

"The gunslinger," Paul said.

"The gunslinger?"

"That's what our staff calls him, the gunslinger. He's never been a problem to anyone at the facility, all he does is walk around doing his quick draw routine," Paul explained.

"It wasn't like that at all."

"What wasn't, Mr. Reuben?"

"I was standing right there the day it happened, center stage when the first gunfight took place in the old west. July 21, 1865 in Springfield, Missouri. That was the day Bill Hickok killed Davis Tutt in the town square at six pm from a distance of seventy-five yards."

"You knew Wild Bill?" Paul asked scooting closer.

"I rode with Bill off and on for a couple years, Wild Bill was just a persona created by magazines and dime novels. Hickok and I spent time in St. Louis and even planned on meeting up in Deadwood. Bill was a hard man, but fair enough if you gave him middle of the road."

"What was the gun fight over--a woman?"

I shook my head no. "Bill Hickok had three passions in life that he shared openly and without objection—poker, whiskey, and women. Pretty much in that order," I explained and gave Hickok and his coarse memory a hard chuckle. "Hell, no, the fight wasn't over a goddamn woman. Bill Hickok was a better man than that. The whole thing started over a damned ol' pocket watch."

Paul laughed and dropped his head in disbelief. "You can't be serious! A pocket watch?"

"Yup, damndest thing I ever saw."

"I'd like to hear about Hickok and your sons if you feel like talking," said Paul leaning back. He crossed his legs and put his hands behind his head, closing his eyes. "Take me away, Reuben."

"Open your mind and feel the thunder, ride the wind and walk with me through reconstruction. Feel the expanding west and relive these wild times with wilder men. Come with me and you will witness the last period of our unspoiled land."

21

The Carolinas
1865

I sit in my train seat and watch as the cold morning stars speed by. The other passengers are asleep and they jostle in their bunks to the hypnotic cadence of metal wheels clinking along these lonely tracks. The soothing percussion of rails and iron wheels lulls the travelers into a falsely constructed dream world, but a far better world than the one filled with the bitter scenes we've shared daily on this route of despair. The land remains scorched for miles on end, and the fields lay blackened with burnt corn crop as if the land itself wore a coating of dark beard stubble. The sun has arisen bright and heatless, day after day, and the entire world's humanity seems to be moving north along these tracks.

We've passed by hordes of wretched foot travelers in various forms of disarray, barefoot and pleading to the passengers as our train slowed by them on steep hillsides. The dead litter the ditches and lay where they had fallen, and still...the living walked on. Dark eyes and hollow stares, cheekbones like razors as they walked together—black or white—one group walking into an uncertain future while the other towards the illusion of their newfound freedom. Clapboard farmhouses were vacant and livestock lay dead with their hams hacked apart by starving refugees. Even the gardens, root cellars, and hen houses were picked clean until nothing was left. These are the sights I saw upon this panoramic landscape of pain.

I disembarked in South Carolina and decided to ride Prophet until I crossed over into Georgia. I'd had enough of trains and the repetitive window scenes of war savagery. But still, I rode by beggars, amputees, and other such mutant varieties of back-road humanity. I ate corn cob soup with freed slaves, slept in tent towns, and shared directions with Confederate deserters as I made my way through the hardship of their broken lives. I rode with famine, I was smoke and pestilence. A dirty man both inside and out, astride a dark horse as if some unknown apocalypse had become my shadow. All thoughts of charity towards humankind were annulled by the time I stumbled upon Wilbur Spitler and his wife, living in squalor at a refugee camp just inside Atlanta. They were holed up in a shanty made from tin stacked against poles lashed together with old telegraph wire. They saw me approaching before I saw them.

"Thy Lord Almighty," said Wilbur Spitler as I rode up to the open front of their hovel. Agnes Spitler crawled out and stood next to her husband as I dismounted. She came over and began to cry and kissed my cheek.

"Did you get my letter?" I asked her. She put her hands to her face and shook her head no.

"No mail is moving into or out of Atlanta. The closest town to get something like mail delivered would be Valdosta. Everything else between here and there is burnt to hell," Wilbur Spitler explained.

"Then you don't know about Jess and Molly—" I had started to say when Wilbur cut me off.

"Oh, we know. That Goddamn Wilhelm Kruger was here a few weeks ago looking for you and the boys. He made sure we knew what had happened to Jess and Molly, and then the little bastard went into great detail about what he did to Three Crows." Wilbur paused for a second and looked at his wife who nodded for him to continue. "He also told us what you did to Hermann and Gunter in return."

I wanted to see where Wilbur Spitler stood. "What do you think about the Krugers now?" I inquired.

He gave me a hard look. "I hope you kill every one of those German sonsabitches," said Wilbur. Agnes gave his shoulder a pinch in objection, but he shook off her hand. "No, Mother, I'll not have it. No call for what was done to Jess and Molly, no damn call for that kind of brutality at all. And I'm sorry to hear about Three Crows," said Wilbur showing me a rare form of compassion. "Wilhelm is probably the worst of the Kruger lot, so kill him slow when you find him. That mutt-faced turd even bragged about what he did to Three Crows, told us how the old fella never said a word when Wilhelm stuck him with his bayonet. He said Three Crows just bled and sang an old Cherokee song until he died."

"Where are my boys?" I asked getting back to my initial concern.

"They're both enrolled at the Phillips Academy in Massachusetts, just outside of Boston. But Confederate currency isn't worth the paper it's printed on these days so there's only enough money left in their account for another month of tuition," said Wilbur.

"Good, then let my boys stay where they are. I'll make good on the tuition when I get to Valdosta. What did you tell Wilhelm Kruger about me and my sons?" I asked. Wilbur started to answer but his wife spoke up.

"I told him you took your boys and headed west like most other sensible folks are doing. He said he'd still hunt you to Hell and back if he had to, and then he rode off without so much as another word. He's a horrid man to look at, that big ole head and those two gaping holes where his nose used to be after it got shot off," said Agnes. Wilbur patted her shoulder.

"Now Aggie, Reuben is here and the boys are safe," he said and looked at me. I could see it in his frail and fragile eyes. Wilbur Spitler was a broken man. He had no means of monetary survival and his bones would be picked clean by those who did. He needed a way out and I would offer Wilbur Spitler what he wanted.

"When the next train comes through this hellhole, I'll buy three tickets to Valdosta," I told them.

"After that?" asked Wilbur a little too quickly.

"After I have money wired to Boston for Luther and Eli's education, I'm putting you two on a train to Massachusetts. You are to raise my boys so they become men of education and prominence. That's what Jess wanted and that's what she'll have. Luther and Eli are to take the Spitler last name instead of mine. As far as my boys are concerned, tell them their father died in the war. I need to know my sons are safe until I finish this business with Wilhelm Kruger."

"Okay," Wilbur said and cleared his throat. He saw his way out and tried to bargain for a better deal. "I made investments just before Sherman came to Atlanta, what of those?" he asked me.

"What kind of investments?"

This time, Wilbur Spitler became the same his old salesman self when he answered me. "I went into business with a man named Will Kellogg. He was running out of land where his plant is located in Michigan so we met last summer and formed a partnership of sorts. He and I started buying farmland here in Georgia to grow corn and planned on shipping the harvest by train to his plant in Battle Creek, Michigan."

I was curious and thought about using this venue as a way of giving Wilbur what he wanted. "What did you plan to do with all that corn?" I asked.

Wilbur gleamed. "We'll take the corn and make toasted flakes out of it. It'll be a breakfast cereal would last forever on a shelf and wouldn't spoil."

"Land will be pennies on the acre until this business of war is over. I'll have the money wired to your account to buy more land, but make no mistake about this partnership between us. Both of you now work for me. Do we understand each other?" I said, eyeing the pair.

Wilbur was caught and he knew it. "I'm not sure I know what you mean, we work for you?" he said, a little too gruffly.

"I am giving you a way out and a way back up the social ladder, but in return you raise my boys. This partnership is that simple, I'm paying you for the responsibility of seeing my sons succeed. If you neglect them or their education in any way, if you ever put your needs before those of my sons...then you alone will answer to me. If you agree, then we have a deal."

Before Wilbur could accept, his wife gave me a stern look and cut in. "We'd raise those boys anyway, Reuben. We'd starve if we had to."

"I appreciate that, but I'm offering you the chance to avoid starving," I said to her.

"I'll make you proud of Luther and Eli," said Wilbur extending his hand. We shook and Agnes hugged us close. I almost felt like I had a family again, almost...but this family I had just bought, they were now my employees.

A whistle sounded in the distant. "Start gathering what you have left, train's coming," I said, as a plume of dull smoke belched skyward.

* * *

I spent two weeks in Valdosta making good on my sons' tuition payments and let Stoddard Quillen handle the travel arrangements and money transfers to help jumpstart Wilbur's corn flake business. I had received a personal telegram from John Mosby, ever the cryptic. "Go west!" was all it said concerning the whereabouts of Wilhelm Kruger. I stepped out of the telegraph office and started across the street towards the café when an old man leaning back in a ratty porch chair stopped me.

"Don't mean to pry, but you've a queersome look about you I've seen 'afore," he said.

I stopped and looked down at him. "What sorta' look would that be?"

"You're not him but you're likely out of his brood," said the old man eyeing me closer.

"Whose brood?"

"Keller Judah himself. You don't have the shunt of white hair he had on his topknot, but you're one of his'n. You got the same miss-matched eyes. Cherokee legend says that ole Keller Judah was touched by the hand of God."

"The Cherokee don't believe in God. But I'd be Reuben, Keller Judah was my great-grandfather."

The man slapped his knee. "I knew it, damn sure did. I saw Keller Judah when I was a young'un. No bigger than a corn nubbin at the time. He was a sight to see, all dressed in buckskins and that dark hair with the white streaks on his crown. Legend says he got the white streaks in his hair when he was struck by lightning while he was fighting against the Iroquois, blew his ass right off the horse and changed the color of his eyes. He still got up and fought those red heathens with his bare hands while his hair was afire. I've heard many a wild story about him, ol' Keller Judah was a mighty fearsome man."

"Only met Keller once, don't know much more about him other than he might've been a pirate," I said.

The old man bobbed his head furiously. "Yes, indeed, a Spanish pirate he was, got himself shipwrecked off the coast of Florida and swam ashore. Story goes he was captured by a tribe of Seminoles and forced to fight in their warrior pits. He butchered a bunch of those dirt worshipping bastards and finally escaped, made his way to the Cherokee lands and took up with their kind."

"Is he still alive?" I cut in.

The old man shrugged. "Damned if I'd know the answer to that, and even if he was alive, Keller would have to be damn near a hundred or more. Not that I'd doubt it for a second. Like I said, he was ornery as the crooked cock on a boar hog and tougher than the warts on a whore's ass."

"You have any idea where he might have settled?" I asked.

The old codger scratched his grizzled chin and thought. "Last I heard he left North Carolina with Chief Richard and went to Texas instead of walking The Trail of Tears. There was a story that circulated around that Chief Richard was killed fight'n at the Alamo, but Keller was never heard from again. No, sir, he was a bigg'un just like you and mean'er than the fires of Hell. Even had tattoos inked on his arms and across the face from his travels to exotic lands. Yes, sir, many a young woman swooned over Keller Judah," said the old timer. "If you happen to make Texas a stop in your worldly travels, ask about Keller down thataway. He was a hard man to forget, gotta' be some folks around those parts that'd remember your great-grandpappy."

"I might just do that when I get the spare time." I thought it over for a second and took a chance. "I was wondering if you might've seen a man I'm looking for. He's an easy feller to spot, got a big head and missing his nose."

The old man made a sour face. "Yup, passed right through here 'bout three weeks ago. Hateful bastard he was, uglier than a mud road to boot. He must've had a bunch of money waiting for him in Missouri."

"Why Missouri?"

"Cause he was always yammering about what a big man he'd be when he got to St. Louis. I think some folks over at Pookie's Tavern finally run him off for cheating at cards." The old fella looked up at me and squinted. "Why are you asking, is that ugly bastard a friend of yours?"

"I wouldn't exactly say he's a friend of mine, but thank you for the information," I said and started to walk away.

The old man held out a scabby hand and said to me, "Hold on now, I could sure use me a bottle of spirits. Ole Sherman and his boys may have burnt everything I ever owned, but their flames never blistered my ability to drink." I dug in my breast pocket and flipped him a silver dollar. Who was I to deny him the solace of whiskey? "Why thank ye' kindly," he said, pocketing the coin.

I ate at the café then returned to the hotel and found Wilbur Spitler in the lobby, holding court in his new social finery. He didn't acknowledge me standing beside him and continued to sell the gathered audience on the importance of his business savvy. It seemed to me that Wilbur and Agnes Spitler were already counting the profits they had yet to earn.

I pulled Wilbur aside by his coat sleeve and spoke abruptly. "I'll be leaving first thing tomorrow morning."

"Why not stay a day or two with me and Aggie. The extra rest wouldn't hurt you." Wilbur said it as if he was selling me a business option. I didn't much care for his false concern or slippery attitude.

"No, you have money in your account and the train fare to Boston is paid for. I've kept my end of our bargain and I have my own personal affairs to attend, fair enough?" I asked extending my hand. When Wilbur Spitler clasped to shake, I clamped down until his hand joints cracked and he winced. "I didn't hear your answer, Wilbur. I said, fair enough?"

"Yes, Reuben, fair enough," he said, gritting his teeth.

I let go of his hand and adjusted my suit jacket. "I'll be gone well before daylight, so pass along my apologies to Agnes for not saying goodbye."

"Yes, of course I will," he said as I started for my room. "Reuben, there's one more thing I'd like to say before you go."

I stopped at the stairs and turned around. "Then go ahead and spit it out."

Wilbur's expression softened. "Jessamine made the right choice...you were a good man to her."

I thought about the story Jess had told me that night at the festival just before we danced. How Wilbur had once arranged her marriage to the very man that murdered her. I let that memory guide my reply. "She was more than a business venture to me, Wilbur. I married your daughter because I loved her."

That night I had a dream in which Jess and Molly were running across a long green field where a battle was taking place. Bullets whizzed past their heads and wildflowers fell from their hair as they ran hand in hand. When the last blossom dropped they made a human cross, and Jess looked at me and mouthed the words: "*I am because we are.*"

The earth grew black and the old Cherokee woman who foretold my future was standing in their place; gathered around her was a horde of ghastly soldiers with horrible wounds. The fighting had stopped and she stared at me with those pale white eyes like rice grains. The soldiers all spun to dust and the fatal crumbs of their life were carried away on a reeking whirlwind. The old Cherokee woman raised a bony finger then repeated my future. "Remember, some will always die so others may live. You will one day become the mountain that life will break itself upon."

I awoke from that dream and left while the night sky hovered moonless and black like a shroud of secrecy. I gave Prophet his lead and let the bay stud stretch his legs out, and the wind felt good on my face as the horse thundered along the dark road like a wraith reborn. Many have said that I abandoned my boys to wander as a murderous and carefree man, and though my reasoning may be considered shallow, I left not for myself, but for the welfare of my boys. All I could offer my sons would be hardship as the clock to mark their time, and calloused hands as a reward for their efforts. If I stayed—my sons would be known as the offspring of a mad man, the children of a murderer with no chance for redemption. The Judah name may have been tarnished by my actions, but Wilbur Spitler would never feel poverty—his type would always travel in the higher circles of society. Although I had the money and the financial means, I could not afford to wear their brand of odor. It was a self-indulgence you either had or you didn't, and Wilbur Spitler wore his greed like mildewed finery.

I would one day see my boys graduate from Harvard and become great men during the Industrial Revolution. I helped them succeed and kept them safe by staying in the periphery of their lives, always introduced to them as an old acquaintance of the Spitler's—a Mr. L. E. Cobb.

In my own hard way, I said good-bye to my sons that morning and disappeared from life. I saw it best to avoid people altogether, electing to ride free and speak rarely. I shunned the main roads that were filled with murderous robbers, and skirted burnt cities where looters and starvation ruled the night. I was seldom seen and heard from less—until I was forced to kill a man after I had crossed the border from Tennessee into Missouri.

He was a foul and drunken carpetbagger who happened upon my camp and made a trashy comment about my choice for supper. I was leaned back against my saddle with a Navy Colt in my lap, fully content on sharing a plate of my victuals with him—but instead of accepting my hospitality, he pulled a jackleg knife from his boot top and came up the hill towards me grinning like a perverted fiend.

"Don't bother trying to be neighborly, I'll just take whatever you got," he said. The off-hand comment pissed me off. But the bastard stood there testing the knife's edge with a dirty thumb while he sucked at his rotten teeth, waiting for me to concede my possessions.

"I'm in no mood for your shit so go away while you're still able," I told him.

He flashed a mouthful of grist-yellow teeth. "Mister, if'n you don't git up and walk on down that road I'll cut your ass to pieces."

"Not tonight you won't," I replied and blew his ass backwards into the roadside ditch. The robber uttered no final words nor twitched an eye. The man had meant to do me harm so I felt no compassion or remorse towards him and the sudden disfavor of his ill-planned enterprise. I burnt a crucifix scar across the back of my hand—and not wanting to finish my meal in the company of men, dead or otherwise—I broke camp and pushed deeper into Missouri.

I changed my route and decided to head towards Springfield, Missouri. Spend a few weeks there, let the situation die down should the bandit's body be found and his untimely demise questioned. I was in bad need of a bath and long overdue for some rest. Prophet seemed to agree on both counts, but the stud's heart leaned more so towards the latter. The years of hard riding were beginning to show on the big bay. Once rested, I'd save us both another cross-country ride and we'd take a train to St. Louis. Passenger trains arrived in the more civilized boroughs of a city, the kind of metropolitan environment a man with no nose would shun. Wilhelm Kruger would be where the hotels and brothels were cheap. He'd be living among the bums and dregs in a red-light district...and I planned to arrive unnoticed.

22

Springfield, Missouri
July 1865

It was mid-July of 1865 when I finally rode into Springfield, Missouri. The countryside still wore the scars of war's aftermath, but the city of Springfield seemed only lightly touched. I took up residence at the Lyon House Hotel and had Prophet stabled in their twelve-stall livery. After a shave and hot bath—and all duded up in my new store-bought clothes—I began to feel more civilized. The hotel lobby was a grand spectacle with its spinning roulette wheels, billiard games, and six poker tables that were set aside for the clientele with serious monetary intentions. I took a seat in the dining section with a cup of coffee and watched a man shuffling a deck of cards. He was sitting alone so I walked closer to scrutinize how his deft hands worked the deck. The man never looked up but must have felt my miss-matched eyes upon him.

"Do you play?" he asked me.

"I don't gamble," I replied, blowing across my cup.

"I didn't ask that, I asked if you played cards," said the man shuffling.

I tried to answer as best I could without insulting him. "I've never played a hand nor had the notion to gamble away my hard-earned money."

The man cut the cards one-handed and introduced himself. "J. B. Hickok," he said and pulled out a chair for me to sit down. "My friends call me Bill, and make no mistake about it, my sharp-tongued friend—every man gambles in some way or another."

I didn't like his sudden observation and stood my ground. "Maybe so, but I'll not put the fate of my personal currency to cards, nor trust the grubby hand that deals them falsely."

He stopped flipping cards over, cocked his head, and looked up at me. I remember he had slate grey eyes. "Your name?" he asked.

"Reuben Judah."

"Well, now, it appears you're calling me a card cheat?"

"I never said you were a cheat," I replied quickly. "But I will say this: I'll not have my ass whipped by a man who plays the game for a living. Brash and honest I may be, but foolish I'm not."

Bill Hickok laughed at my honest rebuttal and motioned for me to sit down. "Well, Reuben Judah, just play me for the hell of it and I'll show you a few tricks of the trade to keep the game honest. Besides, I need the practice to keep my hands sharp for tonight."

"Why tonight?" I asked sitting down.

"Davis Tutt and another shitheel named Lew McCall have the table reserved. So it'll be the two of them, against the one of me."

"Doesn't that mean there's twice the chance to lose all your money?"

He dealt me five cards and smiled. "It just means the stakes are a mite higher. A helluva lot higher than what your sorry ass just brought to my table."

I liked Bill Hickok from the start and enjoyed his glib and cavalier view on the western lifestyle as he saw it. We talked of the recent war, and although we fought on opposite sides of each other—we agreed that when the war ended, the hatchet of animosity was buried with it. Hickok took his time and showed me the intimate secrets of card cheating: marking and counting cards, dealing from the bottom, stacking the deck, and working with partners. Poker was the only true passion I ever saw in the man.

Two men walked up to our table and one of them cleared his greasy throat. "Hey, Horsecock, are you ready to play for money or you gonna' sit there and give out free lessons?" a rude voice asked.

Bill looked up at him and then to me. "Reuben Judah, meet Davis Tutt and Lew McCall. These are the assholes that plan on donating their money to me."

"You're a funny man," said the man named Tutt. He turned and grinned at his cohort. "Well, Horsecock, there's been a change in my plans. I'm only here to back my new partner, Lew McCall."

"Well, Davis, your money is as good as any," Bill said.

Davis Tutt looked at me. "Are you in or out? If you're playing then stay seated and ante up."

Bill smiled and opened his hands toward me. "It's your call, Reuben Judah. Do you wanna' take a chance and ride the bull?"

I stood up and let Lew McCall have my chair. "I believe I'll just sit this one out," I said, stepping away from the table.

"Then it looks like it's just the two of you," muttered Tutt as the cards were cut and dealt.

Bill lost the first few hands then won a large pot with a spade flush. Tutt began to grow more agitated at McCall as the card game and their luck spiraled downward. Hickok showed no emotion nor spoke a word to either man. He just continued to deal and win until his earnings totaled well over two hundred dollars of Tutt's money. McCall was flat busted and Tutt's face twisted in fury as Hickok calmly counted his winnings.

Davis Tutt's mood turned bitter and resentful. "What about the forty dollars you owe me?" he said to Bill Hickok.

"What about it, Davis?"

Tutt tried to humiliate Hickok to recoup his losses. "You still owe me forty dollars for the horse I sold you."

Bill counted out the money owed and slid it across the table. "You mean that ol' nag, Black Nell? It was the worst damn money I ever spent."

Davis Tutt pocketed the debt and looked at Hickok with mean eyes. "What do you mean the worst money you ever spent?"

Hickok tossed back his drink and swallowed before he answered. "That fucking horse you sold me was the dumbest bastard ever to wear a saddle. I even had to teach that ignorant cocksucker how to eat a mouthful of hay and swallow water," said Bill. The gathered crowd of onlookers roared with laughter. Tutt and McCall didn't laugh nor appreciate being the butt end of Hickok's jest.

Tutt stepped beside Hickok and made another allegation to further stir the troubled pot he was brewing. "Well, the horse debt might be settled, but you still owe me thirty-five dollars from another poker game," Tutt accused. McCall stepped beside his financial backer and both men waited for Hickok's reply.

Hickok stopped shuffling and looked up at the man. "I think you're wrong about the amount, Davis. It's only twenty-five dollars and I have the signed memorandum to prove so."

"You're full of shit and you know it, Horsecock. Let's see, how about I just keep this ole pocket watch of yours as collateral," Tutt said taking Hickok's watch off the table.

"You best put my watch back where you got it before I blow a hole through that grubby dickskinner," said Hickok nodding towards the hand clutching his looted timepiece. Davis Tutt pocketed the watch and replied with nothing more than an ugly grin, then started towards the door.

Hickok yelled after the watch thief, "If I see you wearing my pocket watch publicly I'll kill you on the spot." Tutt and McCall responded to Hickok's warning by slamming the lobby door behind them.

Over the next several days, supporters of Tutt began to openly mock Hickok—taunting him by asking for the time or saying Tutt was seen wearing his watch. Tutt's group began following Hickok into the Lyon House Hotel to further ridicule him as he played cards. Bill wanted to avoid a fight and tried to renegotiate a peaceful settlement, but Tutt told Hickok that he'd openly wear his watch the next afternoon in Springfield's town square. It was Tutt's way of saving face while further humiliating Hickok in front of his gambling crowd.

Hickok tapped his empty watchpocket and said to Tutt. "If you wear my watch in that town square then it means dead men can walk."

"Well, I'd give you the proper time to be there and see me wearing it, but you don't have a watch," said Tutt as he left.

I ate breakfast the next morning with Bill in the hotel lobby. The tension between Tutt and Hickok was felt in the stagnant air by everyone who was there. "Bill, I have enough to cover it," I offered.

"Bullshit, it's not about the money," said Bill. He elevated his voice so every patron stopped eating and listened when next he spoke. "It's about the goddamn principal. If that sonofabitch shows up wearing my stolen watch today, I'll blast his ass where he stands," said Hickok loudly. He looked at me then nodded towards my plate. "You best get to eating, your food is gettin' cold."

At five pm, Bill and I were still sitting at our table in the hotel lobby when Tutt walked in. He pulled Hickok's watch from his breastpocket and said to those in attendance: "My, how time flies."

Bill said nothing and we both watched as Tutt walked outside wearing that same ugly grin. Hickok pulled out his Navy Colts and checked the charges. "I've noticed you favor the Navy Colt as well," he said to me.

"Reliable weapons, I've no complaints about them," I answered as he set his pistols on the table.

Bill slid a thumb across his mustache then looked towards the ceiling. "My, how time flies," he said aloud. He closed his eyes and smiled. "That fucking Tutt." Hickok sat in the suicidal silence and rechecked his weapons a final time. He stood and stretched his long arms. "Well, I reckon it's time for me to either cut bait or fish," said Hickok as he started towards the door. He stopped and turned around, pistol in his hand. "You comin' along or you gonna' watch it happen from the window?" he asked me.

"I'll be there," I said following him into the hot summer evening.

Hickok walked to the square in his dark frock coat and calmly eyed each person gathered in the street, looking for Tutt. The crowd scattered to the safety of nearby dwellings, leaving Davis Tutt alone in the northwestern corner of the town square. At a distance of seventy-five yards, Hickok faced Tutt and called out, "Well, Davis, here I am." Hickok cocked his pistol then holstered it butt forward behind the scarlet sash tied around his waist.

He gave Tutt a final warning: "Don't you come across here wearing that watch." Tutt did not reply and stood with his hand on his pistol butt, and for a brief second, neither man spoke nor moved.

Tutt yanked his weapon but Hickok had already pulled his Colt and stood in the deadly distance between them with the pistol barrel planted on his opposite forearm. Davis Tutt fired first and missed his mark. Hickok fired and his bullet struck the sour gambler in the left side of his chest. Tutt's knees buckled and he called out to his supporters, "Well, boys, I'm killed." I watched as he coughed a plume of blood and took a feeble step towards the courthouse, as if he sought some vague pardon for this deadly turn of events, and then Davis Tutt fell dead to the dusty street.

Bill walked over to the dead man and took his watch from the bloody breastpocket. "What time do you have now?" said Hickok to the unblinking corpse.

An arrest warrant was issued the following day for Hickok, and his bail was initially denied. I sent a quick telegraph to Stoddard Quillen and the court then set Hickok's bail at a staggering two thousand dollars. At the time, it was an unattainable sum that most men would never earn in two lifetimes. I posted Hickok's bail and agreed to testify at his trial using a name I saw on the Lyon House ledger when I signed in. As Mr. Eli Armstrong, I gave eyewitness testimony that Bill Hickok had fired in self-defense, as did three other responsible citizens who testified the same. The trial lasted three days but all charges were eventually dropped. Hickok left jail the day following his acquittal and met me at the train station.

He handed me a scribbled piece of paper. "What's this?" I asked.

"My written promissory that I'll make good on the money I owe you for posting my bail."

"Forget it, the last note you wrote for Davis Tutt didn't work out so good."

Hickok laughed then smiled under the brim of his hat. "So what's next for you?" he asked.

"Going by train to St. Louis to find a man."

Hickok pulled out his pocket watch and checked the time, then took his thumbnail and scraped a fleck of blood off the burnished case. "You mind a little extra company?"

"There might be trouble," I said and Hickok shrugged.

"Can't be any worse than it is here."

"Well, then, I'd be obliged to have you," I said and Hickok handed me another sliver of paper. "What's this for?"

Bill gave me an indifferent look then grinned. "Just another promissory note for the train ticket you're gonna' buy me to St. Louis."

By the time we arrived in St. Louis and set up residence at the Planter House Hotel, word had spread of the Springfield shootout and eastern reporters were seeking out Hickok with the promise of money for his side of the story. I stayed in the shadows and left Hickok to his own brand of carnal vice so I could scour the red-light districts looking for Wilhelm Kruger.

"Did you read the awful shit they wrote about me?" Bill asked at breakfast.

"Some of it," I answered.

Hickok gave a chuckle. "Not exactly what I'd call the truth but at least it's getting me some job offers."

"Anything worthwhile?" I asked.

"Nothing I'm interested in at the moment. I'm making more money telling lies to the reporters," he said putting a spoonful of eggs in his mouth.

"What kind of lies?"

Bill held up his hand and finished chewing. "I told them during the war I once shot fifty Confederates with fifty straight shots, told them another time I faced down six armed men in a saloon."

I snorted and wiped my mouth. "And those biscuit heads believed you?"

"Every damn word. Hell, I've been offered good money to

perform on stage from California to New York with Bill Cody himself. If I'd known all this was gonna' happen because I shot one watch-stealing cocksucker, I'd shoot three a day just for shits and giggles."

I thought about his options for a second. "Maybe it'd be a good time to settle down and raise a family. Get fat, grow old, and be happy with the money you've made."

Bill shook his head no. "No, sir, I'd rather chew rusty barbed wire and piss whiskey. Naw, I'll ride this mule until I wear it out." He slid his plate across the table then wiped his mouth. "Any word on that no-nose sonofabitch you've been looking for?"

"Not yet," I said standing.

"Well, I took some liberties on your behalf and had some acquaintances of mine ask around about him. It turns out ol' no-nose Kruger left with two other drifters a month ago to avoid some rather large gambling debts. Men like them have two options—choking at the end of a rope, or you head west and follow the boom towns."

"I'll need to give it some thought before I decide what to do next, Bill."

"Well," said Hickok, standing and dropping his napkin to the plate. "I got an interview this morning with another magazine. After that, I'll put the word out to some of the lower case gamblers headed west and we'll see what happens. If he's in one of the Indian territories they'll find him and get word back to me. If not, we'll go looking for him ourselves."

"I'd appreciate that, Bill. I'll probably just stay in St. Louis for another month or so until I'm sure Wilhelm Kruger is still west of the Mississippi."

"After that?" asked Bill.

"After that I'll head back east for a spell. I have financial affairs to attend and I want to make sure my boys are being taken care of."

Hickok slapped me on the back. "Well, by God, we're here now so let's go have an after-breakfast whiskey and look over our prospects. I'll buy this time," he said.

I followed Bill towards the door and told him the truth as I saw it. As long as Kruger was here in the west, instead of back east, I was in no hurry to find him. I'd leave in a month and take a train to Boston. I felt the need to part ways because I had a premonition that Bill Hickok was running out of time.

Present

"So you went back east to see your twin sons?" asked Paul.

I blinked my eyes to clear the memory and shook my head yes to Paul's question. "I stayed in Boston for six years watching them grow into young men and left again before they started college at Harvard. I had an apartment Stoddard Quillen acquired for me and I retired Prophet to the Quillen farm, the old bay stud deserved that much from me. I had weekend dinners with the Spitler's, but always introduced as Mr. Cobb to the boys."

"When your sons first met you, did either of them remember you as being their father?" Paul inquired. I didn't like these personal questions and stiffened a little before I replied.

"No, and that hurt me. But there is an unspoken bond between a son and his father. When we started talking on a regular basis, they opened up to me a lot more than they would to Wilbur Spitler."

Paul saw my discomfort and thankfully changed the subject. "Did you ever see Wild Bill again?"

"New York, 1873 on the big stage. He and Bill Cody had a play called, 'Scouts of the Plains.' It was truly horrible affair because neither Bill Hickok nor Cody could act worth a damn. The boys and I had dinner with both of them that night. The next morning Hickok invited me to go west with him to Deadwood."

"Did you go to South Dakota?"

"It wasn't even a state back then, just the Dakota Territory. I did eventually accept his offer, but waited until my boys started college before leaving. I got as far as Montana in late July of 1876. The train I was on derailed so I decided to offload and left on a four-year-old gelding that was a gift from Stoddard Quillen. My new horse was named at birth in honor of his sire, The Prophet. The train's derailment cost me three weeks of cross-country travel, and by the time I got to Deadwood, Bill Hickok was dead."

"Did you stay in Deadwood?"

"I was there to see Bill, but since he was gone I didn't stay but a few nights. I was at Nuttal & Mann's Saloon and found out through their grapevine of gamblers that Wilhelm Kruger was headed towards San Francisco. I had no intention of spending the winter in Deadwood so I took off for Texas instead."

Paul scratched his nose. "Why Texas, Mr. Reuben?"

"I had plenty of time back then. Luther and Eli were doing well at Harvard, Kruger was three thousand miles away so I was free to travel and explore. I wanted to find out the truth about my great-grandfather, Keller Judah," I replied.

"Did you find out anything?"

"As a matter of fact I did, I found out that Keller had a place in Texas and lived there until he died. A local school teacher took care of him and wrote dictation for the story he told her about his life. The teacher had apparently taken the manuscript and moved to be with her youngest daughter in San Francisco by the time I got into Texas. Since Kruger was already there, I figured I'd kill two birds with one stone so I headed towards the west coast. I met Teddy Roosevelt when I was passing through North Dakota on my way to San Francisco."

"Was Teddy on the campaign trail?" Paul asked and yawned.

"No, this was a few years before he gave any serious thought to being President. I met Teddy Roosevelt the day I stumbled across Wilhelm Kruger, quite by mistake actually. Kruger was running with a couple of thieves and Roosevelt was hunting them for stealing his river boat. Teddy caught two of the bastards, and as for poor Wilhelm…well, his fate was not so forgiving once I found him. Teddy had just started a ranch and he hired me as his foreman on the spot. A few of the best years I had were on his ranch. I got to see the real west and its fading lifestyle before everything grew too fast and ruined it all. I saw the Native American people as they should have been seen, free and proud. I watched buffalo graze the prairie in numbers so vast they seemed to stretch from horizon to horizon, but even then the changes were coming. I should've known it wouldn't last," I said as Paul stood and stretched his arms.

"Mr. Reuben, I gotta' stop our story here or we'll spend the next two days never leaving our chairs. But, I'd like to come in a bit early tomorrow night and hear about Kruger and Roosevelt if that would be acceptable."

I thought about something Paul had said—now it was, "Our Chairs and Our Story." I waited until he left and countered, "Bring *our* keys when you return."

* * *

I never sleep in the way that others do. I only feel alive at night when I open my secrets to this quiet place, when my brain races in an obsessive muse of daytime reflections. It is only then that I allow myself to slumber in the yesterday of my life, reliving and composing the spent currency of long days gone by. I am only evicted from these memories when upon my thoughts a voluptuous flow of impatience washes the mantle of living nightmares away. It is from the tattered edges of my mental fibers that angry thoughts arise—many things—such as love, hate, revenge, and forgiveness speak their debate for me alone to judge, and who am I to moderate these illicit rhythms of everyday life?

I live this way to adopt a new method of finding solace and comfort, and so it goes from my window. I find in this barometer of transient thoughts, that I am forced to listen.

I hear what this place and those who are confined with me have to say. I contemplate their choices while this foundation shifts on its pillars of discomfort, altering forever the faces whose voices I cannot love. I listen from this window and hear the sunbeams drowned out by the white rain over grim chuckles of thunder. I hear the true cost of those raw emotions I have cast out to accommodate these repetitive memories. I hear the guardsmen talking about wives who break vases in anger and I hear the whispers of deceit from within these crooked walls.

There are worse things in life than being alone with insomnia.

I know there is the real possibility that these tenants of mental weakness will one day override the genius of their hardship. In this harsh world of mine I have come to understand humanity through the eyes of insanity. I sit here staring out my window at the loveless moon and realize that soon—what was sealed with a handshake would be broken by the kiss of misfortune…

Paul Tandy came in wearing a terse smile and walked with his usual sashayed gait to my side. "Good evening, Mr. Reuben," he said taking a chair beside me then grinned his contentment. "I wanted to make sure no one got my chair."

"No one could, it's your chair," I told him.

"So no one but me is allowed to sit beside you?" I nodded my affirmation.

I studied the petite man more closely. Paul was seeking something additional from me. "And what brings you to your chair so early this evening?" I asked.

"Did you forget? We were going to finish our story about Teddy Roosevelt," he said and blushed slightly. "I have always admired the man and for me to have someone like you, someone who can talk about him from firsthand experience…well, it's a rare treat for me."

"Ah, yes, Teddy," I sighed. "But why are you really here?" I asked. My question caught him off-guard.

Paul Tandy stiffened in his chair. "I'm not sure I understand what you mean, Mr. Reuben."

"Why are you in this vile place? You could be anywhere else in this city earning the same living, but you chose this place instead."

"Where else would I go? My father removed me from his house and forbade my mother to contact me. Even before they died, as far as my parents were concerned, I was dead to them. So this place, the patients, and you are all I have. I'll never marry or entertain the possibility of having children, but I am no different than anyone else who ever dreamed of a better life. I still want what every human being on earth has ever wanted since the dawn of time."

"And what would that be?" I asked.

"To be loved and to feel loved," Paul answered and slumped

back in his chair. "You've felt that kind of love with Jessamine, but I never will…so I envy you for that."

For once, it was Paul's turn to catch me off-guard. "Well spoken, Paul. Actually, quite remarkable," I said.

Paul relaxed and lay back with his fingers interlaced behind his head. "I am glad you're satisfied, Mr. Reuben. I'm ready to listen if you want to finish telling me your story," he said and closed his eyes.

"Then feel the concussion of my life and smell the gun-smoke on San Juan Hill. Ride with me and bear witness to the cavalry charge that would one day ignite a legend and forge his path to greatness. Slip back in time when our nation would take its first step towards the greatest period in mankind's history."

Mingo Kane

23

Texas
September, 1882

The news of Bill Hickok's death brought upon me a familiar hardship, and once again I exiled myself from all humanity. I became the gypsy king, a solitary vagrant who ruled invisible men with invisible lives. I was a migrant who worshipped the quiet insanity of western skies and sat beneath their great silence until it drove me sane. I stayed up all night talking to angels who sat perched upon the bashful stars, and by day I followed ghostly vaqueros on their quest to find a more perfect solitude within their loneliness. I slept under stone ledges and watched jagged wires of lightning stretch a path across the skyline before exploding in thunderous brilliance. The swollen creeks roaring with the fury of night, and by daybreak I would sit for hours on end as flowers arose and bloomed from their soggy creek beds like fables.

I made my way through one broad chaparral after another, followed the cold and fluted winds down across vast white salt plains. I rode where cactus shadows stood in the rotting sun like wholesome effigies lost to the voided landscape of their existence. The horse and I wove our way down steep cliffs where pagan hieroglyphs were painted on rock walls, and each story told of savage men who waged war as if they were ordained.

I stopped in small adobe towns that were nothing more than earthen dwellings splattered in the brown desert like a geological fantasy. These were my transient years. A time of reawakening when everything changed and the world seemed to open up. I had reached a point where I had gone as far as I could, and only then did I begin to live again. That's when I learned to love Texas through the eyes of her greatest son.

Captain Richard King
The King Ranch, 1883

By the time I rode into a nameless town near Corpus Christi, the religious mystique of Texas had eased the secret sorrows of my pain. I had found a common ground in the soft shadows and ruthless intolerance of endless thunderstorms rolling through the violent atmosphere. I stopped near the end of town and let the iron red dust settle before I hitched Prophet to a rail, and walked into a ramshackle saloon as the long copper light of dusk fell across the horizon.

The barkeep ambled over and rested an elbow on the rich mahogany bar. "Anything else besides the coffee?" he asked, filling my cup.

"I'm assuming the hotel next door has suitable accommodations?"

"The Steen House?" he asked.

"Yes, sir."

The barkeep slung a buff rag over his shoulder and shook his head. "Most certainly, clean rooms and a free livery service for their guests."

"That's just too perfect," I said and slid my money across the bar to pay for the coffee with a little extra leftover for the barkeep. "Keep the change," I told him.

"Much obliged," he said pocketing the tip. "If there's anything else I can do for you, just ask."

"Matter of fact there is," I said, taking a sip of coffee. "Ever hear of a man named Keller Judah?" The barkeep's manner seized up as did that of other patrons perched on barstools nearby. All physical activity ceased while vigilant ears awakened to hear the man's reply.

The liquor peddler gave me a curious look. "Why are you asking?"

"Keller Judah was my great-grandfather."

The barkeep whistled and a Mexican boy ran to the side of the bar. The barman told the Chico in fluent Spanish to run and fetch the captain while he was still in town. "There might be a gentleman close by who knows something about Keller Judah. Finish your coffee and he'll be along directly," said the man in an easy tone. He gave me a greasy smile and started to walk away when my voice stopped him.

"And who might this captain be?" I asked in perfect Spanish.

"The Captain's the type man who'd want to talk with anyone claiming to be a descendant of Keller Judah," the barkeep answered over his shoulder.

"And he's a man who would have words with anyone claiming as such," a gruff voice said from the doorway. I didn't like the rude accusation by either man, nor did I appreciate the manner in which it was made.

I turned from the bar and faced the man who had spoken. "I'm not here to make bold statements for your entertainment. Keller Judah was my great-grandfather and that's a good enough starting point as any, and since I've covered this ground twice already…let me start by asking, just who the hell are you?"

Three dark-skinned men started through the door in protest until the talker held up his hand. "I'm Captain Richard King and Keller Judah was a friend of mine for twenty years. I didn't catch your name or where you're from."

"Reuben Judah. I was born and raised in Virginia."

The Captain shook his head in acknowledgement. "I'm one of the few men who knew Keller had people in Virginia, so what brings you to his doorstep after all these years?"

"It's a matter of my personal curiosity. The last story I heard, Keller disappeared somewhere in Texas and a school teacher took care of him. But other than that…nada."

"Then you know more than you think," the Captain said sticking out his hand. We shook and his grip was as stout as his build. He started back through the door and said over his shoulder, "I must insist that you stay at my ranch, The Running W."

"I'm obliged," I said following him outside. Captain King stopped at his buggy and turned around.

"Your name sounds familiar. Did you happen to ride with John Mosby?" he asked.

"I did."

"And you would sometimes be known as, 'The Prophet of Cobb Hollow?' "

I looked at the Captain and sighed. "Prophet is the name of my horse and Cobb Hollow is my home. The Prophet of Cobb Hollow is a legend created by a drunken lawyer named Stoddard Quillen. I am wanted for no crime nor have I committed any," I said and looked at Richard King with cool eyes. "And you and I already know that."

"I do?" asked Richard. He let a small grin betray his intent.

It was my turn to grin. "In 1863 John Mosby had me deliver a load of rifles to the Confederates in Texas. Those rifles rode on your steamboat under the neutral flag of Mexico."

"So," said Captain Richard.

"So that gave you the authority to bypass any Union blockades, and all the while your boat was hauling Mosby's rifles tucked away in the bales of your prized Texas cotton."

"Are you a friend of Jesus?" asked the Captain.

I placed a hand over my heart and replied, "I am a Brother."

Richard King laughed and slapped me on the back. "Well, damned if I don't feel like I've just been castrated by my own damn hand," he said getting inside the buggy and giving the driver instructions.

Captain Richard King was a brute of a man both inside and out. He had carved a solitary dream out of the desert, and single-handedly built a walled empire along the San Gertrudis Creek. But once you breeched his tough exterior patina, Captain King's wealth was measured by the compassion he held sacred for the land and its people. We pulled up to where his main ranch house sat upon the pastoral landscape like a feudal castle, and as we talked over a dinner of smoked brisket, a mutual kinship of admiration was born between us.

"Keller had five thousand acres of prime Texas pasture he owned from an old Spanish land grant he had received from General Santa Anna. Keller's family grant is perfectly legal, have no doubt about that, it was awarded to him after the Alamo fell. I had my lawyers pick the document apart when I bought my first tract of land. I needed Keller's property along the San Gertrudis for my stock, but if you knew Keller Judah…he wasn't selling."

"Then how did you get the water rights?" I asked.

Richard King slid his plate back, wiped his mouth, and smiled. His chin whiskers down to his collar bone gave him the appearance of a devilish rogue. "I gave him a chicken," he said. Each member of the King family laughed and shook their heads to lend a quiet credence to Richard's explanation.

"A chicken?" I asked, and Richard laughed.

"Keller told me that if he had a chicken it might drink up all the water and my cattle would have none. But if the chicken would only drink what it needed, then there would be plenty of water for the chicken and my cattle. But he wouldn't know the answer until he had a bird to test his theory. Of course I took him a dozen chickens that evening and by morning Keller Judah stood on my doorstep. 'The chickens drank enough,' was all he said. Keller lived here on my ranch until he died, so that means his five thousand acres is legally yours."

Richard's honest admission caught me off guard. "His land is mine?"

The Captain nodded. "The Spanish land grant Keller had is one of family, and only a family member can buy or sale any property. So it's all yours, but I'd appreciate having the first option to purchase every inch of it back if you decide to sell." The table went silent as each member of the King family awaited my response.

I had no use for the burden of property, nor the hardship that came with it. "Captain Richard, I had thirty thousand acres of prime land once upon a time that was given to me much the same way as your offer. I found out the hard way that getting land is much easier than keeping it. I have no use for Keller's land, and if my great grandfather was taken care of by you and your family, then consider his acreage as payment for services rendered," I said, putting the matter to rest.

Richard King blurted, "You can't just give prime river land away. Are you mad?"

"I'd say if you were to ask the people around Cobb Hollow about my sanity, you'd have the answer you're looking for. So I'll sell you the land for a chicken if it makes you feel all the better."

Richard King slammed his hands flat on the table and everyone jumped when he spoke in that rich Texas drawl. "By God, that's a done deal," he said and nodded towards the door. "Let's you and me head to the porch and sample a glass of my personal bourbon stock."

I followed him towards the door. "I normally avoid the stronger stuff after dinner, but I'd be grateful for a cup of coffee."

"Well, I happen to enjoy an after-dinner whiskey and I'd be insulted if you didn't at least sample one glass of my personal stock," said Richard, stepping onto the broad covered porch. A tray with coffee and all the required condiments was sitting on the table, along with a full sifter of amber-colored liquid. "I do enjoy coffee and bourbon with pleasant company when available. These days, it's rare to have someone I can share it with."

I sat beside Richard in a high backed-chair and accepted a glass of his prized bourbon. "I'd like to hear more about my great-grandfather." The Captain looked at me as he poured two glasses of his prized bourbon.

"I'll make you another deal, you can take your dinner with me each night and then you and I will retire to the porch to drink and talk about Keller," said Richard lighting a cigar and handing me a full glass. "In a few months we'll be taking my private train on our annual ride to Corpus Christi. It's sort of an anniversary celebration we do each year for the cattle roundup, so you can return the favor and entertain me with stories about riding point for John Mosby on the train ride."

"What makes you think I'll be here that long?" I asked taking a sip of his stock whiskey.

"You'll be here, Reuben."

The raw bourbon hit my stomach and I clenched my teeth. "Whew, that packs quite a punch," I said before getting back to the topic at hand. "How do you figure I'll still be on your ranch?"

"You're not the first man to ride across Texas and end up on my ranch. I've seen the same hungry look in your eyes that I've seen in other men. You're like the rest of them, tired and ready to settle down for a while," Richard said and thought for a second. "Besides that, I'll make you the same offer I made for Keller and his chicken."

I was intrigued. "What offer would that be?"

"You and your chicken can live on my ranch for as long as you like," said Richard refilling my glass.

"If I do decide to stay I'll earn my keep and accept no charity, that's not my way. I don't mean it to sound rude, but it is what it is," I replied. The bourbon made my answer come out a little tighter than I intended, but the Captain seemed unfazed and only mildly amused.

"And so it goes," said the Captain. He relit his cigar and shook out the match then grinned. "Well, smartass, tomorrow you can start working cattle with Alvarado Cavatos and the cattlemen I call my *Kineños*. If you survive riding and working with the *Kineños*... you're gonna' earn your keep, and more."

Every day for the next six months I was up two hours before daylight with Prophet saddled, and my breakfast served to me in the saddle. A single burrito made of eggs, peppers, and hot sauce that I ate while riding towards the day's worksite. That was Alvarado Cavatos and the *Kineños* way of life—their entire lives was lived in the saddle. The *Kineños* were to the Captain what the Cherokee had once been to me, both groups were transplanted from their native home to live and work under the banner of our shared freedom. The *Kineños* were the greatest cattle horsemen in the world, and they were faithfully among the most diligent workers I ever saw. Male or female, they had but two missions in life—to serve God and the Captain, and not necessarily in that order. *Kineños* translated to English meant: *the King's People.*

I was working a group of young steers with Alvarado's oldest daughter when her father rode up. Alvarado pulled to a stop and grunted in broken English, "Captain says for you to come see him at the big house." The old man spun around and rode off, never once looking back or acknowledging his daughter sitting beside me.

"My father doesn't waste time with a lot of words," his daughter, Maria, explained. She said the words as if she was apologizing for her father's bluntness. It was the most English Maria had spoken to me in the six months of riding together.

"I was starting to think the lack of conversation ran in the whole damn family," I said peeling Prophet around and riding off before she could reply. Maria was a pretty woman, long black hair that fell to her mid-back and high Spanish cheekbones that highlighted her smile, or darkened her eyes—depending on the mood and moment. Her husband had been killed three years earlier on a cattle drive, so she had taken his position in her father's workforce.

Richard was standing on the porch when I cantered up. "You wanted to see me, Captain?"

He tucked a folded paper into his breastpocket. "Alvarado says you're planning on riding with the herd instead of with me, on my train."

"I've worked these cows for near a year and my intentions are to see the job through," I replied. The Captain seemed disappointed, but there was something else bothering him.

"If my damn upset stomach would allow it, I'd be joining you. I wanted to talk with you about something of minor importance during the train ride up, but since you've made up your mind about driving the cattle to Corpus Christi, it can wait until we get there,' said Richard. He pointed a thick finger at me. "But you're riding back to the ranch with me so we can talk about your days with John Mosby."

"What does minor importance mean?" I asked.

The Captain remained stoic and betrayed nothing while watching Maria working the cattle over my shoulder. "Don't worry about it. If it pans out then I might have everything taken care of before we get back. But if you change your mind about the cattle drive, my private car is still open for the ride up," said the Captain looking from me to Maria. He wore a tight-lipped grin and I knew full well what Richard King was thinking.

"It's not like that, Captain," I said looking over my shoulder towards Maria. "I was married once, not sure I have enough heart left over to ever try it again."

Richard King blew off my response with a casual toss of his hand. "Ah bullshit...you might say that now, but give life a little time and Texas has a way of changing your mind. Right now, you best get back to work or Alvarado Cavatos will have your ass branded and castrated. And make sure you rest up tonight. Tomorrow you're gonna' be driving five thousand head of San Gertrudis cattle through the south Texas brush country."

We left before sunrise and were alone in the back country under skies the color of wet metal when Maria Cavatos caught up to us and spoke to her father. Alvarado motioned me over as his youngest son split from the herd and headed back towards the ranch. "The Captain made a swap; Maria will be riding with you for the cattle drive instead of my son, Jorge," said Alvarado. I only nodded my understanding and went back to work. Alvarado and I knew why the Captain had made the exchange, but we stayed silent in our mutual concern over Richard King's unvoiced agenda.

I spent the majority of my nights riding watch over the herd under a constellation of mute stars that sat above me like a silent audience. Some nights I would stay silent and listen to the young male *Kineños* speaking in soft Spanish to each other about a love yet pledged, other nights I would ride my line while Maria sang old Spanish ballads about young senoritas who were sent away from their true love by cruel step-parents—but I liked it best when I was alone and solitary with my thoughts, thinking about Three Crows, Jessamine, and Molly. Wondering about my sons and what great

189

deeds they might one day accomplish. I thought about myself and how in the entire world—at this point in time—there was no place that I'd rather be.

24

It took three weeks of overland travel to finally make the warm gulf shores of Corpus Christi. The Captain's train had arrived two days prior and a steady stream of workers had transformed the beach into a rousing display of tents, food cooking over open spits, and rows of covered tables laid out for dining. Richard King spared no expense for those he loved and those who gave him an honest day's work.

Maria cut her horse in front of me and whistled. "I'll take the front half of the herd towards the pen and you stay on their opposite flank until the gate's closed," she yelled over the noise and galloped away.

The cattle were driven into the stockyard pens and, keeping with their *Kineños* tradition, the Captain himself closed the gate and got the final tally from Alvarado Cavatos. Richard King pulled his revolver and fired three times into the air. "The day is yours," shouted the Captain.

The men unsaddled their horses and scrambled inside one of the covered tents. Once stripped down to our skivvies, we each emerged and hit the ocean at a dead run to let the salt water refresh tired muscles and soothe our scalded hands. While the men swam, women unpacked trunks filled with their personal belongings and laid out fresh clothes for the cattle-driving *Kineños*.

We swam and soaked in the warm gulf water until the Captain and his wife, Henrietta, called us in for the feast. I stood on the beach and watched as torches were being lit beside the long tables weighted down with steaming food. The unfolding scene took me back to another time and another such banquet, when my life had become wholly livable because of a single dance. I changed into fresh clothes then made myself a plate and stepped out of the serving line to find a secluded spot beyond the festivities. I sat behind a small dune overlooking the ocean, eating my dinner and thinking of Jessamine.

"If I am intruding, my apologies," a voice said. Maria Cavatos walked over with a plate in her hand. "It looks like we appreciate some of the same simple pleasures," she said sitting down in the sand beside me.

"How so?" I asked.

"We would rather eat in peace," she replied looking back towards the tables. The men were enjoying the Captain's bourbon and retelling bawdy stories of the drive.

"Nothing wrong with a man cutting loose and enjoying the taste of fine whiskey," I said putting my plate aside so we could talk.

Maria smiled and looked me in the eyes. "But you're not like the *Kineños*, or other men for that matter. You are more like my father, driven by some internal force to work harder and accomplish more than everyone around you. You are always in control and neither you nor my father is ever out of your element."

I was skeptical of her observation but didn't want to appear rude in my objection. "Maybe so, but it ain't a good way to be most of the time."

Maria gave a soft laugh. "I can tell by your answer that you don't believe me, but I'll prove it. Tell the truth, I'll bet you're sitting here putting more thought into tomorrow's work instead of relaxing."

I shook my head no. "I'm not thinking about today or what might happen tomorrow, Maria."

"Then what *are* you thinking about?"

192

"I was thinking about the first time I ever saw my wife on a beach. Before the war started we both went to visit her relatives and stayed on the coast in North Carolina. My wife Jessamine loved being on the beach at night, walking in the moonlight. She was pregnant with our daughter back then and was too self-conscious to swim during the day. She was so beautiful to look at it took my breath away just to watch her walk in the sand. When I was coming out of the water after we'd finished swimming this evening, that memory struck me and I stood there staring at the empty beach...I guess I almost expected to see her standing on the shore."

Maria's mood changed. "I never knew you were married, Reuben."

"I was once...my wife and daughter were both killed during the war," I explained. Maria relaxed and placed her hand on mine and gave it a squeeze.

"I am sorry to have brought up such a painful memory," she said.

I shrugged off the apology. "It doesn't hurt as bad as it used to. Besides, I think everyone lost someone they loved, or at least a part of themselves to that war." I changed the subject, "I don't mean to make comparisons, but you remind me of my wife."

Maria perked up. "In what way?"

"You and Jess share the same rough exterior you want the world to see, but you both have a softness that truly shines when you think no one is watching. You have your hard opinions and don't mind voicing them, and if feelings get hurt...so be it. I always called it tough love. You're both hard as nails on the outside, but still a complete woman on the inside."

Maria laughed. "I like the sound of your wife. Tell me more about them, if it doesn't bother you."

"Jessamine was a character, strong-willed but had a gentle eye for horse flesh. Molly was just like her mother, curious about everything and wanted to know how it worked," I said and paused while Maria laughed and wiped her mouth. "Molly worried me to death finding and picking up her little *friends*. Frogs, lizards, June-bugs, or snakes, it didn't matter to her grubby little hands. She'd take whatever she caught to an old Cherokee man named Three Crows. The old man would tell her the story of how that animal came to be in the great circle of life, and then it was let go. They all three died together when my house burned."

"In the war?" asked Maria.

"That's what they said. I was away fighting when it happened."

Maria didn't press the issue any further and her eyes softened. "After my husband died, I had to grow up hard and quick. I guess the loneliness and heartache leaves you with a thick skin to protect what's left of your broken heart," Maria said standing and brushing off her dress. It was the first time I noticed she wasn't wearing workpants, chaps, and boots. A white cactus bloom was tucked behind her ear. "Come down and join us when you've finished eating. Come to me and I'll teach you to dance the *Kineños* way," she offered and then leaned down and gave me a kiss on the cheek. "I wanted to give you that and to say thank you...even if you decide not to dance."

The kiss was electric, resurrecting secular feelings that I thought were lost to me forever. "Thank me for what?" I asked as Maria looked over her shoulder towards the festivities.

"It was for letting me work beside you as an equal instead of seeing me as a nuisance, like my father does when I work with him. You've treated me with fairness since the day you started working for us, and that's why I asked the Captain to let me go on the drive instead of my brother, Jorge," she explained. Maria took off her sandals and started walking towards the music. She turned and took a few steps backwards so she could face me, an odd twinkle in her dark eyes. "And if you want another kiss, Reuben Judah, you have to come and dance with me to get it," she said and spun around.

"I haven't danced in twenty years," I hollered after her. Maria kept walking.

"Then it's time you started again," she yelled back.

I should have danced with her that night. I should have gone to Maria's tent and made love to her. I should have wept away my guilt and pain so I could resurrect the sheer beauty of a woman's touch. Instead, I fell asleep where I sat and dreamed of Jessamine. We were walking together on a deserted shoreline, moonbeams dancing on the water like a path of windblown silk. Jess used her toe and wrote in the sand: *I am because we are.* She stood over the words, looking at me and smiling as the waves surged forward and erased everything from the shore, leaving me bathed in darkness. I allowed the vague meaning of that dream to gift-wrap my inhibitions towards staying at the King Ranch. It was Jessamine's way of telling me it was okay to live and love again. But I awoke from that dream and went straight to the hitch-line to saddle Prophet. I was scared of loving again. But I was more afraid of being hurt because of it.

"Wasn't gonna' bother to say goodbye or claim your wages?" a voice asked.

I turned around to face Captain King, fully dressed and sober. "I was gonna' leave you and Maria a note," I explained and changed the subject. "What has you up so early?"

"I've been up most of the night sending telegrams back and forth to Stoddard Quillen on a matter concerning you," said Richard. His statement caught me off guard and made old fears arise. The Captain sensed my apprehension and put my anxiety to rest. "It's nothing too important, just an old acquaintance of yours is on the prowl and Stoddard wanted you to know. I got the telegram back at the ranch before we left, and decided to work with Stoddard to save *you* from yourself."

"Wilhelm Kruger?" I asked. Richard nodded.

"Yes, apparently he's run out of money and now feels you owe him compensation," he explained. I started to protest but Richard held up his hand. "Stoddard has already told me the story of your family, and what you did to the Kruger's. And both of us agree that if you pay Wilhelm Kruger now, you're gonna' be paying him for the rest of your life."

I cinched down the girth strap and straightened my stirrups. "I'm curious to hear about the plan you and Stoddard put together," I said, and cut my eyes directly at the Captain. "And whatever you two decided was done without my consent."

The Captain bristled. "Don't go getting all pissy with me, Reuben.

We had your best interest in mind. With our combined connections, Stoddard and I would rather have the Pinkertons take care of Kruger, and I was thinking that maybe you and Maria can move back to Virginia and manage the Silverbrook Farm I just bought near your hometown in Waynesboro. Stoddard Quillen brokered the land deal and he fully agrees with my thoughts involving you and Maria."

"Sounds to me like you and Stoddard have it all planned out nice and neat. But I'll bet the bottom dollar Stoddard Quillen came out on the better end of your little land deal."

"He wasn't hurting when the final line was signed," said Richard.

I swung into my saddle and gathered the reins. "Where was Wilhelm headed?"

"He was planning on leaving San Francisco in a week or so, and then he'd be headed eastward looking for you and your boys. If he's lucky he'll make North Dakota before winter, but Kruger will have to hold up there till spring or he'll freeze. The trains won't run through that part of the country until spring due to the snow drifts, and there're not many places to stay in the Dakotas until you move closer to St. Louis."

"I'd appreciate it if you'd be the one to tell Maria," I said, pulling Prophet nose to nose with the Captain.

Richard King stood his ground and didn't budge. "Bullshit, you're gonna' tell her yourself in the morning, after you've had the chance to think on this."

"I have thought about it, and to be honest—I might have stayed but Kruger is something I have to take care of, by myself."

Richard cut me off. "I know all about your damned stubbornness, Stoddard told me I'd be lucky to talk any sense at all into that hard head of yours."

"Well Stoddard Quillen is a good one to talk," I shot back. Richard relaxed and tried a softer approach.

"Reuben, everyone sacrificed more than we'd care to admit in that damn war. But don't give up on life. Don't quit on me now."

"I didn't quit on life and I'm not quitting on you, Captain. Everything in my life quit on me."

196

"Goddamn you, Reuben…don't go."

"Captain, I have to…there's no words I possess to explain it, but it's something I gotta' do. I gotta' have some sense of closure before I can go on with my life. And we both know goddamn well that in my place, you'd be doing the same damn thing," I said.

Richard King sighed and stepped aside to let me pass. "Then go ahead and go, do what you gotta' do, but promise me you'll be damn careful about it."

I stuck my hand out and we shook. "Richard, there's not many men I've ever admired, but you're one of them."

He nodded with wet eyes and reminded me. "If you make San Francisco don't forget to look up the school teacher, Suzanne Pease. I've already sent her a telegram about you so she'll give you the book her mother wrote about Keller Judah," said the Captain, walking to the side of Prophet.

"I'll be sure and do that, Captain. Thank you for everything," I said and took a deep breath. I looked out over the quiet water, inhaling the fragrance of salt and sage, my thoughts pulling me like an obscure tide on distant shore.

Richard pushed a wad of currency into my saddle bag along with a sack of provisions and I left as the moon carved a watery path across the velvet sky. It's hard to place a valid reason to account for my actions, but I needed to be alone so I could resurrect and wear the ugliness of my buried pain. I should have stayed, but I had already hardened myself internally. I kept my pain confidential and walked willingly back into my sequestered world. All of my days would again become a mystery of endless misery with the false promise of a peaceful resolution. It was that modality of thought which pushed me further from life. I let past memories rule my days while allowing myself to sleep through the grander times that might have been.

25

North Dakota
Elk Horn Ranch, 1886

It began to feel as if I had launched the final journey of my life, coming ever closer to the tattered edge of my lonely world. I rode back through familiar passes where ghostly bands of Apache still lived in prophetic scenes that were profound in their fundamental magnificence. There is a faithful and internal connection to be made by embracing the uncivilized, so breathless and intense in its immortal and immaculate beauty. It was that silent radiance which spoke to me and caused my inner thoughts to collide with the truth— and those memories I thought I had finally put aside forever—had the strange affinity to remind me that my haunted past was very real. In hindsight, the greatest cost of my revenge was the life I wasted chasing it.

I cleared my head and went back to using the guerilla tactics I learned while riding with John Mosby, wearing travel disguises and stopping just outside of small towns—or waiting until dark before pulling beside family wagons headed westward, asking each dark-faced stranger about a man with no nose. I sent weekly telegrams to Stoddard Quillen inquiring about recent updates, but there were no sightings and it seemed as if Wilhelm Kruger had changed his mind, or maybe I was just lucky enough to still be in front of him…

The cool October days had passed like streamers in a dream when I crossed a small bluff outside of Medora, North Dakota. There was a thin beam of smoke on the far horizon and the faint smell of burnt wood in the crisp November air. Through my spy glass a lone horse stood out like a beacon of ink, on the ground beside the abused animal was something sub-human rolled up in a filthy blanket. I rode into the haphazard camp and decided the person under the blanket was either dead or a fool—but I wasn't going to leave a good horse to starve or freeze. Prophet snorted at the putrid stench coming from under a greasy black hat, covering a dirty male face. The sleeping man farted and rolled over—plugs of weedy grey hair barely covering the liver spots on his large, misshapen head. He hocked forth a clot of phlegm and used his rancid hat as a shade to blot out the sun. I knew who the man was before I ever saw his face.

"Well, kiss my raggedy ass. What say ye now, Reuben Judah? Better you finding me than the four-eyed sonofabitch that's been chasing my ass for near a week or more," said Wilhelm Kruger.

"I'm just as surprised as you are," I said resting a hand on my pistol grip.

"And here I lay thinking you came all this way to pay me in person for what you did to my poor ole family," Kruger said as if this were a joke. He flashed a mouthful of moldy teeth. "Not that I give two shits about them or the family business you burned to the ground. Poppa was a cruel bastard and Gunter wasn't much better."

"What about the compensation for my family, or have you forgotten that?" I asked. Wilhelm Kruger laughed and dropped his hat to the ground. I watched as he slid a hand under the blanket.

"They hellfire, Reuben…that's no reason to—" Kruger started to object. I didn't afford him the chance to finish his protest.

I knew Kruger and his slippery deception. He would keep talking to lull me into a false security then pull his weapon and shoot me from under the blanket. And to that interior thought is wed the exterior intention. I didn't waste time puzzling out the right or wrong, nor did I care about his ill-conceived options at this point.

I emptied my pistol into Wilhelm Kruger and watched without emotion as his body jerked and shook with each impact. I afforded him the same providence he had offered Three Crows. In my eyes, Wilhelm Kruger deserved neither favor nor discrimination, and the impartial justice of western culture was dually applied and executed without remorse.

I took the three black feathers from my saddle bags and pushed them into the gaping holes of Wilhelm Kruger's removed nose. His broad and bulbous head was like a dead planet lost in some unknown space of time, rotten yellow teeth like fingernails of the dead. The Spitlers were right. Wilhelm Kruger was a horrid man to look upon, in life or death.

I heated the cross over his dwindling fire and burnt a mark on my chest above the jagged scar I wore for Jess and Molly. Wilhelm Kruger's blistered wound was now displayed beside the faded stains of his father and brother. I unhobbled his horse and the creature stood sway-backed and tilted pitifully on its thin legs, as if the weight of an unknown world were now lifted free. I fed and watered the animal from my hat then pointed the horse in the direction of Medora, and gave it a smack on the rump. I was headed towards Medora as well and reasoned out that I'd either find the animal in town and cared for, or dead on the trail. But at least I afforded the horse an opportunity to decide its own limited fate...

I left Wilhelm Kruger's body exactly as it lay for the angry world to devour. Three Crows once told me that some men die and their names are remembered, other men die and their names become legend—but the cowards will die forgotten because our world can identify the unseen taint of such men. Wilhelm Kruger's body remained on that shoddy patch of ground for years and no living thing defaced his corpse. His remains leathered and became a riddle to passing settlers where it lay mummified upon the earth as if the land itself had no reason to reclaim him.

I left his campsite and rode half the night under a three-quarter moon that sat like a silent judge directly overhead. There was a solitary lamp giving off a thin cataract of light in the otherwise dark township of Medora. I decided it was best to report Wilhelm Kruger's outcome because I was too damn tired, too damn cold, and too damn stubborn to keep riding through the night. I pulled up and tied Prophet off to the hitchrail then stepped inside the constable's office. Inside, two men were locked in a single cell, one man stood with his arms draped through the bars while the other inmate was asleep on a ragged cot. At the desk, a robust young man with spectacles had his feet propped up, reading a book by the lamplight. I noticed the title and spoke a single word.

"Tolstoy?" I wondered aloud.

The young man put the book down on the table, taking care to mark his place. "Respect was invented to cover the place where love should be," he quoted with his eyes closed.

I recognized the lines and quoted back from the same novel. "If you look for perfection, you'll never be content."

"Anna Karenina," the young man answered loudly, then smacked his meaty hand on the table top. "I'll be damned if the frontier never ceases to amaze me. I never thought it possible that a man would walk into this meager jailhouse and quote Leo Tolstoy," he said rising and walking towards me with his hand stretched out.

"It was bad enough when all we had was ole four-eyes quoting poetry to us, now we got two of'm yammering away. There must be something in the water because these sonsabitches are breeding and multiplying," said the prisoner with his arms draped through the bars.

The bespectacled gent stopped and addressed the convict's crude brand of jailhouse humor. "I thought we had finally reached an agreement about these vulgar comments concerning my eyesight. If they persist, I will be forced to engage in another round of fist-a-cuffs," he said, assuming a boxer's stance.

The inmate on the cot rolled over, one eye already black and swollen shut. "He's a mite queersome to look at, but that little bastard punches harder than a mule can kick. I'd listen to him and shut the hell up," the inmate said to his partner, then rolled back over.

"Now there's a grand nugget of advice," said the young man,

extending his hand to me again. He introduced himself, "Theodore Roosevelt, but my friends call me Teddy."

We shook. "Reuben Judah and I owe the credit for knowing Tolstoy to my sons. I have an early translated copy of Anna Karenina in my saddlebags. It was their gift to me before they left to attend college at Harvard."

"Well, bully for you and your sons," said Roosevelt in a booming voice. "I'm a Harvard man myself, proud member of the Porcellian Club. I got my unauthorized copy of Tolstoy much the same way." He was a bull of a man and it was obvious from the sound of that voice he was born to lead men. "Now tell me, Reuben. What brings you to Medora's constable office at such a late hour?" he asked.

"I'd watch what you say to him," advised the bar-hugging inmate.

"Allow me to apologize for these two uneducated ruffians," Roosevelt explained. He removed his spectacles and started cleaning them with a handkerchief. "I tracked three men for a week after they stole my riverboat. I caught these two, but unfortunately the third hooligan is currently at large."

"The boat thief that got away—is he missing his nose?" I asked. Before Teddy could replace his glasses and answer, the mouthy inmate cut in.

"That's him, name is Wilhelm Kruger. And he's neither my friend nor is that rotten asshole our partner. It's like Pete and I told you from the start," he seemed to plead for Roosevelt's consideration. "Kruger's the one who stole your boat. Pete and I just went along for the ride. Hell, you can't blame either of us for wanting to get closer to St. Louis before winter sets in."

"I'm sure your day to explain our circumstantial differences will come soon enough," answered Roosevelt. Teddy turned back to me. "I've been standing guard over these two in case the locals decided to apply their unique brand of vigilante justice. Now tell me about this gentleman with the missing nose. Do you know of his current whereabouts?" he asked.

"He's about half a day's ride south of town," I said, pointing back towards the prairie.

"I feel certain it's safe to assume that Wilhelm Kruger is currently afoot? I'm only asking this because a riderless horse wandered in a few hours before your arrival. I had the animal fed and assigned a stall at the livery."

"Wilhelm Kruger is dead," I got in before Teddy could expand further on his interrogation.

"You killed him?" Roosevelt questioned.

"I did so out of self-defense," I explained. Both inmates sat up and listened. "I rode into his camp around noon and found Kruger wrapped in his blanket by the fire. I was thinking he was possibly hurt and I might offer assistance. Instead, he tried to rob me at gunpoint."

Roosevelt crossed his arms and squinted. "He fired first I assume?"

I saw no reason to go into great detail and told Roosevelt what he wanted to hear. "He did, from under his blanket and without warning. His shot went wide of its mark and I returned fire to protect myself."

"And you are quite certain Mr. Kruger is expired?"

"He was sporting six holes in his chest and all six holes were leaking when I left," I replied.

"Well, bully for you," said Roosevelt, looking at his prisoners for any objection. "Of course I will need to take your sworn statement for the constable's approval."

"You're not the sheriff?" I asked.

He shook his head no. "I was only deputized long enough to watch these two prisoners until Sheriff Bullock returns. I own the Elk Horn Ranch on the Little Missouri River and just happened to be here with my feet propped up, reading an unauthorized copy of Tolstoy when you walked in."

"Well, kiss my saddle-weary ass," I said and chuckled.

Roosevelt laughed and walked back to the desk then pulled out a sheet of blank stationary. "I've acquired some legal experience so taking your statement shouldn't take us too long." Teddy gave me a wide grin and asked, "Do you play chess by chance?"

"I do, but to be honest I haven't played in years."

"Splendid," said Roosevelt kicking a chair towards me. "Sit down and let's get this unfortunate incident legally put aside. Once I have relinquished my prisoners to Sheriff Bullock—and we have your sworn statement noted and all charges dismissed on the grounds of self-defense, I must insist you allow me the pleasure of providing your breakfast."

Sheriff Bullock signed my written statement without objection and saw no reason to press charges, much less ride back out to investigate and verify Kruger's remains. "Snow's coming so whatever's left of him can wait till the spring thaw," was all the man said. Roosevelt and I left the office as daylight began to illuminate the Dakota plains.

Teddy took a deep breath and exhaled. "I never get tired of seeing this," he said sweeping a hand before the grandeur. "We might as well stop by the Buckboard Café and order a cup of coffee, or maybe something stronger if you're so inclined," he offered and crossed the road.

"Nope, coffee's fine by me," I replied following him across the dirty street. We walked into the café and ordered coffee then stood by the stove warming our hands as the barkeep poured the cups.

"Well, if it ain't ol' four-eyes himself king of the wild frontier," said a dirty man. He was sitting at a table with two other men of the same caliber. The other two drifters looked up and said nothing, then went back to spooning greasy eggs into their mouths.

Teddy looked at me and unbuttoned his jacket. "Go on to the bar and enjoy your coffee, but I would consider it a personal favor if you would keep this pending melee honest," he said handing me his coat. I was already watching the unruly table with vigilant eyes.

"I'll back your play," I replied in a low tone.

Roosevelt walked over to the trio and stood while the filthy denizens were sitting there grinning up at him. I'll admit that I was curious to see the outcome between the seated men and Roosevelt, but I could also understand their ragged way of addressing the young man. Teddy Roosevelt appeared to be somewhat of a greenhorn dandy in his tailored buckskins and fringed jacket. He was articulate,

205

well-spoken, and obliviously educated—but it was the studious-looking spectacles that seemed grossly out of place on the man.

"Gentleman, I can understand the incessant need for humor in your otherwise dull and under-appreciated lives. But I would kindly ask if you would refrain from using my physical appearance as the basis for your tasteless jokes. I find it rather offensive and if you care to think otherwise, then by all means stand up one at a time and voice your objections," Teddy said politely.

"What in the hell do you want me to stand up for? You wanna' dance?" asked the dirty man. The two egg eating men laughed.

"On the contrary, it's so I can enjoy beating your goddamn brains out," said Teddy in an almost casual tone.

The dirty man who first insulted Roosevelt stood up and kicked his chair back. "I'll give you one thing, you little cockweasel, you got a setta' balls for a four-eyed mamma's boy," he said and crossed his arms.

Roosevelt stepped back, cocked his leg, and assumed a pugilist stance. "Prepare to defend yourself," he said bringing up his arms and clenching his fists.

The man laughed. "You go to hell, peckerhead."

Roosevelt threw two quick jabs and the insulter's head snapped back in lyrical obscenity. The other two men at the table lowered their hands to their laps. I pulled one of my Navy Colts and thumbed back the hammer.

"If you two don't put those egg-shoveling dick-skinners back on the table I'll blow a hole through both your asses," I said to them. Both men returned their hands to the tabletop and sat mute as Roosevelt snapped a succession of punches into the swollen face of his adversary. Teddy ducked under a weakly thrown haymaker and answered with a short hook to the man's kidneys. The cowboy's knees buckled and Roosevelt drove a vicious fist to the side of his head knocking the man cock-eyed, face down, and blissfully unconscious. The drifter lay on the floor in a pool of his own blood as if to document these angry men and their violent ways.

"Harvard boxing team, lightweight division," said Roosevelt

looking around. He saw my weapon drawn and looked at the table where the other two sat with their hands perched beside their plates. Roosevelt said to the two men, "I assume this little demonstration has satisfied your curiosity as to my physical capabilities?" The two men said nothing and only nodded. "Grand, then we can dismiss any further need for physical violence," he said, motioning for me to holster my pistol. "You are free to help your friend recover," said Teddy to the men.

"He ain't our goddamn friend," said one of the seated men. "He rides for the Triple Bar W ranch, and we don't care much for neither of'm. The dumb bastard shot his mouth off and got his ass handed back to him. We had nothing in it from the get-go."

"I think it's safe to assume the Triple Bar W should employ men with better manners," said Teddy. Both men smiled. "Are you gainfully employed?" Roosevelt asked them.

"Not currently," they answered.

"I have work available on my Elk Horn ranch if you're interested."

Both men shook their heads no. "We've got a nice little poke put back from our summer wages so we'll just sit tight and ride out the winter here in town instead of riding nurse maid over a frozen herd. But maybe come springtime," said one of the men.

"Splendid," said Roosevelt, returning to where I stood at the bar.

Teddy took a swig of his coffee and swallowed. "Well, what now?" I asked him.

Roosevelt took another sip and shrugged. "What are your options at this point?"

"I just finished working for Captain Richard King, and since the Kruger incident is settled, I'm on the good grace of life's grand offering until my sons graduate from Harvard."

"Excellent," said Teddy clapping me on the back. "I know Richard King personally and he's a rare breed if there ever was one. I'm sure you would have no objections to working as one of my foremen until spring."

"You know nothing about me," I replied.

"I know that anyone who works for Captain King is top notch, and I could use whatever you learned from him to keep my ranch productive. I also know you backed my play when you could have walked away. That tells me you're a man who follows through with his convictions."

"More than you'll ever know," I said.

"By all means, elaborate," he answered quickly.

I drained my coffee and shrugged. "I always figured that if I was in for a penny, I was in for a pound. I don't know any other way to be."

Teddy's voice showed a hint of excitement. "I say that's all the more reason for accepting my offer of a working partnership between us. I have the same high personal standards when it comes to completing my goals. If you want to ride out and see the Elk Horn, we can discuss your employment options."

Roosevelt started towards the door without waiting for my answer. "What about the breakfast you promised?" I asked. He stopped and turned around as if he'd been caught in a lie.

"I apologize, but my steaming cup of morning purgative has taken hold," said Roosevelt, walking faster.

"Your morning what?" I asked following him around back of the café.

"I like a cup of hot coffee in the morning to invigorate my bowels."

I scratched my head as Teddy closed the outhouse door behind him, and then heaved a sigh of relief. "You mean you needed a cup of coffee so you could take a shit before we left?" I asked him through the door.

"Exactly," grunted Roosevelt.

"If I'm gonna' be riding with you, then we need to have a talk about your manner of speaking," I said.

"How so?"

"You need to drop the higher than God Almighty way you speak around these men. Because I'm not pulling my Navy Colt every time some saddle tramp calls you a little four-eyed momma's boy."

A grunt and then chuckle came from inside the privy.

I heard Roosevelt stand up. "Well, I'll be goddamned, I think I've just been insulted," he said through the half-moon opening in the door.

"Take it any way you see fit," I told him and started to walk off.

Roosevelt came through the door tucking his shirttail in. "Hold on, I haven't forgotten your breakfast. If you still want that meal, it'll be served at my ranch if you're so inclined to join me," he answered.

Less than an hour later I was unsaddling Prophet in Roosevelt's barn, thinking to myself once again. In for a penny, in for a pound...

26

New York
1897

It was the first week in May of 1897 and the world still smelled of wintertime. The wind was voiceless and blew with invalid warmth, and it seemed as if the entire city of New York held its breath in anticipation of spring. Raindrops began to fall like delicate hosts descending upon a ballroom, the damp streets aglow with yellow lamplight as dawn slowly dimmed away the bitter black. Electricity had arrived and voided the decay of night, while fashionable trolley cars ambled through the boroughs and made traveling a modern and timeless luxury. I watched the day begin, thinking back on my life and the nameless men who now flooded my thoughts…and I was thinking about Theodore Roosevelt.

Roosevelt was much like the other men who helped carve out the very nature of my life: Three Crows, John Mosby, Hickok, and Richard King—but Roosevelt was different. Teddy was fiercely loyal and he set the example which forced me to become a better man. When we first met in 1886, nature had its own agenda and the clutch of winter held fast and by February of 1887, the Elk Horn's herd was damaged beyond repair, as was Teddy's investment in North Dakota.

It was during the next ten years of our friendship that opposing worlds would begin to collide, unseen forces came into play and gambles were made. Sometimes the strongest craving unravels the very fabric of time, yet what I wanted was placed before me on a platter like some reeking and undeserved reward. But nothing is ever as it seems. Every reward has a price. I plucked the strings of time and certain lives would be forfeit while other lives would echo beyond eternity.

Sagamore Hill, New York
May 6, 1898

After the Elk Horn Ranch was sold I moved back to New York at Teddy's request. The years had done little to slow Roosevelt down—if anything, the man's energy seemed to have multiplied as if he had a fatal deadline with destiny. I had begun to finally unwind and enjoy the sudden comfort city life afforded me in my apartment along the Hudson River. Stoddard Quillen brokered the lease so I could be closer to Luther and Eli. Wilbur Spitler had retired and conceded his shares of our mutual business to the boys, who began to re-industrialize the operation with their Harvard engineering degrees. The boys were in the process of opening a new production line in Boston, and I had just returned to my apartment after having received a guided tour of their new machines. A message from Roosevelt was slid under the door: "Be at Sagamore Hill today at 3 pm—Urgent!"

It was a two-hour ride by horse and trolley to Sagamore Hill. Teddy's second wife, Edith, answered the door when I arrived. "Reuben, please come in. He's in his study so go on in and try to talk some sense into him," she pleaded.

"What's going on?"

Edith Roosevelt shut the door and pushed me forward with her hand. "He'll tell you his plan, and when he does you be sure and talk him out of it."

I went into Roosevelt's study and found him sitting in his high-backed chair, looking out his window with a glass of brandy in his meaty hand. "Nature has always provided me with a relief from the turmoil in my mind," he explained without taking his eyes off the scenery.

I walked over and stood beside Roosevelt who closed his eyes as if he were perpetually asleep. "Don't you think it's a little early to be hitting the hard sauce?" I asked looking at his glass. Roosevelt opened his eyes and looked at me.

"Nonsense," he said, putting the glass down. Then he poured us two cups of coffee. "Let me ask you a question, Reuben. Do you ever sit in the quiet solitude of your day and think back on your life?"

"All men do, Teddy."

"Do you have any regrets? Maybe a tinge of guilt about killing the Kruger men out of revenge?" he asked. Over the years I had told Teddy about my life and no secrets existed between us.

I looked at Roosevelt, took a drink of coffee and sighed. "I think revenge is a place of illusion and it belongs to the past lives we no longer control."

Roosevelt smacked the table with his hand. "Exactly, and yet you were still willing to pay the full price of your conviction. That's what separates men like you and me from all others. We are men of action and resolve."

"To be honest, when I have to kill a man the price of revenge is of no concern to me. When I pull the trigger I'm resigned to that action alone, and it is my intention that the end result will serve a far greater need." I placed my cup on the tray while Teddy contemplated my answer. I didn't like the subject matter of this meeting. Roosevelt seemed oddly distracted and impatient. "So what's this urgency you wanted to see me about?" I asked changing the subject.

Roosevelt seemed to relax and he smiled. "I have two announcements and you are among the first to know," he said taking a sip of his coffee. "First, you are to accompany me to a very special event tonight."

"What kind of event?"

"It's more an assemblage of gentlemen much like you and me.

Unfortunately I cannot disclose any more so you'll just have to trust me on this."

"Okay…what's the second announcement?" I asked.

Teddy gave me that wide smile, set his cup on the tray and clapped me on the shoulder. "I did it," he said.

"Did what?"

"I resigned my commission as Assistant Secretary of the Navy this morning."

"What in the hell for? Have you gone nuts?" I asked, wiping my mouth. "You're a politician, Teddy. That's your job, it's what you do."

"I can assure you that I am in complete control of my faculties. I resigned my commission so I could legally form a volunteer cavalry unit. Plans are being made and we're going to finally assault Cuba. I am asking you to be my first volunteer, and before you say no, bear in mind that I have full authority to personally select my men and this invasion has complete Presidential approval. Any man who rides for me will become one of my *Rough Riders*."

I tried to reason with him. "There's not going to be a war or a battle for that matter, one side or the other, our side or theirs will back down before you set foot on Cuban soil. You're a family man. Why are you so determined to fight in a war all of a sudden?"

"If I am to stay in politics then I have to build a broader platform. To be a great man you must perform great deeds worthy of merit and distinction. Infamy is earned, Reuben. And what better way to earn a nation's admiration than on a field of battle with valorous men beside you?"

"None of that means a goddamn thing if you're killed so forget this nonsense, Teddy."

"Edith put you up to this, didn't she?" he asked.

I tried to look innocent. "Put me up to what, Teddy?"

"Trying to talk me out of it."

I looked out his window and shrugged my indifference. "What does it matter?"

Roosevelt grew serious and began to peddle his political agenda.

"We've been at war with Spain for a month and President McKinley hasn't done a goddamn thing until now. It's going to happen, and I *will* be the first American to set foot on Cuban shores. Because of the climate, we'll meet and select the men for our unit in Texas, and we'll immediately start training once we've filled our ranks. I need the cavalry expertise and guerilla tactics from your days riding with Mosby, so I'll say this again. Will you volunteer for my Rough Riders and help me train the men for war?" he asked.

I wanted to say no, but the thought of battle began calling to me like a chronic echo from my past. "Teddy, in four days my sons will open their new production line and I plan on being in Boston for the event," I tried a final time.

Teddy slapped his knee. "Well, my good man, that's what this secret event is all about. As a matter of fact, we leave for the train station in fifteen minutes and dinner will be served once we arrive on location. I assume you have no objection to eating pork?"

"Nope, ate it all my life."

"Splendid," said Roosevelt heading towards the door. "Now let's go to my closet and examine our choices for evening attire. We need to find you something suitable to wear. Tonight is going to be a grand occasion, and I give you my personal assurance that we'll both attend your sons' opening in four days," he said. Roosevelt turned around, grabbed me by the shoulders with both hands and looked directly into my odd-colored eyes. "But I want your word you'll be on my train to Texas the fifth day, and by God I won't take no for an answer. I mean to have you with me when we land on Cuban soil."

"Teddy," I started to protest and he cut me off.

"Reuben, I'm asking you as a friend. I'm asking because you're the only man I trust to cover my back."

I looked at Roosevelt and then dropped my head. "Goddamn you, Teddy," I said.

"Splendid," said Roosevelt pumping my hand, grinning like a mad jester. "Now step lively, man. We have a prior engagement of considerable importance to attend first off and after that we'll begin a grand adventure in Texas together. I can feel it in my blood and bones, Reuben. This is my destiny…I was born for this invasion."

We left thirty minutes later and rode by train to Boston, then switched to a covered buggy and rode another hour until we stopped two blocks short of our destination. Roosevelt apologized and put a hood of secrecy over my head until we arrived. I was led from the buggy into a building and up a flight of stairs into a great banquet room that echoed with our footsteps. My hood was removed and I stood in a large dining hall, staring at an enormous marble pig with a banjo placed at its cloven feet. Around the room were men with their faces in cowling beneath the plain black robes they all wore.

"Who stands before these Brothers of the Porcellian?" the gathering of men asked in unison.

"Luther Eli Cobb," the unmistakable voice of Roosevelt answered. Though he knew about my earlier life, hearing my alias being used by Teddy was puzzling.

"And what does this man seek?" they asked.

"Admission into our sacred world of Brotherhood," Roosevelt replied.

"This nominee was researched, and his integrity validated before he was brought before these Brothers of Honor?"

"Luther Eli Cobb is pure and worthy," said Roosevelt.

"Is there a second voice to affirm this nomination?" they asked.

"We second the known integrity of Luther Eli Cobb," answered the voices of my sons. Hearing their voices explained why Roosevelt had chosen to use my alias.

"Is Luther Eli Cobb a friend of Jesus?" a cowled man asked.

"He is a Brother," said Roosevelt. I knew then that John Mosby had connections far deeper than I originally thought possible.

"Then let us welcome our Brother and may he be accepted into The Porcellian," the men replied, removing their hoods.

The initiation ritual began and lasted for three days. Among the members were Roosevelt and my sons, politicians, business tycoons, and other noted men of prominence. I was finally accepted into their ranks on the fourth day, and by mid-morning of the fifth—I would be on a train with Lieutenant-Colonel Theodore Roosevelt, headed back towards Texas.

During the train ride, I spent most of my time in Roosevelt's personal car going over training procedures, cavalry tactics, and deciding on the standard equipment each man should have. Teddy immersed himself in coordinating every aspect of his Rough Riders so nothing would be overlooked or left to chance. He called in favors from the wealthy elite, threatened anyone who voiced opposition, personally designed the uniform, and used his political connections to solicit donations. Teddy purchased the best rifles of the day and made it perfectly clear; every Rough Rider selected would exhibit the same high standards he and I expected from ourselves. And it was *that* trait which drew me and other men to Roosevelt. It was his continuous and contagious excitement amid the high standards of excellence he maintained not only for himself, but fully expected from those around him. It's what drew us to ride and fight under Roosevelt's violent banner, and he embraced us because of it.

We met at the Menger Hotel and Bar in San Antonio, Texas, on May 10, 1898 and began our recruitment process. The problem from day one was not selecting the men for the Rough Riders—it was rejecting them. Roosevelt set a strict limit of 2,000 men who would begin training and we would eventually lessen that number to half by way of natural attrition. More than 5,000 men showed up in the first two days. By week's end we had our limit, and the Rough Rider selection process began immediately in the harsh Texas sun. It was Roosevelt's and my way of acclimatizing the Rough Riders for the smothering Cuban summer that lay ahead.

The 2,000 men who made it through the first phase of selection were a mixed lot of cultural diversity: learned men of education, college athletes, cowboys, old west sheriffs, outlaws, bandits, and Native Americans comprised the ranks. During the two weeks of training and selection it became apparent that the men who survived our combative course would become just as independent, strong-willed, and every bit as determined as their new Executive Officer, Theodore Roosevelt.

The final 1060 men who showed exemplary determination during the selection phase were inducted into the 1st United States Volunteer Cavalry at Fort Sam Houston, and issued the standard equipment: uniform consisting of a slouch hat, blue flannel shirt, brown trousers with matching leggings, and boots. The men wore handkerchiefs knotted loosely around their necks and looked exactly as a body of cavalrymen should look. It was self-pride and Roosevelt's unwavering charisma that contributed to the distinction of being selected as one of his Rough Riders.

Afraid of missing the opportunity for his "grand little war," Roosevelt wasted no time in making hasty plans for immediate deployment. We enjoyed a small graduation dinner then loaded a Southern Pacific train on May 28 bound for Tampa, Florida, where we would await our shipping orders.

Just before we deployed to Cuba, I received a handwritten letter from Stoddard Quillen on June 8, 1898. I knew before I read the lines that this was to be his final goodbye. Stoddard's health had declined over the years and his son, William Edward Quillen, was now in charge of my personal affairs. I could picture his bony hand and that roguish smile as he drunkenly penned out this final goodbye.

> *My Dear Friend,*
> *I feel impelled to write this letter that will ultimately fall under your eyes when I am gone. I have no misgivings about my life. Tomorrow is never a guarantee for anyone, least of all me. I have learned a great many things in this long life and the greatest gift of all is what you gave me…to love those around you every day.*
>
> *I do not need the proof that you existed in my life, or that we created a history that will be spoken of long after we both have passed. I have never asked much of you, but I ask this as my final request. Don't be afraid to love again, Reuben. Open your heart and the world will again become limitless.*

The Prophet of Cobb Hollow

*Rest easy dear friend—we have had quite a ride
together and I have no regrets.*
Stoddard

Stoddard Edward Quillen died on June 18, 1898...and he would always be remembered by great men in grander settings than mine. I would be remembered as diabolical—a callous man who stole gold teeth from those he murdered. I was The Prophet of Cobb Hollow, and that fabricated story was Stoddard's greatest jest. It was Stoddard Quillen who breathed life into The Prophet of Cobb Hollow, and with his last breath...he took the truth of it to his grave...

San Juan Hill, Cuba
June 30, 1898

Our orders came on a sweltering Cuban morning and we moved out in single file, paralleling the San Juan River with Roosevelt in the lead. We passed by a gathering of bathing refugees, and to these aborigines, Roosevelt seemed like a hero yet named in this sudden tide of their tropical war. A young Cuban girl crouched naked in the grass with her arms covering her nakedness like a Gauguin painting. Roosevelt and I continued by and she called out to us in Spanish, *"Cuba Libre!"*

Roosevelt looked at me lost in the meaning. "Free Cuba," I translated.

We rode on as the heat mounted and artillery sounded in the distance amid the sporadic gunfire that began to increase in sound and volume. I looked back over my shoulder at the men behind us, their faces shadowed under hat brims hiding grim eyes and clenched jaws, each man mute and lost in his private pre-battle thoughts.

A solitary rider came at us in a full gallop of smoky dust. The soldier slid his horse to a stop and saluted before his mount could right itself. The animal pranced on edgy feet as Roosevelt pulled up and acknowledged the salute. "Sir, there's been a change in orders. Colonel Wood needs you to take your unit and make an assault on Kettle Hill to support the Army regulars pinned down on San Juan

219

Hill," said the soldier crisply.

Roosevelt checked his map then looked at the messenger and gave instructions. "Ride two miles to the rear and rest your mount at the field hospital. Wait there until ordered otherwise," said Teddy to the young soldier. The lad saluted and rode off, all the happier to be out of the bloodshed towards which we were heading. I spat to my left and looked at Roosevelt who had his eyes closed and his fists clenched in contemplation.

"What's wrong?" I asked. Teddy shifted in his saddle and opened his eyes.

"I'm afraid I'll panic when the time comes," said Roosevelt.

I shook my head in objection. "It's too damn soon to panic. Panic when the last few sands of your life are caroming down the hourglass of battle, when the final round is fired and your shirt is stained and you're near dead upon Kettle Hill with no one to close your lifeless eyes. You can panic when your recurring dream involves a white headstone and a comrade weeping…and when you awake—you wonder if the undertaker had his own death in mind when he fashioned your casket. That's when you panic," I said to Teddy. He seemed to relax and regain that hard resolve.

"Do you ever think about dying when you fight in battle?" he asked.

"Shitfire, Teddy, I sometimes want to wrap my arms around a vacant coffin and feel my veins thrum with life. Fear is what I fear most, and that makes me no different than any other man. You included."

Roosevelt clenched his jaw and nodded. "Of course…you're right, Reuben. What now?"

"You best get us all together and give the men a speech because they're gonna' need all the motivation they can get when the shooting starts and blood is being spilled."

Roosevelt whistled and the men rode forward and gathered around him as if he were a resurrected prophet of doom. No sound except that of the lathered mounts stomping their hooves to shake the botflies from their legs. Teddy Roosevelt took the time, starting with me—and looked his Rough Riders in the eye before he spoke in that rich political voice:

"Gentlemen...in the long history of this world, war transpired first in order to have the exploits of gallant men carved into stone. It is the grandest form of honor...and today, we will not shirk from our responsibility. You and I, gentlemen, have shared in the labor of training—and side by side, we shall ride together into battle. I have in my confidence that if we perform our duty, if nothing is neglected, we will be victorious and survive the coming storm of our enemy. It is incumbent upon all of us to conquer not only the satisfaction of our mutual ambitions, and whether with or without me...we *must* leave our mark as courageous men, as American Rough Riders upon the ever changing history of Cuba." Roosevelt finished his speech and cinched his hat down.

The men said nothing and only nodded their understanding, each knowing they had volunteered and no further words were necessary for them to apply their sworn trade of killing. Roosevelt gave the men a few minutes to gather their thoughts before we would cross the river and begin moving towards Kettle Hill. Teddy looked to where I sat in silence, watching smoke unfurl from the verdant hillsides ahead. I was lost in thought, thinking of another charge I had made so many years ago across similar terrain in Manassas, Virginia.

Roosevelt spoke and broke my gathering storm of memories. "Well?" he asked.

"Well, what, Teddy?"

"It wasn't one of my best speeches, but considering the circumstances and the short preparation...how was it?"

"To be honest, I've heard my fair share of pre-battle sermons and one thing I have come to realize. If we win, your words will be remembered for generations by those who heard them and rode with you."

"And if we fail?" he asked.

"Then your words die on the cold lips which spoke them, and your speech stays with those dead ears on the field of battle. It might sound harsh, but it is what it is...and so it goes."

Roosevelt took a deep breath and exhaled through clenched teeth. "Then failure is not an option today. Reuben...if I should fall," he started to add.

"You won't fall, Teddy. I won't let you...now let's get the ranks formed and ready to move out. It's time," I said.

Roosevelt stuck out his hand and we shook. "I'll see you at the summit when we raise the American flag," he said.

"I reckon so, Teddy."

We moved out across the river and broke through the woods on the far bank as rounds thudded on the open ground before us. "Now is the time, press on!" shouted Roosevelt as he spurred his horse forward.

Up the hillside we went, man beside man in mounted fury. The first volley of rounds met our charge and fifty men went down in a clash of hooves and dirt. Upward we pressed into the green hills and the fine tropical mists as if we were men on a crusade towards some metropolis of the dead. On my right two Spanish soldiers ran from a bunker up the hill towards their rear; I shot one with my Winchester and Roosevelt the other. Teddy swung the charge left to stay abreast of the Gatling guns, which were positioned lower than they were instructed and wouldn't be able to provide cover near the top.

I cut away from Roosevelt and rode up to their positions. "Move those damn guns up one hundred yards and train your fire towards the top of that hill!" I shouted to them. No one moved. I brought my Winchester around and leveled it at a young sergeant manning the first Gatling position. "Every man charging up that hill depends on your leadership and ability, so you're either gonna' provide cover fire for our asses...or so help me God, I'll shoot your sorry ass and I'll keep on shooting until I see these goddamn guns moved closer," I said.

Men began to break down the machine guns and run forward into positions around clumps of scrub palm for concealment. It was as if these very plants were here to bear witness to this ever changing movement of battle. I spun around and started back towards Roosevelt, passing men who lay behind their downed and dead mounts providing cover fire for those still riding. I came abreast of Roosevelt and started to yell for him to wait until the Gatling guns were repositioned when the air broke in a vagrant uprising of noise as our machine guns began coughing forth a baptism of death. On the top, the enemy was dressed in their bright red uniforms like obscene marionettes, clattering about with soot-blackened faces of panic.

"The Gatlings!" Roosevelt shouted over his shoulder and rode on ahead. I was a few yards behind him and slouched over the neck of my horse and shot two more Spanish soldiers amid the clamor, chaos, gun-smoke, and screams of nervous mounts.

I realized oddly at that moment, charging up a long green hill towards enemy positions, that I was where I belonged as my veins thrummed with life. It was intoxicating and unnerving at the same time. It was sensory overload, the clang of gun bolts and the shouts of combatants mixed fearfully with the sound of artillery and the groans of those who fell and now lay dying beneath the feet of charging men and their steeds. The splendid uniform of the Rough Riders sweaty and now defaced with dust and blood. It would be this audacious charge up Kettle Hill that would carve a path of greatness for the suicide messiah we followed. These were my thoughts as the ash swirled around our mounts and drifted upon the breeze like dead snowflakes. All that was beautiful in the known world had disappeared, and what was now visible was the inevitable response to war that had awakened the dormant and secular beast in all men.

Roosevelt came to a wire fence forty yards from the peak, dismounted, and hit the ground running towards the summit on foot, I and four other Rough Riders beside him when we reached the top. Roosevelt waved his hat above his head and the men below us cheered while still under enemy fire.

Roosevelt took enough time to catch his breath and then ordered another charge, and without waiting for a reply, he broke across the open ground towards San Juan Hill on foot with me and the four others following. In the chaos and amid deafening abuse of conflict, no one but me and those close to Roosevelt ever heard his order.

I caught up to Roosevelt, who was hunkered down in a ditch, firing over a broken fence post. "Next time you give a goddamn order to charge, you best make damn sure everyone hears it," I yelled.

Roosevelt looked over his shoulder and saw we were alone. He cursed and moved back down the hillside waving his arms like a maddened priest. Once his command became general knowledge to those below our position, the Rough Riders came forth in their finery of war like a legion of horribles cast out from hell itself. It was as unavoidable as the rising tide, a miracle of self-sacrifice and the indomitable bulldog spirit of Teddy Roosevelt that both hillsides were taken by the Rough Riders.

By nightfall, both San Juan and Kettle Hill remained under Rough Rider control as Spanish soldiers retreated towards the Cuban coast. By July 17, the Spanish would surrender and be gone from the island, earning Roosevelt his place in history. Less than a month later, Teddy and I would be back in New York, sipping looted Cuban rum in his study at Sagamore Hill. The stepping stones of Teddy's success were laid before him, and as I expected—Theodore Roosevelt did not tread lightly upon them.

27

Present

"Absolutely breathtaking, Mr. Reuben," said Paul.

"Yes, it was."

Paul clasped his hands and almost seemed to swoon. "Roosevelt sounds just as I imagined him, so charming and debonair, while being courageous and somewhat of a wild ruffian at heart."

I nodded my head in acknowledgement. "That he was. Teddy was what every man wanted to be. He was the best friend I ever had and one of the few men I not only admired, but was completely devoted to."

Paul's mood seemed to darken. "Mr. Reuben, I'll be gone for a few months to attend more school," he said and leaned forward. "I won't be here, but tomorrow morning we're getting a new inmate by the name of Bernard Tobias. Mind you he is by no means insane, just an utterly brutal drunkard. He'll be here for a two week court-appointed evaluation, and likely discharged after that."

"What's his crime?" I asked.

Paul made a sound of disgust and closed his eyes. "He held his infant son's head to a hot woodstove and burnt his face because he was crying."

I was curious as to Paul's intentions for telling me this. "And why is this important to me?"

Paul's brow wrinkled with concern. "Mr. Reuben, this new man is a beast. He's large and heavily muscled and has a violent temper to go with his size. I think it's best to step lightly around Mr. Tobias and let the staff do their job if it becomes necessary to intervene," he cautioned.

"We'll see," I said and changed the subject. "Why more school?"

Paul's mood lightened. "I need to complete an eight week advanced study program and pass the state test to receive my psychological qualification in nursing." I looked at him lost in his explanation. "It means more money if I pass," he explained.

I wanted to test his monetary devotion. "And money is important to you?"

"It's important to everyone, Mr. Reuben."

"More so to some than others," I replied and Paul chuckled.

"Very true," he said and yawned. "So what happens next in your life? It'll give me something to look forward to when I return."

"My sons were married less than a month apart. Luther had three boys and Eli had three girls. They lived, raised their families, and died less than a mile from each other."

Paul looked confused. "So you moved to Boston when you got back from Cuba?"

I shook my head no. "I stayed in New York, but traveled back and forth between there and Boston to visit Luther and Eli. I began to enjoy watching my son's families grow, but I got too comfortable. I relaxed and began to savor the quiet life until I got the Kruger letter from Germany."

"That's when you volunteered to fight in World War One?"

"Yes, but I had to call in a favor from Roosevelt to be accepted into the ranks due to my age. That's when I was sent to France and served side by side with the finest soldier I ever met." I wanted to know more about Paul. Time was closing in upon me. "What of *your* family, Paul? I know so little about you, so let's start with your mother?" I asked, changing the subject from me to him. Paul's eyes widened and then closed slightly.

"Not much to tell, Mr. Reuben. My mother immigrated to this country as an infant, and both of her parents died of the flu before she could walk. Her name was Hilda. She was a hard woman to be around most of the time. She grew up in an orphanage and learned the secretarial trade at a vocational school. She and my father met at the accounting firm where they both worked, and the rest is pretty much dull history," Paul answered. I could tell the subject made him defensive and uncomfortable. Good for Paul. Uncomfortable kept him honest.

"No brothers or sisters?" I asked.

Paul shook his head no. "No siblings or cousins that I know of. Other than this job, I have nothing left in my life since the passing of my parents over two years ago." Paul gave me an odd appreciative look. "I guess we share that commonality between us," he said, standing up and stretching his thin arms.

"What do you think we share?" I asked. Paul looked down at me, a thin smile on his waxen lips.

"I guess neither one of us turned out to be exactly what our fathers wanted us to be. Parental rejection is a hard lesson to learn for a child, no matter the circumstances or age," he replied.

I looked up and held his eyes. "Perhaps we do share a small commonality after all."

"Perhaps we do at that, Mr. Reuben." Paul took out his keys and looked down the hall. "I need to finish my rounds and fill out the paperwork for school before I clock out. Just remember to walk lightly around Mr. Tobias."

"Walk lightly, indeed," I replied as Paul slipped back into his thankless world of insanity.

* * *

I watched the rain as it sliced down my window in jagged patterns; how I hated the rain. In the Argonne Forest it rained every day; how horrid the mud was when mixed with blood and human remains. Cement of the dead. The earth lovers say there is a subtle compliancy in rain, a gentle and natural cleansing of the land. It is

227

a lie. There is no cleansing salvation to these false droplets. Kill it all…kill the rain.

The sound of bed slippers shuffling on the floor, I watched as a new man skated his way on temperamental feet towards the craft table. All others on this block were asleep, but what is night to the blind? The new man arrived yesterday to our mentally infected domicile and, like me, he is a holdover from the First World War. He walks the corridor with his hands touching the mortared lines of the wall, letting their length guide him along the baseboard with the fingers he now uses for eyes. Thirteen short and scuffled steps to the end of the hallway and thirteen mortared lines that mark the boundary of his eternal night.

I watch him walk in that cautious gait of the blind, feet that trundle and scuff along, unsure and never leaving the ground as they feel their way to the dark cadence of this delicate hour. Those pristine fingers now rule his dark world, and what say he when they are too calloused and the days of their use are gone forever. How blind will his world be then, and what of his colorless dreams? I watched him sit at the craft table and begin weaving a basket, the deft fingers creating what only his static mind may see while he remains mute in his artistic contemplation. The doctors at this asylum have peddled the art form of basket weaving as therapy for the soldiers.

It was prescribed as a remedial curative for those soldiers diagnosed with a form of shell shock insanity, and that therapeutic craft would forevermore become a moniker to mark the insane— "basket case."

"You fought in the war?" I asked. The blind man turned his head and searched, ears suddenly alert and tracing the sound of my voice until his scarred face met mine.

He blinked his dead and sightless eyes. "I was there, and damn those who sent us to that horrible place. The only regret I live with from before the mustard gas claimed my eyes is that the last sight I saw on this earth was war being waged, and men were dying because of it. I don't think I'll ever kill the horrible vision of that day."

I could see the dismantled conflict behind his abstract eyes of darkness. I understood him and his sightless plight of disfavor. Who better than me to judge another man's suffering? War called forth the hard hands of man, as hard as God's own hands—and the vigilant cruelties they formed came long before Eden's paradise was ever tainted by the serpent's false blessing.

I thought about what the blind soldier had said and remembered the acrid yellow smoke of mustard gas, wafting like cold fingers of the dead through those muddy trenches in France. Taking a life in those wretched trenches was up close and personal. It had a morbid passion about it.

The finest cruelties of mankind were waged in those murderous ruts. One side would sound its bugle and men would spill forth from their trenches as if the great maw of this earth had retched them forth. The gross barrage of weapons firing and artillery putting out a deadly bedrock of lead while the soldiers fell like wingless butterflies in a synchronized obscenity, the wink of smoke from a rifle and the deadly puff of dust that echoed back when the round slapped meat.

And all the dreams of a wasted youth became banished forever as another nameless kid fell. The expression on their young faces the same each time, wonderment—as if their innocence made them invincible to death and this sudden pain was a lie…and they were so close to you. Close enough to read their thoughts when the small lozenges of lead entered their body and they crumpled so lifeless to the field. Pain has a universal language and all men of battle will one day speak its tongue.

But it was once the ammunition ran out, when there came a charge of screaming madmen, like Vikings with their eyes wide and running towards you with fixed bayonets. That was when the real murder began in the close quarters of your trench.

There was a controlled chaos to it, like fighting drunks in a tomb. The grunts of pain as knives or bayonets entered flesh, and the suctioning sound as the blade was yanked free, the bodies stacking up like muddy cocoons underfoot, already succumbed to the earth that would soon enough claim them forever. And it is the *fear* of death which drives you to kill when you face the brutality of closed order conflict—there are two options and you're forced to choose—you either murder every man you face, or join those at your feet.

One side waves a flag of truce so the living can venture across the muddy pasture of death, men weeping while searching each corpse as if the bodies themselves had fallen from the cliffs of Heaven. The soldiers on both sides attended this gruesome task while swapping food and cigarettes with each other, as if this were halftime at some festive sporting event.

The dead are buried in the fallow ground between the trenches while men clean their weapons of death and await nightfall. In those dark hours of respite is when the illumination flares are fired overhead, dropping back to the earth under silk canopies like tarnished angels of doom, while below their soft light, men readied themselves for another night of killing.

Three Crows was right when he said common dirt was worth its weight in gold if the right man or government coveted it. It was worth killing for in France. It is still hard for me to believe how many lives were lost, and all for the fifty feet of dirt between our trenches. I have come to understand there are men who fight in battle and there are men who wage war. I can only imagine there must be a separate Hell for those who waged war.

The blind soldier finished his basket, turned it upside down on the table and walked back the way he came, fingers brushing the walls as he passed Paul Tandy before disappearing into his dark room and the darker prospects that faced him.

* * *

"Mr. Reuben, so good to see you again," said Paul, taking his usual seat. I could tell by his stiff and upright posture that he was excited.

"Did you pass your test?" I asked.

"I did," he almost squealed out the reply. "And even better than that, I got a nice fat raise. Besides, isn't money supposed to be the root of all evil?"

"Money is not the root of evil," I corrected.

"Then what is?" asked Paul taking the bait.

"The lack of it," I replied. Paul chuckled.

"Touché," Paul laughed and then grew serious. "Tell me something, Mr. Reuben. How did you do it?"

"Do what?" I asked innocently.

"Take care of Mr. Tobias?"

I smirked. "Simple logistics, really. The crazies in this place listen to me and they hear my whispers at night when the others are asleep. Perhaps someone kicked the table by accident and a leg came loose, and by the next day all is forgotten. I think it was less than two days after he arrived that I found myself with a foot on Mr. Tobias' throat, watching with some pleasure as he choked merrily upon his shattered teeth."

"The report said he fell out of bed and must have rolled over. After that, asphyxiation by the obstruction of teeth was the corner's conclusion," Paul explained.

I gave Paul a thin smile. "Oh, I can attest to the fact that that brutal sonofabitch fell out of bed when the table leg came crashing down across his face. And I can further assure you Mr. Tobias was quite surprised and suffered greatly."

Paul seemed to accept the cruelty of my explanation and relaxed. He leaned back and asked a little too casually, "I don't suppose any of this bothers you at all, does it?"

"Does what bother me?" I asked.

"You honestly don't care or give it a second thought. Don't you worry about going to Hell and burning for eternity?" asked Paul.

"The only thing that burns in Hell is the part of your soul that once controlled the living…your memories, your great loves, and the false belief that your gift of life will extinguish the fires before you ever arrive."

"Jesus, that's a dreadful outlook on eternity. There's always enough time to change," Paul tried to reason.

I slid my chair around to face him and lowered my voice. "I've fought in three great wars and countless smaller conflicts. I have ridden beside men into armed conflict with everything from horses and swords, to cannons, tanks, and even airplanes. I've seen life and death, up close and personal…and I was raised by the purest people on earth. In my long life I have loved only one woman with an unquenchable passion that could *never* be felt, much less understood by men of lesser caliber."

"Easy, Mr. Reuben," Paul replied patting the air with his hands to calm me down. "I didn't mean to offend you. It was just a random question, I was curious because no one at this facility wanted any part of that child-burning maniac; even our direct care staff was petrified of Mr. Tobias."

I closed my eyes and recited a quote: "And I heard the voice of the Lord saying, whom shall I send, and who will go for us? Then I said, here I am…send me."

"Is that a piece of scripture from the Bible?" asked Paul.

"Isaiah 6:8."

Paul relaxed back into his chair. "I guess that verse means some will always go forth and do what others never will," he said and then added, "Before I left for school you were telling me about the greatest soldier you ever served with."

"His name was Eton Swackhammer," I replied as Paul propped his feet up on my windowsill. The uncaring gesture irked me.

"Take your feet off my windowsill, you're blocking my view," I told him.

Paul dropped his feet quickly and apologized. "I beg your pardon, Mr. Reuben. So tell me about Eton Swackhammer and World War One."

I brushed the dirt from my window and placed my index finger on his forehead. "I was there in the beginning and I will be there when it ends. I am the alpha and the omega, the first and the last…I am the beginning, and I am the end."

28

Sagamore Hill, New York
May 4, 1918

These long days of spring now shift the tides of winter like a sacred mantra praying a new color into being. But in the hopeful finality of these cruel years, there is less time for an *outsider* in my son's lives—they have their own fresh families to raise. Wilber and Agnes Spitler will not survive another year and it is in the shadow of these lonely days that I am forced to reminisce.

I take no solace in revisiting the past. Good or bad, my memories pass in sequence like shy glances, fleeting faces caught in a bashful crowd. The good recollections become my tragic tunes that soften with time. But there are those buried memories that beg for my violation, they demand their share of nurturing abuse like a resurrected virgin. I was content to live out my days and die alone, but my world was never ready for peace. Looking out my apartment window at the dark silhouettes lining the street under bitter lamplight, I reread the letter again.

> *Reuben,*
> *It has come to my attention the three remaining*
> *female members of the Kruger family have male*

*heirs currently enlisted with the German military.
Viktor Mueller, Gerhard Fromm, and Rudolf Hauer
are the only male descendants of Hermann Kruger.*

*I received an international notice today. (The
postmark is from a village near the Argonne Forest,
in France). Quite simply, it was addressed to you but
my office was used for postal delivery. It appears
the aforementioned (male) descendants of Hermann
Kruger, upon completion of their combined war duty
in France, will gain voyage to America and reclaim
their family's land. The final line stated the Judah
line of ancestry will be eradicated.*

*If you so desire, and upon your approval, I will
gladly handle this situation through our government's
legal system.*

*I am at your disposal,
William E. Quillen, Esq.*

I sent a telegram with my terse reply.

*I'll be at your office in two days' time to manage
this situation personally.*

There was only one man I trusted enough to help me…Teddy
Roosevelt.

* * *

I arrived at Sagamore Hill the following day around mid-morning
and was met at the door by Edith Roosevelt. "Reuben, it has been
months since you stopped by. I hope everything is alright? Is Teddy
expecting you?" she asked, giving me a hug.

We parted and I lowered my voice. I wanted Edith's approval
first. "Actually no, I wanted to ask *your* permission first."

"My permission for what?" she asked.

"I'd like to borrow Teddy for three days…I'd like to take him to
where I grew up in Virginia," I explained. Edith Roosevelt's mood
lightened.

"I think that's a marvelous idea," she said. Edith raised her hands and made a hooking motion for emphasis. "The day Teddy left public office he was supposed to be retired, out of government and politics for good. The old Lion has been a surly curse to live around this winter, so if he chooses not to go with you. I'll either shoot him in his sleep or go on a hunger strike. Likely both," said Edith with an edge to her voice. "He's in his study so we'll both go in."

We went into the large book-bound study and found Teddy sitting at his desk furiously scribbling notes in a ledger. "Reuben... damn man, I thought you had forsaken me or died," he said getting up. We shook hands and hugged.

"Good to see you, Teddy."

Roosevelt grabbed my arms and held me fast. "Have I done something to offend you?" he asked.

"No...why on earth would you ask something like that?"

Teddy gave me that wide grin. "Then you have no excuse for not stopping by and seeing me," said Roosevelt, punching my shoulder. Edith cleared her throat.

"Theodore," she interrupted. "Reuben has decided to visit his home in Virginia and has invited you to accompany him. I highly suggest you accept his gracious invitation or Reuben will attest to my swift reprisal should you elect to decline."

"Reprisal?" Roosevelt asked looking at me.

I hid my grin and shrugged in defeat. "Edith said if you don't go with me she'll either shoot you in your sleep or start a hunger strike...likely both."

Roosevelt looked from me to his wife, then looked back at me and shook his head. "I can fully appreciate why you have remained a confirmed bachelor," he said. I laughed but Edith Roosevelt did not crack a smile.

"Theodore Roosevelt, you will leave this house for a few days or I'll personally have you removed by force. Whatever this country may need of you today, can wait until tomorrow," she admonished.

Teddy raised his hands and tried to barter a way out. "Edith, I have to finish this report for the Department of the Interior on annexing more land for our National Park system. It's due in five days."

Edith stood her ground. She looked at me and crossed her arms. "When will you be back at Sagamore Hill?"

"Three days…four at the most," I replied.

Edith tapped her foot then looked at her husband and squinted. "It's settled, you're going," she said and left the room without another word. We watched as Edith left the room and slammed the door in exasperation.

"I'd charge San Juan Hill all over again rather than cross that woman," said Roosevelt.

"She's good to you, Teddy. Consider yourself lucky; most men will never find someone like Edith."

Teddy nodded and chuckled. "I know, but I do love to irritate her from time to time. It keeps her on her toes. You know damn good and well I could never say no to you."

"Then why did you buck at my offer?" I asked.

"Consider it a lesson within the power shift of marriage between the sexes," Teddy said as if all men should know this fact.

"I couldn't agree more. Why in the hell do you think I went to Edith first?" I replied.

"You rotten pig-eating bastard," joked Roosevelt. He grew serious. "Now, what do we need and when are we leaving?"

"I have reservations for us to leave by train this evening. I think it's probably best if we're on horseback while in Virginia, so we can either take two horses from your stable or try to rent a couple fresh mounts when we get there."

Roosevelt opened the study door. "Bullshit, why rent a crippled or half-broke nag when I have quality bloodlines in my stable. Speaking of which, I have just the horse for you…it was to be a gift this summer. But why wait when there's no time like the present," he said.

We went to the barn and walked to the third stall. Teddy opened the sliding door and led a solid black gelding out into the open corral. The animal was tall and well-muscled and so black it seemed devoid of eyes. "Goddamn, what a horse," I said and whistled.

"I got him as a two year-old jumper from a horse farm in upstate New York. I don't want you to be offended, but I named him Prophet and he's all yours," said Roosevelt, handing me the lead line.

I looked the animal over and noted aloud. "Though his namesake is long dead, I think the big bay stud would be proud. Thank you, Teddy," I said. We shook hands and I knew then, like Three Crows—I was living my third life, riding my third horse, and walking my third and final path.

We left Sagamore Hill on the freshly saddled mounts and as we passed his main gate, Roosevelt muttered, "I remember a time when I could jump a five-rail fence on this very horse. Nowadays, we're both just as content to ride around at our own leisure. Where has the time taken us, and to what end do we face?"

I looked at Roosevelt as our horses plodded along. "John Mosby and our Rangers had a saying about the things in life we could not change, but were forced to endure anyway."

"What was that?"

"It is what it is...and so it goes," I replied.

"True enough," said Roosevelt as the vastness of New York City came into view. We stopped and Teddy pointed towards the sprawling scene of urbanized structure. "When I look at New York I cannot remember my life without electricity, automobiles, or a trolley system. I look at how modern our days have become and cannot fathom, for the life of me...remembering a happier time in my life than the winter you and I spent in North Dakota, on the Elk Horn."

We started forward again and I nodded my head in agreement. "Yes, sir, but everything changes, Teddy...with or without our consent."

"It is what it is," Roosevelt added.

"And so it goes," I finished.

* * *

We offloaded our train in Staunton, Virginia and checked into

The Jackson Hotel before saddling up and moving east along the mountains. The long blue-spiked ridges seemed to awaken and offer us a glimpse inside these terrestrial manifestations. We rode in a silent consciousness until I began to relay the names of familiar landmarks and retold stories of local history to Roosevelt. We cut a course along a stony path where trees with deep hatchet marks followed the ridgeline, marking the boundary line of my property.

"How many acres do you own in these mountains?" Teddy finally asked.

"I was initially given a 30,000 acre allotment by the Cherokee. A few years ago I bought another two thousand acres by paying the back taxes on an additional tract of joining property. It was a parcel once owned by an old German family named Kruger."

"You own 32,000 acres, so why on earth would you want to live in a congested city when you have all of this natural wealth to enjoy every day. It's incredible," remarked Roosevelt.

"Wait until we get to the top and walk out on the Bee Rocks. The view from that point alone is worth the ride," I answered guiding my horse around a narrow twist in the path.

The trail leading down to the Bee Rocks was overgrown and faint as a windblown kiss. We dismounted and began picking our way through the tangle of mountain laurel until we came out onto the wide plateau of the stony Bee Rocks. The view from the rocky abutment had not changed in a thousand years. The Shenandoah Valley stretched out before us in its intensity as the South River split the scene like an abstract mark upon the unspoiled landscape.

"Dear Lord, I can only imagine what the first man who stood here must have thought," whispered Roosevelt as if his words were a part of a prayer.

"Probably much the same thoughts you and I are having right now," I said and paused until Teddy turned around. He wore that wide confident grin.

"Breathtaking," he said slapping his chest as if to free it from demons.

"I'm glad you approve, Teddy. Because it's all yours," I said.

Roosevelt took a step back, unsure if he had heard me correctly. "Well, I mean I want you to have my land annexed into one of your National Forests. I made a promise to an old man a long time ago and I'd like to make sure the Cherokee's land stays unspoiled. Otherwise these mountains will be timbered and ruined forever."

Teddy thought for a second and objected. "Reuben, my budget for purchasing land is extremely low right now."

I spoke before Teddy could further his opposition. "The price is non-negotiable, and the terms of my land deal will not only provide you with a curiosity, but the price itself will be more than acceptable to you and the government."

Roosevelt walked in a tight circle of confusion and sputtered. "I don't know what to say?"

"Say yes," I replied.

"Of course I'll say yes. I'm not a damn fool…but why?"

I took a deep breath and let it out slow. "It's a long story, but trust me. I got far more than I bargained for when I accepted this land from Three Crows and the Cherokee."

"My God, just how far does your land extend from these rocks?" asked Roosevelt, twisting around.

I pointed and swept my hand in an arc towards the imaginary boundaries. "It's a two-day ride in any direction from the Bee Rocks," I said and started moving back through the thicket. "We'll come back tomorrow if we have the time, but right now we have an appointment at the law office of Quillen and Quillen. I've already had all the papers drawn up, so in a few hours you and the government will be the proud owners of Cobb Hollow."

Roosevelt bought copies of several newspapers to read on the train ride back, but would periodically drop his reading material and look over his paper at me, and remark, "I bought 32,000 acres of land for a handful of dirt. Utterly brilliant. Both historical and epic," he would say to me.

We arrived back at Sagamore in the late evening and unsaddled the horses before walking to the main house. Teddy went in with his usual swagger and swept Edith up in his arms. "The old lion has returned to his den," he said, flashing that brilliant smile.

"It appears he has," Edith laughed as Teddy put her down. She turned to me and smiled. "Thank you for bringing the old bull-moose back," she said and winked.

"It was my pleasure, Edith," I said with a sarcastic bow that was meant more for Teddy.

"We had a grand time, Edith. Wait until you hear about our little land deal. You won't believe me; it is simply genius," said Roosevelt.

I cut back in to finish my business. "Edith, if I could trouble you with a final request before I leave."

"Of course, Reuben. What is it?"

"If I could have a few private moments with Teddy, I'd be forever in your debt."

She used her hand and shooed us towards the study. "I'll have coffee brought in as soon as it's ready," she said. Teddy gave her a kiss and opened the door to his study.

Roosevelt filled two glasses and we stood looking out his window sipping peach-flavored brandy, talking about the great men in our combined lives. I waited until Teddy was on his third glass of brandy before I spoke. "Close to twenty years ago we stood in this very office when you asked me to go with you to Cuba," I said for openers.

Roosevelt took another sip of his brandy and nodded. "They thought we were crazy, but you and I created history."

"That's why I'm here…this is the second request I told you about before we left for Virginia. I want you to write me a letter of recommendation."

"Of course, Reuben…anything. What's the letter for?" asked Roosevelt.

"I want to enlist in the Army and be immediately shipped to France on the western front."

Roosevelt sputtered and then slapped me on the shoulder. "For a minute I thought you were serious," he said and laughed. "Now I know how you must have felt twenty years ago when I told you I'd just resigned my naval commission."

"I'm dead serious, Teddy."

Roosevelt downed the remaining contents of his glass in one gulp and his face lost all humor. "Are you completely mad? You're too damn old, Reuben. I'll admit you don't look a day over forty but that's beside the point. I'm twenty years *your* junior and they told me I was too old. If you're serious, then you are…you're mad, completely mad."

"If memory serves me correctly, I said much the same thing when you told me you had just resigned your commission." Roosevelt slumped.

"That was different and you know it. Goddamn you, Reuben. Don't you dare do this to me."

I played my final trump card. "You asked me as a friend…now I'm asking you."

"You sonofabitch," said Roosevelt dropping his head.

"It's not about me, Teddy."

Roosevelt thought, then made his proposal. "I have connections with the 77th Division here in New York. I know their commander, Major Charles Whittlesey who presently commands the 308th Infantry Regiment. I'll have a courier deliver a personal letter, signed by my hand. But you owe me as well—first you must pass a physical given by my personal physician," Roosevelt bargained. The mellow effects of his brandy disappeared and the familiar gusto returned. "And secondly, I want to know why? You owe me that much, Reuben."

I thought about my reply. "I have to finish what was started long ago," I explained. But it was only half the truth and we both knew it. Roosevelt understood more about my past than he let on, but didn't press my explanation any further. He and I were too much alike.

"If by some miracle you pass the physical," said Roosevelt tapping his chin and thinking aloud. "I know the 308th Infantry Regiment is planning to send a non-combat advanced party to work directly with the French in preparation for the arrival of their main force. How soon do you want to leave?" he asked.

"As soon as possible."

Teddy raised his hands in defeat and dropped them to his sides. "Okay, I'll take care of it. But only if you pass the physical," he agreed and started towards the door.

"Thank you," I replied.

Roosevelt stopped at the door and turned around with an odd and curious look. "Reuben, I love you like a brother. But there's something I have wanted to ask you for twenty years."

"Go ahead, Teddy."

Roosevelt thought for a second, searching for the proper words. "After we took San Juan Hill, that first night when we were dug into our defensive position…while everyone was asleep, you were still up. I watched you remove your shirt and heat a cross necklace over a cook fire and burn almost two dozen scars across your torso."

"And you want to know why?" I asked.

"I wasn't the only Rough Rider watching you that night. I think we were all a little hyped up from that bloody charge," Roosevelt explained.

"I guess you could say it provides my inner conflict with a sense of balance. It's an old habit, and nothing more than that."

Roosevelt stood there staring at me. He took off his spectacles and gave me a hug. "You go and have a bully time. Just be careful. I want you back here at Sagamore so I can hear all the details of modern warfare. Do we agree?" he asked. Teddy opened the door and we stepped into the hallway. I was beginning to feel the stimulation from war's windblown whisper. I wanted to turn away, but I could not. The nimbus of war called to me like a snake charmer…

"Agreed," I replied.

* * *

I was assigned to Company A, 308th Infantry Regiment as an enlisted liaison to France. I would be part of an attachment with thirty junior officers assigned to the American Expeditionary Force.

We awoke well before dawn on June 3, 1918 and stood in the shipyard checking our packs and supplies, ensuring we carried what was needed to bring about the birth of our dormant aggression.

242

Brightly dressed women mingled among the men, hugging them and wishing each the good fortune only those who face impending battle can appreciate. Sweet smell of perfume wafted through the early air as the moon struggled across the fading black glass of night. The feminine scent followed us to the loading plank where women rose up on their toes and kissed their sworn loves a final time.

The soldiers who were returning home from the war unloaded the ship and stood in shabby ranks watching the new recruits ready themselves to leave. The abused and battle-hardened veterans looked on with vacant eyes as if they saw a secret image none save themselves could see. As if they saw those reminiscent shades of long-dead comrades whose memories and glory fell silent beneath marble stones etched with their names.

I watched the young soldiers load the ship with smiles and a final boastful remark of courage to their loved ones. False bravado. That would change for all of them. The vanity of youth is a constant reminder that death is the silent creditor of equality. Most of these men would die with their dreams unfulfilled and unbeknownst to the young officers, eighty percent of their ranks would never leave France alive, and those who did survive the war would be scarred—both inside and out—forever.

We stowed our gear in the hold and claimed bunks like school kids on a sleep-over. The officers were not quite sure what to make of the old enlisted man locked within their ranks. Once word traveled through their group that I had ridden with Roosevelt, as he was greatly admired and rightly so, I was accepted and badgered with questions as if my words held a hidden talisman that might offer them protection. At night I listened to them and their talk about life and love. I did not reach out to the young officers for friendship nor did I offer my companionship. I remained mute about my life to avoid the closeness I knew would end with a bullet or worse. And whatever vagrant dreams these hopefuls may have had would be lost upon the troubled waters which brought them to these foreign shores. We docked at Saint Nazaire, France on June 13, 1918 and I was shipped straightaway to the front, as an observer to help plan and coordinate the main assault. I knew when I saw the trenches and the machine gun positions, the horrible tanks that rumbled like mechanical monsters and the airplanes that buzzed the sky. I knew that man had created something more diabolical than words—and when I saw the long rows of freshly dug graves...I knew this war had become a tally sheet of expenditures through attrition.

29

Eton Swackhammer
Argonne Forest, France
World War I
October, 1918

By the time our main force arrived in mid-September, the unusual ability of my memory had provided me with an unexpected advantage. I first learned to pronounce single words and then pieced together phrases, memorizing exactly how each syllable was enunciated by the foreign soldier teaching me—in three months I was semi-fluent in French, Italian, German, and Spanish. My multilingual capabilities landed me with a military warrior whose unwavering leadership would become legendary. His name was Eton Swackhammer, and he was the finest soldier I ever knew or served with. No history will be written of him, save these words now scribed by my hand.

"You smoke?" Swackhammer asked when we met.

"After seeing this shit every damn day for the last three months, I do now," I said. He lit two cigarettes and handed me one.

"Is it that bad at the front?" he asked, taking a drag. Swackhammer exhaled and looked me in the eye, waiting for the answer.

I took a hit off the cigarette and exhaled twin jets of smoke out my nostrils. I returned his stare. "I've never seen anything like it. It's bad," I replied and took another drag. "I've been here for three months and seen more senseless deaths than you could imagine. If you want to survive and help save the lives of your men you'd best listen to me. I can help you get them up to snuff but there's no guarantee. Make no mistake, men are gonna' die, and with winter coming…it's gonna' get a helluva lot worse before it gets better."

"Fuck me running," said Eton, snuffing out his butt.

I looked at Swackhammer and shrugged. Nothing was going to change except the demand for freshly dug American graves. "It is what it is…and so it goes," I said.

"Then you and I had better get to work. I'll let the men get settled tonight, but starting tomorrow…" said Eton looking directly at me. He broke into an evil grin. "Tomorrow morning you and I are gonna' become a couple of mean sonsabitches. If we're gonna' save their lives, then we gotta' put the fear of God into their young asses and turn those kids into killers before they see the front lines."

"How long before they're planning on sending us to the front?" I asked rubbing my nose.

"Two weeks if we're lucky," Swackhammer replied. I started to protest but he raised a hand. "Save your breath, Reuben. I've already argued my point and it was hushed before I had the chance to explain. One thing you gotta' realize if you haven't already, we've got a bunch of medal seekers for officers. I give it two weeks before we see the front, three weeks at best, but I'll lay even odds we get volunteered to go sooner than that."

I shook my head, thinking about how many lives would be sacrificed for the honor of wearing a tin disc wrapped in pretty ribbons on a uniform. "They'll get their medals alright, but a lot of lives will pay the price. It's not worth it; nothing is," I said.

Swackhammer only shrugged. "Tell the officers that, like you said…it is what it is."

"And so it goes," I finished.

The men of A Company, 308th Infantry Regiment, were like Eton Swackhammer in one distinct way; they were all a mixed lot of streetwise New Yorkers. They earned their passage to manhood fighting in the back alleys of Hell's Kitchen and the Bronx. These men had learned the art of being recreational hoodlums before they learned to read or write, if they ever did. I was tossed into ranks that were comprised of: Italians, Puerto Ricans, Irish, Jewish, and other mixed lots of mongrel Americans that would ultimately earn the respect of a nation.

They may have belonged to the military, but they were Eton Swackhammer's men, and though he would save some of their lives, each soldier would learn to hate the man they would ultimately come to love.

The following morning life began to move again as the military clock began ticking down. Time sped up. Everything became strict and structured—and every second, of every minute, of every day belonged to Sergeant-Major Eton Swackhammer. Up well before dawn, he had the men running assault and gun drills until noon chow. And then we were moving again, always moving…over and over…Eton ever present as if he alone was tasked with their right to live or die, standing over the men in judgment and pointing out what they did wrong.

A young Irish kid plopped down in the mud at our feet. "Not fucking fast enough, you dumb Irish mick. Get up and do it the fuck again," snapped Swackhammer. He walked to the next line of soldiers cussing as the young Irish lad got wearily to his feet.

The kid looked at me and wiped the mud from his face and cursed. "Goddamn Swackhammer, there's no pleasing that big bastard," he said to me. If he wanted sympathy or a friend to take his side—he received neither from me.

The boy needed to toughen up before he saw the shithole we would soon be knee deep in. I offered the kid a rare piece of advice. "You best remember this as I'll not say it again. A General has his thoughts on how war should be fought, but when you take a man like Eton Swackhammer…he has the foresight of how a battle should be won. The way he sees it, the more lives he saves on our side means the more lives we can take on their side."

"Well, pardon me all to hell if I don't jump up and kick my heels, but this ain't exactly what I bargained for," said the soldier plodding off. I watched him stomp away and thought to myself, "You never get what you bargained for in war."

Swackhammer was ultimately right. Less than two weeks after they arrived and the new ranks were assembled, every American doughboy was sent to the front. The Germans lined up across the muddy field and watched the new arrivals wade into the muddy trenches. They held their fire and allowed the former to leave without firing a shot.

"Why ain't the krauts shooting at us?" a private asked.

Swackhammer spoke up, "Why would they wanna' waste their ammunition now? Those goddamn sausage-eaters are gonna' have plenty of fresh meat to kill soon enough."

"Goddamn," someone muttered down the line. Just after daybreak the following morning we found out just how right Swackhammer was.

* * *

In wartime I never worried about yesterday. To me it was an unearned history, and anything that had happened could not be undone. My concern was always for tomorrow. I could make tomorrow a better place and a better world by killing as many of them as I could. But the first time we charged across that field in the Argonne Forest, I realized that when you went to work in a slaughterhouse somebody had to be the butcher. On most days it was me doing the butchering. But on that day, the Germans stepped up to the bloody task.

Swackhammer walked down the long trenches, the mud making sucking sounds as his feet clomped the half-frozen slurry. There was no time for Eton to romanticize war to the dirty young faces staring at him, no smoke and mirrors to glamorize what was about to happen. It is a torturous time, waiting and looking to each other for reassurance when none was to be had. Swackhammer made sure our minds were taken off the gruesome task, barking instructions as if his words were suddenly of holy origin.

"Take the time to write down your particulars on a piece of paper—blood type, allergies, your name, and the contact info for a loved one. Stay low when you exit the pit, the lower you get the better chance you have of staying under their fire line. If you're hit stay put and try not to move, the more you move the more chance you give the krauts to put another round in you. The medics will be busy so do your best to stop the bleeding and someone will get to you when the shooting stops. If you're hit bad, make your peace with God and know that we will come back for you…we will not leave you behind," Eton said. He looked up and down the rows of grim-faced doughboys crouched under their helmets. "Are there any questions?"

A red-haired soldier named Gilson who had the nervous habit of cracking his finger knuckles spoke up. "When do we move?" he asked, flexing his digits.

"Sometime around daybreak is the best answer I can give. When the word comes down to go over the top you'll be the first to know. Anything else?" asked Swackhammer. None spoke and the men remained quiet in their contemplation of things to come, the boasting and false bravery suddenly gone from their young faces. This was real. Men were going to die on this day—and for many, it would be their first and final initiation into the grand scheme of war.

I sat down on an empty ammo crate beside Swackhammer. He lit two cigarettes and handed me one. We both took long drags and exhaled our smoke towards the open sky to further estimate the wind direction. "You know this is gonna' be bad," I said.

"I figure they didn't bring us over here for tap dancing lessons," said Eton, watching our new lieutenant walk up. Neither one of us bothered to get up or salute. Lieutenant Mabry stood over us and waited for Swackhammer to stand. Eton never moved and continued to enjoy his smoke.

"Ten minutes," Mabry finally said. "If you haven't gotten your men squared away, you have a little time to do it now."

"Exactly what are our orders?" asked Eton.

Mabry stiffened at the question, as if the answer might undermine his shaky authority. "To advance and hold our position with the French in support of our left flank."

"That's just wonderful," exhaled Swackhammer. He snuffed out his cigarette. "I'm not real keen on trusting those fucking cheese-eaters. I take it you've made all necessary coordinations with the French?"

Mabry nodded and said, "Down to the smallest detail."

"You better hope so," said Eton getting up. I stood beside him as men down the ranks stood and rechecked their weapons a final time. "Let me ask you something, Lieutenant Mabry. Exactly where in the hell are you gonna' be ten minutes from now when shit starts hitting the fan?" asked Eton.

Mabry's face reddened. "I'll be right here, coordinating your movements and calling out directions as the men assault the German positions," he said, as if his role in this foray were far more important than dying.

Swackhammer patted Mabry on the shoulder. "Good for you, Lieutenant," said Eton, cinching down the chin strap to his helmet. "Just don't forget to duck, sir. I'd hate to think something tragic might happen to you while we're out there getting our asses shot off." The men down the line snickered and followed Swackhammer's lead and tightened down their chin straps.

It began an hour after daybreak when our big artillery guns broke the grim morning silence. The sound of incoming shells like whistling stones dropping into a deep, dark well. A farm pond off in the distance where turtles lay on logs sunning themselves, an odd scene indeed as the amphibians sat watching this spectacle of man before they dropped like dumplings back into the water.

I inhaled the carnal scent of war, breathing it in. I belonged here, in this place of dying. My blood had turned to dust and it seemed to me that I needed war to breathe. To exist. To thrive in the world I was now wed to. A series of whistles sounded from one end of the trench while bugles blew from the far side. Men started spilling out of the muddy ruts and were cut down before they could stand.

Swackhammer yelled down the line as men started to scramble

towards the lip of our trench, "Hold fast and wait until the next barrage of artillery starts impacting!"

"Are you fucking crazy?" someone yelled back.

"Just goddamn do what the hell you're told!" Eton yelled back. The buzzing sound of bullets began ripping through the air over our heads like torn silk, smacking the muddy bank above our heads. "When those arty rounds start exploding, the krauts will have their heads down and it'll get you out of these murder ruts. After that, keep firing and moving and listen to me for orders. Are we clear?" The men nodded and waited. Some with their eyes clenched shut, as if to fleece this sudden malady from existence. Others sat writing a last-minute letter to loved ones at home, silently hoping that the stationary would be found on their body and mailed out along with their corpse.

Another series of dull thumps sounded in the distant like a base drum. I flicked my safety off and waited for Eton's order. "Get ready," I told the man next to me. The soldier said nothing and only nodded.

The heavy rounds shook the earth upon impact. Men stumbled to keep their footing and most put a hand out to steady themselves from the rapid concussion of air. "Now goddammit…move!" yelled Swackhammer, sliding belly first over the rim of our pit.

The Germans regained their momentary loss of discipline and opened up from their gun pits, the rounds like sideways raindrops striking all about the scared and crawling men. Snipers began taking single shots at soldiers peeking over their trench for a better view, two heads snapped back and ensured it was the last sight those young Americans would ever see. As men lay dying on the bloody field, they would call out names of family members unfamiliar to us. Others called out, "God help me!" And I knew that today, God was absent and wouldn't be answering his personal messages.

The charge lasted thirty minutes and the men who survived the call for us to retreat had a better grasp of battle. It became clear to each and every soldier that this war had become a silent teacher, and the more you learned—the more silent you became because of it.

Swackhammer crawled back to our trench and slid headfirst over the side. He and I sat down with our backs against the muddy bank, our uniforms rotten with the blood and brain matter of our comrades. "How many do you think we lost?" Eton asked me.

"I saw at least twenty go down soon as they left the trench and at least twice that many on the field. The krauts will call for a truce in an hour or so to remove their dead and wounded. We'll know more about our losses then," I replied. I turned my head and blew the mud and water from my nose and watched Swackhammer closely. Eton crocked his head, trying to locate a crunching noise. "What's wrong?" I asked.

"What in the hell is that damn crunching noise?" he asked.

"Corpse rats," I said pointing to a muddy and blackened rodent above our pit. "They eat whatever meat is left over from the bodies. Get used to seeing them because they're gonna' get used to seeing you, one way or another," I replied.

Swackhammer looked up at the strange sky hovering above this strange land. He dropped his head and whispered, "This ain't right, Reuben."

"I'll not argue that," I said as Mabry walked up.

"I didn't foresee the mud as being an obstacle. What did you see from your vantage point?" asked Mabry squatting down in front of our position. His uniform was still clean.

Eton looked at Mabry and rubbed his face to free it from the gore. "I'm sure it's hard to see everything from the trench, but I'll try my best to clue you in. Out there," said Swackhammer pointing beyond the trench. "When you're out there in no man's land you realize those are real bullets being fired and what's lying on those stretchers is real fucking bodies. That's what I saw from my vantage point, sir."

"What do you think we should do next?" asked Mabry. He wasn't ready for this. None of us were.

Swackhammer gritted his teeth. "I'm not going to sugar-coat it for you, sir. I suggest you find out if the French have secured our left flank, because if they haven't, we're fucking surrounded. And that

252

means all of us are cut off from any chance of resupply," answered Swackhammer.

"I'll send another runner out," said Mabry.

"How many men have you already sent out?" asked Eton.

"This will be the third."

Swackhammer lost his military bearing. "Jesus fucking Christ, sir! Did it ever occur to you the krauts already have control of our left flank, and maybe...just maybe...you're doing nothing but sending our men straight into German gun barrels?"

"I'll try sending out a courier pigeon this time," said Mabry, hoping to find some agreement with Eton to perhaps win him and the men over. It didn't work.

Swackhammer tapped his head. "That's just genius," he said to Mabry, while rolling his eyes at me. "Birds are one thing but men and supplies are running low. So it would behoove you to correct this situation with the fucking cheese-eaters, or every one of us is gonna' end up dead."

"It's not that drastic," said Mabry, standing and kicking the mud from his otherwise clean boots.

He started to walk off when Swackhammer called out to Mabry in a casual tone. "Not that drastic? Then you won't mind leading the next charge...sir."

"I'll do my job and you do yours," answered Mabry from the far end of our trench.

Swackhammer looked at me. "He's gonna' get us all killed."

"Don't worry about it," I said as Eton spat a glob of mud from his mouth. "The krauts can't hold out forever."

"Nor can we," Eton replied as it started to rain.

It continued to rain for three days, and each morning we would slog across the field to face withering fire, and at night we'd stand under the illumination flares amid the constant barrages as we buried our dead. The trenches filled with water and became holes of torture to the living, smelling of rotten feet, human decay, and body odor—all of which seemed to emanate from the scratched and scarred soil. And to the soldiers who sat crouched in these wet piss pits of war, loneliness became an unforgiveable starvation of the soul. The thoughts of revenge became secondary to just staying alive. In the dark seconds before we charged into the hailstorm of military-ordered murder, our hopes became something foreign altogether—a forbidden truth or perhaps some unspeakable taboo. But eventually, each man felt the inner evil of himself, and killing became an attractive accomplice to this newfound nature.

Four days straight and still it rained in soggy bone-cursing misery. Our unit was preparing to charge again in vain hope of breaking through the German lines. We were low on men, food, water, and most of all, moral. I watched as the Germans locked and loaded their weapons with precision and without rancor. Time stood still as they sat watching and waiting for us to move across the rancid field they were defending. I was close enough to look into their eyes—eyes that had seen death and knew that it traveled on their cold bullets.

Swackhammer pulled up beside me and plopped down. "If we don't break through their lines this time, we're fucked," he hissed.

"No luck with Lieutenant Mabry?" I replied. But I already knew the answer.

"That bumblehead has sent out six pigeons today and watched each one get blasted out of the sky by the fucking sausage-eaters. We've lost two hundred men and there's only enough water to get our asses through the night."

I thought for a second. "Eton, I've been here for three months and I know where a creek is just beyond the German lines on their right flank. I think I can slip through and get enough water to hold us out."

Swackhammer shook his head in objection. "Too risky."

I don't know why, but when Eton said it was too risky, we both stopped and let the words sink in and then we began to laugh at the stupidity of our dire situation. Swackhammer composed himself as men down the ranks looked on as if they were denied the punch line of a private joke. "I'll make you a deal, Reuben," Eton finally said.

"I'm listening."

"If we don't make it through their lines, and providing both of us ain't killed in the process, you can go then. Fair enough?" Eton offered.

"Sounds good," I replied as we both watched Mabry put a whistle to his lips. "Here we go again," I muttered under my breath. We flicked the safeties off and dug our feet in for better traction.

"It is what it is," Eton said grabbing a hand hold.

"And so it goes," I replied as whistles began to blow.

"Are you sure Sgt. Judah can make it across to the creek and back again with fresh water?" asked Mabry.

Swackhammer and I sat in the Lieutenant's bunker. Eton looked at the man and made a counter-offer. "It's either gonna' be me, you, or Reuben that's gotta' go," said Swackhammer nodding to where I sat in silence. "And since Reuben is the only one who can speak German, he's the best choice for pulling this off."

"If we can wait it out another week," Mabry tried to counter.

Swackhammer cut him off. "Sir, you need to get your ass squared away. The last messenger bird you sent out was shot down, and the fucking krauts sent out their own pigeon with a different drop zone grid for our resupply. All of our ammo, food, and water were dropped right in their damn laps. Now the sausage-eaters have enough supplies to last them through Christmas. We have enough water to last us through the night and you want us to hold out for another week without a resupply. Are you fucking serious? It's gonna' happen tonight, sir. So what's it gonna be? Would your conscience feel better if we drew straws to decide whose ass we put on the line?"

Mabry was boxed in and he knew it. "Okay…Reuben can go," he said and then looked us both in the eyes apologizing. "I'm sorry… this was my father's idea, me being here and fighting for the glory of our family name."

Swackhammer stood up and looked down at Mabry. "With all due respect, fuck your father and his family name."

* * *

The German prisoner was crouched in the mud with Pvt. Gilson standing over him when Swackhammer and I walked up. The red-haired kid was green Irish to the bone with a temper to match. He looked at Swackhammer and grinned. "Swack, you just say the word and I'll send this bastard to sauerkraut Heaven," he said. Gilson touched the muzzle against the head of his prisoner and dropped the safety. The young German closed his eyes and began to pray.

"If you pull that trigger I'll send your grubby ass into the field to bury him by yourself," Swackhammer growled.

"What's a matter, you getting soft?" the red-haired kid asked.

"Pull the trigger and find out," Eton snapped and stepped chest to chest with Gilson.

"Fuck it, why don't you two cook him a sit-down dinner and powder his little ass while you're at it. We don't have enough food to feed ourselves, and both of you know we sure as hell can't send this sonofabitch back to his side," said Gilson. He slogged off as Eton offered the German kid a smoke.

"Nein," said the boy.

I spoke to him in German. "How old are you?"

"Sixteen," he replied. Hands shaking as the violent outcome he expected seemed to draw closer to the end of his young life.

"Do you want to live?" I asked. He shook his head up and down vigorously. "Then do as I say and you'll live to see the sun rise again."

"I'll do anything," the kid said.

"Good, now strip down and give me your uniform," I said. The boy hesitated, unsure of this odd request. Gilson sat watching us from his position. I nodded towards the red-haired kid. "You can either give me your uniform or I'll have Gilson come back and we'll take the uniform off your corpse." The prisoner stood and disrobed without further protest.

I stood in front of Eton in full German attire. Swackhammer looked me over. "The uniform will get you in, but how are you planning on getting back out?"

"The tanks haven't been able to move in this mud since it started raining but their ruts have gotten deeper. I think I can crawl in those tank trails and make the round trip," I said and looked directly at Eton. "There's only one thing that I'm worried about."

"What's that?" asked Swackhammer lighting a cigarette.

"Getting my ass shot off by a trigger happy kid like Gilson."

"I'll take care of that and make sure we don't launch any flares tonight, but I can't speak for the krauts. How are you planning on carrying all that water?"

I pulled out a length of tripwire. "I'll tie as many canteens to one end of this as I can and carry the other end with me. You tie a separate piece to the canteens as well, and once I get all of them filled, I'll give your cord a tug and you can pull the water back to your trench," I explained, adjusting the new uniform.

"Where are you gonna' be?" asked Swackhammer, jetting two streams of smoke from his nose.

I thought about the Krugers. "I'll be back before daylight...once I'm over there, I have some personal business to settle."

"Okay, just don't do anything stupid," he said. I nodded and unwound one end of the tripwire and put it in my teeth. Swackhammer took the other end and tied it to a string of tethered canteens. He looked at me and grinned. "You ready?"

"I reckon so, Eton."

Swackhammer smacked me on the back. "Then get your ass over there, you ugly bastard. I'm getting thirsty," he said as I slid over the rim of our trench.

I kept my head low and pulled myself through the slime, inch by wet soggy inch. I could hear the Germans talking and their conversations were no different than ours. Both sides were tired of fighting and killing. I passed by their positions, and as their voices became fainter, the sound of rippling water grew louder. I stopped at the creek's edge and lay there as if I were dead, listening to the night sounds for any sign of alarm, making sure no sentries were close before I unscrewed the canteen caps and began filling them with precious water. I gave Swackhammer's tripwire a tug and the bottled water slid silently back to our side. I dipped my head into the cold stream and drank my fill. I needed the extra hydration. The night was just getting started for me.

I turned and started back, crawling more slowly until I made the edge of the German trenches. I kept my head down and waited until a sentry walking his post passed by and then I slid silently into their pit. Their side or ours the trenches smelled the same and the misery seemed to compound the brutal effects of warfare. I waited until I heard the sentry's cloggy steps coming towards me and sat back.

"All quiet?" I asked the guard in German.

"Nothing moving but the rats," he said, stopping. Sentries were all alike. Any conversation was a welcomed relief from the doldrums of staying awake.

"How long have you been here?" I asked.

"Six months, but I have leave coming to me next week." He leaned close to get a better look at who he was talking to. I saw him wrinkle his nose. "I don't remember seeing you."

"I've only been here a week," I said and looked around. Trying to appear as nothing more than a scared confused comrade. "I've been trying to find my cousins but haven't had any luck so far."

"I know pretty much everyone in this shithole; what's their names?" asked the sentry.

"Viktor Mueller, Gerhard Fromm, and Rudolf Hauer."

The guard recognized the names and his mood changed from light to sour. "Go to the end of this trench and you'll find Captain Mueller's bunker on the left. The other two are here but I'm not sure which line they're in," he replied and then resumed his duty without another word.

I watched him disappear down the soggy trench and knew from our conversation and the abrupt change in his attitude, there was no love for the Kruger family by their own countrymen. I trudged through the mud, listening to the men talk as I passed by. It was odd for so many to be up and alert at such an early hour. As I drew closer to Viktor Mueller's bunker it became apparent from the bits and pieces of fragmented conversations—the Germans were going to throw everything they had at our side—first thing tomorrow morning at daybreak.

I couldn't waste the time, but I was close enough to the bunker to see if Viktor Mueller was one of Hermann Kruger's ancestors. I slipped inside the dank bunker, the smell like that of a dungeon or the entrance to a mineshaft. Mueller was crouched over the snub of a candle writing something down on paper. He didn't look up. "Yes?" he said.

"I have a message, Captain," I said moving to the edge of an ammo crate he was using for a desktop. Viktor Mueller looked up, waiting for my delivery. I could see the same heavy jowls and piggish eyes of Hermann Kruger staring up at me.

"Well, don't just stand there looking stupid. What's the message?" he asked gruffly and went back to his scratch pad.

I pulled the brass knuckled trench knife Swackhammer had given me free of its sheath. "The message is simple, Herr Captain." He looked back up at me and I smiled. "Reuben Shadrack Judah sends his regards," I answered and brought the knife blade down through the top of his head. Viktor Mueller's eyes bulged and he tried opening his mouth that was now pinned to the lower jaw by my knifeblade.

I took whatever paperwork I found, along with three large bars of chocolate and left his bunker much the same way as I came. At the opening, I stuck three black pigeon feathers into the timbered doorframe and went back through the dark trench towards our own lines. Swackhammer met me at the far end of our pit. He was grinning as I slid over the side into the muck and mire.

I took a deep breath and looked into his grinning face. "We got to move, Eton." Swackhammer dropped his grin.

"What's going on?" he asked.

"When daylight breaks the Germans are gonna' send everything they have at us."

"Fuck," Eton swore. "There's three thousand of them and less than five hundred of us. We might be able to stop them once. But anything after that, and we're all dead."

"Maybe not," I said and thought more about our sudden plight

259

of disfavor. "If we can get our machine guns to hold their fire while the riflemen open up on the first wave of krauts from our trench, we might have a chance."

"That's suicide," Swackhammer shook his head in objection. "Once they make it inside our trench we'll be outnumbered and outgunned and it'll be a matter of time until we're all dead, or prisoners."

"Not necessarily, Eton. We can keep half our men on the ground behind our trench and let the first wave of krauts make it to our pit. Once they're in our trench, just give the order to fire the machine guns and the second wave of krauts will get cut down. After that, have the men behind the pit drop back inside and it'll be like shooting fish in a barrel."

"Too risky," said Eton.

"We got three hours before we find out. Unless you got something better," I replied and handed Eton a slab of chocolate.

He grinned and opened the wrapper then shoved a chunk inside his mouth. He closed his eyes and chewed then smiled. "At least I'll die with chocolate in my mouth instead of mud and shit." Swackhammer swallowed and broke off another chunk. "We'll do it your way, Reuben. We don't have any choice and right now we're out of options."

Eton handed me a chunk of candy. I stuck it in my mouth and let the rich chocolate melt. "Let's finish this complimentary German breakfast and then we'll get busy. We've got a lot to do and not enough time to waste enjoying German chocolate and talking about old times," I told him.

Swackhammer laughed. "You know, I'm starting to like you more and more."

I swallowed my chocolate and leaned back, closing my eyes. "Don't get too damn comfy, Eton. It's not like we're gonna' start holding hands and swapping spit."

Swackhammer chuckled and stood up. "You've been up all night so grab some sleep. I'll start getting things put together and wake you when it's time. Good enough?"

I tipped my helmet down and shoved my hands into the deep coat pockets. "Good enough, Swack."

I lay back and closed my eyes, briefly…only for a second. Then Swackhammer was there shaking me awake. Clouds above me edged in pink as a fine mist fell like a blanket of grief. It was close to being that time, when you first awaken and discover yourself lying in the mud, limp, head in that watered down slurry of stink. The earth itself seems to become a genuine alien force, where life upon it has no resonance. When the land begins to feel like this, all things elemental and inhuman will be measured.

Behind our trench men lay flat on their stomachs, rifle to the side. Machine guns were fully loaded and cleaned, sitting in silence. Men were waiting in the grim darkness like a horde of unruly vagabonds, while across the field those who waited for their own brand of unknown fate seemed darker yet—the eerie space between the trenches like a field of sport waiting for a game to commence.

Swackhammer walked up and down the lines hissing to the men. "Let the first wave come to within twenty paces before you open up. Some of the krauts will go down but not all of them. Any German that enters this trench dies. Do we understand?" No words, just half-hearted nods from the men. "When the krauts get inside our trench the men behind us will reinforce our position while the machine guns open up on the second wave that crosses the field. Make no mistake about what's gonna' happen today…if we don't stop the Germans this morning, there's not going to be a tomorrow."

Eton finished and came back to where I was sitting. "What about the German kid?" he asked. I had forgotten about the boy and told Eton to have him brought to our position.

The German kid was half-frozen and wearing nothing but a set of rancid pants. If there was fear in his eyes it did not show, the trenches had mentally broken the boy. I spoke in a low easy tone to him. "I'm sending you back to your side the way you are. My advice is to stumble through the mud reaching out with your hands to find the way. Act like your blind from mustard gas until you make it back to your trench. If your superiors believe you, it might give you a brief ticket back home." The German kid looked at me and said nothing. "Do you understand?" I asked him. He dipped his head and only nodded before Swackhammer shoved him naked and trembling over the lip and told him to get his ass moving.

We heard bolts drop on rifles and Swackhammer called out down the line. "Let him go," he ordered as German artillery opened up and began delivering a bone crushing barrage. And it seemed then as if God himself were hidden out of sight and was recreating mankind from the very earth itself. Germans arose and came at our lines five rows thick, eyes wide as they charged across the muddy field.

"Let'm come!" screamed Swackhammer. He and I stood and braced ourselves, dropping our safeties and waiting until the time was right. There were so many coming at us you couldn't miss. "Oh, dear God," I heard Eton whisper just before he fired. And then the world erupted into a sacred wind of destruction.

The tender scenes of youth vanished, and to try and put these tragic scenes of warfare into words is to try and reconfigure each second. I belonged to the men charging across the field and they would soon belong to me, letting the silence spread as they gained momentum and I began talking to it. Not yet. Wait. Let them get a little closer. The biggest fear is when that silence answers back. Under the caustic sky we fought nameless men with hardened stares. The first charge showed the Germans their mistake while the second charge would show ours. The breath of desire and the crunch of bones and the dead faces that belonged to those shattered bodies lay everywhere.

It seemed to never end. From the earth and air the krauts poured into us, into our trenches, and they would soon pour themselves into our nightmares. I looked to my left and saw Eton Swackhammer stab two men, shoot three with his sidearm and stomp one into the mud under his feet. And even this was normal to us, as if it all were a part of another day in the short-lived lives of grunts. You come to understand that things are learned in war the civilized world cannot teach you. How to light a cigarette in a rainstorm, how to bury a body in mud, how to take your trench knife and remove a blackened toe because of trench rot. But most of all you learned how to kill with indifference.

The sound of bugles blowing and the Germans running back the way they came, pitching forward in the mud as they were shot in the back. Some shot down by their own side in this acidic fog of war. Swackhammer's booming voice yelling above the melee to cease-fire and save ammo for the next time. And it suddenly occurred to me that it was always the next time. The next time was all that invaded our minds.

The Germans stayed silent for two days as our supplies dwindled down to nothing. Once again I went back to the creek and filled canteens, then dropped into the German trenches, taking whatever I could find. Half-eaten rations, cigarettes, chocolate, and I took one more life.

I found Gerhard Fromm to be more like his uncle, Gunter Kruger. The men around him stayed away from where he slept... but on this night he would never awaken. I put three black feathers in the gaping wound across his throat and dipped my index finger in his blood and wrote a single word on his forehead—"Prophet." I wanted Rudolf Hauer, the last man of the Kruger clan, to know I was not only here. I was coming back.

I made it back to our side and was half-asleep when Swackhammer came stomping down the duckboard. "See if you can talk some sense into that hardheaded bastard, Reuben."

"Who?" I asked and yawned.

"Our fearless lieutenant," he answered, plopping down beside me.

"About what?"

"The dumb bastard is going to order another over-the-top charge across that murder field," Swackhammer said, shaking his head.

"That's insanity. We don't have enough men and we'll be cut down before we get out of this muddy trench."

"I know, Reuben...I know."

I walked over to where Mabry stood surveying the ground beyond our trench, as if something new might arise from the earth and change his warped mind. "Get your men ready to move, Judah. We're going over the top at nightfall," he said.

"Do you think that's a good idea considering how many men we've already lost?"

"Those were my orders," Mabry said with a shrug.

"Yeah, well, just remember it's the officers who get fat off orders, but it's the grunts that get slaughtered because of them. You go ahead and send us," I said and pointed toward the field. "But do me one favor, sir."

"What's that, Sgt. Judah?"

"Why don't you nut up and lead the charge, that way while we're trampling the wounded and hurdling the dead you'll be right beside us for a change," I replied and walked back to where Swackhammer stood.

"Well?" asked Eton.

"We're going over the top again, and if that yellow bastard isn't with us when we go I'll personally shoot him if we make it back alive," I said and Eton grinned.

"If you don't shoot that waddling little fuck-waffle, I will." We both laughed in the way that condemned men laugh when facing the gallows. "Let me ask you something, do you happen to know what day it is?" asked Swackhammer.

"November tenth…why?"

"I don't know, for some reason I thought I heard church bells ringing last night," he said as Mabry walked over dressed for battle.

Mabry cinched down his chin strap and said in a voice weak with apprehension. "Get the men ready and let them know I'm leading the assault this time." I knew he was trying to fit in, but men like Lt. Mabry were out of their element in the mud, the blood, and the killing. He belonged in a choir, a cushy office, or a grand social setting with comfort and security.

"We're all thrilled to have you with us, sir," said Swackhammer. He grinned at Mabry and added. "A word of advice, don't use the whistle this time."

"Why?" asked Mabry, suddenly curious about this battle etiquette.

"The sausage-eaters know that only our officers blow the whistles while their side blows a bugle. It makes you a fine target for those sauerkraut-eating sonsabitches on the other side." Mabry said nothing in return, but as Eton and I walked back to our positions—I watched as Mabry tucked the silver plated whistle inside his starched shirt top.

The evening fell as silver storms rained down from the black coals of Heaven. Eton and I sat watching in silence as the burnt flagstaffs fluttered in the bitter wind of war's greatest gamble. Swackhammer looked over and exhaled a plume of stale smoke, rain dripping from the brim of his helmet. "You think you're ever gonna' leave this war alive, Reuben?"

"I reckon I'll be here until a bayonet or bullet finds me. And then my bones will be left to those relics of the magnificent. We all face the prospect that life will stop giving us a chance to live," I whispered getting to my feet.

"Then what happens?"

I shrugged my uncertainty. "I don't know, Eton. I haven't got that far yet."

Swackhammer stood up and stretched. "Well, lemme know when you do."

Mabry yelled down the line. "Be ready, one minute until we move!"

A soldier down the dark ranks yelled back. "Say it a little louder, you dumb bastard, I don't think the krauts heard you." Men laughed in the gloom as flares whooshed towards the stars.

"Now!" Mabry yelled and climbed over the trench into the waiting gun muzzles.

Mabry wasn't cut out for war but it waited for him. He died thirty feet from the pit. No calls for help, just dead. Dropped by a single round as if the strings of his life were measured and cut before they were full length. As we charged past him I looked down at his body; my sons and even their children were older than Lieutenant Alvin Simpson Mabry. All the dreams and fears gone as Mabry joined the ranks of those who would never grow old. We made it to within fifteen feet of the German line, but they held fast and sent us running back through the bodies, blood, and barbed wire. In less than three minutes thirteen men died, including our lieutenant. I crawled back to our trench and put the last piece of chocolate into my mouth and watched as Eton came down the muddy line with his usual air of swagger.

"You're a fucking legend," said Swackhammer dropping down beside me.

"How do you figure?"

He pulled out a scrap piece of paper. "We found this on a dead kraut," he explained.

"What does it say?"

"It's a poem about you," Eton said.

"Me?"

Swackhammer read the words.

> "You feel him brushing lightly,
> Barely there…like a ghost from the fog,
>
> A faint outline.
> A trick of the eye.
> A fleeting shadow.
>
> He's silent like the mist.
> And nothing will stop…
> The Prophet."

"You know every kraut over there is gonna' hate you for this," said Eton, handing me a cigarette.

"Let'm hate me so long as they fear me coming," I said, leaning over to catch a light from him.

"Reuben, I've seen you use that cross you wear around your neck to burn yourself after each battle. Can I ask you why?"

"It helps me keep my conscious clean."

Swackhammer thought for a second then asked an odd question. Even for him. "Why are you here?"

266

The Prophet of Cobb Hollow

"I told you, the Krugers were planning on hunting me and my family so I saved them the trouble." Eton shook his head and lit his cigarette. In the long nights we had talked and Swackhammer knew more about me than most men ever would.

"No, Reuben, it's more than that. More than just your need for revenge." Swackhammer looked at me and squinted, as if to better see what manner of man was beside him. "You like it, don't you?"

"Like what, Eton?"

"War," he said.

I took a drag off my cigarette and shrugged. "I guess I've done this for so long I've gotten used to it."

"Were you born with those different-colored eyes?" asked Eton, changing the conversation to a lighter subject.

"Nope, a damn mule kicked me in the head when I was a kid and put me in a coma for three months. When I woke up my eyes had changed color. I had to pass a complete physical before I could enlist to fight over here. It was a pain in the ass process, but the doctors found an agent in my blood that attacks any disease or infection. It wasn't enough to keep me out of the Army, but it was a curiosity to them all the same. They told me the mule kick must've messed up a gland or something in my brain."

"The hell you say," said Swackhammer, snuffing out his smoke.

"Yup, and that mule kick improved my memory. Made it almost perfect," I added finishing my smoke.

"Fuck that," Eton swore. "I hope to forget this damn place and everything about it. Maybe I will, but you won't ever have that option."

I dropped my cigarette butt to a mud puddle between our feet. "Nothing I can do about it now, it is what it is."

Swackhammer nodded and grinned. "And so it goes."

"And so it goes," I said.

He thought for a second and made a personal observation. "Do you ever wonder if the rifle is evil or is it the man that wields it?" asked Swackhammer.

"Eton, it's not the hand that holds the rifle or the finger that touches off the trigger."

"What is it then?"

"It is the evil which lies within the men who will use it, and the ability of the mind to accept what this war has made them do." I replied. Swackhammer shook his head in disgust and then kicked the frozen ground with the toe of his boot.

"I was wrong when I told you I had the option of forgetting. You can't forget all of this," he said nodding towards the grave-lined field. "You can't forget what you did and everything you saw…not fucking ever," said Eton, rolling and lighting two more cigarettes.

"Then we got no other choice but to live with it," I answered.

Eton handed me one of the lit cigarettes and I watched as he took a long satisfied pull off his. Swackhammer exhaled a plume of grey smoke and looked out across the frozen and muddy field. The pending twilight sent amber waves of light across the ground like fools gold as big guns somewhere in the far distance rumbled and roared. Even in our personal lull in action, war was still going on without us.

"Yeah, well," said Eton, grinning at me, "I guess it could be worse."

"How so?" I asked. Swackhammer slapped me on the back and laughed.

"We could be on the other side of this field wondering the same goddamn thing."

30

Argonne Forest, France
November 11, 1918

Midnight is a time when those who remain among the living are locked within the solitude and turmoil of their past lives. The wee hours when the cries from nightmares only add to the savage air that seeps into the dementia-fueled minds of combatants. The air erupted into a whoosh as a gossamer tail of a German flare soared overheard and then broke into an odd light, the ghostly face of Swackhammer beside me.

Eton cracked an eye and looked over at me. "Here we go again," he said. We were groggy and tired, mentally broken and spent. And we both carried the weight of loss and responsibility on our conscience.

"Look at that dumb bastard," someone down the line said.

Swackhammer and I peered above the pit and on the gloomy field stood the German boy I had sent back to his side of this conflict. The kid stood pale white and half-naked in the murky light of the flare, as if he were a mystic and was preordained to lead us away from this awful place.

"What in the hell is he doing, committing suicide?" asked Eton.

"Maybe he missed us?" I replied.

Before we could make any further assessment the German kid came running at us, half-naked and maddened. I could see in his crazed eyes that life no longer had any value, much less any meaning to him. He was nothing more than a shirtless and barefooted martyr, a sacrificial lamb used to hide the enemy charge that came roaring behind him. He was shot less than two feet from our trench as he pitched a grenade into the hovel we had called home. Swackhammer dropped to his knees and frantically searched the mud for the grenade as men scrambled away.

In those precious seconds before the grenade exploded, Eton Swackhammer did something beyond that of mortal love for his fellow man. And all who were there would never forget. He stood up and shoved me back then turned to face me, the oddest look on his blood-stained face. It was as if he was saying he was sorry without words, with his eyes and actions alone. Slight grin as he widened his stance and stood spread-eagled, shielding me and the other men. The grenade detonated and shrapnel tore into Eton Swackhammer's body, the concussion blowing me from the trench onto the muddy field, both tone-deaf and stunned. I lay there dazed and unmoving as German foot soldiers jumped over my limp body and entered our pit. I could hear the clash of metal and gnash of teeth clenched in combat, but I could not move.

Bugles sounded and the same German boots jumped back over my body as they retreated back to their side of conflict. I sat up as sound began to recalibrate the scene in slow moving waves, the land itself churning under me in choppy gestures of time. I crawled back into the trench and slid headfirst into Eton's body. I rolled him over and he blinked, each eye movement slow and precise. Swackhammer's uniform was in shreds, buttons from his jacket blown into his upper torso. I pulled him close and whispered into his ear that all men should know of at least one man like him, and unless they have…their life would never be fulfilled. I told him I would not leave his side, and I would not let him be forgotten. Eton Swackhammer smiled thinly through the pain and whispered his final words to me: "Freedom is cheap to those who forget its cost."

His eyes closed slightly as if he were contemplating the very nature of this silent darkness of death that now claimed him. The act of war is wedded to the interior of man and the man who strives in that unholy matrimony will forever see himself as a killer. I watched as fiery life in Swackhammer's eyes glazed until the farther prism of death took him from me, and I looked out across the broken field at the horror of what was left.

The dead lay broken and mutilated upon the shallow ground where cadaverous arms arose from the pale and frozen earth like the shattered legs of egrets. Men gathered around their comrades like disciples before a pagan cross, heads lowered in the burnt and solemn light of the fading moon as if they were praying back into being their fallen saviors, cries and moans drifting over the scene from the field hospital where surgeons applied their awful trade of sawing bones. The glow of cigarettes, a hiss of exhaled smoke hiding grim eyes…the night-breath of war.

I pulled Eton's head close. The wet dog smell of his hair, as if he were a faithful fireside companion—asleep and drying out after a long day in the rain. I clenched my eyes shut and fought back a sob, and another…and then I wept hard bitter tears. I cried for Eton Swackhammer and I cried for Jessamine, Molly, and Three Crows. I wept for myself and what I had become, I wept for what I denied, and what might have been. Inside the trenches none spoke, but the very soul of every soldier wept silently with me—they wept to free themselves of their grief amidst this unforgiving tide of war.

It was in this moment of anguish that I broke with reason. I spun my rifle around and put the muddy barrel in my mouth, the bitter taste of wet metal sending shocks through my teeth. I dropped the safety and pushed the trigger with my thumb. I heard the firing pin strike the primer and felt the vibration against the roof of my mouth. Nothing happened. I ejected the spent round and inspected the case, small dimple in the primer but the round had misfired. And whether it was the rain soaked powder or God's own hand that spared me—I would never again give thought to using my own treasonous hand.

I stayed with Eton Swackhammer through the night. The rain had finally stopped, as if Eton's death was the sacrifice which made it so. I touched his cold head and realized he had already passed through the portals of death into the Great Halls of Valhalla. The budding sun sent the first veins of light out across the field and I wondered if our enemies felt the same sad loss. A horse-drawn wagon creaked by in the half-lit murk of the day with its soiled cargo of abused and shattered flesh—a sullen trolley of discarded and broken dolls. Frozen dead—the final fare for each passenger so costly, and yet so free.

I waited until the cart pulled beside my position, the driver a black man free of the burdens of war and only bound to the silent graves of his labor. I looked down at Swackhammer's waxen face as if a miracle might happen, but none did.

"It's time to let him go, mistah," said the black man.

"I know, give me another minute."

The black drover sat back and tilted his head. "Take your time, lessen you wanna' bury him here like some of the other soldiers do."

I shook my head. "No, anywhere but here...I'm not going to bury him in this damn place. He deserves better than this."

"Maybe it's what he would have wanted. I hear that all the time from soldiers when they bury one of their own. I reckon to some of you boys, it's better to be with the men you fought beside than be buried with a passel of strangers."

"Maybe," I said standing up. The black man got down and helped me load Eton. I looked at the elder man and told him. "His name was Eton Swackhammer and he deserves to be where the people who didn't fight over here will know how great he was."

"I'll not argue your reasoning," said the black man climbing back to his perch. He gathered his reins and looked down at me. "But it seems to me that folks back home are quick to love a soldier when they're away fighting a war...but damned if their memory don't get a little fuzzy once those soldiers get back home. I reckon it's easy to thank a veteran for serving, but not so damn easy to understand what it cost them."

I looked at the black man and gave him a salute. "Mister, you're the smartest sonofabitch on this battlefield."

He smiled and returned my salute. "Maybe so, but it don't pay me a penny more."

"Treat Eton with respect, that's all I ask," I said as he drove towards his next morbid addition.

I walked back through the awful mud to my retched trench and sat back, waiting once again in that space between the fighting and killing. It is an awful wait because it forces you to crave what you cannot have—a wagon ride of death or a cool dip in the icy stream of life. Like the forgotten touch of a female hand, you become content with the unknown and forgotten. I had to be disconnected from my life to be connected to war, and in the midst of trying to reconnect—I was still in debt to this endless repetition. I remembered the tense sensation of Swackhammer's cold skin. I wondered what he had secretly craved in those last hours before the killing had started again, just before his life was snuffed out by a half-naked kid of the same horrible conflict…I hope they both found it.

Bells started ringing in distant towns, no sound save that of the thrumming gongs and the dull heartbeat of scared and war-scarred men. More towns followed and icy bells rang all down through the long and bloody trenches. "Something happened," someone down the line muttered.

A German cried out across the field in perfect English. "It's over!"

Cautious heads peered above the trench, watching with a mixture of hope and curiosity as German soldiers crawled from their horrible ruts and began clapping each other on the back. Some lit cigarettes while others drank as they looked towards us, their sworn enemy, and smiled like forgiving saints.

"Hold your fire," a voice called out. "We're getting the official word now."

Men cheered and hands were raised when the announcement was made general, the war ended on the eleventh hour of the eleventh day, in the eleventh month of 1918. Soldiers from all sides met in the field and hugged each other as if they were lost comrades only now reunited by some unknown act of fate. I stayed in my trench and watched with some amazement at this unfolding spectacle. It was the first time in almost a year that I witnessed men celebrating life, instead of taking it. I sat back in the mud and unloaded my rifle. I stood up and took the weapon by the barrel and broke it in half over an empty ration crate. I took off my helmet and unbuttoned my jacket top. I closed my eyes and swore an oath…I would *never* kill again.

Night after long night, until I left France, I would have the same dream where I looked out over the corpse-riddled field between our trenches. The dream began to fester, like a diabolical experiment gone wrong. The last night before I boarded my ship to leave France, the dream was different. I drifted off and slept in that space between the living world and the one beyond. I dreamed the dead would arise from their shallow battlefield graves, clawing their way through the cold and barren ground as it they were some monster race called forth to destroy the world. They would fight again, horrible scenes of mutilation until a single man remained. Unto to him was given the task of burying these retched creatures once again. The remaining soldier stood alone and triumphant, and then he turned to me.

"It's your turn, Reuben," the shade would say.

It was the same lone soldier I would see night after night for the rest of my life. It was Eton Swackhammer. He would lay down his shovel and a vacant hole in the earth would swallow him as if he were a part of nature and the land itself.

Many years later I would offload another ship and revisit that horrid field. Now it is covered with red poppy flowers and the grass is so green it hurts the eyes. But I was there, and to this day I can still feel the decay. The earth is still red with blood, and the memory of how Swackhammer died shall forever scar the image…Sometimes the beauty you see today is but an illusion of yesterday's deceit.

Maybe I should have buried Swackhammer with our friends and brothers. Maybe I should have buried Eton in my nightmares—but I never did.

All my life it feels as if I've been alone. Many times I've faced death in battle with no one to know. I would look into the eyes and faces of others in the cold dark reaches of war, and I would see those soldiers holding their dying brothers in the night, but death always passed me by. I hope Valhalla is like the great feasting hall of my dreams. I hope to see my friends there so I can shake their hands once again. I hope to share the same bond we created so long ago, and it is my prayer that the soft tempers of time have diminished the harsh necessities of those battles we waged together.

I will never forget the sound of Swackhammer's booming voice so loud it shook the gold out of pockets and snuffed the vagrant dreams from sleep. I would like to sit behind a slab of unmarked cemetery stone and smoke a cigarette with Eton Swackhammer once again. I would like, just once, to sleep through the night and not wake up screaming and thirsty from nightmares beyond war's infinite measure. I would like not to think about rewriting my life and remembering the horrors that afflict me through this vast velocity of time. I am not thinking about submitting. I am not thinking about the enduring lust of mortal men. I am not thinking about forgiveness or revenge. I am thinking about how the full moon once lit the way for angry men to fight for each other. I am not thinking about their deaths…I am thinking about their lives.

Mingo Kane

31

Paris, France
January 6, 1919

The day before my unit departed from France I received a telegram with five crushing words: *"The old Lion is dead."* It was a simple message from Teddy Roosevelt's son, Archibald. My oldest living friend had died in his sleep from an apparent blood clot. Seven days later I would be in the middle of the Atlantic when I would receive yet another telegram. This time from, William Quillen:

> *Reuben,*
> *It is with deep regret that I find myself the bearer of ill tidings. Your sons, Luther and Eli, passed this morning less than one hour apart, a result of complications due to the influenza pandemic. If I could have bestowed this grievous chore upon another I surely would have, but I felt compelled, as both friend and colleague, to accept this duty.*
> *I am respectfully at your disposal,*
> *William Quillen, Esq.*

There are, within a man's tortured soul—those things which he is unable verbalize. They remain unto him alone, a segregated grief. These are the memories I cannot suppress nor articulate within the abode of these written words. The perfect smile of Luther and Eli, the exact color of their eyes, and the pitch of their combined voices. These are the unburied recollections that will torment me forever. I hid my pain upon the sea and prayed each moment to die, to extinguish myself into the colors that first stained the heavens and earth. I rusted away and slowly became a different species. The ocean was my final surrender to life—it loved and hated, it was soft and vicious. It set boundaries each day and broke them the next. I had reached the rocky bottom of my dark well and found a trap door—I went through and never came back. I ran and kept running. Further and further, scorching everything I touched like a stillborn Phoenix rebirthing in the flames of my damnation.

I spent a year in the Amazon and lived among the Yanomami tribe in a place where human life remained pure and undiscovered. I had to become lost in their world before I could be found in mine. I sailed on the edge of loneliness where time passed unearned and unnamed. I was a sorcerer of the sea, free to wander with nothing but the wrath of unlived imagination to guide my way.

I jumped ship in Portugal and rode an oil tanker to Tangiers. Became first mate on a cargo ship bound for Greece and two years later I was in Tuscany. I made port in Spain and sat in solitude off the coast of Barcelona, watching true passion unfold through the nets of simple fishermen. I stood on a mountaintop in Tibet, listening to the chanting monks praying their religion to life. I walked across blue glaciers, unable to capture or share their cold and wordless beauty... it would take a thousand daybreaks, when the sky and water came screaming together. It took a thousand twilights, watching the sun dissolve into the horizon like a silent sabbatical. Only then did I begin to heal. But no matter how far I ran. No matter the distance or the years. Somehow, I always ran back to myself.

The thirteenth ship I was aboard docked in San Francisco, on October 2, 1939. I had run into myself again, and this time—I would not escape. I hadn't touched American soil in twenty years so I allowed my curiosity to reclaim the past. There was a link missing in the tattered pages of my life. A final unsolved mystery. I went ashore to find my only connection to a family I had never known, to find and restore the truth of myself through his lost world of words. I wanted to find his book and rediscover my great grandfather... Keller Judah.

Present

Paul Tandy was crying. "My God, Mr. Reuben. You've seen so much pain and suffering it sickens the heart," he said wiping his eyes with a shirtsleeve.

"Only the living suffer. The dead share a forgiveness we are not yet a part of."

"How could you live with this loss for so many years?" asked Paul.

I started coughing. The air in this sanitarium was damp and stagnant and my lungs were feeling the cost. "What other choice did I have?"

A wash of cold air swept into the room as the door opened and the janitor pushed a floor buffer into the hall. We halted our conversation as he began polishing the floors and I watched the man sway with his machine as if he were dancing with some odd form of artificial life. "That means you arrived in San Francisco only a few months before you were placed at our facility," Paul said over the racket.

I started to reply but the floor buffer drowned out my words. I coughed again and spoke louder. "I miss the quiet," I said to Paul.

"The quiet?" he asked.

"When I lived with Three Crows it was always quiet. It didn't matter the time of day or the hour of night, it was so quiet you could hear the flutter of a candle flame or the whippoorwill's call as it cut through the mountains and echoed back." I wanted to take my fingers and plug my ears. I shook my head in sadness. "Quiet is gone. It's always noisy these days with the automobile engines, airplanes, machines, and other such nuisances. In this long life of mine I have seen these changes and these are my words, visit the world one thousand years from now and stone will again become the commerce of mankind. Only then will it be quiet."

"Mr. Reuben, I think you're exactly right." I hacked up a clot of phlegm and Paul leaned forward. "Mr. Reuben, let me call the infirmary and have you checked out. It sounds like your lungs are pretty congested."

I waved off the concern. "What once was dust will be so again. The world changes and we have no choice but to change with it. Like all things in my life, this cough will pass," I said covering my mouth. But I knew it wouldn't. I knew my time was slipping.

Paul gave me a curious look and asked me an odd question. "Mr. Reuben, are you afraid of dying?"

I started to laugh and coughed instead. Paul patted my back until I waved him off. "I have lived longer than three normal men and this is what I have learned. There are two questions that will be asked as long as creatures have intelligent thoughts. Where did we come from, and what happens after we die? One question will be answered and the other never will."

"Which question has no answer?"

"Our source of animation…if man were to find the exact origin of all life it would negate our existence within it."

"And death?" asked Paul.

"What comes after death will be answered once," I replied.

We sat listening to the thrum of the buffer until Paul changed the subject. "Did you ever find Keller Judah's book?" he asked.

"I read his story, but I never had the opportunity to purchase the book."

Paul looked at me and pursed his lips. "If you read the book, then why didn't you buy it?"

"The book was in the possession of Suzanne Pease and her nephew, Richard. I left their residence the night I read Keller's story to buy a train ticket back to New York. My plans were to return for the book before my train left the following morning. I was headed home to pay my respects to Teddy, and of course I would visit my sons. They were buried side by side. I wanted Luther and Eli to know the truth about me. I wanted to tell them how sorry I was… it was something I had to do. Of course, I never made my departure time the following day. As you already know, Rudolf Hauer ensured I would never return home."

"The man who tried to rob you?" asked Paul.

"In a sense, I suppose he was," I replied.

Paul stood and kicked the stiffness from his legs and yawned. "Mr. Reuben, I have next week off," he said and looked down at me with compassionate eyes—genuine and unclouded. Paul Tandy truly cared. "If you feel like your lungs are getting worse, I'll leave the doctor a note before I clock out asking him to see you immediately."

"I will keep that in mind…thank you, Paul."

"You're welcome, Reuben. I'll see you in a week so we can pick back up with your story."

"My final chapter is almost written," I said and Paul stopped.

"The final chapter?" he asked.

"Every story has to end or it would be no story at all," I replied. Paul averted his eyes and lowered his head. I could see then, he knew I was dying. "I promise to give you another week. Besides, we're all connected to the same story with the same perfect ending," I reassured him.

"It is what it is," he said touching my hand. Paul let his keys brush my arm as he went back to the devilish trade of his useless world.

I watched Paul Tandy walk down the long hallway, through the puddles of sad light until he disappeared. "And so it goes," I whispered after him.

* * *

This window is dying and my reflection distorts itself in the wet bruise of these passionless nights. The face staring back is haggard and tired, worn with age and etched with sadness. It is an ugly face with no hint of the young perfection, sadly lost and gone forever in this nightly anthem of afterthoughts. It forces me to ask myself, 'Did that face ever exist at all?' The reflection never lies and a blank page is always full of truth.

I have finally accepted it is useless to struggle further in this retched retreat of mental defiance. The cries of anguish which once aroused my anger have become the closing tune to this bitter melody. If I could find my voice, I would gladly sing along.

There's no reward to this curse of longevity and endurance, it wears me down as this new world comes vaulting ever faster and forward. I would have gone mad by now, but I was always mad to begin with. Mad at everything.

The world has begun to close before me. The magic is gone. I have no dreams left in this emptiness as the mechanism of my life slowly spirals downward. I am void of mind and soul. No urgency required. Death is patient. Tapping its cheap foot while politely asking me without words: "Are you ready?"

"Mr. Reuben, are you okay?" asked Paul. I didn't hear him come in. He bent forward and inspected my face. "You're pale and sweaty, and I think you should get some sleep. We can pick up your story and talk tomorrow night instead."

"With age—sleep becomes optional," I replied. "Besides, ask for me tomorrow and you shall find me a grave man." Paul smiled.

"Mercutio, from Romeo and Juliet," he said.

"Well done, Paul." He smiled and shook his compassionate head.

"I still think you should plan on spending a few days in the infirmary, just to be on the safe side."

"My plans are being made, perhaps in a day or two," I said and coughed weakly. I looked up at Paul and saw the concern in his eyes. "Paul, would you happen to know what day it is?" I asked.

"October 29, 1955."

"Thank you, soon another year passes for me," I whispered more to myself.

Paul seemed to change. He grew serious. "Mr. Reuben, you asked me once why I was here. I'd like to ask you the same question."

I gave Paul Tandy a weak smile. "You don't know? You haven't figured it out by now? In an odd way, you and I are here for the same reason…to finish writing my final chapter."

Paul shook his head in objection. "I want to hear what happens next in your life, and I'll help you write it. But I think you need to be on bed rest, Mr. Reuben," he started to plead further when I stopped him.

"No. I'm only tired, Paul. Nothing more."

Paul slumped into the chair. "Okay, Mr. Reuben. But tomorrow we're starting an IV and getting you on a round of antibiotics. If that doesn't work we'll make plans to see our in-house physician."

"Rest assured, dear fellow. Plans have been made," I said.

Paul accepted my response and relaxed back into his chair. "I admit I'm very curious to hear the end," he said in a drowsy voice.

I looked at Paul with his sleepy eyes and tranquil face. He did not know who he was in the slow scheme of this struggling world. Paul Tandy had listened to every word, and still he was blind to the truth. I leaned close his ear and let my frail voice guide him...

"You have always held the key I was forbidden to touch, and you alone can unlock the door and allow my light to fade from these fine mists of past conflicts. I am on the razor's edge, stay with me on this closing line of descent. The well of my life has a final offering to drown out the flagrant mortality within these defeated walls."

32

San Francisco
October, 1939

The clamor of progressive advancement welcomed me like an unwanted host when I stepped off the ship and headed into the city. I breathed in the cool morning air and was overcome by the rush of popular humanity moving en masse to the slow slaughter of their work schedule. The noise peddlers were busy yelling out the false pledges of their trade, while the newsboys honked out the headlines over the smell of fish and rotting produce. No matter how far I had traveled, sea ports had changed little the world over.

Up the steep walkways I went, passing by shop-windows where reflections moved like living merchandise, across busy streets where trolley rails sat buried in the gleaming beds of cobblestones. I meandered through the markets where patrons sat beneath canopies sipping coffee and watching the shadows spread their inky blackness against the rooftops. I found myself in the heart of San Francisco where muddled dreams clouded over the bay like a biblical curse.

I stopped a well-dressed gentleman on a street corner and asked where suitable accommodations might be found. He gave one look at my seafaring attire and wrinkled his uppity nose. "You won't find anything in your meager price range here. Try looking for something a little closer to the docks."

"And exactly what is my price range?" I asked him. He responded with a look that betrayed his segregated world of the have and the have not's. I walked on through the bustle of city life until I found a men's clothing and accessory shop.

Bells clanged as I went through the door and was greeted by the familiar odor of shoe polish and leather. The proprietor gestured with his chin and asked, "Can I help you with something?"

"I need to purchase a new wardrobe, something more fitting with the times," I replied. The promise of a sale changed his attitude and manners now found their rightful place.

"Of course, sir. Please step over to the mirror and let's see what we have on the rack to accommodate your individual tastes," said the tailor. He stepped lively and gestured towards the racks of shirts and suit jackets with his clean white hand.

An hour later I left with three pairs of gabardine slacks, ties, four shirts, and a camelhair dress coat with matching necessities. The tailor gave me directions and I followed the concrete veins of sidewalks into the city's heart where the sheer size of modern density overcame the skyline. I checked into The Westin St. Francis Hotel and spent the evening in a posh room watching my first American night in two decades, staring out the window at the never-ending movement of street life.

I sat for hours trying to formulate words that did not exist while watching the expansion of street life I never thought possible. The young skipped about with a privileged air of youth and innocence, while the elderly trundled by them on clawed and misshapen feet that had long ago lost the fruit of their virtue. And it is these ever-changing scenes of life, which first drew me to windows—I could learn from them and feel through the glass when the lonely streets offered guidance to the loneliest of souls.

I was crossing the hotel's front lobby the next morning as employees stood in earnest making polite invites to the guests in their trade for tips. "Cab for you, sir?" a bellboy asked me.

I was about to decline his offer when a stout, jowly man cut me off. "Excuse me, sir. I couldn't help but noticing you're new to San Francisco. I would like to offer you—" he started to say.

"Did we happen to serve together in the war?" I asked him.

"Doubtful," he replied uneasily.

"Then perhaps we have sailed the world's oceans together?"

"Highly unlikely," he huffed in growing agitation.

"I didn't think so," I said and squared into him. "In that case, we're not friends and you have nothing of interest to offer me, so save your sales barter for those who have the time and ears for it. I don't give two shits about your guaranteed pledges of health, wealth, or prosperity. If any of the bullshit you're peddling to honest people actually worked, your ass wouldn't be here. My advice is to either enlist and serve your country, or change professions. Good day to you, sir," I said and left him slack-jawed and dumbfounded where he stood.

I moved to where the receptionist stood behind the lobby counter. "Would you happen to know where the nearest telegraph office might be?" I asked her.

She looked up from her register with tight lips, eyes half-closed in thought. "I'm not sure, the new telephone systems pretty much closed down the old telegraph offices. Would you rather make a phone call?" she asked. The receptionist saw my confusion and explained the process and pointed me to the complimentary lobby phone for personal use.

I stepped to the small booth and put the receiver to my ear, a dull drumming sound followed by a female voice. "Operator, how may I direct your call?" she cooed.

"I'd like to make a call to Waynesboro, Virginia."

"Name of the person or party receiving your call?" the operator asked in a professional voice.

"The law office of William Quillen," I replied.

"Please hold while I connect your call," she answered.

There was a slight pause and the same drumming noise followed by a click and another female voice. "Quillen and Quillen."

"I'd like to speak with William," I told her.

"He's rather busy. May I ask who's calling?"

"Reuben Judah."

There was a pause before she replied." Mr. Judah, please hold while I transfer your call."

Before I could speak, William Quillen's voice came over the line. "Reuben, my God, man…where in the hell are you?" he asked. William had inherited the same rich baritone voice of his father.

"I'm still in San Francisco for the moment. I'll likely head to New York tomorrow so I can pay my respects to Teddy and my sons. After that, I'm coming home…I just wanted to let you know before I arrived," I told him. I listened as William Quillen took a deep breath before he replied.

"Ok, Reuben…but listen to me first. I haven't heard a thing from you in three months, so let me catch you up to date. The last telegram I received said you'd be docking in San Francisco sometime in early October. Rudolf Hauer was at my office less than a month ago wanting to see the deeds to the old Kruger property," William explained with some urgency.

"How was it handled?" I asked.

"I produced the deed transfers from Teddy Roosevelt to the United States and relayed to him that all of the land was now a federally funded National Forest. He tried to pursue it further with another lawyer, who promptly told him his office would not entertain his request or hear his argument—three days later my office was broken in to and vandalized. Nothing was taken except a single sheet of notes that was torn from my personal ledger."

"I'm done with all of that and the Kruger family. I'm ready to come home," I said into the phone piece.

"I'm glad to hear that, Reuben. But I want you to listen to me, it took me a day to remember what was on that torn ledger sheet."

"And?" I asked, but I already knew.

"It was the last telegram transaction you sent me three months ago. Rudolf Hauer hasn't been seen since the night my office was ransacked," William said and then paused for a second. "Let me ask you something. Did you check into a hotel using your name?"

"I did."

"Damn," William swore. "Okay, listen to me, Reuben. Just to be on the safe side, I want you to check out of that hotel and check into another one. From now on, I want you to go back to using the name, Luther Eli Cobb."

"Okay." I was already thinking, slipping back into old habits I had sworn off. "What does this Rudolf Hauer look like?" I asked.

"He's a man of medium height, stout, with close-set eyes above a pudgy nose. He looks nothing like the old Kruger family members, except for the big head."

I looked around for the stout man who had just stopped me. Other than the hotel employees, the lobby was empty. "I'm making train reservations to leave first thing tomorrow morning. I'll call you from the station before I board."

"Okay, Reuben. Just be careful," said William. I waited on my end until the telephone line clicked to dead space.

The trolley lurched upon the long rail sleeves and rumbled down through the city streets where mill stacks belched out the closing day's productivity. Automobiles zipped by as the trolley bell clanged its sad soliloquy of caution so passengers could disembark towards the end of their day. I watched old things pass as galleries of people plodded along like fortune seekers. Overhead an airplane buzzed the sky with its payload of human refugees being transported to a far better destination than they likely deserved.

I stepped off the trolley and walked the last two blocks in the feathered twilight to the location I had written down on a dinner napkin. I had found the address of Ms. Suzanne Pease in the telephone directory and made arrangements to visit her residence. I knocked on the door and was greeted by a young man. "Can I help you?" he asked eyeing me, as if he were waiting for a gaudy sales pitch.

"Richard, who is it?" a woman's voice asked from inside. The young man looked at me, waiting for an introduction.

I took the hint. "I do beg your pardon, I'm Reuben Judah. Ms. Pease and I spoke earlier today on the telephone."

The young man recognized my name and stepped aside. "Please come in, Aunt Susie has been expecting you," he said closing the door behind me. I followed him down a dim hallway and into a large sitting room. "Please make yourself comfortable, I'm Aunt Susie's nephew, Richard Pease."

We shook hands. "Nice to make your acquaintance, Richard," I said as a small woman with iron gray hair stopped in the doorway.

Suzanne Pease covered her face and began to cry. She wiped her eyes and apologized. "I'm so sorry, Mr. Judah. But when I first saw you standing there I thought it was Keller," she explained and looked closely at my face through her spectacles. "Mr. Judah, you are the living portrait of your great-grandfather. Please sit down and make yourself at home, we have so much to talk about."

"Thank you, and please call me, Reuben," I said and took the offered chair. "You actually knew Keller?"

"Oh my yes, I was thirteen when he died. Keller Judah was the deadliest man in Texas when he was younger. He helped my mother raise me and he was oddly, the kindest man I ever knew."

"I only met him once, and even then he made quite an impression on me."

She nodded and smiled. "He had the same effect on anyone who ever knew him," Ms. Pease said and pointed towards my face. "You have the same odd-colored eyes and the same intense look behind them. Keller told me his eyes changed color when he was struck by the lightning bolt that gave him the white streak in his hair. It was so odd—as he aged and the rest of his hair turned white, the white streak did the opposite and turned black. My mother would coax the stories out of him and then she'd write down everything he said in short hand," she explained and pulled out a box from under her couch. "Mother and I transcribed Keller's story when we moved out here to care for Richard after my sister died from the flu. It's all in here," she said, handing me the manuscript.

I opened the plain box and pulled out a rich, leather-bound book. The pages were hand-written in exquisite penmanship. Mrs. Pease stood and cleared her throat. I was embarrassed for forgetting she was still in the room. "I'm sorry," I apologized and stood up. "I've just waited a long time to read about my great-grandfather."

"Please sit down, Mr. Judah. It's quite alright. I was going to make a pot of fresh coffee and leave you alone for a spell. It'll give you a little time to read some of Keller's story in private. It truly is a remarkable biography about a remarkable man. The original copy you have is hand-written, but there's another copy in the box that's typed out for easier reading."

"Thank you," I said as she started to leave.

Ms. Pease stopped at the door and turned around. "Before I forget, there's a picture of Keller with me as a child sitting on his lap inside the front cover. My mother put it there, it's the only picture of Keller Judah that I know of," she said and bowed politely out of the room.

I opened the book and removed the wax paper; inside was an old tintype picture. I looked at the defiant man sitting in the wicker chair, and then I looked at myself in the mirror hanging on the wall. Ms. Pease was right. We were almost physically identical in both looks and body structure. I carefully put the picture back in the paper and began reading:

"In the year of our Lord, 1749, I was the only Spanish survivor to make it ashore. All others have perished upon the stormy and troubled seas. I am a castaway. A solitary man facing an unknown and uncharted land with savages such as I have never seen."

I continued reading until Ms. Pease and her nephew returned to the room. "Mr. Judah, I apologize for interrupting. But you've been here for over two hours and the time is rather late," Richard Pease interrupted.

I closed the book and stood. "I'm sorry. I had no idea of the time. Perhaps I could return early tomorrow morning, and if you and Ms. Pease have no objections—I would very much like to purchase one of your copies."

Ms. Pease spoke before her nephew could reply. "I think the books are rightfully yours; they're about your great-grandfather. You should have them."

"Ms. Pease," I started to protest when she cut me off.

"I insist," she said and looked at her nephew. "Wrap the books up so Reuben can pick them up in the morning."

I walked across the room and shook her hand and accepted her offer of coffee the following morning. "I'll call before I return tomorrow," I said, putting my hat on.

I left the train station and walked back towards the location of my hotel, I had changed twice that day before visiting the Pease residence. Late summer toads were on the roadways and sidewalks, soaking up any fading warmth they could from the heatless stones before they retired to their cold-blooded dens. Lamplights winked and hummed in its nightly ritual, casting slimy light on a host of slugs that littered the sidewalk like a plague.

"I thought you might be making train reservations," a male voice said. A thick shadow stepped from the darkness and into the splotchy light, his outline vaguely familiar. It was the stout gentleman I had spoken with in the hotel lobby.

I stopped and eyed the man. "I reckon you're Rudolf Hauer."

He smiled and tipped his hat as if we were mildly acquainted, large misshapen head like that of his dead kin. "I see my reputation precedes me, or perhaps your thieving attorney warned you I was planning a visit."

"It doesn't really matter, you're here now," I said easily, trying to control my temper and avoid this situation.

"I am here, and I assume you know the reason why," he said in a guttural voice.

I did understand his reason, and I nodded my head. "You're here for revenge, and it's the same thought which drove me all these years. But I'll tell you this," I said to him. He stepped back and wore a tight-lipped grin as he listened. "It's not worth it. I ruined all the promise I could have had in this world, spoiled everything because once the hate was gone my pain was still there. Just walk away and forget this. You and I both know our families have suffered and spilled enough blood to last three lifetimes."

He clucked his tongue as if he were summoning a child or

beckoning a common dog. "You're just an old man who wants the easy way out," he said losing the smile. "Well, there's no way out this time."

I had sworn an oath to never kill again, made a vow the violence had finally ended when Eton Swackhammer died. I had hoped to put away all things in my callous past and live my remaining years trying to further man, rather than killing him. But it would not be this way or any other way. Rudolf Hauer was standing before me, and he meant to take my life.

I took a cautious step back, to allow myself enough distance to react. "Just let this go while you still can. I've no intention of killing you, or anyone else...ever again," I said to the man.

He shook his globular head and laughed at me. "You just don't get it. I've done my checking and you don't have a damn thing worth taking. You're a broken down old man with no land or family left to give two shits about you." He stopped talking and his face tightened, turning darker in his late night objective. "And just to let you know, it wasn't my brothers who sent that letter to William Quillen's office...it was me. They had no intention of coming to America," he said and twisted the handle on his walking cane. A metal knife-blade flashed in the wicked lamplight.

I shook my right arm free of the jacket and whipped it around my left forearm for protection. "Then come ahead you big-headed sonofabitch, but remember what I said and take it to Hell with you."

"Remember what?" he asked.

"At least I tried, goddammit."

A young couple stopped across the street and watched the pending fight. The man yelled over to where we were facing each other. "Should I call for a police officer?" he asked. The woman stepped behind her man and peered over his shoulder as if some unknown reckoning were about to take place.

Instead of answering the man's offer of help, Rudolf Hauer looked at me with eyes that gleamed of recklessness. "Since I won't be getting a fucking penny from you, I'll give you this as payment for my two brothers," he said taking a swipe at me with his knife.

To survive a life or death fight you have to let go of wanting to live. You have to accept there is no changing the action of your opponent, and when you finally understand the simplicity of this propaganda—you will understand the magic of killing. Combat begins with half-truths or accusations and ends with death or a handshake. There is no other way.

"Stop this nonsense immediately...the police have been notified," yelled the man from across the street.

Rudolf Hauer looked towards the couple, breaking eye contact just long enough for me to make a slap at his knife hand and move into the road. I needed more distance so I could keep my body away from the wall. I didn't want to be pinned against it. "For an old man, you're quicker than I thought," he said skipping into the street on cautious feet.

I took a defensive stance and eyed the man. "You're no spring chicken, so I'll say this again. Forget this foolishness and go about your business," I said, trying one last time to avoid killing him. "The police are on the way, go now and I'll tell the officer a drunken kid tried to rob me." I could see no change in his guarded stance or aggressive demeanor. His intent remained the same. Rudolf Hauer meant to kill me. I watched as he stepped further into the street to block me from escaping.

"Don't try running, I'll only stick your yellow ass in the back," he said walking towards me.

I watched him come closer and readied myself. I had no intention of running ever again. "You've come all this way for it...so here it is," I said to him.

Rudolf Hauer mistook the meaning of my words, thinking I had resigned to my fate. He grunted and lunged forward in a mist of bitterness, as if he were skewering a prize. I caught his wrist with my left hand and clamped down. He slid the knife-blade across the bundled jacket trying to hack into my protected wrist. I gave his arm a downward twist and took the big German to his knees, he looked up and started to yell out when my free hand clamped around his exposed throat. The years of sailing, working with ropes and hoists on the long voyages across the hard ocean had strengthened my grip. I pinched my fingers together like a vise, the whites of his eyes turning red as blood vessels ruptured, his windpipe crushing in my hand like eggshells.

The knife slid from his struggling hand and I kicked it to the gutter and listened to it clang away to the labyrinth of piping below. Rudolf Hauer brought his hands up and tried to push himself away from me. He was getting weaker. Fading softly. I could feel his fingers loosen their grip and melt away from my arm. And still I held on, clenching down tighter on the neck until his face begin to purple like a wet and rotten blossom. His mouth opened and the frail life of Rudolf Hauer slowly wheezed out.

The lady across the street screamed, her man began yelling at me. "Hold on there, I think he's down and had enough…let him up, you're killing him!"

Rudolf Hauer was dead. I released his pulpy throat and wiped my hands off on the wet crease of his trouser legs. I knew then…I would never change. There was no future for me until I learned to let go of my past. I looked down at the dead man and thought about the violent life I had lived. I had fought in three wars, countless other conflicts on distant continents and I still craved the blood, how bitter the venom of its bite. The slow poison working its mental magic forever. So many paths I could have traveled, yet my life had become a straight line from there to here with nothing but scorched imagery between those inflective points of time.

Whistles began blowing as two men in uniforms bobbed towards the street where I stood. The young couple stopping them at the corner to give their eyewitness account of the gruesome homicide. The young man pointed at me as he talked while the woman hid behind him as if I were a threat to all life itself.

The two flatfoots crossed the road and stopped a few feet shy of me. "Do you have any weapons on you?" one asked. The other unsnapping his holster flap, hand on the pistol butt.

"I am unarmed," I said holding my hands aloft. They relaxed.

"Mind telling me what in the hell happened here?" he asked as his partner bent to check the corpse. He looked up at the officer questioning me. "He's dead, throat's been crushed or bashed in," he said, looking at me from his knees.

"His throat was probably mashed in our struggle. This bastard tried to rob and kill me and he got what every thief deserves. So if you two gentlemen will make note of this, I'll be on my way. I have a train to catch first thing tomorrow morning," I said to them both.

The officer questioning me pulled out a set of handcuffs while his partner stood and walked around behind me. "You're not going anywhere my friend. You've just admitted to murdering a man. So that means you're under arrest until we get this sorted out," he said.

His partner took one of my hands and pinned it to my back, "Just hold still, old fella, this won't take but a second," he said almost politely.

I tried reasoning with them. "There's no cause for this, it was self-defense. He had a knife."

"Where's the knife?" asked the older officer looking about.

"I knocked it out of his hand and kicked it to the sewer," I told him.

The other officer cocked his capped head and nodded towards the waste water pouring through the gutter opening. "I don't see us finding the knife down there, so the arrest stands," he said. His partner grinned and led me forward my shirt sleeve.

I pulled up and looked at both men. Hard hands went to their nightsticks as they stood waiting. "Thirty years ago people would've bought me a drink and congratulated me for ridding the world of that German bastard," I said as they pulled me towards the curb. A flashing set of red lights were coming towards us, the reflection on the wet streets like moving blood.

"Yeah, well, that was thirty years ago, grandpa," said the youngest officer lighting a cigarette, "I hate to tell you, but this ain't the old west and you're not Wild Bill Hickok."

"No, sir," I said as the wagon stopped and the officers opened the rear door flaps. "Bill Hickok would've shot his ass right where he stood."

"Reuben, it's good to hear your voice again," said William Quillen.

"I'm in jail." There was a long pause.

"Rudolf Hauer found you?" asked William.

"Yeah...he's dead."

"Ok, I'm assuming he came at you first. So we have premeditation and self-defense in our corner. Do you have a court date for your arraignment hearing?"

"Tomorrow morning."

William started talking in a quick, rapid-fire manner. "Okay, I need to work fast on my end, so let me explain the process and then I want you to do exactly what I say. Tomorrow morning at your arraignment the prosecuting attorney will state the charges against you. The defense attorney I'll hire to represent you will plead not guilty."

"Okay," I said.

"Now, you're not wanted for any crime so bail will be set and I'll have it paid once the amount is posted. Once you're out, I want you to find me a location for the sanitarium San Francisco uses for their criminal inmates," William almost whispered into the telephone.

I was confused about his motivation. "What for?"

"If I can get your charges reduced to involuntary manslaughter by reason of temporary insanity, you'll do six months or less and be back out on the street. It's better than serving five to ten years in a penitentiary for second-degree murder. I'll have your attorney argue the insanity plea when you go back to court for your preliminary hearing."

"So after tomorrow I'll be free until the second court date?" I asked.

"Yes, but this is very important. At both court appearances I don't want you to say anything at all, let your attorney do the talking. Just keep your head down and don't make eye contact with anyone in the court room. We have got to convince the judge of our insanity plea to make this work," William explained.

I thought for a second and decided my fate. "If it's insanity you want...then it's insanity you'll get."

This was William Quillen's arena. I could feel the confidence in his voice. "Good enough, Reuben. I'll have you out of there by sundown tomorrow. Once you get through your second court appearance and a trial date is set, I'll be there to handle your case personally. Do as I say and everything is going to work out."

"I have no doubt," I replied. The connection went dead as a prison bell began ringing.

"Telephones are off, time's up," said the attending officer.

I met my attorney just before I was led into the court room the following morning. He was more disheveled than I was. Shoulders stooped as if the weight of the justice system itself had become the unbalanced scales of affliction to him. Nasally voice when he asked if I knew what was about to happen. I only nodded and followed him into the broad room where my life had become nothing more than the strike of a judge's gavel. The bailiff went through his ceremony of reciting the case number and the crime committed by Luther Eli Cobb. My attorney argued that his client was facing an absurd charge, and though I agreed with my attorney's reasoning—this wasn't the first time I had faced a biased society and their impartial laws. The judge listened and saw no reason to deny my bail, which he smugly set at two hundred dollars. I was a free man before the sun had set over the cold San Francisco bay—two weeks later I would make my final stand in the very same courtroom and be sentenced to life.

33

"I read the newspaper article, Mr. Reuben. You set the district attorney and the entire courtroom on fire. What the paper didn't say was how you got the gasoline into the building," Paul said, chuckling.

"I went to a hospital supply store and bought a woman's douche. I filled it with gas and ran the rubber tube down my jacket sleeve. The district attorney catching on fire was an accident. I only sprayed the courtroom floor and struck a match to it; that's when the dumb bastard jumped the bench and tried to stomping it out and caught his pant legs on fire. I watched that stupid sonofabitch dancing and slapping his burning legs while cussing me. It was the funniest damn thing I'd seen in a long time and I busted out laughing. It wasn't hard to convict me after that, but like the other choices I've made in my life, I got a helluva lot more than I bargained for," I said and chuckled feebly.

"You didn't have to start that fire in court. You and I both know it. You had a different reason, another motive…why did you do it?" asked Paul.

"You know exactly why I did it, Paul. I belong here."

Paul shook his head in objection—his face serious and intense.

"No, it's more than that. You could have walked away a free man. You choose this place as punishment, same as me."

I looked at Paul and the outline of his delicate face. It was almost too feminine, like the sad comfort of a pillow. He had grown and matured, gotten tougher. Paul was going to be alright when this was over. "Do you want to hear the honest truth, Paul?"

"I think you owe me that much, Mr. Reuben," he said scooting closer.

"The biggest regret I have lived with all these years is not about the personal loss I've suffered, and it's not about this imprisonment."

"Then tell me the truth, Mr. Reuben. Please, just once, tell me the truth," Paul almost pleaded.

"It's about my personal choice of self-exile. It's about the loneliness that comes with the fear of ever loving again. I didn't have to fight in the war and leave Jessamine, but I did. My remorse was never about Jess being killed. It's the guilt I've had to carry for not staying with Jess and dying with her and Molly. I could have stayed with Richard King, married Maria and learned to appreciate the love of friends and family. But I ran. I should've been the one to take the grenade that killed Eton Swackhammer, but instead he saved my life out of love. A love I didn't understand, much less appreciate or deserve until he was gone. I sit at this window each night asking myself—was I ever worthy. All those I have ever loved are gone so there are no answers left for me. That's why I am here, Paul. I'm an old man with no place to go. I'm alone…and I'm scared."

Tears carved a path down Paul Tandy's fragile face. "Mr. Reuben, you're the only friend I have. You're the only person who ever stood up for me when everyone else in my life turned their backs…and…" He wanted to continue but choked back a sob instead.

"And?" I asked.

Paul composed himself. "And no matter what you might think of yourself, you're a good man. That's what I see and it's what all the people who ever loved you saw. All of us saw the same thing you've denied all these years. We saw the goodness you tried to hide. And each one of us loved you in our own way because of it."

I looked at his face, so soft. Innocent and honest. The taut wrinkles around his eyes were the lines of an unspoken hardship. I put a finger to his cheek and brought away a single tear. I held my finger up and looked at the small, salty drop. "The honest truth of love is found inside a tear." Paul lowered his head, avoiding my eyes. "Look at me," I said to him. He looked up and held my stare. "You're a good man, Paul Tandy…and you have been a friend to me when none could be found."

"Thank you for saying so, Mr. Reuben. But still, you could have left this place. You had the money and the connections. Why did you stay all of these years?"

"I knew I couldn't leave through the doors; if I did, this vile place would have haunted me forever. The only way I could ever be free of this place was to pass through the walls," I said to him.

Paul wiped his face and smiled. "You can't just walk through cinder blocks and concrete," he said trying to lighten the air. He was avoiding the subject, but he knew. Paul Tandy was the only one with the key to unlock these diseased walls.

I smiled back at Paul Tandy. "Tomorrow is a special day so come to work an hour early. Make sure you're off the clock…it's my birthday and I have a gift for you."

"A gift?" Paul asked with wide eyes.

I gave his hand a gentle squeeze. "Bring your keys tomorrow night and I'll make all your dreams come true."

34

October 31, 1955
11:00pm

I have endured and survived the hardships of three separate lifetimes. It has become an unbearable affliction. I never asked for war; war came to my doorstep with the false promise of peace. So many years of killing because of it, each death is forever stitched into the reflection of a silence and solitude beyond my reach. The divine providence of my youth has faded, and I now stand in the shadow of my warring sun. I have outlived them all. There is none alive who will object to this final discord of consequences. These are the final words so written by my hand.

My story is complete and I now put The Prophet of Cobb Hollow to rest.

Reuben Shadrack Judah
The Prophet of Cobb Hollow

San Francisco
1975—The Present
8:30am

I closed Reuben Judah's book and poured myself another glass of scotch. The sun was rising over the bay with pink blossoms of light on soft gray clouds, a shroud of fog hugging and huffing over the water like a stain upon existence. I had unwrapped the long slow walk of Reuben Judah's sad life, learned the secrets and truth behind The Prophet of Cobb Hollow.

I lifted my glass and made a toast to Paul Tandy and his guarded secrets. I kept the glass raised out of respect for Three Crows, John Mosby, Bill Hickok, Roosevelt, and Eton Swackhammer. Lastly, I lifted the glass higher and made a separate toast to Reuben Shadrack Judah and the painted dreams of his life. I did not judge him or the blood sacrifices he had wagered. Once his hate was gone, Reuben had to face the pain it had left behind, and there was something almost suicidal about watching it unfold through his jaded words.

I tipped my glass and swallowed, closing my eyes and thinking how Reuben's life had collapsed under the silent riches he willingly hid from himself and the world. Reuben had only valued his life when he knew it would end on his terms. Paul Tandy was right. Reuben's story was never about war and loss. It was about love.

About the Author

Mingo Kane was born and raised in the Shenandoah Valley of Virginia. After high school he left the Blue Ridge Mountains, and entered the United States Army where he served as a sniper with Bravo Company, 1st/75th (Airborne) Rangers.

During his military career he traveled and explored the world, survived a Blackhawk helicopter crash, and endured some of the Army's most demanding training.

Mingo is now retired and has enjoyed a host of unique occupations: bouncer, contract security specialist, first-class high voltage lineman, and now a full time writer. An avid outdoorsman and long-range shooter, he can be found hunting or fishing the mountains near his home when he's not at work on his latest novel.

To find out more about Mingo Kane, visit his Facebook, Goodreads, or Amazon author page(s).

OTHER TITLES FROM FIRESHIP PRESS

CHARLATAN

How do you keep the love of the King of France?

1676. In a hovel in the centre of Paris, the fortune-teller La Voisin holds a black mass, summoning the devil to help an unnamed client keep the love of the King of France, Louis XIV.

Three years later, Athénaïs, Madame de Montespan, the King's glamorous mistress, is nearly forty. She has borne Louis seven children but now seethes with rage as he falls for eighteen-year-old, Angélique de Fontanges.

At the same time, police chief La Reynie and his young assistant Bezons have uncovered a network of fortune-tellers and poisoners operating in the city. Athénaïs does not know it, but she is about to named as a favoured client of the infamous La Voisin.

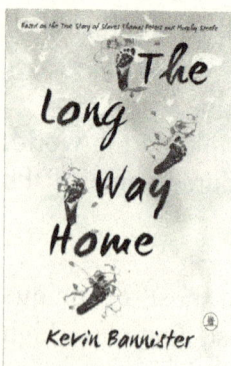

The Long Way Home

Set in the turbulent times of the War of Independence, *The Long Way Home* follows the lives of Thomas Peters and Murphy Steele who are friends, former slaves, fellows-in-arms and leaders of the Black Brigade. Their real-life story is an epic adventure tale as they battle bounty hunters, racism, poverty and epidemic in their adopted country after the war.

The Long Way Home has resonated with readers around the world as an unforgettable account of courage, hope and determination triumphing over despair and injustice. Thomas Peters, thoughtful and charismatic, and Murphy Steele, strong and impulsive, lead their followers on an inspirational search for a place where they can be free.

"Kevin Bannister's *The Long Way Home* is a novel that grabs your attention from the start and keeps you riveted to the last word."
—Dr. Daniel N. Paul, C.M., O.N.S., LLD, DLIT, Mi'kmaq eldering, author of *We Were Not The Savages*, Order of Canada recipient, journalist and lecturer

For the Finest in Nautical and Historical Fiction and Non-Fiction
www.FireshipPress.com

Interesting • Informative • Authoritative

All Fireship Press books are available
through FireshipPress.com, Amazon.com and
other leading bookstores and wholesalers worldwide.

CPSIA information can be obtained
at www.ICGtesting.com
Printed in the USA
BVOW08s0226260117

474532BV00001B/82/P